SIMON PETER ROACH

TARA
THE
FORBIDDEN FRUIT

© Copyright 2004 Simon Roach.
All rights reserved. No part of this publication may be reproduced, stored in a retrieval system, or transmitted, in any form or by any means, electronic, mechanical, photocopying, recording, or otherwise, without the written prior permission of the author.

Note for Librarians: a cataloguing record for this book that includes Dewey Decimal Classification and US Library of Congress numbers is available from the Library and Archives of Canada. The complete cataloguing record can be obtained from their online database at:
www.collectionscanada.ca/amicus/index-e.html
ISBN 1-4120-3903-7
Printed in Victoria, BC, Canada

TRAFFORD

Offices in Canada, USA, Ireland, UK and Spain
This book was published *on-demand* in cooperation with Trafford Publishing. On-demand publishing is a unique process and service of making a book available for retail sale to the public taking advantage of on-demand manufacturing and Internet marketing. On-demand publishing includes promotions, retail sales, manufacturing, order fulfilment, accounting and collecting royalties on behalf of the author.
Book sales for North America and international:
Trafford Publishing, 6E–2333 Government St.,
Victoria, BC v8t 4p4 CANADA
phone 250 383 6864 (toll-free 1 888 232 4444)
fax 250 383 6804; email to orders@trafford.com
Book sales in Europe:
Trafford Publishing (UK) Ltd., Enterprise House, Wistaston Road Business Centre,
Wistaston Road, Crewe, Cheshire cw2 7rp UNITED KINGDOM
phone 01270 251 396 (local rate 0845 230 9601)
facsimile 01270 254 983; orders.uk@trafford.com
Order online at:
www.trafford.com/robots/04-1711.html

10 9 8 7 6 5 4 3 2 1

Dedicated to
Martha Serrano-Roach and Dorothy Roach
"A vision just a vision if it only in your head.
If no one gets to hear it; it's as good as dead."

Master Storyteller
The Art of Words

CONTENTS

Prologue

Part I   Alpha and Omega - 7

Part II   Ritual - 18

Part III   Creation of Passions - 28

Part IV   To Have To Hold - 59

Part V   Time After Time - 104

Part VI   Eyes of the Beholders - 145

Part VII   Dangerous Affairs - 197

Part VIII   Delusion of Trust - 239

Part IX   The Soul's of Lovers - 273

Part X   Yearning - 310

Part XI   Vanishing Affair - 373

Part XII   To Hell and Back - 397

Part XIII   The Eyes of Love - 426

Prologue

One shouldn't explore in places, which they are not unwilling to accept its customs or beliefs. This was the case of a man name Alexander, a person which views of the world as pure logic and reasoning, the supernatural was of no importance to him, just a toy of the powerful and a cage of the weak minded. Unfortunately he would soon discover and collide into the ill-logical rims of the forbidden love. As life's lines between black and white would become even more blurred. Only the world of gray and darkness remains replacing Alexander's controlled world. Through his pending encounters an exquisite woman named Tara would come into his life and turn it upside down. Unknown to Tara, the destiny before her would transport to become the world of long forgotten Voodooist. Conflicting with the age of computers and technologies, Alexander discovers Tara's world which still dealt with the ancient art of black magic and supernatural to be a powerful impact to control.

Crushing into Tara's destiny to become High Priestess on her coming birthday was unknown to her. The main Pond in this deadly game is a close friend of Tara named Jeanne. An attractive New Yorker, she is Tara's true blue companion. Yet she too will witness the horrifying discovery of her best friend's trial and tribulations. Jeanne will soon become the instrument which thrush the two lovers together. The three will be consumed into the world of the supernatural, a world of unexplained wonders of voodooist. Little was Alexander aware of the awesome physic powers confronting him. A power rivaling any whom dare opposed it, sometimes with their own life, and where the world of the supernatural and fearful voodoo dominated practically everyone's soul, yet through it all, there stood a beam of hope. Their love was the love of man and women, spouting forth strength of the human heart and soul. Even though both would be threaten and personally assaulted, time after time, the two lovers only hope of life would rely on whether the passion for each other would prevail over and the overwhelming forces set to destroy them.

As they struggle for their own lives, Tara would be forced to come into her own physic supremacy before time, before understanding clearly just what she was about to release within very dept of her soul. She is forced to use unknown physic powers passed to her by the High Priestess which cares for her all of her natural life, La Veanna, a true Quadroon woman of the Black region of New Orleans; a place of erotic pleasures, mystery, and danger where few outsiders weren't allowed to venture, and for those who did, they never returned the same, if they didn't vanish from the face of the earth. It was a trip which they took at their own peril.

The year was the modern age. Alexander, an over worked and greatly stress computer network specialist decided to vacation in New Orleans, encountering what was known throughout, The Black Region, and the Forbidden Fruit known to everyone as Tara, herself a Quadroon woman? Yet the two lovers were from completely different worlds, now forced to face the reality of life; for their love for each other would suffer and La Veanna would use every power she possess to end it, for Tara was born to be Queen.

PART I

Alpha and Omega

It was April 11, 1980, St. Louis, Missouri -- Saint Mary Infirmary -- late night. There was a tempest in the city. Suddenly a bolt of lighting flashed directly in front of the building as the winds continue howling violently across the front steps. Above a lonely streetlamp beams its flickering light upon the sidewalk. High in the night's skies one could see the heavens cursing the world. Below, two female nurses dressed as nuns raced out of the hard rain and into the infirmary's front door. Suddenly an ambulance appeared approaching down the lonely street with sirens screaming away. It suddenly halts in front the building as a driver leaps out and his partner hurriedly followed suit.

They threw the rear double doors open searching for their passenger. Before them, a very pregnant woman screaming in labor pains. The contractions had become closer and her water was about to burst. Harry, one of the drivers and partner carted her into the infirmary passed the nurses.

TARA THE FORBIDDEN FRUIT - 8

An hour later in the maternity wardroom the room is lit with hovering bright lights. The instruments for operation lay neatly in their tray, a heart-machine near an operating table that is cover with fresh sheets, and oxygen tanks nearby just in case. Through the double doors the pregnant women rolls in still screaming out foul language. The doctor and nurses look stun but concerned. They had done plenty of births, but is one was different? This one was totally mysterious. This one had a sense of peril to them all. All knew that only the mother or the child would live after this birth.

The pregnant woman is having her baby with complications as they place her on the operating table hurriedly. "Mrs. Anthony, we have to deliver the baby now or it's possible we may lose the both of you," the doctor shouted to his patent.

The nurse whispers, "The bleeding isn't stopping, doctor. I don't understand it? I mean this shouldn't be happening? I think we're going to lose the child!"

"Not if I can help it, dammit!" He replied. "We have to quite her down, relax her in some way? But we need her awake."

The Doctor Carson and nurse work feverishly to save the child. The heart machine indicator for the woman beeps wildly then…flat lines. The doctor attempts to restart the heart but it is too late through shock.

"Doctor, the mother is dead. We must try to save the child."

"I don't understand?" He whispered in shock.

"Doctor the child still has a chance, right?"

"Sure, yes save the child." He replied perplexed, "The child…"

The doctor delivered a baby boy healthy and well. After a slap on the ass, the baby cries taking in the air of life. Quickly the baby was taken away leaving its mother forever resting, never to greet his mother again.

Later shortly after in the infirmary's baby intensive care unit, there were rolls of empty baby crabs in a low lit room. Huge bay windows over looked the south end of the infirmary as the hard rain continued pounding, fighting to get in. Suddenly there came a bolt of lighting hitting the window, the clamor raddled the room and leaves the window pains shattered in a thousand pieces, yet strangely standing. In the far corner is a dim light over the newborn's crab.

Meanwhile at the Doctor Carson's office nearby, he was busy filling out the death certificate from the ID founded on the woman. Strange there was no phone number anywhere to be found, no one to contact. It was as if the women came out of nowhere to leave her mark on the world. Then there came feverish knocks at his door. A nurse addresses him in hurried frightening fashion and by her expression he could see she was in shock.

"Doctor Carson?"

"Yes?" He asked.

"Your needed in the Children Infirmary," she answered.

"What now?" He asked, "Can't you see I'm busy?"

"Please you have to see this for yourself!" She shouted.

"The child?" Doctor Carson asked. "Tell me?"

"Yes, but there is more," she added.

"What more could happen tonight?"

"You have to see this with your own eyes, please come now!"

Doctor Carson nods and follows.

Shortly later, both the nurse and Doctor Carson enter the room unaware of what just happened. Before them were the shattered window panes reaching to the ceiling ready to fall upon the child. It was a miracle the glass didn't enter the room, yet it only stood there waiting to strike its fatal blow. There was a slight glow coming from the child in its crab, not was very bright one but all could see it slightly. The staff now looked on confused and shocked. The same glowing appeared to them resting upon the windows as to shield the child. Slowly Doctor Carson moved to the child with the nurse who picked the baby up and examines him.

"Doctor, what shall we name him?" The Nurses asked.

"Since seeing him was a sign of relief, and there is no other relative, let's name him, Alexander Anthony." He replied.

"Well Alexander, welcome to this imperfect world," the nurse voiced oddly.

The baby begins to cry as they moved away from the window. Behind came a loud clash of shattered glass from the windows. Stun, both look around only to view a totally destroyed area where once a crab stood.

"You don't think…" the nurses voiced as she held him caringly.

"Don't be silly, nurse," Doctor Carson quickly answered.

Alexander began to cry…

TARA THE FORBIDDEN FRUIT - 12

Meanwhile, on that same abnormal night, in the city of New Orleans, Louisiana on Dumaine Street, an ancient wooden wall clock struck midnight setting forth an unwelcoming chain of events. It was an obscure night in a somber land of Black Magic. A place of it dominance, of Voodooism prevailing over all it consumed. A night of strange beginnings or a night endings, no one would be sure. The action was at a place called The Old Brickyard. The inside surrounding walls was dressed in old peeling wall paper of faded red roses. There was a faded calendar indicating the month of April. Strangely upon it was a particular date was circled, the 11th in what seemed to be…red blood.

The temperature steamed hot, bellowing extremely humid climate and constantly produced unbearable discomfort to those not born there. Any outsider with the notion that the night air would cool things off and grant them relief, were sadly mistaken. This place, this infernal region with its River of Hell like the Styx was the back ground to what was to come, a place of everlasting fire where the religious and the divine dare not undertake. It is located just south of the state of Missouri and known throughout the world for its elegance and pleasurable ness, it invites the foolish. To the naive eyes it was impossible until it was too late to view its ideal paradise, and to the inelegance and the monstrous shade of life hidden from them. Through the world's eyes it was viewed for its ideal of paradise. It would provide pleasure and well as pain.

"Dammit, kill her!" The mother cried in room at the Old Brickyard.

The suddenly there came an unnerving flow of screams shattering the mute night. Her screams were so loud that some say it woke up heavens. That she created such a scream that the walls rattled with fear. That everyone in the room felt her horror.

"Damn you all, what have you done to me!" She screamed, "No-no-no-no-no, destroy it before she knows. Before she has a chance to enter this world, before it's too late to turn back the evil within her; for your own sakes, listen to me, please!"

"Shut up bitch," A woman cried, "Let the birth processed."

The only other response came from unwelcoming cheers sprouting, huzza, hurrah and yell's of rejoice, sounds of the few which were honored to witness the birth before them. Nearby the expected Quadroon woman continued to shout at the top of her lungs from fear. The room seems a home for evil spirits. Some later would square there were creator such as demon's shadows within the room rooming freely, also watching. While other later would vow they seen specter like visions and phantoms of unearthly nature. As for the expected woman, she could not postpone the birth any longer. Now she had delivered a female child from her now listless body; for this female infant possess extraordinary psychic ability to control all among her.

Before anyone could act in response on her request of pure anxiety, before anyone could hear another bellow from her chapped lips; there appeared two red dots in the darkness of the far corner. What seemed to be a man slowly stepped out of the shadows as if he were a mischievous sprite. The expected woman looked on shaking her head, trying desperately to view him clearly through darkness of the room. Finally her unwilling eyes adjusted to the darkness as the Quadroon man stepped closer into the moon light from the window. A true member of the voodoo tribe, he was possessed. His eyes were locked upon the baby's every move lying now just between her legs. Suddenly he snatched the new born away only uttering, "They await the child now!" His deep and strong tone voice was enough to force everyone to back away in chilling fearful anxiety. In his massive arms he ran leaving the room hurriedly with the female baby. Having no regards for anyone in his way, and his well built frame of a body; it was apparent he would receive no detractors.

Meanwhile the mother screams in anguish, but she was in no position to extinguish any resistant. Now she feared retribution and knew what was next, death. Her weak body suddenly began to become motionless. First her toes and fingers, next her smooth long legs, and followed by the arms. She attempted to struggle out of bed but with no success. Her chest and neck soon became motionless, leaving only her eye motion. They could only roll around wildly at the ceiling then tears ran from them. She again knew it was time. She thought she heard minstrel, suddenly a distance trumpeter company by other musicians. Soon her mind began to wander off uttering to herself, "The melody is so-so sweet. It's like fantasia." Suddenly what was so sweet halted leaving a drummer softly pounding his instrument as she pasted away. The room was now harmonious as the witness left slowly and quietly.

Out of the Brickyard house, the lonely streets seemed to bellow-up stream causing the area to become murky. The moon in the towering sky was lustrous for the night, casting eerie shadows as if there were someone hiding. He glanced upwards at the moon with distaste and a hard grimace. Suddenly there appeared growing dark clouds rolling in like an ocean, no, more like a tempest. Soon the moon once bright was engulfed before his very eyes by dark storm clouds. It was not the heavens doing but the baby, trying out her powers; playing God. The steam itself was now a thick mist as the man's eyes return to normal. Unfortunately his massive body was being controlled by an unknown force. For clear reasons the Quadroon man was afraid of the baby he was carrying. Surely he could easily terminate its life. Even though pound-for-pound there was no man who he feared, but strangely this little child weighting under five pounds made him fear her with her psyche supremacy. Born with powers beyond normal humans, she was part human and part God; the child possessed supernatural powers. Her intellectual mind was developing at an extreme paste adjusting to her psychological will.

He started sensing the child was an abomination upon this earth, wishing he wasn't chosen to transport this child of unbelievable psychic abilities. It was on the scale of supernatural. He knew the child had powers in the form of dominance of mind manipulation over him. He knew he was being directed from within his own consciousness, yet how could this be? His thoughts desperately struggled from within. Glancing down at the child he noticed her gazing at him with conviction as if mocking him.

Shortly later he transported her through the strident woods in the Quadroon area. The child spoke not a word nor made a sound, but her eyes, yes were those stabbing eyes like glacial. They were the instruments of her channeling commands to him. She displayed one of many supernatural abilities which would be her unmistakable trade mark upon this earth. With the total eclipse of the moon and sky, the Quadroon man continued forcefully through enormous troublesome undergrowth. His skin was shining because of sweat pouring out of his body. Still with his arms and his strong bountiful hands, he held the child with care. Suddenly, with a roar and a loud earth awakening crack of thunder which engulfed the night's sky caught his attention. Then with a sure charge of electricity the cloudburst unleash upon them. It seemed like thousand of tiny needles falling heavily against his muscular frame. Most of all he dare not glance upward; for the sounds of the downpour presented hissing filling his ears.

PART II
Ritual

The downpour was so hard to him, it caused him benightedness. Still he could view a clearing up ahead with many discordant brushes surrounding it. With one hand, he wiped the rain out of his eyes to get a better look. Only the eyes filled back up with rain fall as his face displayed total apprehension. Again he peeked to notice a man-throne made out of pieces of wood, more like tree bark. He disembarked onto the clearing discovering the soil was fantastically dry, which fascinated him greatly.

"The rain hasn't fallen upon this burial ground, why?" He murmured.

Slowly he moves in even closer, now pleased that at least the downpour was obstructed. Though it only caused him to ponder by what supernatural force? There was surely a ghostly spirit present.

A sudden and eerie karma befell him. He now knew where the infant lead him to. The place was established as a "Voodoo Ceremony." With the infant still resting and perched tightly in his huge and massive arms, he approaches ever so slowly upon the unholy grounds resolute caution for his life.

"Give the child to me!" A voice whispered out of nowhere to him.

Now frighten nearly out of his mind; he glances uncontrollably behind him. But no one was present to pass the infant to. He wasn't sure whether he ever heard a voice, may be it was just the rain. He thought.

"Give the female infant to me!" A female voice utter louder this time and with more regiment. The sound of the command this time was more passionate and powerful, something he surely took note.

Cautiously he turned towards the border of rain behind him. Suddenly a flash of blinding lighting bellowed from the center of the area causing him to rethink his action of running. When he turned again there stood a beautiful woman, radiant and dry, wearing a deep red and blue wrap. With grace she extended her arms outward towards him. Behind him appeared another woman just as attractive and dress similar. Her skin was smooth and dark as she watches the both of them.

"Pass the infant to her now," she ordered in an undemanding tone.

Petrified by misgivings, he was unable to respond. Then the infant strangely gaze at him with rage. He was out numbered passing on the infant now with haste. Surely he didn't wish to anger the infant's new guardians.

"You must go now, Gama!" A heaver and coarse voice shouted from the direction of the man-made throne causing him to withdraw quickly, leaving the infant with them. He scarcely knew what was about to happen. Rushing out of the clearing the downpour began again, but extraordinarily only outside the clearing. Some paranormal influence was holding back the downpour as torches bellowed its glowing flames amongst the site, some supernatural bending field of some source? He was afraid to look anymore. Instead he opted to run back to wrench he came.

Truly the principal race of the worshippers was Mulattoes and Quadroon nature.

This night unlike any other night, the Voodoo Queen, who would soon preside over the ceremonial and ritual dance of the cult? It was well known that Voodoo Doctors occupied secondary positions in the voodoo hierarchy. All also knew if they were to stay healthy they would follow her orders and without any hesitation.

Later, Gama returns at the Old Brickyard, the rains had strangely halted, much to his relief. Several police cars and the Cornier were working around the building. There, he discovered the woman which gave birth earlier was founded dead inside. Confused, the cornier could not figure out why she hadn't shown any signs of ever having a child? For eight months she was with child he was sure of it. The Cornier knew of disappearing children but this was a mystery and better left that way. What he didn't know everyone else knew. The residents could sense it in the air. The eclipse clouds that once blocked off now opened with the moon just as bright as before. The police officers questioned everyone in the area about the peculiar death but with no helpful results. When they questioned Gama of what he knew about the woman, he refused to assist in investigation. It matter not what questions were pressed upon him, he did not reveal what he knew, fearing retribution. Also knowing better than to utter what he surely knew of the, unholy birth, opting to move away with speed from the area and leaving behind the Old Brickyard; for his task was accomplished.

Meanwhile that same night at the ritual site, the ceremony was about to begin. There were males and females, old and young, dark skinned and light skinned-handsome mulatresses and quadroons about the fires. With them, a half dozen white men and seven women joined. In the middle of the opening was a burning fierce fire, as it cast a lurid light over the scene. Each woman had a white kerchief tied around the forehead, though the heads of latter were covered by the traditional Madras handkerchief, with its seven artistic points, upturned to heaven. In a little while the company, some seventy in all, had assembled. On an oblong table about eight feet in length and six in width. There stood thought live cats. But when touched, the most philosophical of all the sense, they were fine specimens of taxidermy. Admirably stuffed they were, too.

    In the center of the table was a cypress sapling, some five feet in height, planted in center of a firkin or keg? Immediately behind the cypress, and towering above it, was a black doll with a dress variegated by cabalistic signs and emblems, and a necklace of the vertebrae of snakes around her neck, from which depended an alligator's fang encased in silver.

    A quadroon man was astride of a cylinder made of thin cypress stave hooped with brass and headed by sheepskin. With two sticks he droned away a monotonous "ra-ta-ta-ra-ta," while on his left a black skinned mansa sat on a low stool, whop with two sheep shank bones, and a female with the leg bones of a buzzard, beat an accompaniment on the sides discord. Some two feet from these arch musicians squatted a young dark skin woman vigorously twirling a long calabash. It was made of Louisiana gourds a foot and a half long and filled with peddles.

At a given signal the four initiates form a crescent before La Veanna, who was evidently the high priestess or voudou queen. She made cabalistic signs over them and the new born child, and sprinkled them vigorously with liquid from a calabash in her hand, muttering under her breath. She raised her hand and the quadroon man dismounted from his cylinder, and from some hidden receptacle in or behind the large black doll, drew a gigantic snake, which he brandished wildly aloft.

The quadroon man talked and whispered to it strangely. Yet at every word the reptile, with undulating body and lambent tongue, seemed to acknowledge the dominion body asserted over it. In the meantime, with arms crossed and reverent eyes, the initiates had now formed a crescent around him. He now compelled the snake to stand upright for about ten inches of its body. In that position the quadroon man passed the snake over the heads and over the initiates, repeating at each pass the words which constitute the name of an African sect, "Voudou Magnian."

A deep howl of exultation broke from every part of the opening. The quadroon man moved back to his tam-tam, his accompanier's right and left and the gourd musician with his rattle. Boards were laid for a supper-table. No benches, no seats of any kind. Some squatted on their haunches, others reclined. Before stood a clay vase, with capacious and rounded belly, and a small spout, out of which the revelers drank wine or tafia (sugar-cane rum). An old woman removed the boards then swept away the debris of the feast, and left space to dance. As the guest stood up, the quadroon man went to the altar to the priestess.

He shouted, "The Fetish-worship!" and again drew forth the snake.

He forced it to writhe and wriggle over and around the company, uttering, "Voudou! Voudo Magnian!"

He then twirled the snake around his head and dexterously cast it into the blazing pile. Such a yell arose no words can describe. Also the rude instruments took up their discord, mixed with yells.

The new born female was then placed out of sight from the voices by the High Priestess La Veanna. By some unknown supernatural powers by her, a spell was placed upon the new born. La Veanna was over a hundred years of age, blind, and soon would be replaced. The chorus of Tara's yell had entered the mad shouts of Africa. Then came a general call for dance, as the new born began to mature before their eyes! The baby's body began the change at an alarming rate, turning, bending and stretching to grow against nature its self. Suddenly there was an appearance of engulfing bizarre reddish like smoke, which swilled wildly about her coming from nowhere. There seemed to be flashes of self yet contained lighting from within its being. Then smoke appeared from below a once barren spot of earth. It began to turn from a deep reddish color to white and finally to black until it suddenly shielded her completely from all view.

Up sprang, Tara!

She was a magnificent specimen of human flesh. A leggy, tall, smooth skinned woman with a long damp hair appeared. She was wrapped just in a wisp of silky orange fabric draped against her body, exquisitely sensual.

Suddenly, an unholy scream, no, more like a howling from a wild animal came from her. Then quite as the hardness of the cry became a softness of acceptance. With her body waving and undulating like the quadroon man's snake a perfect Semiramis from the jungles of

Africa. The baby was now totally transformed into a grown woman of 24 years of age, if not in mind. Confining herself to a spot not more than two feet in space, Tara began to sway on one and the other side. Gradually the undulating motion was imparted to her from the ankles to her forehead. Then she tore the handkerchief from her forehead. This was a signal, for the whole assembly sprang forward and entered the dance wildly.

Tara moved away and sat next to La Veanna. Both watched the dancers move uncontrollably. The beat of the drum, alone with other instrument, swelled louder and ever louder. Under the passion of hours, the women tore off their garments, and entirely nude, continued dancing, as if they were snakes wriggling. Above all of this, the orgies would have become frightful for any outsiders. Brushing Tara's beautiful black hair, La Veanna stared at her chosen replacement from birth.

She uttered softly, "Within twenty-five years you will replace me, like I have replaced ones before the turn of time its self. You are truly exquisite, just like I was before, Tara."

Tara did not understand, she couldn't understand. Her mind was devoid, open to receive whatever La Veanna chose to place into it.

TARA THE FORBIDDEN FRUIT - 27

Tara did however sense of the invisible presence of his majesty, Satan. The night among his voudou worshippers, he played.

Still there was another vision of an unknown man. But there was something forcing La Veanna hand now, another child born on the same night at the same time in a state called Missouri and a city named St. Louis; for she foreseen the future and seen him as an irritation. Surely this child could not derail her plans for Tara, she thought. She would never allow this vision to come true, but she also knew vision had a way of coming true regardless of the best intentions.

PART III

Creation of Passions

Twenty-four years later…2004

Alexander rested in his office, his chair now completely turned towards the bay windows, and his work going unattended; his mind flowed in and out. To look at him, one would never consider him the threat of which La Veanna was afraid. Yet the uncontrolled events were being set into motion. He was born the same night as Tara and in total conflict. Though they didn't know that their paths cross, both lives would change dramatically. It started right here in his office complex downtown. Before him were a host of reports. It was a neither hot and humid summer, a day which Alexander didn't wish nor care to be inside working on a demanding network for some undeserving client with money to burn. With the continued stress of the position, it soon took its toll upon him, mentally. And he was looking for a speedy way out. For the past three years there was no one in his life accept a very close friend, Jimmy. The only one he could speak to.

Jimmy was concern and continued to push Alexander to take a vacation, sometime even setting him up with blind-dates which ended mostly in disaster. He visited his friend's office that morning and would change his life forever...

"Alexander, please have this report done by the end of the day," a female coworker voiced over a huge file upon his desk.

There lied several other file too which had to be done since the recent merger.

"Just what I needed, more work," Alexander murmured.

"Like a hole in the head?" The female staffer asked jokingly. "To bad you just can't make it vanished, then maybe you'll have peace?"

"Yeah."

"Sorry for that, but I was told you know what to do with these reports," she added.

"Consolidate, consolidate," he replied with a half smile.

She left him alone shaking her head.

Alexander had been working day and most nights just trying to clear his and others work around the office. But this time he had had enough. The department was short staffed from downsizing and there were no signs of any let up in the near future.

That night Jimmy noticed his Alexander's office light still on. The other workers had already left for the weekend. Peering in he'd noticed his friend working. Entering and observing the craziness' of the situation, he sat on the couch near the window and watched him work. After a few minutes Alexander looks up to him. His face displayed a long want of slumber.

"Thought you've went home," Alexander spoke, "What time is it anyway?"

"Near midnight, my overworked friend," Jimmy replied.

"Great. Only four more hours to go before the weekend," Alexander added.

"Alex? Didn't you hear me about the other day?"

"What?" Alexander asked.

"You need a vacation and soon." He replied.

Alexander didn't blame Jimmy for the over flow of work. He too had doubled the work he had. Yet Alexander ponder why him? Why is it always him who has to do these reports at the last minute? He begun to feel strongly that others in the office should do their own jobs then maybe, just maybe it would not be so stressful on him, wishful thinking?

"What the hell am I doing here anyway?" Alexander asked exhausted.

"Look, don't yell at me, friend?" Jimmy shouted back, "Besides, what the hell is a matter with you? You act as if you were forced into this chair. You accepted the job of your own freewill. No one placed a gun to your head."

Alexander was in no mood for plain truth from his best friend or anyone for the matter. True, he was an expert in networking and a well know computer wiz. Still he had feelings which were not expressed, needed to be. The problem was that there was no one he felt worth while to love. All his life he felt that he was saving himself for someone special, someone strangely not of this earth. The other females for whom he was aware of could only be considered good friends, something that they wanted no part of. Then there was Jimmy known in circles as the Match Maker of the office. He felt strongly that it was his job to get his best friend paired up. Alexander paid Jimmy no attention and proceeded to walk strangely towards his office bay windows. He was tired, weak and totally drained from the everyday slaving at his desk. The week had been a rough one to handle.

"What's the matter?" Jimmy asked.

"Look Jimmy, nothing," he voiced thinking.

"Tell me, friend."

"There's nothing for me to say about my actions."

"You're a very tired man," Jimmy said jokingly.

He knew Jimmy was staring at him,

"Shit what am I to do?" Alexander asked.

"Listen, Alex why don't you just take the damn long vacation? It will do you much good to get far away from this place. Fuck, you have the time! I'll say two months, right?" He stated as he begin strengthen up Alexander's desk.

Jimmy was right and he knew it. He needed to get away fast.

"Ok-ok, my true friend, a vacation it is!"

"Then it's settled?" Jimmy asked.

"Your wish is my command, anything to keep you off my back. Besides, I do have the spare time and all." Suddenly he began to ponder over how to take it. Taking any kind of vacation he'd never considered. He then would have to face being alone for the first time, a frightening prospect. His machines have always been there for him, their logic and reasoning was their gift to him. There were no gray lines, just on and off decisions. Human reaction was out of the question and not considered a factor in his life.

"Where do you prescribe I go?" He added bluntly, yet with withdraws sensitivity. Knowing he has experience traveling throughout the world, before, during and after his brief military days in the army. Now in his early twenties and still unmarried, there was nothing halting him taking off.

Jimmy viewed him backing out of the furlough and had to act forthwith. "Why not, New Orleans?"

"What?"

"Yeah, New Orleans! At this time of year, there is no place better, have you been there before?" Jimmy voiced smiling. "Better yet, why not the French Quarter?"

"Are you serous?" He asked startled.

"The French Quarter," Jimmy stated again.

Alexander gazed up at Jimmy's proposition then glanced upon his less attractive selection of work load upon his desk, glancing at Jimmy again pondering his decision.

"Why the Hell not," Alexander said. "I'll tell you what. I shall depart this weekend, good enough for you?" He now returned to his window, as feelings consumed his body and thoughts.

Jimmy moved over and sat at his desk. "New Orleans ready or not, here's Alexander!" Then playfully he began to spin around in Alexander's chair. Suddenly he stops and uttered, "Look, you'll thank me for this just wait and see."

"Famous last words," Alexander said under his breath.

"What?"

"Nothing," Alexander said.

"One more thing, before your aware of it, your whole life may just change? I mean a love may just enter your lonely life. The life of logic reasoning will be out the window and romance will take consume you if your lucky," Jimmy said.

Alexander quickly turned towards him bellowing, "For the good or for the bad, that's what I'm truly afraid."

"What do you mean?" Jimmy asked bewildered. "Not those dreams again of this Forbidden Fruit? Not that woman of your nightmares coming to take you away?"

"Yes," Alexander said wondering.

"Those damn dreams are just that, dreams," Jimmy said.

"Their omens to me."

"Oh I'm scared of this supernatural junk," Jimmy joked.

"It's no joke. It's hunted me ever since I can remember and recently the dreams are stronger, clearer, and sharper in images," Alexander replied. "But her face is still forbidden to me, not yet willing to cast light on itself?"

"What do you mean sharper?"

"Last night I dreamt there was a shape of a female. I couldn't get her face, just a shape view with a cabbie cap."

"A cabbie cap?" Jimmy asked.

"Yeah, then the image faded away as if it was never there?"

"May be you better leave before the weekend?" Jimmy asked.

"No, I'll finish what I can by tonight and you can do the rest."

Jimmy nodded then joked, "I believe your entire life will change on this trip, my friend."

Little was Alexander aware that his best friend's words would haunt him to this day, incinerate all his passion by way of Tara.

That night, Alexander was busy trying to pack what little clothes he had for the trip. Didn't have time to shop, didn't care, and didn't really conceive that he would be taking a vacation. But his dreams were pulling him in that direction. Something he couldn't get a clear hold upon in his consciousness, something strangely beautiful and haunting yet dangerous? Alexander peered out of his bedroom window into the late night sky. There was a shooting star streaking across the panorama background of stars. Maybe? He thought. Maybe it was a sign of some sought, but he was not one to believe in the supernatural; facts and logic was his world and all that mattered. As the Circus Master voices; Get ready for the thrill of all time.

    Saturday morning, Jimmy arrived at his apartment early and assuring he would not turn back on taking the trip; the night before they got into a heated argument about his life. Jimmy's campaign to get him a mate if not in married was getting old. He soul interest was to introduce him to someone who would care for him. It was clear that Alexander's well ordered apartment needed a woman's touch. Alexander moved into the living room then replaced the CD back into its jacket. Waving to his friend it was time to go as he viewed his watch. He was sorry for assuming that everyone was out to get him. Working too long would cause you to think that way without rest. He thought. Alexander gave his apologies to him for yelling so abruptly. For the record, he not looking for anyone and all he desired was a long peaceful rest, far away from any computers and stupid rules. He again strongly express that he was not looking for anyone. Jimmy just stood there watching him pickup his bags not uttering a word. He knew when to leave well enough along. What use would it help anyway? Alexander had locked his heart away from all women and devoted his life, at least he thought to an ideal one man's island. Jimmy was right about him to that point. He was a person who didn't mix words and he admired him for that.

Everything was in its place and not a trace of dust was found. A sign of a sick man Jimmy pondered. Besides, this place needs a women's touch, it needs to be lived in. That very ideal did not amuse Alexander one bit and he displayed it strongly. Jimmy's view of a successful relationship was to date ten women a month and felt it made him an expert on the women. Alexander moving into his kitchen for some orange juice pointed out that just because he desire to live alone and not date doesn't mean he preferred it that way. If the circumstance comes along that he may find just that right female then maybe.

Jimmy quickly turned towards his direction after placing a compact disk into the CD player. To actually hear his friend thinking about finding someone was a wonder in itself. A man solely dedicated to his computer programs, now seeking a mate? Jimmy was shocked after his many attempts. Either Alexander was too busy or too picky, neither one was just right for him. He continued in a skeptical manner uttering, "You are willing to allow a female into this totally modern apartment of yours; to mess with your computer 'Marilyn?' Sleep in your always neat bed?" Jimmy asked. "That I got to see with my own eyes before I die."

Alexander had heard enough.

"You are now crossing the line, enough is enough?"

"Fine with me," Jimmy spoke smiling. "Just having a little fun at your expense, don't be so hard on yourself."

"Let's get out of here." Alexander voiced, upset over the issue. "You act as if I didn't have a life."

"You do now," Jimmy joked helping him out the door.

.

Hours later both arrived at the airport much against Alexander's will. Though he decided not to express his distaste, his stomach felt as if it were an ocean with flowing waves of sickness. He faded in and out as if he was like in a lifejacket, and some poor soul grasping on the life on the high seas. He found pulling himself from his work was a challenging endeavor. When most people would be overjoyed for the fortune in doing so, he guessed it was his protection blanket in a funny sought of way. Alexander's work couldn't hurt his heart the way a woman could. He knew Jimmy had driven him to the airport fearing he would chicken out. Pondering whether he would purposely miss his flight. May be if Jimmy wasn't there he just may have? He thought.

They never had the chance to test that hypothesis.

With every step Jimmy followed him, pushing him on jokingly. It started to seem as if he were under guard by his close attention. Jimmy may have been right all along come to think of it.

They soon viewed the lobby with unwelcoming surprise. Even with its huge corridors it still couldn't accommodate the continued on-slot of weekend travelers. It was as if the air war fares were on again. Reality hit him after Alexander received his ticket at the check-in counter. The lady was very pleasant to him as she confirmed his ticket, rushes of travelers, males, females of all sorts; all pushing, shoving and running seemly in every direction, like a cattle-rush out of control. Like gypsy restless of the world around them. Lost souls it seemed more to him like lost souls never finding any peace. For they too were as he, trying desperately to escape the everyday life in a fish bowl of technology, to at least attempt to see something new; to just stop and smell the roses.

Suddenly, Jimmy broke his thoughts. "Here allow me to assist you," he voiced. Then followed by uttering, "Say, what hell is this? Where are the rest of your bags?" His voice now concerned about Alexander's true intentions.

He responded quickly yet very tired, "What? Are you blind or something?" Alexander pointed in the direction of the two small bags at his feet voicing.

"You got to be joking?" Jimmy asked stun.

"No, I think not my friend. This is all I'll need, any objection?"

"No, just as long as you get on that plane."

"Yeah that too," Alexander replied sadly.

Jimmy shuck his head from side to side opting to accept at least his friend was going on the airplane. He knew Alexander's feelings; any more clothes would be out of the question. If he needed to add to your apparel there's many stores in New Orleans.

"You are staying the entire month, right?" Jimmy asked.

"Sure," Alexander answered stun.

"Flight-108 leaving for New Orleans, now departing at gate twelve! We Repeat! Flight-108 leaving for

New Orleans, now departing at gate 12. Passenger please boards your plane, thank you!" A voice bellowed over the airwaves in the terminal forcing their conversation to be halted abruptly.

"That's your flight my friend, you better get moving and no turning back this time," Jimmy joked.

Alexander was finally taking the much needed vacation.

"I know," he replied.

"Oh! Wait, I have something for you."

"What, hurry my flight is leaving."

"Oh, yeah, here it is. Look, I know you were expecting some stupid toy or something for me. But I just wanted you to know-well-take the damn thing!"

Jimmy thrust in his hands a bizarre looking silver charm.

"What's this!?"

"I found it at your front door this morning in a fancy box lined in blue velvet. Thought someone was giving you a going away gift or something so I brought it with me. The return address is a P.O. Box in New Orleans. Say may be you can track it down while your there, it could be interesting knowing the source. The note had no return home address on it or anything." Jimmy explained. "It just said with love."

The Passion Charm was a half of inch in size and made of pure silver. Upon it were some strange very detailed cravings over it of ancient art work dating back over a hundredth years. On the front there was words craved in French. A tiny red spot in the shape of a heart with an arrow through it rested in the center of the charm. There seemed to be tiny angels craved on the back. Finally the chain was made of fine silver strain string.

"What is it?" Alexander asked.

"Called a Passion Charm."

"You're sure?" He asked wondering.

Yes, a friend of mine from Haiti had one just like it with less detail and he claims it's magic." Jimmy replied. "This one looks a lot older and valuable?"

"You're kidding, right?" Alexander asked.

"Not playing my friend. You're supposed to wear it during your journeys to the unknown far places and before you ask why you should need it; your plane is going to leave you if you don't hurry."

"Ok, I'm going!"

"Good bye,"

"See you in two months," Alexander voice as he backed into the crowd waving.

"Get some rest!" He expressed strongly as he laughed and waved farewell to him.

What was Alexander to do? He didn't know what to say to him and gave him a kindhearted hug in the middle of the corridor. Which no one even noticed for they too were too much in a dash to get to their own planes?

Later aboard the plane, he sat back tranquil for a change. Always conservative in what he did, now to suddenly continue a trip to New Orleans without planning it would be a first for Alexander. Yet the Passion Charm remained upon his mind as he began to laugh at its supposed desire effects. Considering such a piece of silver which was shaped like a candy heart, it surely couldn't bring him any luck in (affaire d'amour). Who ever sent it surely didn't mean for it to land in his hands. He would have cast it in the thrash like he would do any change letter, but what the Hell? It was a gift from the heart of his best friend in life. May be, just may be he might get lucky? Soon his eyes became heavy as the rush of the morning had taken its toll upon Alexander, forcing him to sleep for the short flight to New Orleans.

Yet unaware of what would soon befall him.

Meanwhile in New Orleans, there were laughing going on in Tara's bedroom.

Outside Jeanne had just arrived in co-own a model taxi. The two converted the late model red Mercedes convertible into a taxi to earn some spending money. She only knew Tara for only one year since moving from California for a peaceful life. La Veanna didn't care much for her smartness but Tara needed a friend. It wasn't necessary for her to knock as she would just enter, speaking with Tara's grandmother, La Veanna. She entered the home glanced at La Veanna then hurry on up the stairs to Tara's room. It was then that she heard strange laughing, something was wrong? More peculiar than before, as Tara's laughing seemed out of place? Outside her room Jeanne stops to listen outside the door. There, she could square she heard laughing from another from the inside. As she adjusted her ears upon the door to listen closer it suddenly open. The thrush of it almost caused her to fall into Tara's leggy legs.

"What wrong with you?" Tara asked.

"Uh, nothing?"

"Then why are you pressed upon my door?"

"Was I?" Jeanne played it off.

"Don't shit me!" Tara shouted then grabbed her with great strength, pressing her back against the wall. She was like a wild woman out of control and very dangerous. Jeanne had never seen anything like it, pure unexpected rage coming from once lovable Tara. She was frightened as Tara's eyes seem to turn black then suddenly lighter, turning back to their original color.

"Please yet me down, Tara," she shouted shaking all over.

La Veanna heard the hard thumb and moved to the bottom of the stairs.

"Is there anything wrong up there?" She shouted. "Tara answer me right now!"

Suddenly Tara relaxed realizing that she was scaring her only true comrade; that it was happing again without warming. It was as if she was possessed. "Jeanne, I'm sorry, I'm sorry," Tara cried as this time her tone began remorseless than suddenly faded to a more acceptable tone.

"You're scaring me," Jeanne voiced.

Jeanne had just turned twenty-four years old, a cocky redhead with a great figure for the beach she so often visited. She never went anywhere without her sunglasses to shield her aimless eyes. Her physical appearance could destroy any veteran surfer's concentration as she worn her cutoffs and sky blue roll up blouse. A very attractive female who could hold her own with any female rival accept the unknown before her. Threw out her life, Jeanne had never came a cross a situation such as this.

"I'm sorry," Tara pleaded. "I lost my mind for a minute."

"More than that I'm afraid," Jeanne added.

"I won't happen again, I promise."

"What won't happen again?" Jeanne asked pulling away shaking, caring for her friend. "I still don't know what happen here?"

"I'll explain another time."

"That's not good enough, Tara"

"Please trust me for now. Maybe then I too will understand, we will both laugh at it all?"

Jeanne nodded.

"Thanks," Tara replied.

She gazed upon Tara's appearance and what she was wearing. That being a pale blue long dress from her dead mother's collection compliments of her grandmother La Veanna.

Jeanne took control and order Tara to dress more fashionable. This was truly against her grandmother's wishes. Even though La Veanna was blind from birth, she had an uncanning ability to visualize her surroundings. The two young ladies knew it took hard work to keep in shape and they should not be afraid to show it. They would go and sweat it out at the health club; Jeanne always argued to point strongly. Instead Tara pulled her into the bed room, afraid her grandmother may hear her sexual openness. Tara knew her grandmother would not allow her to expose her body in such a provocative manner; she didn't need this kind of heat and true, Jeanne was bringing her into the twenty-first century behind her grandmother's back or so she thought. For nearly nothing that La Veanna didn't know or her spies didn't inform her of concerning her granddaughter behavior about town.

"Well, aren't you going to change?" Jeanne asked.

"I don't know?" Tara answered banish fully.

Jeanne asked. "What do you mean, you don't know? Why do we have to go through every time I come here?"

"I'm not sure?" Tara answered. "I wanted to but I couldn't."

"You don't want to wear that old dress? That crazy!" Jeanne said.

"Ok, ok I'll find something!"

"Better hurry or we may miss some good fares," Jeanne joked, "and good men!"

"That's all you think about, girlfriend." Jeanne voiced. "What else?"

"Me lately," Tara added. "Lately I've been having this same dream of a man."

"A man, do tell." Jeanne said sitting on the edge of the bed.

"Well he is wearing a black pair of jean and a white shirt. He is handsome with short jet-black sassy hair. Above us are birds flying in a control manner. Suddenly I see him and begin to sweat, my body again to get aroused from his presents. Then suddenly as he comes into my life, he is taken away from me by unknown forces," Tara explained. "Jeanne, I run to help him but something is holding me back?"

"Can you see what?" Jeanne asked.

"I huge black doll," Tara answered. "Then everything goes blank."

"I'm not psychologist, but you have issues here," Jeanne voiced. "Someone or something is trying to tell you something."

"May be one day I will finish the dream."

"Right now you have to finish dressing," Jeanne said.

Tara was truly breath taking and a breath of fresh air for the locals. Though she and Jeanne workout a lot, she looked well off without it. Placing on her short shirt and black low pump, along with a large man white dress shirt, she looked like a dream come true. Her breast naturally pointed upward leaving an impressive lasting imprint. Skillfully, she tied the bottom around her perfect small waist and rolled up the sleeves. Tara thoroughly illustrated the easygoing charm that typified gentle days; reminding any male that it can be best to take the joys of spring lying down, and firm.

Jeanne pulled her top off the display her breast too voicing, "Tara, you as firm as me. The men will fall all over you!"

Tara just blushed.

"We better get going before your grandmother objects again"

"Ok, you know how she feels about you dressing modern." Jeanne said. "I could never figure out how she tells what you're wearing?"

They ease quietly out the front door without saying good bye. La Veanna sat in the living room facing the front window. From outside Tara could see her strangely sitting there listening. Jeanne saw her too but pushed Tara playfully to move on, but something kept sticking in her mind, Jeanne had to get it out. She decided to press Tara for the answers now free from the listening ears of her grandmother.

"Tara, earlier in your room before I had arrived…"
"Yes?"
"…what was all that laughter going on? Don't tell me it wasn't you!" Jeanne asked.

"I can't tell you yet, and I'm not sure myself?" Tara replied.

"That's not good enough, Tara."

Tara only responded as usual stating she knew of nothing of which Jeanne spoke.

Jeanne pressed the issues and Tara denied it strongly again.

"You have to tell me this time," Jeanne asked. "No more hiding."

"Please not now!" Tara cried.

"You remember when we first met?" Jeanne asked.

Tara nodded to confirm she did.

"Jeanne, it was at the abandon cabin a year ago. I was by myself just resting, just enjoying the peace when you came along."

"Thanks a lot!" Jeanne voiced.

"No! You know what I mean," Tara quickly added smiling.

"Yes, I remember I was lost?" She followed up, "I remember it clearly..."

One year ago…

Jeanne spoke aloud to herself confused over traveling for hours in a circle in the swamps. Suddenly there stood before her in the distant a long forgotten slave cabin, in mint condition. Before it, a small pond with white flower trees surroundings. As she approached there was strange laughter from a female voice. She was just pleased that at least she had found someone to help her find her way back home. The sweat was now pouring down her neck onto her firm heated breast. The heat had become nearly unbearable now. Each step Jeanne took seemed to zap her energy. It was nothing like California's heat which for the most part dry. This was humid and very uncomfortable heat, the kind which made your clothes stick to you; it had her struggling for air.

Slowly Jeanne struggled painfully through the shrubbery, peering to see who was there. As she approached closer all became quite and still. Only the wind seemed to move around her and itself only created more discomfort. Strangely there was the absent of bird's noises. In fact there was absents of any creature of any sought? Above her, what was once a bright sunny day now turned strangely dusk? Again she tried to look up at the sky but the trees were so thick above her that they blocked out the once radiant sun. For a moment her fears were telling her to turn back, yet there was no turning back now, there was nowhere to go but forward into the unknown. Clearly unwilling to read the signs, Jeanne didn't know better as she entered the world of the supernatural.

Danger was ahead now and she pondered over moving forward. There seemed like light of some sought breaking though the trees ahead. No, more like a beam of light to a specific clearing. But how can that be she struggled with? Her thoughts kept rushing at her and playing tricks on the mind. It now became an unseen force pulling her ever so close. For a while the air surrounding her seemed thick and nearly impossible to breathe. Her heart pounded rapidly to maintain her needs. But after resting a bit she adjusted to it, never taking her eyes off the beam of light near the abandon lone slave cabin.

"Shit!" Jeanne shouted aloud as she stumped her toe.

Curiosity now took over for trepidation. Each step moved her unwilling and sweating body closer and closer. Now she had a clear view of the cabin as she approached from the rear. Suddenly her nerves began to show themselves, as her hands began to tremble. Her sunglasses fell off her face and she never noticed. Her mind was locked in misgivings. It was too late to turn back now. Too late forget what was happening to her.

Too damn late for all!

Suddenly out of the corner of her eyes she thought she saw a figure flying above the tree lines. All pale in color, but trying to get a fix on it, it strangely vanished from sight. But what she did see was that it had red flaming eyes and heard laughter. She thought.

Even though she had a great tan, one could not guess it because of anxiety. Her skin became pale with fear. She felt it was a total lost, now. Whatever was there she would have to face. She was at the cabin and moved around to the front. Slowly she peeked around the corner and befell, Tara, a sexual diva. She was bathing in the small pond alone only a few feet from her.

"Excuse me," Jeanne whispered in a nervous tone.

No reply.

Tara seemed in a trance and void of her presents. Whatever was there was gone now. Without warning the woman abruptly turned towards her. The glare was haunting and controlling in nature. The pond she was in was strangely clear.

Again she uttered, "Excuse me, I'm lost and wondered."

Suddenly the attractive and arousing figured woman roses out of the pond nude. She walked ever so gracefully towards the shore, not paying Jeanne any attention. She passed her and into the cabin. There was a bizarre glitter upon her entire body, a bright hazing type of glow accompanied by a low humming sound from no unknown origin. Suddenly she noticed Tara was not wet from the pond and coated in a hazy soft mist; which surrounded her perfect body. Like the story of the lady in the pond story, one of her favorite novels. Each step Tara placed down was like a goddess entering a room to welcoming her subjects.

The stun Jeanne gazed on with exalted intrigue, her mind jumping every-which-away on the proper reaction.

Yet the entire vista was beautiful and yet magical. Suddenly there was a sweet aroma in the air and a low sound of singing she thought? Never have she seen anything like it or heard such a song. Never has she seen the likes of Tara in any case.

    Jeanne had seen plenty troubles in her short span of time, more than she should had, one reason that she left California. The stress, the over driving competition, people climbing over other people to gain their little foolish rewards of life and not even remembering what its all was for in the first place? She had had enough of the games of life, of the agony of the big city. But her mind was still there. She could never escape. But seeing Tara Somehow took away the bad memory of her past, it was a magical.

    The shrubbery bowed silently to Tara. Jeanne was at a lost for words for the first time. Not sure what to make of it? The beam of light seemed to follow the nude woman into the cabin then vanished. Suddenly the Sun bellowed its heat as before. She had forgotten it ever being there with the show before her. Another thing that was abnormal was there were no drips of water, nor foot prints upon the ground by the woman.

At this time Jeanne decided she whether be lost then to face whatever was happening. She turned and started back.

"Don't go," Tara voice in a low tone asked sadly.

"What?" Jeanne asked.

"Please don't go," Tara said.

"I don't understand?" Jeanne asked again.

"Please don't go, please…" Tara replied.

Jeanne slowly turned around to view the nude woman now dressing in blue jeans and a white shirt. She was exceptionally beautiful to behold. Tara's eyes were a beautiful hazel brown and hard to break away. Her lips seem so innocent yet full of life. She long jet black hair was alike a crown upon her. Everything about her was perfect to behold.

"I have to go," Jeanne responded half frighten of what she had seemed.

"Are you lost?" Tara asked.

"I'm not sure anymore," Jeanne replied, "What the Hell is going on?"

"You look lost," she uttered to her.

"Who are you?" Jeanne asked.

"My name is Tara and yours?"

No reply.

"You do have a name?" Tara asked.

"Sure, sure, it's Jeanne and I'm lost," she replied surprising herself.

"Hi, Jeanne."

"You, do you live here, Tara?" Jeanne asked wondering.

"No. But for some strange reason I come here, that's all?"

"Just what is this place to you?" Jeanne asked.

No response.

"Please someone has to make reason of this?"

"You can call it, A little privacy and a little treasure!" Tara replied. "Surprisingly I find it so easy to talk with you, Jeanne?"

"Many people say that to me, I'm not sure why?" Jeanne replied. "I can be a real bitch at times."

"Well, pleasure meeting you, Jeanne."

"You to, I think?" She said.

"You know something?"

"Yes." Jeanne asked.

"Sometimes I wake up feeling as if someone was controlling me? It scares me sometime just go to sleep. I feel like a part of me is fighting another deep within myself. Jeanne, the simplest way to say it is my heart knows what best for me, yet I guess as now and always I end here and it's a place which keeps me safe," Tara uttered in a half daze. She too felt trust in Jeanne.

"Strange, who is controlling you?" Jeanne asked.

"Don't know yet."

"You know another thing; I feel there's someone out there just waiting for me. I'm sure of it!"

Later they were conversing as if nothing had ever happen. Jeanne found a new friend though a little strange sometimes. Reluctantly she decide to pay no attention to what she thought she may have seen, and opting clearly to place it as her imagination playing tricks on her. Also claiming too much heat was the cause for the illusions. Tara had shown Jeanne the way back to the road willingly and during the trip the ladies got to know one another. Yet each time Jeanne would ask Tara of her childhood, she only received silence. Strangely Tara couldn't remember her past. So Jeanne just let well enough alone. If her new friend blocked out his past, there must have been a good reason. It was not her place to probe.

PART IV

Chances Are

"Sir-Sir, we have landed." A soft voice came to him, awaking Alexander from his deep hibernation.

Glancing upward towards the soft tone of her voice, he viewed an airline host named Karen. He glances out of the always too small windows of the plane and started to ponder if anyone could actually fit through such an insignificant hole.

"Sir?" She asked.

"Oh thanks," he replied then proceeded out of the plane.

Later Alexander reached the terminal. The area to him seemed like a fiery furnace with temperate reaching near hundred degrees. Soon Alexander was stepping down the terminal in a hurry to rid himself of the ever growing crowd and concern why he had to come here? To him it was a sorry state and bad timing to come this time of year.

"A person could bake in this humid weather!" He loudly voiced.

Alexander was overheard by an attractive 24 year old young diva, smartest, sexiest, and most savvy woman he'd ever seen. She drove a taxi with her redhead friend, both wearing taxi caps. Gazing at him the lady voiced strongly, "Maybe you should give my home a try before scrapping us completely?"

"What?" He replied stunned.

"Well, we somehow managed to tolerate the heat just fine. I'm sure your be able to adjust to it, give it a chance," she commented from behind surprised him, causing him to jump from Tara's seductive voice. Then glancing in the direction of the sounds, he viewed a vision of delight. Her hair was long and sassy, black as a moonless night and well suited for the climate of the region. With skin so smooth and clear with an even tone color engulfing her complete body. She was totally captivating to behold. She was a jewel of exceptional beauty and innocent charm with a splash of lust build in to drive men crazy.

Alexander was in love the first time he laid eyes upon her. She was at least 6 feet in height with a perfect frame of a body. What she had would set anyone to answer her beckon call. With Tara's firm full breast which hadn't been touch by man, she was a virgin in all ways. They pointed through the thin shirt she was wearing, arousing him so. Never had he meet any woman who gripped him so. A little breeze which was passing off her brought even a more delightful fragrance of sweetness from her. And he consumed ever bit of the essence willingly.

He was never a believer of love at first sight, but this he could not denied! His eyes locked on to Tara's eyes and hers to Alexander.

Jeanne knew from the start what was happening and was very pleased at their reaction towards each other. She vowed to herself get these two lovers together at all cost. She had never seen Tara act so responsive towards any man they met. This was truly a good sign, she pondered.

Alexander finally utter, "I'm sorry for the remarks about your home, and if your heart has any hope for me, forgive me?"

His tone was expressed deeply to her as he smiled at the vision of love. Tara looked on with the same interest and desire. Her lips parted just slightly breathing in much needed air, and moist and inviting to him to approach them. But something suddenly pulled her back. Her heart which was first racing at an alarming rate eased down now. Yet her mind still dreamed of him holding her.

"I think I love you?" She murmured in a very low tone.

"What?" He asked surprised.

"Tara?" Jeanne shouted stun herself.

He requested her to repeat what she'd foolishly bellowed out, only sadly catching part of it. She refused and opting to just smile in confusion of wanting him.

"Tara, you don't even know his name," Jeanne quickly covered for her friend. "Just forget what was said. Tara is a bit confused I think?"

Tara stood there in silence not even knowing his name. Yet something was surely wrong.

"What do you think, girlfriend?" Jeanne whispered.

"What?" Tara asked.

"He's handsome and have very appealing to the eyes, don't you think?"

"There something about those eyes that bother me, Jeanne," Tara voiced playing off her feelings with humor. She discovered an overwhelming desire of closeness towards him. It would have been a great falsehood to act as if there weren't any feelings and both knew it.

Alexander and Tara became mentally and physically attractive to each other in a very short period of time, chance meeting.

"We better go now," Tara voiced backing off.

"Yeah, I think we better," Jeanne added.

"Fine," Tara followed still eyes locked on him.

TARA THE FORBIDDEN FRUIT - 63

"Time to go girlfriend," Jeanne whispered as she had to pull away Tara from his side.

Both he and Tara just watched each other sending chills down each other's back.

"Forgive me?" He yelled once more.

Tara finally responded softly, "All is forgiven."

"Well...I hope to see you again." He said.

Tara nodded, sadly waved to him. Her eyes seemed to want to cry for him. Then a sudden jerk from Jeanne forced her along.

"Why did you do that?" Tara yelled at her.

"Look, I know what I'm doing and it's best for you!" Jeanne uttered hurriedly Tara down the corridor.

Alexander wasn't sure what to make of this? But he was too tired now and hurried back to pickup his bags. Yet his mind began to wonder what the young ladies names were, expectedly the one hurried pulled away? Finally he decided if it was meant to be, they will meet each other again. In his heart he knew faith would see to it that the special lady again would cross his path. It was meant to be. Tara had surely captured his heart and Jeanne's sudden actions only left him pondering of what could be?

Meanwhile Tara was very upset with Jeanne's actions too. She pulling her way from Alexander at the time they were really connecting. Never had Tara met such an interesting man with no connection to her past. Her expression was one of contempt towards her supposed to be best friend, Jeanne.

"Why did you do that?" Tara asked in a tantrum.

"Let me explain," Jeanne responded.

"No, first you push me into dates that don't workout then. Then finally I meet someone who stirs me up inside so; I don't understand you, Jeanne?"

"Wait a minute!"

"What?"

"Hold it right there!" Jeanne yelled back catching the attention of those in the parking lot near their taxi. "You like him, don't you?"

"You drove him away from me, did you forget?" Tara replied.

"No, I didn't. I mean you really cherish him?"

Tara looked suddenly ashamed by her own actions. She had always been a person who could control her rage. Even when other men call out to them walking around the airport, it would never faze her. But this was something new. Something she strangely had never felt so strongly about for some reason. She wanted him and Jeanne had clearly intruded in their enthusiasm.

Tara looked up at Jeanne with passion, whispering as if ashamed, "I told him, I loved him, Jeanne."

"What?"

"I mean, I told him but he didn't hear me well. At least I think he didn't?" Tara said.

"Tell you what," Jeanne replied. "That's not like you, Tara."

"Don't you think I know that?" Tara followed upset, "Don't why I said it? But it just felt it had to be said!"

"While it's out now."

"Jeanne, I just had too." Tara replied.

"But you only met him a few minutes go," Jeanne added.

"I know, I know ... but it as if I've known him long ago. I just have this bizarre yearning, feeling about him. Like...like...damn!" Tara cursed.

"Get it out," Jeanne said.

"I don't understand it myself, but I need him inside," Tara pleaded.

To say Jeanne was shocked would be an under statement. She could square she saw tears coming from Tara's eyes. This was a special moment in Tara life, one which would affect her very being. Tara quickly turned in embarrassment moving the driver side of their taxi. Jeanne knew what she was doing, plotting all the time to get them together. She found Alexander to be attractive too, but reserved that right to herself. It was a plus for Tara to desire him so and she had to hurry to put matchmaking into motion. There was little time to pull this off so she had to work fast.

Meanwhile the soaring heat was making Alexander very uncomfortable and he was struggling trying to carry him bag. Finally making it to the taxi loading area, he didn't know where to go but that was fine. He knew wherever it was, would have to be away from the modern world. Something unknown was pulling to him in the location where Tara and Jeanne stood. Maybe he thought it was faith to see Tara again so soon? For a chance to see Tara again he wasn't willing to allow her to leave without knowing more. Quickly he waved at them to stop and receiving just that. Tara noticed him immediately and gazed at Jeanne, now knowing why they left in such a hurry. A huge smile broke on Tara's beautiful face in tribute to her friend.

"Thanks," she whispers in Jeanne's ears.

Jeanne leaps to Alexander's side.

"Say! Waiting to ride with us?" She called out.

He nodded.

Jeanne's red hair shining brightly in the Sun's beams caught the little breeze slightly before him.

Alexander just stood there speechless as he gazing at Tara's beauty again. Jeanne repeated her statement, but still he looked on as if in a trance. He was rational man but this not what he had expected out of the vacation. His mind was not sure what he was walking in? Alexander knew he was walking the line.

"Sorry, yes!" He voiced with a smile.

"Thought you were suffering from a heat stoke," Jeanne joked.

"Can you escort me to the French Quarters, that if it's not out of your way?" He asked.

Jeanne replied, "Sure! We can take you to the front door. That's our job. Jump in before we change your mind."

She then opened the back door allowing him in with their blessing.

Suddenly Tara became strangely silent and passive. She seemed very nervous by his present there. From within herself, she wasn't sure why but Alexander represent her future? Only that she knew it was wrong. A chilly breeze passed over her body from nowhere? Tara just prayed he would change his mind about going now.

Crying out of anxiety, "There are places to stay and more secured for you near the airport."

"I know but this place interest me," Alexander joked.

"There are a lot better hotels," Tara added.

Jeanne noticed her denial over his request. "Wait a minute! Just what's going on here, Tara?" She asked.

"Nothing, just thought he wanted better, that's all," she replied. "There are better sites."

"You just do the driving this time and I'll tend the customer," Jeanne joked. "You've never turned down a customer's request before."

Alexander rested in the backseat as they drove off. He could see Tara watching him through the rearview mirror every now and then. Once are twice they would give each other a smile.

Tara admired the way he dressed. Tall as he was; his black jeans fitted him well. His strong chest and the white rolled up shirt only added to his mystic. But it was the way he walked. The way his waist moved with his black leather belt highlighting his well shaped body. Again she gave him a smile of acceptance and inviting smirk.

"I'm sorry but I don't know your name?" He asked.

"What's yours?" Jeanne asked turning around to him.

"Alex, Alexander," he answered.

Tara didn't reply to his request strangely. An overwhelming feeling came over her causing her to with withdraw. Somehow, Tara felt an abnormal flow of je ne sais quoi coming from him.

"Sorry Alexander, I don't know what has gotten into her lately," Jeanne jumped in. "Never mind her, my name is Jeanne and this suddenly silent lady ... and my partner is Tara."

"Who's ideal for the taxi?" He asked.

She voiced looking oddly at her friend, "We usually drive this taxi a couple of hours a day to take the rest off." Then Jeanne turned back around upset over Tara's denial and refusal to speak. She punched Tara secretly at her side.

"What about you, Tara? What occupies the rest of your day? Could it be some man of your dreams?" He asked trying to see her face back through the rear view mirror.

"Nothing, I'm a virgin when it comes to going out," Tara said.

Alexander gazed at with great interest and returned the smile. He was satisfied to lean back willingly, resting back and engulfing her alluring scent placed upon her body. Slowly he was being drawn into her world, her mysterious world.

Tara again looked back at him voicing softly, "Well ... where do you wish to board at? Uptown?"

"I'm not sure," he answered.

She hoped he would be near her somehow. She couldn't explain why? Her body began to tremble without warning being in his present. She struggle to keep her composure as scent of him consumed her too. This was a man out for her heart and she knew it.

"My friend, Jimmy Arthur said to try somewhere in the Quadroon section. Say that it would be an adventure to remember, also that I would see things never seen before."

"Jimmy Arthur?" Tara asked.

"Yes a longtime friend of my childhood," he answered. "Say if I ever needed to trust someone, it would be him. I trust him with my life. Countless of times he has been there for me and that go a long way back and a long with me."

Suddenly the car jolted onto wrong traffic lane and onto coming traffic. Tara didn't even notice it until Jeanne shouted at her to watch out! All was stun by now and a massive truck was head directly in their path. Then something strange happen, Tara glaze at the on coming truck with passion as sweat poured from her face. Her raven color hair appeared to fare up as if the wind gust at it. Her eyes became sparkling as if the sunshine had bounce upon the lake. Suddenly the truck halted just a car length before them, allowing Tara to speed to the right side of the truck and avoiding a fatal crush. She quickly returned back on the right side of the road a little confused and dazed but in control now. Still shocked Alexander and Jeanne pondered over the strange out come, as they both felt their Maker was coming.

"Is everyone alright?" Tara asked.

"Fine I think?" Alexander replied shaken.

"What the hell was that about!?" Jeanne asked Tara.

"I'm sorry for that," she replied. "The steering wheel got stuck." She continued to drive as if all was well, but it was not.

"The steering wheel?" Jeanne spoke, "It never happened to me?"

"There's always a first time, Jeanne."

Jeanne looked on confused and bewildered over Tara's strange behavior. She opted to question the matter later as not to frighten Alexander.

Tara became oddly withdrawn again.

"Maybe you should let drive?" Jeanne asked.

"No, no I'm fine now," she said in a low tone. "I'll take you wherever you wish to go."

"Say, I know just the place you seek, Alexander. This is your lucky day!" Jeanne added looking ahead now. Her willingness to keep them together would soon come at a price.

Tara bellowed at her friend, "No! Not that place!"

"Yes, if he desires to go, let him!" Jeanne voiced back smiling.

"Please take me there, ok?" Alexander pleaded with Tara.

"Very well then if you desire," Tara answered accepting their faith unwillingly.

Jeanne felt the attraction of her sassy raven color hair friend to him and wasn't allowing Tara to let him get away. The location they were headed for, she was well aware that Tara lived in that part of town. Therefore her plan was to place Alexander right in her everyday path. Unfortunately, Jeanne didn't know about Tara's strange past. Nor that Tara for some reason unknown to her could not remember her childhood for good reasons. What it was or even aware of what she was horribly groomed to be.

Hours later they soon drove down a street called Dumaine Street. In sight was an ancient red brick boarding house around the 1700's, a haunting looking place to be direct.

"There! That's the place," Jeanne yelled wildly pointing out of the car window.

Tara acted as if she wanted to keep driving.

Suddenly Jeanne yelled again, "Quick, pull over Tara or we'll pass it! The steering will again?"

Alexander glanced out the window in a hurry to get a full view of the place. Though it was ancient, it didn't bother him as much as it seemed to torment Tara's soul.

"It's ancient. I give you that," his only reply echo his true feelings.

"You like?" Jeanne asked.

"Are you two sure someone actual lives there?"

Jeanne nodded.

His concern grew even more in his voice. Wondering if he'd made a mistake coming there. But at this point he would almost give anything to stay near Tara.

Jeanne voiced quickly, "Oh someone stays there all right. Isn't that correct, Tara?"

She did not, could not answer her at first. She was abnormally frightened to a fever pitch of the residence.

"Tara, are you all right?" Jeanne asked.

"Yes, I was supposed to be born there all," she uttered.

"You don't say," Alexander voiced in joy of actually renting a room at the same place of her birth. Still the way Tara answered him was in a reluctant manner caused him to gaze at her strongly wondering why she was, unsure. Thoughts passed across his mind, were it because of bad memories or what?

The trio drove even closer to the brickyard. The closer Alexander got, enable him to see the place was restore to its fine splendor form of yesterday. As soon as the three gotten out of the old Mercedes taxi, Tara became chilly and weak, causing her to shiver. Even though the temperature was a hundred degrees she could not shake the eerie feeling. It was the first time she had ever venture this close the place of her birth.

"What's wrong?" Alexander asked.

"I'm not sure but there's something malicious about this place, I'm sure of it!" Tara said strangely, forcing him to ask again.

"What evil?" He asked.

Tara replied, "It's nothing."

"What do you mean it's nothing?"

Jeanne jumped in citing, "There are a lot supernatural stories coming from this area about voodoo. You know the ones we see in the movies and books. But don't let it get to you, you're here to relax and have fun."

"Well I'm a logical man," he added.

"It's always dangerous when you play in other people's playground without knowing the rules. Please be careful while you're here," Tara voiced with concern.

"I will."

"Well, we better get you settle, never mind my thoughts," Tara voiced. "They tend to wonder at times." Yet her bones were trying to tell her something true. There was a dangerous haunting comma surrounding the residence. Tara's gazed wildly at the outside of the building, trying to figure out what she was experiencing.

"Look, you two are so silly. You know what this place was?" Jeanne interceded, "The place used to be some abandoned slave auction house, rumor has it. But I'm not certain about it? I only know it's an inexpensive place to stay, and everyone could save money." She paused then utter in a very low tone, "Though strangely no one is ever here?"

"Next thing you'll tell me is, there are spirits there," he joked.

Tara suddenly stared at him as if she knew something horrible. Watching him lifting his bag, she stood there puzzled and continued to fear for his safety not knowing why? Yet she managed to smile towards his direction, a sign of joy in meeting him, but the phobia remained.

"While aren't you going to say goodbye?" Alexander asked.

"I hope you enjoy your stay here," Tara responded.

"That goes double for me." Jeanne added.

He paused and looked as if he were headed for prison.

"Will I see both of you later?" He asked.

"You bet," Jeanne said happily.

"What about you, Tara?" He asked wanting Tara's reaction to his request greatly.

"Alexander, tell you what, why don't Jeanne and I pick you up tonight," she spoke with concern for his well being, always staying on the driver side of the taxi. Then as he nodded he headed in with the agreement for a much wanted meeting with them.

"What time?" He asked happily.

"Tara added, "Let's said about 7:00pm this evening?"

"Fine, I'll see you then," he answered.

Alexander was totally glad to meet Tara and Jeanne. They created a special kind of understanding among each other in such a short time. Jeanne truly the matchmaker for them, but they were unaware of their conversation being observed intensely from a short distant across the parkway.

La Veanna, Queen of Voodoo knew of his coming in visions. She demanded that Tara, her un-godly granddaughter be watched throughout her life. This task was bestowed to a local Voodoo doctor named Doctor Walker. He flourished as a mind-reader and dabbler in astrology and for special magical effects sold shells and peddles which had been soaked for three days in evil-smelling oil rendered from snakes, lizards, and frogs. He was a huge coal-black man with a completely tattooed face. Doctor Walker observer every movement and every word said by them. His skills included reading lips, watching as if it were his own life in the balance. Finally he came to the conclusion of what he had seen wasn't good for their people. Knowing the time was the spring, the time of the long awaited particular birthday of Tara. A birthday which meant she would soon take her place as High Priestess, like it or not. It was ordain before her birth.

Nearby Tara through her telepathic powers felt Doctor Walker presents in the area and became very uncomfortable and nervous. Suddenly she glanced at Alexander expressing also that they had to leave.

"Don't worry about anything," she cried seeing his uneasiness about being left there. "We'll protect you if any bad ghost attacks you."

"You are joking?" Alexander asked.

"Tara just playing," Jeanne said.

Strangely, he could sense what she was feeling partly.

"We'll see you later," Tara added then peeled off and left him behind at the boarding house alone.

In the car the two discuss what had happen. Tara refused to enlighten Jeanne of her feelings. Yet she could not block out the feelings of danger about the residence. For her life was a troubled one with blackouts and continue nightmares of an afterlife which played on her mentality. It only confused her more as her birthday approached.

    At the time they left him there, Alexander was somewhat apprehensive about the whole thing. Uttering to myself aloud, "Here's goes nothing." He took a very deep breath, choked on his nervousness and proceeds into the structure. Inside he could not help notice the enormous collections of African art upon the beautifully printed walls and on the floor below him. The designs were exceptional to the human eyes with colors bright and lavish. Alexander looked for assistants but founded none. Suddenly an icy chill fell upon his body without warning. Before him was a check-in counter which seemed to be out of place, may be placed there hastily? He continued to glimpse around the huge lobby, finally deciding to approach the desk.

    With a digital camera he presided to take some pictures of his surroundings. There was a room just to the right with a blue violet crushed curtain covering the doorway. He could hear voices from behind it and decide to approach it with interest. Just as he was about to open it suddenly the curtain flew half way open. Before him were two huge size men with painted faces. One had on a black hat with a feather in it, wearing a brown suit. The other dressed in a dark blue suit with tie and had ear rings. Upon both their neck were a charm like piece hanging. Before them there was a table with powered of assorted colors and they seemed to be mixing them in small bottles carefully. Quickly they blocked Alexander's view and backed him away from the curtain. The man in the black suit removed a huge knife from his jacket. The other took a pair of huge blades and together they approach Alexander to harm him. What he had seemed was a clear mistake and would cost him his life.

"May I help you Sir?" A voice blasted out of nowhere to him.

Turning around, there was no one oddly present behind him. Then as he turned around to face the desk, there stood an old Mulatress woman about ninety years of age gazing at him with cold steel eyes, watching him as if he had no right to be there. The sudden sight of her hard glare startles him; for a moment he thought his spirit jumped out of his body.

"What's the matter?" She said roughly.

"You scared the hell out of me!" He shouted.

"I surely doubt that, young man," she added. "Hell is not here."

He added still jumpy, "Say, where did you come from anyway? It was as if you've appeared out of nowhere?"

No reply and only a gaze preceded his request.

Placing his bag down he uttered, "Well, I'm looking for a room for a month or two if you please."

Still her eyes and wrinkled face had a ghostly expression of non-expression. Deep wrinkles of advance age. He leaned over and the 'Passion Charm' which Jimmy had given him fell loose from his neck. It quickly dropped towards the ground settling at the old woman's feet. A sudden change of demeanor came upon her. One could say of astonishment and even fright from the likelihood of it being in his very possession. Fortunately, she misunderstood the charm to be from La Veanna to allow him to stay there; for it belonged to Tara. Anything else, he may have died there.

She stated in a perplexity of tones, "I'm sorry for being rude to you and hoped you will not report me."

The two men slowly backed away and returned behind the curtain.

Alexander felt at ease with their reaction and took no notice of its nature nor assumed what it meant. His mind was too tired to focus on anything now. Taking it as a vindication of her actions before, feeling it was part of the house hospitality and dismissing it. She fell upon her old weak keens before him in forgiveness. The sudden reaction from her shocked him tremendously.

"Hey, what are you doing? That's all right, please. Look, all I only wish is a room. Now please get up from the floor, your too old to be doing this," Alexander uttered worrying about her and helping her up.

The old Mulatress woman handed him back the charm in her trembling hands thanking him. Slowly and in discomfort, she moves around the desk in a humble matter. Pulling from under the desk, she removed a special key and passed it him, slightly smiling. There were tears of joy now coming from her once cold eyes. With her fingers she pointed to the register for him to sign in, uttering, "You're in room three on the second floor."

"Thank you," Alexander voiced signing the book.

"Hope you enjoy your stay," she spoke in a frighten tone.

He quickly proceeded to his long awaited room, still engulfed with astonishment over what had happen. His mind wasn't too clear to seek out what had transpired. Rest was what he severely needed as he tiredly made it up the stairs.

Moments later, entering his room there strangely seemed to be a feeling of eerie spirits, evil or good natured he wasn't sure. Opting to cast it off as nerves, he thought it may be a ridiculous feeling, yet it was there for a brief moment.

"Mind must be playing tricks on me?" Alexander whispered to himself.

Soon the strange ghastly feelings passed rather quickly. The room was still oddly in the same fashion it were over twenty-four years ago, maybe even since it was built, a hundred year ago with the same simple brass bed and faded prints upon its walls. Little was he aware of the room rented was the same place of Tara's birth. May be that is why he thought he felt her presents there. Listless from the trip, he placed his bag down, jumped upon the bed and decided to get some rest before the awaited evening with the ladies. Knowing later he would see the radiant, Tara and stylish Jeanne. The thought of them brought a huge grin which was missing from his wearisome face. For it took no time for Alexander to drift soundly in a deep appreciated slumber.

TARA THE FORBIDDEN FRUIT - 84

Meanwhile not far from his restful hibernation in a wooded area, there sat a two-story brick house. This was a special home owned by the Voodoo Queen, La Veanna, appointed grandmother of Tara. There, she pursued her powers over her subjects. Also living there was Tara which dwelled there because of La Veanna's illness of old age, for soon it would be time to pass on the throne to Tara. Both La Veanna and the Doctor Walker were practitioners of black magic, and derived substantial incomes from the sale of charms, amulets, and magical powers, all guaranteed, to cure, the purchaser's every ailment, to grant his or hers desire, and to confound or destroy their enemies. With this knowledge, La Veanna had taught Tara all she knew, placing it deep in her subconscious mind. This was preformed as she slept in a soundless trance. She would slowly come into these powers as her birthday neared. Any sudden shock before than could cause enormous uncertainty!

Later that evening about 1:00 pm, Tara and Jeanne was preparing to leave when a knock came at the front door. Coming down the stairs, both ladies hurried to answer it. Tara suddenly halted for a moment. Her action freeze Jeanne which was behind her.

Jeanne cried, "What's the matter? Are you going the answer the door?"

Tara's psychic feeling was pulling her back. Jeanne asked again and Tara moved on unwillingly. Slowly she turned the door knob to except what she thought was evil.

"I wish to speak with your grandmother," A tattooed face man spoke.

"Doctor Walker?" Tara asked.

"Where is she, Tara?" Doctor Walker smiled in a scandalous matter.

But before Tara could even reply or even turn around, there stood her grandmother as she stepped out of the darkness. She stood firm at the man known as Doctor Walker. Tara noticed the position was so intense it made even her look twice. With a swift change of expression, La Veanna smiled to relax her granddaughter's nerves.

"Now my dear, you and your little friend, Jeanne move along. Hurry now ladies. I have some things to attend to," she voiced forcing them out of the door with her fragile hands.

"But grandmother?" Tara asked.

"See you later," they replied as obliging her.

Outside on the porch the two ladies continue their conversation. Still Tara felt unease seeing Doctor Walker at their dwelling. He had never been seen in person though she had felt his present numerous times. There was something dangerous about the tattooed man which frightens her. Now Jeanne was full of questions about Doctor Walker and Tara found it hard to evade them.

"How is it that the tattooed man knew your name?" Jeanne asked. "And what business he has with your great grandmother?"

"I'm not sure, he seems to know everything," she replied all the time feeling his unscrupulous nature.

"You're not telling me what you know?" Jeanne asked.

"Look we have a meeting before meeting Alexander and we have to go cross town for several hours first," Tara played off the questions.

"Ok, may be you tell me the whole story one day," Jeanne added as they drove off the mood changed to hostility as the front door closed.

La Veanna's eyes became a deep yellow tone. Upset over Doctor Walker's unexpected appearance at her home, their late nightly rendezvous to control the consciousness of Tara was now in danger. The total nerves of him to surface at her home while Tara was still present causes only confusion to the grand plan of her birth right. In a terrible rage Doctor Walker had to face La Veanna. Her main concern hindered upon why must he come here at such a critical phase of the process? She long sensed the evil-smelling oil renderings from the snake, lizards, and frogs he carried with him. Doctor Walker quickly explained the meeting of her granddaughter with the stranger of another city. Yet she already was aware and at the same time feared of their closeness.

Doctor Walker warned of the yet jeopardy of the closeness and the ceremony that were to happen. Clearly he respected La Veanna even though she was blind at birth. Most native in the surrounding area claimed she could do things better than ones with perfect sight. That she embodies a sixth sense enabling her to explore beyond the rim of the fourth dimension. She continued to gaze in the doctor's direction. She finally instructed him to end the relationship with all speed. But the Doctor Walker stun at the order complained about any possible interference from Tara. His concern surrounded what if she protects him? La Veanna could not give him an answer to that now. There were still confusing thoughts on Tara's abilities. Could she or could not have mastered total control of her psychic powers so soon? La Veanna still possessed part of Tara's consciousness if not completely. But if it by chance happened, she too feared that if Tara were forced into her new role as queen too soon, she could become a threat to all.

La Veanna bellowed, "Take care of Alexander!"

"What of Tara?" He asked again.

"I will deal with my granddaughter," she replied, "It is not of your concern, Doctor Walker. She is not to be harmed! She is not to know of this pending action, understand?"

"Yes, I will force him home," he responded shaking.

"Where is this man?"

"He resides at the Old Brick House," he answered.

"I see, take care of him right away!"

"Shall I kill him?" Doctor Walker asked.

La Veanna paused then in a muttering voice slowly, "Yes."

With that statement Doctor Walker departed her home hurriedly to perform his task.

Much later Doctor Walker headed towards Alexander's dwelling to place a "gris-gris" at his room door. The celebrated "gris-gris," the most feared of all Voodoo magic were to be used on him. Earlier that evening, Doctor Walker gathered what he needed to make a "gris-gris." It was composed of anything more than a little cotton and leather bag filled with powered brick, yellow ochre, and cayenne pepper, with the occasional addition of nail paring, hair, and bits of reptile skin.

As he arrived there with his horrible gift no one in the brickyard as the word got out to certain caretaker of the house. Quietly he moved up the stairs always gaze at the upper floors as not to be caught. The hallway was dark and oddly silent. There, he carefully placed on the doorstep in the dark hallway his gift of terror, and assured the "gris-gris" was supposed to work incalculable harm to the occupant of the room. Alexander took two glasses of water from a vase near his bed and began to undress. A few minutes later he began to get a sudden fever. He only assumed it was from the swelling heat of the area unaware of the "gris-gris" being placed at his outer door. This continued for an hour, psych agony, suffering, delirium, and numbness took over. The room to him seemed like a Turkish bath. He continued to sweat as the black magic pressed on incandescing him. Alexander's attempts to rise were a total failure. His legs were as though they were paralyzed, insensible to touch.

After continues attempts somehow he only managed to pull himself off the bed and towards the window. He dragged himself along the floor and pulled himself up by the chair. Wishing to get some fresh air to clear his bedazzle mind, he looked out of the window now, but his eyes could not focus. All he could see was a glare of the sunset down for the evening. Suddenly the room surrounding him began to swirl at an alarming rate until he dropped to the floor unconscious.

Later that evening around 7:00pm driving up at the brickyard was Tara and Jeanne arriving and unaware of Alexander's pending death. Tara sensed something was improper quickly. The neck of her hair was tingling with possibility. A sudden pain struck at her very core of emotion almost doubling her up. She strangely felt a clairvoyant connection of conscious thought with Alexander. It was as if she could see through his eyes and feel the anguish he was enduring. This ability of consciousness with others had never manifested so strongly before and was hard to address or brush off in her mind.

Suddenly she cried, "Hurry Jeanne!"

"What wrong?" She asked.

"It's Alexander!"

"What about him? How can you tell?" Jeanne asked in a confusing tone.

"We just have to hurry," she replied, "His is in jeopardy!"

"Look Tara, I know that you sometimes get these strange feelings and I turn a blind eye to them, but this one bothers me a great deal," Jeanne voiced.

"You have to just believe me."

"Ok, I'll go along with this, but you have some explaining to do after this," Jeanne cried then nodded.

"Anything, just we have to go now!" Tara shouted leading the way with Jeanne flowing closely.

Inside the Brick House all the light are oddly out. Jeanne took two candles on the counter and lit it. The glow of the candle made the huge room seem magical and fearful. Suddenly Tara felt as if someone or something was watching them. Flashes of her past suddenly evaded her thoughts at an alarming rate, too swiftly for her to comprehend. Tara stubbles off her nerves and continued on with Jeanne's help. Rushing up the stairs to his room, Tara suddenly halted a few steps from Alexander's room. Never had she been inside since her birth and the surrounding confused her thoughts. There was a slight aroma with a sweet taste in the small corridor causing her to proceed with care. Her heart was pushing her on now and the great interest she had in Alexander. There stood the old woman gazing every so bizarre at the "gris-gris" bag resting at the foot of the door. Tara was frozen in her steps at the site strange woman with Jeanne at her side in silence.

"What doing, old woman?" Jeanne asked.

Tara only looked on with astonishment.

"Tara, say something?" Jeanne asked.

"Why are you here?" Tara finally asked.

Now her mind started to address what was being seen and her processing skills took over. Discovering strangely she knew of the bag for no apparent reason, never to her knowledge having to come upon one before, yet her intellect knew of its powers.

"Open the door!" Tara ordered, forcing the old woman to fellow.

The old woman entered the room voicing, "You must hurry immediately to the Voodoo queen to procure a counter-charm."

"What is she talking?" Jeanne asked.

Jeanne saw Tara dazed and took things into her own hands. Suddenly she threw the woman out of the room and slammed the door rudely behind her.

"What some people would say," Jeanne uttered upset and concerned.

The spunky Jeanne was herself not a believer of the supernatural scene, but recent events did cause her to rethink some of the rejection to a higher degree of certainty.

By now Alexander was still out cold next to his bed. His breathing was heavy and heart beating at an alarming rate. His eyes lids were shaking as he was in a trance. Tara screamed for Jeanne's aid as they helped him back onto the bed. It was evident the first time was they needed get his fever down. So Jeanne through Tara's order dumped the water from the vase and hurried out to get cold water. Tara remained as her soft hands continue touching and rubbing carefully Alexander's heated forehead. They were now left alone for the first time and both knew he was dying. The signs were strong that he didn't have long to live. Tara began to display hurting tears as she held Alexander tight upon the bed waiting for Jeanne return. Suddenly he gazed at her awaking but still dazed. He still couldn't speak or signal her of his feelings, but Tara knew they desired each other.

Tara also knew well that nothing humanly was wrong him as she exam him closely. The only trouble now was that she was losing him quickly. She once looked around the room viewing that this was the same room she was born in. Without warming suddenly the special magic powers of healing which were locked deep inside her unleashed upon him. Strangely the feelings she had for him caused Tara to be overtaken in the powerful form of spells and incantations while in a trance. This allowed her voodoo sorcery to overcome the efforts of another who wished Alexander great harm. Tara gently placed his head upon the pillow. She keen beside Alexander's bed and began to concentrate.

There was an unknown force in room which consumed her very soul, and at the same time supplying her with psychic powers. The tranquility was now horribly broken and the war of black magic now engaged. Spirit evil or good took over the room placing the lovers in some kind of fourth dimension limbo of some sought. As Hell's fires sprouted across the room, below them it was they could see the River of Hell. The entire room took on a hellish pandemonium of torment. Gusting winds came into the room in a rushing and strong breeze from the ocean, during a hailstorm. Yet there were no ocean! Alexander was now an unwilling witness to the forbidden power of the supernatural. His absorbing of the rapid changing events was overwhelming in his weaken condition and just before blacking out he heard Tara yelling.

Tara cried out," "Houm! Dance Calinda! Voudou Magnian!"

Suddenly Alexander's body started to rise like baked bread in an oven over his bed, floating in midair. Even Tara wasn't aware of what was happening about her. Her feelings for him and her own impregnable determination took over her mind to control the events. It was clear that at La Veanna's home she too could feel majestic power in the air. She was not pleased and feared losing control of Tara. Clearly this was not the way she planned the event. And clearly she needed special help from another near more dangerous adversary to change the tide then she, something she was reluctant to call upon.

Back at the Brick house Tara bellowed again, "Aie! Aie! Dance Calinda!" And again the winds blew stronger and more directly coming from the Hell's fires which had consumed the room. Finally, Alexander's body began its decline back upon his bed and all the ailing had cleared. Alexander was stun and now clearly out of peril from the high fever as the winds abruptly halted. Through Tara's actions were of an Empathic nature, she had adsorbed all his agony, and all his afflictions, transporting it out him to herself; then slowly discharging it telepathy out of her. Tara had felt his discomfort deeply as it drained most of the life force out of her, and knowing as she cried that she was risking her own life for him. Still Tara knew inside Alexander was the one. She too had come out of the trance, only to fall upon her love's chest from exhaustion. The nearly full extensions of her psychic powers were pushed greatly, forcing Tara to the point she was not accustomed to. She telepathic powers were now controlling the events to secure her will.

A few moments later Jeanne returned. "What the hell is happening in here?" Jeanne shouted rushing into the disorganized room. It appeared as if a tornado had left its calling card there. The only winds remaining was a soft cool breeze coming into the room; out of the ordinary because the air was very humid and hot outside. She rushed to the window and quickly closed it. Then notice strangely that Tara was out cold on Alexander's bed.

"Wake up lady," she uttered, "Tara are you all right?"

No reply.

Jeanne reached over shaking her best friend's head trying to bring her around, but only woke Alexander.

"What happen here?" She asked.

Alexander not feeling any after affects of the high fever. Nor had he remember undergoing such a dramatic event. He thought it was all a nightmare of a dream. Tara upon him, tired from some unknown event caught his attention as her lifeless moved a little.

"What happen here?" He asked. "Why, what's wrong with Tara?"

"I'm not sure of anything now," Jeanne respond placing vase on the table.

"What a mess!" He uttered first from his mouth, glanced at Tara resting there, "Jeanne, why are you and Tara in my room?"

Jeanne was at lost for word for the first time in her life. The look she displayed was one of confusion.

"Well?" Alexander asked again.

She gave it a try voicing, "Look, all I was told was to get cold water for your fever by Tara. So you see I'm as much in the dark as much as you are? Wait, don't you feel sick?" She suddenly noticed Alexander fresh from rest. Not a trace of fever was present.

"No, I feel perfectly well and oddly rejuvenated." He answered. "What about Tara's condition?"

"I'm not sure?" Jeanne said.

Alexander stood up wandering about her request. She asked him for his help with Tara, placing her in the chair near the window as she eyes slowly open. The first words coming from her mouth were "Alexander."

"I'm here, Tara," he voiced.

Suddenly she leaped up cling onto him with passion as if she had lost him forever. There were small tears coming from her beautiful eyes as she quickly wiped them away, desperately attempting to not expose herself and her true feelings too soon. She couldn't restrain her heated soft hands, placing them upon his strong featured face.

Tara's eyes gazed into his as she whispered, "You're all right...my...love?"

Her reaction had confirmed his thoughts about her. Tara desired him as much as he desired her.

"Don't worry about me. What about you?" He asked overly concerned about her well being. Still seeing a trace of true tears remaining, uttering, "Just what were you doing in my room? And why wasn't I aware of it?"

Tara responded halfheartedly, "The landlady allowed us in while you are sleeping."

"I see."

"You don't mind, do you?" Looking at each of them, Jeanne expressing confusion and Tara displaying part denial, bewilderment; for now, whatever happened he would back off.

"Well I guess its ok for now. I better get dress. I guess the landlady will clean this place up?" Alexander said.

"She will," Tara answered staring with contempt at the old woman.

The old woman nodded in shame.

But for Tara, her nightmare had just started as flashback ran across her mind of the passed events. For some unknown reason she could vision her grandmother's face. The bizarre thing about it all was the face was smiling? Yet Tara wisely decided to keep it within herself until she could get a better understanding of the signs. Jeanne viewed all of this with part joy of them accepting their feelings and the other part; she didn't know what the hell to make of it?

Tara yelled, "Let's get out of here. The house keeper will take care of the room."

The other two nodded in agreement.

"That's right! We promise you a tour and we have a whole area to show you, Alexander," Jeanne added as he went behind a dressing wall to change.

Shortly later Jeanne pulled him along insisting that they hurry to catch the night's events. By the time the trio was on their way Alexander was brisk up in confusion, he was dazed still a bit; trying to control his reasoning of the situation with less achievement than before; this was clearly beyond reality. Tara on the other hand remained astound about the unnatural events surrounding the room herself, just what was real or just a nightmare; it only left to the imagination for now. Her psyche battled over the just what was real, what was true; what were horribly just her mind playing tricks. Outside everything was in walking distant from the Brick House as they decided to leave the taxi around the corner. Much to the pleasure of all, it was a delight to see the areas most tours never viewed. The moment allowed and gave Alexander more of a personal contact with Tara closely at his side.

The next few days the relationship was in full swing between the lovers. Alexander took some time to get know La Veanna deciding on his own to visit her without the knowledge of Tara or Jeanne. He caught a taxi over to Tara's home midday looking for a good conversation with La Veanna. He approached the porch with good intention when suddenly he felt a panic attack. It was as if someone was playing with his mind. For each step he took towards the house, the more anxiety to overcome. Yet determined he knocked on the door. It took a few minutes before the door slowly opened peculiarly without assistance. Stun he peeked in unsure if it was his imagination playing tricks on him.

"Come in, young man," La Veanna voiced sitting in the living room. Standing behind her was a young attractive woman barely dressed in a light blue dress, seeing through the garment the pointed nipples of excitement. The girl noticed and precipitated with a sexual smile.

"Hello, I'm Alexander," he voiced.

"We know of you," the girl cited.

La Veanna nodded.

"Well, I was in the neighborhood and wanted to meet you for myself," he explained. "Tara wanted me to wait, but I had to see you alone."

"You're dating my granddaughter?" La Veanna asked.

"We are dating each other," he answered.

"Let her touch your face?" the girl asked. "She is blind and can tell a lot from touching."

"Ok, I guess," he replied unsure.

La Veanna reached out and touched him as if seeing through to his mind. Alexander soon noticed he was becoming dazed. It was like a La Veanna was absorbing his thoughts, his very soul. Behind him was the attractive girl, preventing him from backing away. She wraps her warm arms around him, touching him and exciting him.

"Wait, I didn't come here for this?" Alexander voiced.

"I was just positioning you," she answered.

"Is that what you call it?" He shouted upset.

La Veanna's mind control was powerful and demanding, yet he broke away upset over the ordeal of being tested. The conversation went downhill from there. For ever positive point he brought up about their relationship, La Veanna shot it down abruptly. It soon came apparent that he was not welcome there. Checking his watch he decided to depart before dark. Strangely, La Veanna made no move against him knowing that Tara would arrive soon. Instead, he offered him a ride back and he took the offer. They said their goodbye and the girl escorted him to the door and to her car. La Veanna disturb, yelled, "This affaire d'amour must be halted! My granddaughter must not prance into this man's life. I will not have it!" She had foreseen the predestination of their meeting each other through Tara's dreams and feared its results. Aware one day and that day may be soon; she would have to oppose Tara's desires for him. But it would certainly be a last result. Once it came to the forefront; Tara would know of her grandmother true calling "Queen of Voodoo" with evidence of the secret had been locked up in her large bedroom. Never had Tara been allowed in the bedroom, strangely never had it not been locked from her. Within its walls lied Tara's true complete past of black magic and domination.

PART V
Time After Time

Shortly after Alexander's visit there was another closeness which wished to be avoided, hurrying down the path and arriving at Tara's home, Doctor Walker stood there winded. The messenger had failed in his important mission and what he had feared had come true; the coming of Tara's psychic powers. There was still a great amount of sunlight that late evening, as the sweat from the humidity shown on his arms and face. At La Veanna's home, Doctor Walker had to illuminate just what transpired earlier at the brickyard. Unfortunately, both knew now it was a mistake to attempt to separate the Tara from him and the damage was done. In a room of such a rich remembrance of her birth, La Veanna should have known it could trigger her powers. That Doctor Walker's influence was no match for Tara's dominance of psychic abilities; even though Tara was not sure how and to what boundaries she was capable of using them? Still when it came to implementing it, something unseen took over Tara to protect the one she loved, Alexander.

The Walker had never seen La Veanna in such a rage.

Pulling back in concern for his own life, he paid no attention to what he was backing into as he collided against an antiquated lamp table. Upon it was a stain glass beautiful lamp. It was given to her by Tara a year ago. Though La Veanna was blinded, Tara described it to perfection as a reminder of her past. The sudden crash of it caught her attention as she slowly turned towards its finally resting place shattered beyond repair.

"Beauty!" She muttered to herself, smiling. "Yes...beauty!"

"I'm sorry," Doctor Walker cried.

She turned back facing him, smiling.

"Doctor Walker, I want you to contact Mai Dede." She ordered him. "Don't worry about that damn lamp!"

"Are you sure?" He asked.

She nodded with reservation.

Mai Dede of which she spoke of was a lower queen herself under her. Mai Dede was a Voodoo queen in her own right and a true quadroon woman. Who if it weren't for Tara being the chosen one, she would be the next High Priestess; a position which she desired majestically. Quickly he bowed and hurried on his way, relieved that La

Veanna allowed him grace in his foul up of the matter, very graceful.

Mai Dede was twenty-three years of age, younger than Tara and Alexander. Though she came from Santo Domingo, her meeting of Voodoos was held in the old Dumaine Street brickyard near the same area of his hotel of Alexander. Mai Dede, whom for several years had attempted considerable headway in her schemes of rebellion against La Veanna; yet with each attempt La Veanna met the situation in a characteristically masterful manner. Strangely, never did La Veanna wanted to exterminate the young queen's life. She knew Mai Dede would play a more important roll yet to come. She sent Doctor Walker on his way to the greedy heirs. Walker knew that   Mai Dede would relish over showing her psychic powers over Tara's. He and La Veanna only hoped when the time presented itself, Tara would meet the task head on against her; using force against force in an attempt to end the affair between them.

Later, arriving at Mai Dede's town-house, Doctor Walker approached it with caution, attempting desperately not to offend the powerful queen, well aware she possesses nearly as much telepathic supremacy as the queen which sent him. Mai Dede always had good taste in clothes and a fine taste of the good life. Truly her living area reflected that with one of the finest town-houses on the block. Doctor Walker entered the front gate which gave loud scream due to rust. The front red and white rose garden was in full bloom along the pathway the house. There were several servants working in the garden pruning the flowers. One, an old woman gazed at as if she was in a trance then quickly returned to her work. He hesitated at the door displaying the anxiety he always felt around her. Now he wondered whether to hit hard upon the stain glass door to get her attention? Finally he opted to tap softly as possible. After four taps, he withdrew a bit with misgivings. The door began to open at a snail's pace; before stood a young woman dress in white to greet him, a house servant fourth teen years of age, named Siva.

"You are expected," Siva said.

"May I come in?" Doctor Walker asked.

She nodded allowing him to follow her into a nearby den.

"You are to remain here," Aaron said then closed the den's door behind her. "You are not to leave this room, understand?"

Doctor Walker stood there looking around with interest. He had never been inside of the town-house before. He soon noticed the room was modern and void of voodoo items. Suddenly the door opened revealing the radiant Mai Dede. She was wearing bright color clothes. Her eyes were deep and passionate to any who befell them, pure sexual diva.

"What do you want little...doctor?" She asked. "No! I am aware of what brings you here. La Veanna needs me doesn't she? She tests me!" She whispered strangely into the humid air.

Walker forced his mouth to whisper, "Then you will do it?"

Mai Dede paused moving to the study's door.

"Siva, come in here and bring the stroll," Mai Dede ordered.

"La Veanna, needs your answer," Doctor Walker said.

Soon Siva returned with a small stroll and handed it to Doctor Walker.

"Do not open it, sir. It is for La Veanna," Mai Dede replied. "Now take this to her."

"What about Alexander?" He asked.

But she did not reply and peered out the window into the sky; directly into the blazing sun; never bated an eye. If it wasn't for Tara, it would surely be "She" who would become the next queen; Mai Dede thoughts wondered. Turning her attention back to the Walker, she was willing to listen to what his orders were from La Veanna. But Mai Dede had other plans in mind too. In turn, Doctor Walker related the dilemma to her as she agreed surely to intervene. She laughed at the situation with abandonment having heard enough she suddenly ordered him out the house and slammed the door in his tattooed face. The harsh closing almost shattered the stain glass door with its impact. Feeling there was nothing more he could express on the situation. Mai Dede had quickly tired of his voice. Though her task was clear, there was nothing to deny her now. La Veanna would in the past forbid her from attacking the unaware Tara. Now the flood gates were opened! Mai Dede mocked Tara's grandmother for so long, always felt unappreciated by her.

Now resting upon her stairway, she smiled seductively.

"Are you concerned about the La Veanna discovering you sent Alexander the charm?" Siva asked.

"Not at all, it could never be traced back to me," Mai Dede said.

Mai Dede was the one who sent the charm to Alexander and now the plan was coming together to rid of

Tara. Through visions she had seen Alexander around town with Tara earlier. She also felt a peculiar sexual attraction towards him, convinced that it would be a feather in her cap to pull away Tara's new found and only yearning more than to simply kill him as planned before. Aware it would deeply cut into Tara's willing heart with great affliction; the game was on.

"Yeah...," Mai Dede voiced to Siva.

"I don't understand," Siva said.

"A vulnerable spot indeed I've discovered and it is time to play, my dear Tara," Mai Dede joked. "Get me my drink."

Siva returned with drink in hand.

"Hand it here," Mai Dede ordered. "What I do you need not understand, my dear, dismiss!"

Siva handed her the drink and went back cleaning.

Slowly with her right index finger, she moved it along the rim of the chalice, forcing a light humming from its bows. Like an obsession, Mai Dade's reasoning began to focus upon Alexander. She knew he would not be able to deny her. Seeing it as a revelation of what is to be; the key to the throne itself. Her consciousness started to reflect the way he walked; strongly and so assure of himself, the way Alexander would present himself; sharp dressing with a flare of boyish charm. But his weakness, which consumed him was his analytical thinking, a liability which would play to his disadvantage and her leverage over him, she thought. With strong view to his mentality, the key would be the unpredictable of passion and she had plenty of it. Now Alexander would be the weapon to finally get to Tara's heart. She laughed wildly in a loud array of tones. It was a devilish sound carrying though out the modern town-house like never before.

Several days passed Alexander was in the wooded area exploring. The sun beams somehow founded its way through the high wet-lands trees. There was little creature running along his feet as he step unexpectedly upon their space. Wearing a pair of black jeans and light white rolled up shirt, he was becoming more accustomed with his surrounding. Ever where he looked the scene was Mother Nature at her best, numerous arrays of colors placed before him. He was totally convinced the trip was doing him a world of good. He didn't even miss "Marilyn" his home computer; replacing her were a gorgeous woman which he felt a lost for by the name of Tara. As for the charm, he placed it away never considering displaying it to Tara for her opinion, mistake of great importance.

La Veanna had sent Tara alone into the city on task. The only time they were apart that day.

Later Alexander alone felt weaken from the heat and stumble on an unknown path in the swamp. Exhausted, he sat upon a huge black stone. Strangely it didn't seem to belong there? Yet he rested upon it. Suddenly he began wiping his irritated eyes, the more he wiped the more agony he encountered. His body still was resting against the black stone which was about six feet in height and seven feet in width, round in shape. As he attempted to pull away, his leg gave way under him. The once solid ground now was like soft clay. There seemed to be a short supply of air to breathe causing his thoughts to struggle. Off in the distant there was someone with perfect vision. She knew just what was happening. Laughing quietly, she looked on with intrigue, but hunger for his death. Mai Dede appeared performing her telepathic powers upon him, and by all observation, it was going as promised. The stone was made to draw his life force out of him. Fortunately just a few yards away Jeanne was coming through the woods. Since Tara had the taxi, she felt it was a good day to find him. Suddenly she thought she could hear choking ahead, like some one being desperately attempting to regain air.

"Who's there?" She uttered, only heard the continued choking sounds. Slowly she pushed the leaves and branches which obstructed her view, only to behold Alexander. Finally Jeanne removed the last of the leave. Now on his back Alexander could only look on. Jeanne screamed his name out of fear seeing the great anguish. Mai Dede on the other hand viewed Jeanne coming into the area unexpectedly. Frowning with displeasure, she cursed her interference. But there was nothing she could do for now but retreat in silence. She finally withdrew from the worrisome task; it to her was no more fun and vowing to deal with Jeanne meddling with her affairs. After her hurried departure the air suddenly return to Alexander's mouth; shocked of actually losing it.

Jeanne asked, "Are you right?"

He still couldn't speak but nodded his head for her help.

"Now just what are you doing out here in the woods? A person could collide something he or she weren't meant to see. You could have gotten hurt," Jeanne expressed with great concern.

"Had to get out for awhile," Alexander replied.

"There are a lot of bizarre happenings out here. Even I don't venture it at night," She added in a zealous matter.

"Have to remember that," he voiced sitting up.

By this time Alexander was moved from near the huge stone and laid upon Jeanne's thighs.

"What....what happen?" Alexander asked.

"I'm not sure?" She answered. "Are you alright?"

"Fine, I guess?"

"That's good! You had me scared," Jeanne voiced holding him.

He waved to her uttering, "Help me up, ok."

Jeanne pulled him up with care. Still he stood there a little stun over the ordeal. "Place your arm around my waist," she instructed him. The two began to move back to the brickyard.

Later resting upon his bed, Alexander recovered from the earlier ordeal in the swamp. He thanked Jeanne and was glad she shown up. The two had a long extended conversation about adjusting there and just who to trust. On the nightstand was a cold puncher of lemonade brought earlier by the old woman. Jeanne poured them both a drink as the conversation became more focus towards her life. It was no big secret why she came to New Orleans, a point she express openly.

"Why this place?" He asked Jeanne.

Alexander moved towards the switch and turning on the ceiling fan. Its blades moved slowly cooling off the room. Jeanne looked at him with trust and a need to express herself. It was somewhat different talking to male friend who wasn't trying to get under her dress and fuck her. She dearly welcomed the change. She didn't know why, only feeling she had to start somewhere, why not New Orleans?

"What about you? And don't tell me it was a sudden thought," Jeanne asked.

He smiled knowing that it was right on the spot. Yet he pulled away from the question. The more they talked, the more they trusted each other. But opted suddenly Jeanne became very withdrawn for a time; wearing her off-white sundress climbed into his bed as she gazed into his eyes.

"Alexander," she uttered in a low caring tone.

"Yes?"

"Tara is my best friend," she said.

"I know," he responded puzzled.

"We...we are like sisters, she and I."

"What are you trying to say, Jeanne?" Alexander asked.

"I love her very much and I don't want her to get hurt, I mean kicked around like a play doll," she voiced.

"Look, I've never met anyone like Tara. Sure I've dated but with no success,' he voiced than paused, "but that day all three of us met...I fell in love with Tara right there. Never have my very soul cried for anyone so...so...strongly."

Jeanne smiled.

"Look, Jeanne...I will never hurt Tara or allow anyone to."

Hearing that statement she smiled more, convinced that he was a man of his words and heart. Giving him a hug, Jeanne gave her blessing. Playing matchmaker and finally making a match for Tara was a perfect ending to her day. She kissed Alexander explaining she had to find Tara. Leaving the room, Jeanne looked back voicing, "You really love her, don't you?"

He smiled uttering, "Don't tell her! I want to do that myself. And most of all don't tell her about what happen today, promise?"

Jeanne nodded in agreement exultant that things were going to workout. She added one more words of advice, "The next time you have the urge to go into the swamps, just call us. You know by now we are your escort, ok?"

He smiled waving his hands for her to go on.

As the door closed he relaxed thinking about his date with Tara later that night.

It is hard not to notice the fame of New Orleans as the gayest place on the North American Continent. And Tara was a part of it all. As days passed Tara and Alexander became more and more involved with each other, with their hearts pounding at an alarming rate it was hard to conceal the affection they want to show to one another. A true testimony to devoted love at first sight, there was no keeping them apart. Though the city was known for the unrestrained merriment of the Mardi Gras Festival, there remained plenty for them to see and do. Even though the festival had pasted, there Jeanne made sure of their fun. Also with an escort whom represented the essence of such a world was indeed, a special added gift to Alexander and Tara was a vision to him. She had shown him dance-houses, and other low resorts reared their fantastic structures of prosperity. Yet she avoided a street called Basin Street? It was notorious known throughout as a veritable cesspool of sin, was principally because of the prevalence of prostitution, which secretly in turn was owing to the tolerance with it was regarded by authorities and people generally. Yet he wanted to know more. May be he should have left it alone.

"What is Basin Street really like?" Alexander asked with curiosity.

Tara replied enraged, "The only locality in the city where decent people do not live,"

"Who said?" Jeanne asked.

"That's what my grandmother told me. I guess you desire to go there?" Tara asked him. The way she voiced it made him think first before replying. Noticing the sadness upon her fair face; it appeared as if all the pleasure they started with suddenly ran from her. And Alexander couldn't allow that to happen.

"No," he replied, seeing the smile upon Tara's face gave an astonished and unexpected response.

Jeanne next to Tara smiled with acceptance of his decision not to go there. Across the street was a binder selling teddy bears of numerous colors. A little girl from the booth ran over to them with a few. She offered one at a good price as Alexander handed over the money. With a smile he presented a black one to Tara with his love. The gift was well received and soon after followed by a lustful kiss. There was a full moon shining upon them as he and Tara hugged each other with affection. It was then that Tara decided to expose them to an exclusive swamp area outside the town that night.

Shortly later there in the backwoods they expectedly came upon   Mai Dede. She was singing a beautiful ballet which seem to full the night humid air. Strangely she was bathing in pond similar as the one Jeanne discovered Tara last year. The pond was of clear fresh water, very unusual in the first place to be there. Jeanne and Alexander moved closer as the moon light was like a spotlight upon Mai Dede's perfectly formed body. Tara pulled back aware of Mai Dede's clear deceptions.

Mai Dede had never met Alexander personally before and close up he was much more attractive then she had imagine. Suddenly the task of taking him away from Tara was more pleasurable.

"Hi, bet your Alexander?" She uttered with a huge smile.

"And you are?" He asked.

"Mai, Mai Dede."

"Born here?" He asked.

"All my life and before," she said.

"Before?" He asked.

"Never mind. Say, would you...well...would you care to join me?"

He looked at both ladies with a stun reaction to Mai Dede's alluring and tempting request. Tara had already shown her disapproval at Mai Dede's intention.

Suddenly Mai Dede whispered towards Alexander's direction, "I'm sure Tara wouldn't mind. Beside, we're old friends here and like to share."

"Old friends?" Tara joked.

"We're all old friends here, ladies?" Mai Dede voiced. "I promise not to bite any of you."

All three was speechless by the sight.

Alexander couldn't help but find pleasures of beholding Mai Dede in the nude. The sound of her voice was strangely drawing him in gently just as any male. The continued flirtation towards him only added to gaining more of his watchfulness. Tara became more steamed every minute she view the foreplay of emotions between them. This time Mai Dede had pushed her too far. A strong wind began to blow behind her as if it was a wall of raging gust, but it kept its distant; oddly waiting for her command. Tara never knew it was of her own doing, her subconscious was brewing all around her. Though Jeanne and Alexander were confused about just what was happening? Mai Dede knew how was to play it well.

Tara gazed at Mai Dede now figuring out what she was attempting to do. She would not allow Mai Dede an opportunity to make her out to be a monster.

Tara shouted, "No! He wouldn't care to join you, whore!"

She without speaking anymore stormed from the sight of them agitated and suppressing her uncontrollable anger. Alexander wondered why she left so abruptly, as Mai Dede still played with his mind and interested him greatly for some unknown reason? Not that he felt the same about her as for Tara, there was something appealing...something...bewitching and magical? He knew not what? Jeanne stood as an innocent bystander. Mai Dede was a very seductive and well structured lady. The clear pond only induced him to watch closer, controlling his very thoughts. Alexander couldn't break free from watching this bountiful lady. But something was wrong? It was reasonable she could have any man she desired. Mai Dede's beauty was known to kill a man that didn't please her; like a black widow spider after making love. Yet there was something alluring and abnormal about her. Her tone was as smooth as Tara's tone. She stood about 5"11, with a gorgeous face and captivating green sparking eyes.

Sponging the moisture off in a sexual manner only highlighted Mai Dede's heated assets even more. The sassy tone in her voice was direct yet not direct. But his feelings was for Tara and well apparent to Mai Dede. Still he was man and she an alluring woman, the opposite sex. The more Mai Dede talked the salty the conversation become.

"Look, Mai Dede? We must be leaving," Alexander voiced wondering why he hadn't left.

"To bad," Mai Dede joked. "At least you're not a believer of paranoia. We're all not that bad."

"Tara is waiting for us," he added perplexed.

Mai Dede only responded in an arousing voice, "That very unfortunate for the both of us." she paused looking at Jeanne which was still near his side. "Are you sure you have to leave? I do think Tara is a big girl now."

"Sorry I really must be leaving," he answered in an unsure tone. Suddenly she waved him closer and he obliged intrigue by her emotions. Again she waved him even closer. Jeanne watched him move closer but refused to interfere. Mai Dede smiled ever so willingly to him connecting his thoughts with hers.

"Well...take care, Alexander. I know we shall see each other again, it's our destiny, love," she whispered touching his hands and placing them upon her beautiful bronzed face.

"Destiny?" He asked.

"The next time you are left alone, will you visualize me?" Mai Dede whispered to him. "The size in your pants claimed you will, my love."

"I can't promise you that," he followed up.

Suddenly she stood up revealing all her majestic beauty and radiated warmth, speaking as if she knew something from within. But for some unknown reason, he found himself unable to move? His thoughts were attempting to tell him to leave, yet they were being controlled.

Alexander found himself gazing towards the pond. The sparkles from the water reflected off her nude body seemed to be as one? Suddenly a push against his back moved him on by Jeanne.

"Nice try, Mai, but not tonight," Jeanne voiced. "Lets get going lover boy. There's a very concerned and foolhardy best friend waiting for you."

Mai Dede frowned playfully.

"I'll say goodbye to Mai for you. Good by Mai. Not this one, he's already taken," Jeanne added.

Mai Dede just smiled at Jeanne statement with contempt. She had found out what she was looking for; her own psychic powers were enough to trick him, if not hold him.

Alexander and Jeanne caught up with the now enraged Tara, who was stumping about. She wasn't sure of just what to do about the exchange between them? When Alexander finally laid eyes upon her, his mind now focus on her, though the nude body of Mai Dede did gain a space. The trance placed upon him was now gone completely. Tara's magical gifts were infinitely superior to those of Mai Dede; often her supremacy would threaten Mai Dede.

Still she refused to use her mind controlling powers to master his love. The only thing which she demanded was awareness of his true love. Wishing the true love she was offering to him, no spells or black magic was the way which she desired. As the trio walked through the woods, all was peaceful and calm. Alexander gazed at Tara wondering how lucky he was to discover her so soon. She too had beauty, charm and especially grace, not to mention great symmetry of a figure. Her lips were red as a rose, bright and savvy. Surely one of the most beautiful ladies around, but doesn't flaunt her assets. Yet Tara was a heroine who took charge; curious and not afraid to explore the unknown. Her past reaction only intrigued him to witness the hot-tempered animal underneath her beauty. Even though by profession she drove a taxi, it was a godsend which gained admittance to homes of fashionable people, where she learned many secrets which she never hesitated to use, but never to her own advantage. Not like her counterpart, Mai Dede who gained from every scandalous affair financially.

Jeanne seen they needed to talk alone, to allow their affection for the other to heal the faction of lust. The silence was overwhelming to be around as the expression upon Tara's facing warden such action.

"I'll catch you two later and from the looks of things, you better watch it Alexander," Jeanne whispered in his ears. Jeanne moved off with little fanfare, waving to Tara to relax more.

Tara obliged nodding.

They must work this problem out themselves, Jeanne thought to herself moving slowly from the two lovers.

He was lost for words in explaining his earlier action with Mai Dede, a first for him. Finally after an hour of walking the silence was broken, but not from Tara. It had to come from him.

"Jeanne's good person isn't she?" He asked to the still enraged Tara. She glanced at him with concern understanding what he was trying to accomplish. Laughing within herself, she felt sorry for the way she had acted. Now she had a chance to get close to him again, discovering whatever he had done she would still love him.

"Yes, she is," Tara answered. "Though I sometimes I wonder if she knows me too well. Jeanne has really helped me to adjust. I never would know what to do if she was gone. She is my only friend."

"I see," he voiced.

Tara touched his face and smiled. "Now, I'm lucky to have you, Alexander," she voiced.

He nodded. .

"I so blessed; first we became friends, now we're friends in love and will never be alone, Alex."

Tara's commit was a welcoming statement to him as Tara pass on an half smile, but still something puzzled her? Tara suddenly placed her small hands upon his, gripping them and now returning an even larger smile.

"You're not mad at me? Even thought I should be at you, but I just can't be. Mai Dede...has also lured men her way," Tara said in a very quietly,

"I understand," Alexander followed. "She has the right equipment."

Tara gazed at him stopping, Alexander in his track and turned the confused man to face her. "What Mai Dede attempted to do means nothing to me, understand? Mai Dede is a beautiful woman, I gave her that, but I figure love should come from the heart, that all." Tara said. "Now I want to show you something very important to me." She kissed him with great passion.

"What is it?" Alexander asked with interests.

"Just wait and come along," she responded laughing. "You'll love it, I promise…"

"Where are you taking me?"

Tara cried playfully, "Please...in time you will see."

"I could think of better things to do with you," he joked.

"Bet you could, my love," Tara cried pulling him along joyfully. "Trust me, I would never cause you any harm."

"Bet you say that to all the guys?" He asked jokingly.

Tara suddenly stopped, causing him to trip upon her. She stared at him with conviction. "Alexander, please believe me when I tell you that I would never harm you or allow any harm to come to you. If I knew it could, surely I would leave you!"

"Wait," he uttered facing her, "Never say that!"

She gazed at him speaking in a low sure tone, "Ok."

They kissed each other with great passion again and held on for dear life.

Soon they came upon a queer site, like a ceremony site. There, he viewed before him numerous ritual objects laying around. All were neatly placed in some sought of order. He noticed that more then anything, since patterns were his specialty. But what followed disturbed him greatly, setting the terms of his suspicions about Tara. Alexander retrieved a certain round object and Tara oddly became enraged, shouting at him with misgivings. Her reaction was more like a tantrum of great proportions screaming, "Please, Alexander put back!"

"Why?" He asked jokingly.

"Trust me, because it's not of this world," she cried. "You don't know what you have there. You don't know what you're dealing with here!"

Looking at the bizarre piece which resembled an oval large ring with feathers surrounded it. He started to play with it carelessly; throwing it high in the sky and catching it with the same abandon. Then Alexander started to mock her as he dance foolhardy around Tara with it. Suddenly and without any warning she became frighten. Yet he didn't notice it and thought she was just playing along with him. Tara began to become provoke by his reckless actions. Her beautiful body began shaking uncontrollably at each time he danced around her. Tara bellowed with fear, "Stop! Please stop! You...you don't know what it's doing to me...it taking control of me..." Winds started to howl from every direction as before with Mai Dede and this time it did get his attention quickly, gazing at Tara with great concern using her telepathic powers; this time he halted as the irregular winds died down to their once wild form. Tara suddenly rushed at him and grabbed the object from his hand. Within the same movement, she returned the object to its rightful place. Alexander could only watch with amazement of her actions with the winds being a big question mark to him.

"What was that?" He asked stun gazing on curiously.

"We must leave this place, now!" She instructed him, "Lets go before..."

"Before what?" Alexander asked.

"Shouldn't have brought you here, should have known better," she said eyeing area as if some being of unseen nature as waiting.

Tara leaded him out to a small brook nearby. Whatever happen there with Tara, he was wrong in acting like an ass. He thought to himself as the silence which he received from her disconcerted him greatly. Turning to Tara and seeing tears coming slowly from her romantic eyes, there must be something he could do? He thought with fervor.

"Look, I'm sorry for what happen at the site, which I'm not too sure just what I witness there? I seems as if your apart of all this in some way? Tell me what is it with you and this place?" He asked demanding a reply.

Tara only glanced at her own reflection in the brook. She decided to rest upon a huge smooth stone, similar to one he ran into before. Its shape was flat and laid positioned over the brook. It was time to come clean with feeling, that if they were to extend their relationship, he had to understand her people and mostly their way of life.

Alexander's world with seen factors and figures are fine for its limitations. Contrary to Tara's world which is seduced by the unseen, sometimes visible to man and the dark side, comparing it to mid-evil times when people believed in charmers, magicians, and conjuror, how could he compare his world with hers? Those things were well before Alexander's time and don't exist in this modern world, which grown out of such sorcery, and replaced it illogically. Tara just gazed at him, forcing him to ponder over what they were to face if their relationship were expand beyond friendship. He smiled confused for a bit. True, his world now rely on computers and logic but time have a way of moving on and leaving the past behind. But before him stood Tara; a believers of the past and soon to be guardian.

She asked directly. "You perceive the believer as crazes."

He nodded.

Tara seen that getting through to him would be difficult, reached out touching his hands with the utmost feelings of concern. A glow passed through her to him of affection and desire. It was like nothing Alexander had ever felt. Then staring deep into his logical and warm eyes she spoke, "Alexander, my logical mind love, the point I'm trying to convince you of is that we here have never changed. That...that Voodoo medicine, witch doctors, and sorceress still control this place will never change."

"Wait a minute here, next you will be telling me, you believe in incantation, hoodoo, jinks, and the witches of Endor," he voiced. "Why don't I just say the magic words 'Open-Sesame!"

Alexander expressed with great skepticism of Tara's stand on the subject.

"Dammit, Alexander!" Tara screamed not too please at his at his response. "This is not a game! These people are capable of hurting you!"

"You can't expect me to go along with this?" He asked. "There's nothing that can't be explained."

"You don't know what you're up against here, do you?" She asked.

"Up against isn't the word here, is it?"

She got up irritated, walking away then suddenly turned towards him. Slowly she moved towards him with the most forthright expression she could muster. "Please put aside your logic, rational, stupid, wait I'm sorry, reasonable way of dealing with this. Now try, just try to scrutinize things from our prospective. Alexander, don't be blind by what you cannot see or touch."

"What do you mean?" He asked.

"The supremacy it not there, but, resides in the psyche. You know how wondrous it could be? Most people around here believe strongly in such worship. In some ways, I do. That is all I'm telling you. It could be deadliest of ways if not controlled," Tara said.

"We're not in the Middle Ages," he said.

Taking a deep breath she tried again.

"The people here deal in the pure world of the paranormal, spirits, and specters. These people and their ways can hurt you."

"I must respect their belief?" He asked.

"Alexander, you must respect their beliefs."

They knew there may not be any historical records of its introduction of Voodoo worship, but it must have occurred at an early date.

Alexander was totally lost for words. He was sure she wasn't apart of the voodoo ceremony. Still Tara didn't dismiss her range of involvement, opting Alexander to come to the conclusion that the situation was complex and truly deadly if not handle correctly.

"Tara, now I need to know the truth," he voiced, "Are you in someway connected to any of this paranormal or voodoo world?" His eyes never left her face.

Tara slowly backed away from him strangely. She just stared at Alexander perplexed without returning his thoughts. Slowly from her full red lips she uttered with caution, "Alexander, do you believe in future state?"

"You mean life after death?" He asked with uncertainty in his voice.

"Yes." She added.

"I don't know?" He answered. "I guess there is always the possibilities under extreme situation allowing the fact it did really happen."

Tara came closer to her love, kissing him with great passion while stroking his short soft black hair. "I've been here all my life and seen things no one would ever believe. To turn a blind eye to it would be foolish," she said.

He pushed Tara back a bit to view her seriousness.

"No and yes to your question of death," she answered. "I don't know how to explain it, just know I'm not apart of their world; but I cannot just close my eyes to what happens around me either. Yet Alexander, I've seem to be drawn to this world of the paranormal in some weird and wonderful fashion…funny yeah?" She smile was now uncomfortable to say the least with an uneasy laugh.

Alexander had entered her world and forced her comfort the very issues she numerous times attempt to avoided. Tara's mind was locked in on her cultural ways and to their mythology. Suddenly he didn't know her, as a feeling of bewilderment consumed him. He was reminded that he was an outsider looking in, but he couldn't leave her. He just couldn't. He wanted Tara badly and if she claimed she was from another planet; it would not have faze him one bit. Tara's was starting to sound stranger by the minute. Opting not to hear anymore he pressed his full lips onto hers with sensitivity and love. Tara responded with a lasting embrace upon him. Part confused by his reaction of what she had said and her desire to continue, she passed on what was happening to them now. He could stir up her emotion so easily by his look of delight and his touch of warmth upon her very soul. With his arms around her small waist, something no man could ever do; Tara held him as if her life depended on it. Yet what she had expressed earlier puzzled him?

"Tara, wait a minute, why did you say that you love me?" He asked.

Tara smiled then pressed her fingers upon his chest playfully. "Well I wanted to see how you would respond if I told you first," she jested.

Gazing at her, Alexander noticed her reactions were one of being afraid of rejection. Suddenly she placed her head upon his chest with apprehension. But his expression was in the most favorable manner, this much to Tara's delight and pleasure. She gazed into his eyes to hear the words themselves. There were slight traces of tears coming from her richly soft eyes. Each was demanding his utmost attention.

"I will return your love happily, Tara," Alexander said. "When you left me, I was lost inside."

"I know we just met but I missed you today," she said. "Fore I felt the same as you, my love."

He was aware that it was a short time since we've known each other, but he felt the passion too. These words pleased Tara and brought on a huge smile of enormous lightheartedness over her radiant face. Now she was a lost for words as she desperately attempted to conceal unsuccessfully her rapture. With tears in Tara's eyes and her apologetic attempt to wipe them away as more just replaced them, she wanted to parade him with the rest of the area.

"I've been here with you all by myself," she added.

"I like it that way," Alexander responded.

"No, I'm sorry."

Turning her back to him, Tara rested upon his chest as she pulled Alexander's strong hands around her. Gazing towards the sky above them, Tara whispered, "The clouds are gorgeous to behold, Alexander."

He smiled as he held Tara tightly with affection. Below them there was a blue and yellow flower next to them and he bent down; plucked it and presented it to Tara. She thanked him by rolling the back of her head against him in approval in a sexual manner.

"Maybe this lady only desires to keep you to herself?" She asked turning quickly to place herself back in front of him.

"Truly you jest, my lady?" He asked.

"Me lord, I jest not for I love thee," she joked.

"That I honor thee with all my love forever," he joked back.

"But if you want to leave then we shall explore the town like never before. Places I'm willing to show you that no out-of-towner was aware of? Ready." Tara asked in a happy state.

"Not so fast," Alexander answered. "Not just yet if you don't mind?" He replied smiling, holding her, expressing his feelings with a gaze and a much heated passionate ever engulfing kiss.

"I like that," Tara mourned.

Then he followed up with a whisper, "In a few minutes. I'm consumed by your beauty and your everlasting love, tonight we shall become lover forever."

She replied in an erotic tone, "That's nice of you to say and very smart, Alexander." Tara smiled and agreed by caressing him tighter in majestic and arousing appreciation.

"You make it easy," he said.

"I was hoping you would say that," she voiced romantically in his ears. There's no telling what Tara would do to quench her thirst for infinite sexual bliss that night.

"My true pleasure, Tara," he added.

"Alex...can I ask you something?" She asked. "I mean it's just a little thing."

He nodded.

Tara move away from her love. Then looked up at him with conviction she voiced, "I don't know how to say this? Never mind here goes nothing; it's about Mai Dede the lady we met earlier at the pond."

"There's nothing to be concern about her, It was just curiosity that got best of me," he explained, "I love you only."

"I'm not concern about Mai Dede playfulness with men. You must understand she is very dangerous and has great dominance over people here. For reason unknown to me, Mai Dede hates me with a passion and I wish I knew why? Tara explained. "Don't ask her, ok!"

He read what Tara was saying wrong responding, "Mai Dede is beautiful to behold and there is something about her, something which catches a man's consciousness. But she is all looks and that is all, to me." He'd hoped to assure Tara of his devoted love for her only. Though he didn't understand what she was trying to warn him of the peril. What she did hear brought on a gleam of joy from her face. He was pleased to see the expression of anxiety leave that beautiful face of hers.

"Is there anything more bothering you?" Alexander asked.

"Well...one more thing," she replied.

"What?"

"If you ever witness something you don't understand or abnormal. Would you please attempt to see it through with an open mind? Would you promise me that before making judgment?" Tara asked strongly, yet in a concerned tone.

"What could be stranger then Mai Dede taking a bath in a pond of thought clear water and the moon shinning overhead," he joked. "Tara, everything is perfect between you and me. Now unless you are one of those Voodoo Queens we were discussing then we have a problem."

"That isn't funny," she said finding it in bad taste and expressed it had no humor in his outburst. Yet she moved to offer an even stranger reply, "I hope for both of our sakes."

This caused Alexander to ponder deeply. Feeling there was something abnormal about Tara. Something he couldn't see in her beautiful face then there was the abnormal condition at the ritual site. Tara rested upon the flat rock with her thoughts as he approached her willingly. Her thoughts were now for no reason in conflict of her affection towards Alexander. She knew she I loved him so, yet couldn't stay away from him to keep him out of peril. Their desire to make love was unduly a factor neither could resist. Tara thoughts were overwhelming as she struggle with arousing hunger. It couldn't be happening to her, but it was. Alexander continued to kiss Tara's warm and vibrate lips. Willingly she responded and in a desirable matter, leaving no questions to what she hungered of him. Tara continued to fight the feelings of him in her mind, losing at every turn.

Tara greatest concern now was that his love would discover that she was a virgin. Her thoughts ranged from hopelessness and blissful existence. What made it so difficult was that Tara was a perpetually horny being with him. She was sexy, and very elegant, always wore flowing capes, black pumps, and short skirt. Her silk shirts would be open almost to the waist, the cleft between her braless breast so warm and inviting. The perfume she dabbed in that forbidden zone made his nostrils quiver and his cock pulse. He could feel her beat through the panties' thin crotch. Her hands slid up Alexander's arms to stroke his shoulders, leaving a light trail with her nails. He felt his cock strain in his jeans as her lush body pressed against him. Her fingers entwined behind his neck; her bronzed thighs rubbed against his waist as he lifted her hips against him. As he placed her on the cool black stone, they eagerly began to strip off their clothes. He groans as her firm tits, their bronze nipples fully erect, broke free of her flimsy blouse.

"Oh, Alex, I've waited so long for this," Tara cried, tears running down her beautiful eyes.

Slowly she glided under him. Tara's legs spread enticingly and her back arched as she thrust her dripping virgin pussy against his hard cock, welcoming him into her.

He spread her legs further apart and knelt between them, savoring the sweet, pungent fragrance of her love juices, which glistened against her smooth thighs. Alexander rubbed his thumbs over her hard nipples and her firm belly, then slid them down the inside of her thighs and began to trace teasing circle around her stiff clitoris.

"Now, now," Tara groaned.

Tara's lovely vagina was still throbbing as Alexander slid his aching cock deeply into her. Her thigh muscles engulfed him for nearly over an hour until they both came together. Alexander and Tara were throwing caution to the wind and indulged themselves in a feast for the senses that only they knew how to temper the fiery. Tara, the once shy young woman was now becoming sexually unstoppable when she discovered Alexander true love, for the more she indulged, the more active she sarcoma to him.

Sneaking a peek at them was a hot voyeur named Mai Dede. Unaware they were being observed by her in the pond she was bathing in; their every word and erotic action was being collected by her devilish mind. Mai Dede had used the pond as a paranormal window to track the two. In her mind she was plotting their demise as she whispered aloud to herself, "My dear friends, we must surely meet again, as you dear Tara, your throne is a good as mines, for no one would welcome a queen who is weak." Suddenly she began to smile slashing the pond which reflected the scene of the two until they were gone.

Meanwhile…

"So will I see you, tomorrow? And the next day after and the next?" Alexander asked as Tara rested in his warm arms.

She laughed expressing joy voicing, "Yes...yes!" Her face had signs of her bathing in the afterglow. Slowly her moved towards him to kiss him again but paused citing; they had better go now. Both seemed disappointed that it had to end, but darkness was approaching rapidly as the moon was being covered by dark clouds. After getting dressed Tara bent down to him voicing, "Alexander, I do love you so, but please remember what I've told you about the people here."

Still he brushed it off as foolishness. She stared at his stubbornness crying, "Your so in love. You can't see what is before you." Tara pouted with a smile but still sweetly upset over his rational attitude. "Alexander, would you die for me?"

He felt as if she were joking, never responding.

She feared for his life and sensed strongly misfortune ahead for them.

PART VI
Eyes of the Beholders

Days passed as the lovers discovered each other but had another seeking their destruction. During the day Tara was sitting on her grandmother's porch resting alone, daydreaming of the next time she and Alexander will meet again. The sun was doing its best to fowl the moment, but Tara still enjoys the peacefulness until...

"Hey Girlfriend?" Mai Dede greeted her pulling into Tara's driveway in front of her residence. She climbs out of the car and addressed Tara smiling. The mimesis was armed with knowledge of their adoration for each other, and the weakness it also brings. But what she didn't consider was what their adoration offered, strength.

The expression on Tara's face expressed it disapproval of her presents there. Still Mai Dede came closer, wearing a bright yellow sun dress compared to Tara's jeans and white blouse. Apparently Mai Dede was well suited to trap whomever she chosen; a fact which brought great distrust from Tara. She had just finished out cleaning the front yard for her grandmother, still her beautiful expanded beyond a biological boundary and Mai Dede knew it. Sitting on the porch with a hoe in her hand, Tara demanded to know what the vixen desired; she had never been over before. Mai Dede glanced at the hoe then bravely sat next to Tara. She gazed out at the yard smiling at Tara accomplishment in her task. The dirt upon Tara's face was combined with sweat running down to her cheek.

"When are you ever going to hire help around here," Mai Dede asked in a joking manner. "I can send over some of my servants if needed."

"We'll do just fine without them," Tara said.

"Just offering some assistance."

"What do you want, Mai?" Tara asked upset.

Mai pulled away a bit, acting as if she were shock at she words.

"My, you've been working too hard. Too much sun, I guess or love?" Mai Dede joked.

"You're not wanted here," Tara interjected.

"Or is it your glad to see an old friend?" She joked.

"Your not my friend nor ever will be."

"Don't be like that, girlfriend," Mai Dede replied in a low tone.

"Jeanne is my only friend, remember that," Tara added.

"I don't know why you're so visible lately...nights not fun?"

Mai Dede stood up, walked off the porch then turned gracefully. With a seductive tone she added, "Where is your other friend, Alexander?"

She then eased back down next to Tara's side.

"What other friend?" Tara asked blushing.

"I know you have been getting much heat over seeing him from the locals and specially your grandmother," Mai Dede voiced. "He is an outer-towner, not one of us, my dear. There will be a dangerous price to pay if you continue this shameful relationship."

"What are you getting at?" Tara asked.

"Alexander may be the fox in the hunt here?" Mai Dede said.

Tara didn't reply knowing better than to play along with Mai Dede's mind games. Still she was in love and now acceptable to deep feelings of the heart.

Mai Dede added, "Maybe I can help you with sometimes...if you...let me."

Tara wanted none of that.

"Whatever delirium coming my way, I'll find my own way out of it," Tara voiced, "As far as Alexander, that is whom your speaking of? He is doing well here. And I caution you to leave him alone."

Tara knew that in order to conquer Mai Dede, she had to be very very vigilant. Mai Dede placed her hands upon her breast teasing Tara about Alexander's fondling her.

"Was it as good for you as it has been for me? He was the first, wasn't he, you can tell me, girlfriend."

Tara desperately attempted to hold her rage in at Mai Dede's continued punching of her relationship with Alexander, as temperatures were at a boiling point.

"I wasn't amused at the way you first met him," Tara voiced.

"Whatever do you mean?" She asked, "Oh, the pond."

"Yes."

She replied sinfully. "Oh that! It was so long ago, I must have forgotten," she joked.

Tara reclined back, against the pole uttering, "Don't push me, Mai. You would not like it when I get angry."

"Oh, do I see the devil spirit within you, child?" Mai Dede said.

Tara took a deep breath then smiled at Mai Dede, much to her surprise. "It won't work. He won't come to you like the others," she express smiling.

"Surely you jest about him," Mai Dede voiced.

"I've noticed you talking with him lot when I'm not there. Leave him alone, I'm warning you," Tara said upset over the ordeal.

"Poor little Tara," Mai Dede joked.

"What's your point?"

"You've played the role of the desperate damsel so long that reality beginning to blur for you, dear," she answered.

"You are the desperate one, Mai."

"You think he's in love with you. But you've got another thing coming. Alexander is just a man and they think only with one thing. And you've had a tasted of it yourself. Grow up! They think with their dicks not their minds like us. Not as long as that tool between their legs can move," Mai Dede voiced upset. "I bet he couldn't keep his hands off of you and you, him? Let me tell you one thing, little girl raised into a woman before your time."

Tara listened with little interest until the last part of the statement by Mai Dede.

"What do you mean a woman before my time? What do you know about my childhood?" Tara asked. "Why is it I don't remember anything about it, no records, no pictures; nothing?"

Mai Dede made an oversight opted to change the subject.

"Tell me what you meant!" Tara repeated.

"I will not, not now, girlfriend," she answered. "But in time you will know."

As many times she questioned Mai Dede. The more Mai Dede skillfully avoided the issue masterfully leading Tara to nowhere. Finally she had enough, leaping up away from Mai Dede in frustration. Oddly her attempt to use her consciousness abilities on Mai Dede's mind was blocked?

"Nice try, but I'm just as capable as you are, Tara," Mai Dede said.

"You have the power?"

Mai Dede nodded smiling.

"You don't know anything. You play with man as if they were your private toys," Tara bellowed upset, "Well Alexander is not like them. He loves me and nothing you or anyone can do to pull us apart."

The two ladies pulled their tempers in for a moment, each taking a breather to regroup. Tara had held her own very well against the street-wise nemesis. Though they both possessed telepathic powers, Mai Dede was used to such skills in the art, as for Tara, she was just coming into the art of such skills, a virgin in every form.

"Maybe him fucking you like a young bull changed you in some way, I don't know, but whatever he did to you will not last," Mai Dede cited, suddenly walked off from Tara after that statement.

Her statement did leave Tara bewilder over the issue. If it was any sexual desires, it was her which demanded it so much.

Mai Dede added one more thing citing, "Little girl who desires this stranger so much. Once he'd shown you the way to come, you will be his slave forever. It will make you twist from the need of it. It will make you hungry for his tool every waken hour, that if you can rest. Yes...I see it in your eyes all right...yes..."

Walking down to her car, Mai Dede had discovered what she came there for, the information of Alexander. Tara's heart was soft now and consumed by his emotions. Now Tara was ready for the fall. With a slight turn of the head, Mai Dede noticed La Veanna sitting at the front window listening to the heated exchanged all the time. The blind grandmother of Tara's was totally please on two folds. First, Mai Dede was up to the task of finishing Alexander, second, in a strange way Tara had proven herself as an admirable adversary against the likes of Mai Dede. Yet one thing did displease her. Mai Dede almost stated the nature of Tara's birth before its time. It would have been a costly mistake at such a time. As for Alexander being Tara's first love, she was pleased it was someone whom loved her granddaughter, but it was unfortunate that he had to die so soon after their romantic encounter.

Tara had left him alone as she and Jeanne went to work. Much to Tara's intention this was a serious mistake; as Mai Dede took full advantage of her absent.

Alexander received a strange call from Mai Dede that morning request his present that night, a prefect well plan call as his protectors were working. Most of the time in which Tara was absent, Mai Dede filled the void. Though she played it well, Mai Dede never made any sexual moves towards Alexander for fear of running him away. This played well to the point of him trusting her and accepting her help adjusting in town, much to Tara's objection and dismay. From the first time he laid eyes upon her, Mai Dede consumed his interest. Everything about her was different from Tara. She was the very being of biological desire and passion. The way she moved was one of endless motions of erotic pleasures. Alexander knew she was no good for him, but she intrigue him so in every way. She was persuasive, hot blooded, and strong; a quality he admired. Anytime Mai Dede was around, Alexander could feel the aura of her undeniable presents. He knew of her scent, of her eyes, of possibly her intention. Yet deep inside his soul knew what he lust for. Yet Tara respect for him never wavered. He knew Mai Dede was no damn good for him, and he was unaware that he was walking a dangerous line.

    Alexander should have seen the complexities of Mai Dede's brilliant plan when she called that day. He had pickup the phone expecting Tara but only heard silence.

    "Who is this?" He asked on the phone.

    Silence.

    "Will you stop playing in this line," he bellowed upset by the continued playing of hang ups.

    "Alex?" Mai Dede finally spoke.

    He knew it was Mai testing his convictions.

    "Why are you playing games?" He asked.

    "You know who this is? You don't need to know my name. It's embedded in your mind." The persuasive tone of her voice trapped him in her web of indulgence.

    Alexander began to hang up the phone.

With a seductive voice Mai Dede whispered, "What are you doing tonight?"

"No sure?"

"Well...why not meet me outside if your not frighten of being alone with me."

He joke it off assuming her playful nature voicing, "I'll see you out front."

"No!" Mai Dede shouted, "I'll meet you two blocks down at the corner. There something very important you need to know, about Tara."

He agreed.

"Just for the record, don't tell anyone where you're going," she said.

"Our secret?" He asked.

"You can say that," Mai Dede replied smartly.

Alexander enjoyed seeing Mai Dede and her sexual overture which seemed to float from her power of speech. It was an arousing experience to behold. Arriving two blocks away as requested, he noticed Mai Dede resting against a wall which lead to an alley way. She waved to him to come to her in an eager manner.

"What this all about?" He asked confused about actions. Though he'd seen Mai Dede acted strangely so many times before, this time was bedazzling.

"What do you mean, wrong?" Mai Dede asked smiling like a cat trapping a mouse in a corner. "Nothings wrong."

"Then why are you acting in a strange manner?"

"That's what you think. Come here," she voiced in a heated manner, pulling him close to her, but abruptly he refused.

"You know better? Tara is my love and not you."

"Pity isn't?" She responded pouting sweetly.

"Thanks anyway," he expressed taking a breather. She was gorgeous to behold, and her eyes were surely lustful.

It took all his might to resist the irresistible Mai Dede. It was the way she approached him, there was something different about this woman, dangerous. Alexander knew inside that she was no good for him, filled with passion and lust. The way she moved, her body created a persuasive machine of sexual tension.

"I'm sorry," he voiced. "Your manipulation isn't working."

"So this is where we're heading?" Mai Dede asked dejectedly. "Pity." She touched him with passion.

"Still friends?" He asked.

"Let me get back to you on that. Can you wait here a moment?" Mai Dede asked as she signaled to a car across the street.

"Sure?"

"I need to get something before we go." She called out.

"Fine," Alexander agreed as he stood there at the mouth of the alley unaware of what was about to happen.

Shortly a man appeared approaching him out of the alley as two others were passing him along the mouth of the alley. Mai Dede was nowhere to be founded. She had successfully lured him away from the Brickyard and onto the side streets. The two suddenly halted in front of him strangely. But before he could react they grabbed him as another took a pipe to his head. Alexander was out cold from the blunt blow to the head and dragged into a waiting car. The kidnappers were successful to this venture and looked to have had plenty of practice. What they were going to do with him was left to the imagination.

Hours later, Alexander found himself bounded then taken to an old cabin somewhere deep in the woods. The car pulled up to the cabin as he was blindfolded. Still dazed from the earlier blow, his intelligence battled over if whether Mai Dede had something to do with it or not? By all accounts it seemed she would gain the most in being the architect of the kidnapping, but Alexander just could not be certain? There were other things to consider, like figuring out how to reverse this dilemma? He was bonded and blindfolded since being placed in the car, though there was now a wrap upon his head stopping the bleeding. The kidnappers roughly threw him down on a chair, warning him to remain silent. Alexander wished to leave before thing got dangerous, yet he wasn't too sure what to make of this? The whole situation was unusual to him. If it wasn't the physical factor of him being tide, blindfolded and a painful thrush into reality, physical anguish would go way in time, but the ropes reminded him it was existence or bereavement. Somehow he had to get through to these men gathering that the situation was becoming unbearable.

    The room around was dusty and the wallpaper were peeling from aging and neglect. A single candle was lit and placed on a table, the illumination created an eerie feeling as it exposed the surrounding. The floor was made of wood as Alexander steps made was cranking sound due to rotten wood. The windows surrounding the room a total of five were covered with tattered white cotton lace. There rested a small table in the center of the room before him with deep-rooted medicine of the past. There was a bright green curtain hanging over the doorway behind him, as eyes peered at the action which befell him. Those eyes were the tool of his faith for the moment. The situation was grim and his faith was up in the air. He had exasperated the locals with his flaunting of affection with Tara. It was only a matter of time before he would gain their uncontrollable wrath, for tonight was clearly the beginning of his possible execution. The eyes which peered from behind the green curtain had the commanding force to decide his life at a moment notice.

Meanwhile that night on the other side of town Tara and Jeanne were eating in the airports eatery. The night's fares were good and they gain nice amount of currency to prove it. The taste of Tara's rice made her withdraw from it, pushing it aside in an upset manner. Nothing was wrong with the meal just her appetite failed her tonight. What should have been enjoyment over good fares, turned into aimlessness? Tara's mystifying actions stirred Jeanne's attention. It was clear Tara not herself getting upset over a small matter of cuisine.

"You're acting very peculiar, tonight, Tara," Jeanne said.

Tara just glared out at the incoming flights which they had done countless times.

"Alexander came in on one of those flights. He came into my life and rocked to hell out of it. Jeanne, sometimes I wonder was it meant to be, was it right," Softly she voiced.

"Tara, where all this resentment coming from?" Jeanne asked.

"Jeanne, love hurt so much," Tara replied.

Jeanne glanced at the flights herself then tried to ease Tara's emotional hangover. Surely she was going through the agony of withdraws from being unable to see him. Then there was the erotic Mai Dede making a physically powerful play on him. Whether Alexander could weather the storm remained to be seen by both. The odds were against him as other men suffered from the out come.

"Look Tara, Alexander loves you," Jeanne said.

"I know that, but it hurts sometimes. I need him so much, it gives me a stomach-ache," she cried. "Jeanne, I don't like this feeling yet I strangely desire it all. May be Mai Dede was right."

"Relax now, you'll see him later. I promise."

"You don't understand. I believe he is in danger knowing me," Tara pointed out. "I've notice how people act when were together. They point figure and spread rumors over our attraction to each other."

"What?" Jeanne asked.

"I don't know what kind of danger, but I know it's pending."

Jeanne then reclined upon the chair, only seeing that Tara was acting foolishly over it all. A roar of a jet passed over them on its way back to its origin halting their conversation. Suddenly Tara felt it was like Alexander was leaving her all alone. She gazed at Jeanne deep in thought in a pool of conflicting emotions.

"Jeanne, I would give Alexander anything he asked for and all my time. I just hope there's no one else in his life. I couldn't take that, I just couldn't!" Tara said pounding the table.

Jeanne placed her hands upon Tara's in comfort expressing that everything would go well for them. But Tara's strong feelings had tide into his. Tara's impression was not of losing him but the harm coming towards him. She just couldn't control it into focus.

Meanwhile at the cabin in the swamp, Alexander had his hand full preventing his possible death.

"Look gentlemen, I don't know what to make of this? You don't frighten me. Please remove this damn blindfold from my eyes, if you don't mind!" He shouted.

Suddenly he was knocked to the floor and forced feed a drink. It didn't take long before he became dizzy and disorganized. Still he fought his consciousness from going out, totally unaware of what about to happen to him, coming to a horrible conclusion he was surely in a fine mess of difficulty. With one last strong scream he shouted, "Let me up!" Sadly his shouting was in a losing cause. Knowing his captors were of huge size and not to be reckoned with, he had to try something? "Just what do you want from me?" He pleaded.

Finally he heard a voice even though he couldn't who was speaking. At least there was a response to his request. A strong yet whisper came to his ears, "You are not of this land, Alexander."

"I know that!" He shouted.

"Alexander, we only desire for you to go home. Just go back where you belong," the female voice cried traveling through his unwilling consciousness.

"I will not leave Tara," he responded.

"Your willingness is admirable, but foolish," she said. "Sadly, you leave us no other option."

Appearing from behind the emerald curtain was a man with tattoos over his face, Doctor Walker. Accompanying him were four beautiful young women. Each had a white handkerchief tied around their foreheads. It was the traditional Madras handkerchief, with its seven artistic points, upturned to heaven. Alexander now could smell the ladies fragrance of perfume and thought he smelled it before.

He cried, "This is some kind of voodoo ritual?"

"You seek the truth and now you will get it, Alexander."

"What are you going to do now?" He asked.

The captors didn't reply, making him even more nerves.

Alexander considered himself not one of the gullible clients that could be harmed by some stupid incantation. But they still proceeded with the ceremony despite his strong will power of the mind. Whatever he'd imagine which his possible death was; they had other plans for him. Doctor Walker presented some enchantment dust, which was forced internally into his mouth against his will. It contain a generous proportion of strong cathartic, and would cause him frequently anguish. Alexander struggled to no avail and was forced again to take more; for each time he forced it out, more was applied. Again he coughed it up and more was poured in causing him to blackout.

Mai Dede now entered the small room smiling. Unfortunately there was more to come. She possessed the vast knowledge of strange and subtle poisons, which she dispensed with great abandon when she pleased. Gradually she induced some into Alexander's mouth, defying any detection and would cause him to waste away and die of exhaustion within the night.

"Take him back to his room," Mai Dede ordered. "Let him expire in his own bed." She then kissed him gently on the same mouth which she placed the poisons, not caring of its effects.

Quickly the quadroon men followed her orders without question. A huge smile came upon Mai Dede's face, one of satisfaction of a job well done, and the best part was he was unaware of her complete involvement if it should be unsuccessful. Deep inside her, Mai Dede had become fascinated with him. Though a little too logical for her taste, Alexander was a refreshing change to her past tortured. Gazing at him, she pulled back her thoughts to reality, something Alexander had failed to do. The limp body of Tara's lover was lifted into the car and drove back to the brickyard to waste away, and by daybreak La Veanna would be pleased at their actions.

During the same time while driving, Tara had suddenly had a disturbing vision of her love being drugged by someone's hand. Jeanne was with her as always during working hours and most time afterwards had no clue. Many times that night, Tara had acted peculiar to her, citing unclear visions. Jeanne soon noticed Tara's expression of pandemonium. Luckily she was driving that night because Tara went into an eccentric state of mind, more like a daze of endlessness.

"Hey girlfriend, what's wrong?" She asked. "You look as if you've seen a ghost or something?"

"Something wrong," Tara voiced shaking.

Jeanne concerned glance every now and then on the road ahead. Suddenly Tara grabbed her hands with force.

"Where to?" Jeanne asked.

"Drive to the Brickyard."

"Why?" Jeanne asked. "We still have more fares to collect. Besides that's over five miles in the opposite direction."

"Don't ask me any question now. Please hurry, Jeanne!"

Tara's eyes were full of agony.

"What are you feeling?" Jeanne asked. "What do you see? Dammit tell me what you see!"

"Alexander is in anguish," Tara answered.

Jeanne nodded knowing better than to question her.

Not wishing to ask Tara anymore questions about her actions, the close friend pressing on the gas and driving ever faster towards the Brickyard five miles away. Jeanne decided to reserve judgment on her friend's extraordinary state of mind. Strangely she came to depend on her insight on other matters, even though Tara refused to gamble with it. One thing, she knew Tara was surely addicted to him more than she thought. Noticing Tara's actions on several peculiar events which should be questioned themselves, the pieces were coming together in Jeanne's mind. By the time they arrived at the Brickyard it was after midnight. Quickly they viewed three colossal of men leaving Alexander's hotel. Tara recklessly leaped out of the car shouting to Jeanne to stay in the car and to wait upon her return. She hurriedly rushed up the stairs without any concerns of her own life. Tara was first comforted by a man who quickly ran the other way afraid of her powers. Still she entered the forbidden room of her past.

Alexander's bedroom was shadowy and eerie now. There she sadly discovered him neatly undressed and placed in his bed like he was a baby resting in his cradle, but she knew better. She quickly noticed the bleeding of his forehead from the earlier blow. With a damp cool towel, she attended the cut. His blood was spattered upon her white blouse but he didn't care. Slowly and with worry, Tara climbed upon his bed. Tears rolled down her face fearing the worse.

She called out in a low tone of uncertainly, "Alexander?"

No reply.

With no positive sign of response coming from him, Tara placed his head upon her lap with great care. Checking his eyes and looking over his body for any harm other than the bleeding form the head, she discovered the deep incisions on his wrist made by ropes.

"Alexander, what have they done to you?" She asked aloud, rubbing his wounds gently.

Tara started to fear the worse from his non-response. Immediately she sensed a sickening smell from the room, similar to before; her mind knew what had to be done. The evil-smelling oil rendering from snake, lizards, and frogs consumed her thoughts. Surely she knew they were the signs of Doctor Walker and he soon would be her target of revenge. Yet he was known not to have such harmful knowledge of magnitude, there had to be a conspiracy aiding him? Just who was involved could come from a many of angles, just too many factors for Tara to consider. Therefore it had to come from one of the known Voodoo queens in the area, but which one? Tara gazed around the room with apprehension.

As before Tara went into a trance. Like second nature, she used her psychic powers with much ease this time, growing accustomed to supremacy within herself.

She bellows out a song.

"Hounsi-ya-yo, dogwel, dogwe,

Dogwel, dogwel, diab au corps,

Dogwel, dogwel, diab au corps.

Dogwel, dogwel, diab au corps," repeating it three times.

Beginning with her loving hands upon his, a strange blinding white glow traveled freely up his arms. The life given energy continued until it consumed his entire body. The only view remaining of Alexander was a glaring bright white light. Tara's face grew pale in color from the connection of his affliction. Veins in her arms and face pop to alarming size, then settled. This time it passed quickly a sign of her ability to rid his body of the deadly poisons.

Clearly this was an indication that she was accepting the powers given to her at birth; a sign of coming of age to the paranormal. Slowly the color returned in her beautiful face and the glow which was once bright faded into the hours of darkness. She was still fatigued from the ordeal, as Alexander began to awaken. All the poisons which as placed inside his body was strangely gone? The glow of Tara's sweaty face was now above him and Tara's arms around him. Still weak, his concentration began to clear. A huge caring smile fell upon Tara's face of relief; delighted that he was out of the woods for now. Her telepathic supremacy had not failed her gladly but only became stronger at each demanding challenge.

"I love you," she whispered quietly to him in a cautious tone, "My love, I cannot protect you forever here."

Alexander glanced up and tried to reach for her. But his body was too weak from the painful ordeal. Instead he fell back upon his bed unable to respond. Tara gazed at him and kissed him deeply, placing him in a deep slumber with her enchantment. Tara's supremacy of her consciousness forced him to instantly relax. With Alexander resting in Tara's lap, she whispered, "I shall stay with you tonight. I must assure you will be all right through the remaining night, my foolish love."

She had committed herself to watch over him that night from harm.

"No one will ever harm you again!" She vowed aloud.

Meanwhile Jeanne sat in their taxi as ordered. She had seen the bright light from the window, but now knew to allow Tara her space to work her supernatural forces unabated.

What's happening up there? Jeanne pondered. First Tara rushes her over there then tells her to stay in the car. When she looked up at Alexander's room, a bright glow suddenly appears then disappears.

Jeanne was becoming impatience outside waiting such a long period of time. Tossing her baseball cap onto the seat, she opted not to wait any longer, rushing into the building then up the stairs to his room; only to discover them both fast asleep in his bed. It was a perfect representation of love the way they relaxed upon each other. Jeanne looked around the dark room. At least the room was in better shape then before. Maybe it was time she thought to allow them to engulf the attraction alone. Jeanne slow backed out of the room; leaving them alone to themselves and smiling to herself.

"Well I better be getting home and calling it a night. See you guys tomorrow," she whispered at them while departing from the room.

Across the street all was not well. Standing there was Mai Dede, watching and waiting for screams which never came. Only to realize she had failed to rid Alexander from this earth. There were no scream, nor cries coming from his window. But there was always a tomorrow for her to reach her objective. Mai Dede had no option but to allow Tara and her lover peace for the night. Laughing discretely, slowly the vixen backed off into the shadows of the alley viewing Jeanne coming out of the hotel; now was not time to be discovered.

The sun was blazing early the next morning as the residence along the street went about their way in front of the Brickyard. Some knew of the events of last night while other opted to turn a blind eye. There was strong rapping coming at his door the next morning. As Alexander turned over the morning awaken by the knocking. He was well greeted with Tara at his side awakening too. She smiled at him pleased to know he was alright, that last night foul play didn't leave any side effects.

"Good morning," Alexander voiced.

"Good morning yourself, my love," Tara replied.

Tara sat up checking the time.

"Shall I see whomever it is at this ungodly hour?" She asked.

He nodded thanking her. Still his body was still a little weak. "Did we ...?" He asked smiling confused.

"If we did, I wouldn't be getting up from your side, my love," she answered, "I would still be on top!"

"Very funny," he joked.

Tara pulled his white shirt off a hanger and sexually danced slowly towards the door. She had nothing under it and teased him as she moved from the bed. Her hair was wildly over her face creating a great look of sexuality. "Another time, love-boy," she added reaching for the door knob.

Opening the door there stood Jeanne with a happy smile welcoming the morning.

"Well I hope the two of you got some sleep?" She joked.

"What sleep?" Tara asked rubbing her sleepily eyes.

"Hi Alex, and good morning," Jeanne voiced.

He looked up as he sat up in the bed. "Jeanne?"

"Now Tara, we have fares to collect. It's not going to get done with you making love with Alexander night and day."

Tara smiled glancing at him. "I don't know about that?"

"Nether do I, Jeanne. Maybe you better come back later," he joked. "We have some unfinished business."

"Is that what you call it?" Tara voiced throwing a pillow at him out of fun voicing. "Oh Jeanne, I'll be ready soon. But hold your voice down if you have pity for my ears. For some reason my senses seemed heighten?"

"You have to explain last night?" He asked. "Why in the hell were they trying to kill me, last night for being with you?"

"Who's trying to kill?" Jeanne asked looking stun.

"Please let me do some investigation, guys," Tara pleaded.

"Wait, I'm at a lost here?" Jeanne asked.

"I'm in the same boat," Alexander said.

No reply from Tara.

"What really happened last night?" Jeanne asked drinking a glass of water. She faced Tara with conviction.

"Please Jeanne?" Tara voiced upset. "I need time!"

"Well while you're seeking more time, Alexander's life is closing in on him. We need some answer now?" Jeanne asked.

Tara paced the floor debating over what to say? She knew only a little of the events and none of the reasons for the acts of deadly intent towards Alexander. She explained that Mai Dede had her hand prints all over the past events, yet no proof. As for Doctor Walker, he had to be getting his orders from a higher origin, maybe her own grandmother? As the two listened to Tara explanations, they soon managed to ease up a bit on her. She was at a lost as well as them on who was pulling the string here? It became clear to all that time would play an important role. First Tara and Jeanne would investigate the slave quarters where Alexander was brought to, second Tara would speak with her grandmother over what part if any she was playing? Alexander was still too weak to join them in their investigation and had to remain in bed.

Leaping onto his bed and hugging him with great affection, Tara kissed him.

"I have to leave you for a little while, forgive me?" She asked.

He nodded.

The lovers kissed each other deep and very longing until Jeanne pulled Tara off him expressing it was time to leave. Tara sadly got dress to leave him there. Still some answers to why he was taken last night puzzled his mind? But Tara eluded his questioning with every fiber of her being. Finally with great pressure she promised to address them later that night. He was still too weak to demand anymore from her relaxing back in his bed. Tara moved over to him and kissed him farewell for the morning and so did Jeanne.

Tara reluctantly left the room.

"See you later dear, wish me luck and remember I will not allow you to get harmed anymore."

Then they were gone.

Alexander slowly got up and moved his exhausted body to the window. There he observed the two ladies going to their taxi. Tara gazed up at him smiling and throwing him a kiss. Then quickly climb into the vehicle and drove way.

Pondering over the past, Alexander returned in the room and sat near the window. He struggled over what had happen to him. The kidnapping was playing wildly on his mind. Those who took him by force last night weren't playing and ordered him to leave New Orleans. Clearly the demand to leave Tara alone must have come from her grandmother La Veanna. Why was Tara protecting La Veanna? What part was La Veanna playing? He was still in amazement over the whole ordeal. The local people must be insane to attempt such a murder. He thought to himself upset over the physical action and the attempted poisoning of his body. But then something struck him?

Why wasn't he dead?

Why was it Tara who was always there to aid him?

What of Mai Dede's roll in all of this?

Who was La Veanna and where was she during all of this?

And most of all, what is the secret Tara was hiding?

Suddenly he felt ineffective and lightheaded almost falling out of the open window. Quickly Alexander staggered back to the comfort of his bed. His intelligence was too confused to attempt to piece it all together. What he needed now was simply more rest. Alexander pulled the sheets over him, resting his head slowly upon the pillows. A smile came over his bedazzle face. There he smelled Tara's fragrance in the pillow, a very pleasant scent indeed, sweet and lively. Yet his mind stayed in perplexity to what was pending? The room seemed to gyrate around him and he had enough of trying to figure it all out. The anguish of the night before had a great after affect; keeping him down. Alexander just covered his head under the sheets and fell asleep.

Later that morning Tara and Jeanne were as promised investigating.

"Where do we go first?" Jeanne asked.

"I have to go home," Tara answered.

"I'll come with you. I...think you will have some explaining to your grandmother?" Jeanne voiced in an uncertain tone.

Tara stared at her muttering, "Might as well face the music now than later. It's not going to get any easier if I should stay away another day, Jeanne. I never stayed away from home before, never stood up to her."

"Your right about that," she replied.

An hour later they drove up to Tara's home. There was uneasiness about the place.

"Well, here we are," Jeanne voiced. "I see Doctor Walker here again."

"Don't remind me," Tara said.

With what was before them, Tara was surely in for a harsh time. Sitting on the porch was Doctor Walker eyeing Tara's arrival with distaste. But that didn't matter as much as La Veanna standing beside him. It was apparent they were her welcoming committee, her judges; which waited most the night for Tara's return. Her grandmother always knew Tara was an impulsive young woman if let to her own will. Jeanne did her no help advancing her head first into the world before time. The last year was a struggled just maintaining control over her granddaughter's consciousness. Now since meeting Alexander, which she had vision at Tara's birth, had now came to past. Slowly and in a listless manner, Tara walked towards the porch. Suddenly she pulled Jeanne by the arms to accompany her.

"Ok, I'm coming!" Jeanne shouted.

"You better, you got me into this," Tara replied.

With rage, La Veanna bellowed, "Where have you've been all night, young lady? Tara, you do stay here under my rules or have you forgotten?" The expression upon her face was of great disappointment of Tara considered recklessness with her affair with Alexander. Not just because she stayed out all night, but whom she was with. Jeanne attempted to eases the situation by casting a joke at the wrong time. Yet it failed upon deaf ears of all around and received just the opposite, scorn. La Veanna raised her ivory cane towards them.

"You, Tara come with me now!" She shouted. Wait, as for your friend..."

"Wait, you now her name? It's Jeanne," Tara shouted back for the first time ever.

"What?" Doctor Walker cried shocked at her rage.

"Grandmother, you know her name," Tara jump to the aid of Jeanne. "There's no need for that tone in your voice."

La Veanna was stun by Tara's directness. Suddenly she stormed back into the house. Jeanne was shocked too by Tara's shouting at her grandmother, very shocked.

"What are you doing?" Jeanne asked.

"What I've should have done a long time ago," Tara replied. "If she has something to do with the attempt on Alexander's life, I want to know? Dammit, I want to know everything about my life! Jeanne there has been too many secret surrounding my life and I've had enough."

"But Tara, your shouting at your grandmother," she replied confused. "You get more with sweetness than the other way. Your new found freedom will come at a cost if you're not careful."

"Strangely I feel stronger and free for the first time in my life, Jeanne," Tara said smiling. "The night away has done something wonderful to me; it's made me, made me…independent."

"Independence or not, remember La Veanna is still your grandmother, she deserves some respect no matter what role she is playing here," Jeanne whispered. "Ease down, my friend. Ease down for there is more than one to achieve your goals here, get my drift?"

Suddenly Tara halted her assault on La Veanna, opting to dismiss the whole action with a deep sigh of relief. She looked towards the front door, the door of her grandmother worried about her feelings. Thinking her tantrum may have went over the line? Tara clinched her fists in rebellion attempting to hold in her antagonism. Yet her eyes displayed shame inside them. La Veanna was blind but still could feel her anguish. Slowly she turned around after having her back to Tara.

"You come in the house now, young lady," she said this softer. "Jeanne, you are to remain out here with Doctor Walker."

"Jeanne?" Tara asked.

"Now come along, my dear," La Veanna voiced with a level temper.

Jeanne pushed her from the back, forcing Tara to move.

"I'll just do as she requested and wait for you out here, where it's safe. Ok?" She whispered into Tara's ear. The expression upon Jeanne's face was one of uncertainty for her friend. But this was one time Tara was her own person. There was an uneasy feeling engulfing Jeanne as she was left on the porch. Doctor Walker was bizarrely staring at the Sun. It became obvious the two had nothing in common and there was no need to generate the association. Her main concern was Tara, as La Veanna looked and acted towards her granddaughter with trepidation over the affair.

Inside the house, La Veanna had placed her granddaughter's things in the corridor; displaying that she desired her to leave at once. Tara discovered her bags and a few personal things, understanding what was at stake. It was a despondent attempt to by La Veanna to control Tara, forcing the issue by threatening to throw her out on the street; rejecting her at each attempt of trying to make peace with her. Tara stood there in the dark totally in turmoil, forcing herself to make some of sense of the matter. Though it didn't matter whether she lived there or not La Veanna raised her hand and suddenly struck Tara upon her face with extreme force. Tara went smashing into a tall mirror, causing her to glare at her with contempt, shaking her head enraged.

Tara bellowed in bewilderment, "Grandmother, you don't mean this! What's all the fuss? So I stayed out one night. You've never acted in such a matter."

"You disobeyed me, child!" La Veanna shouted.

"You hit me for the first and last time!" Tara shouted.

"You are still my descendant," La Veanna said waving her cane.

"I am not a child!" Tara shouted back. "Dammit, I'm twenty-four years old and you treat me like a child, grandmother. You have no right in placing me into a corner trying to run my life. You have not right to alter my life."

Suddenly La Veanna's head turned to follow Tara's voice and profanity. Tara noticed it immediately voicing, "I'm sorry for that. But I'm not a child anymore, grandmother. Remember my next birthday is coming soon and I like to spend it with Alexander. Understand I have the right to do as I please."

"Not with him!" La Veanna replied.

"You mean Alexander?"

"He is trouble, Tara," La Veanna said. "I have foreseen danger in him. This man wasn't supposed to be part of our life."

Tara paused looking for a reaction from La Veanna.

"No grandmother, there must be some more to this which your not exposing to me? What is it you want from me?" Tara asked.

There was silence in the house not heard before.

"Tell my grandmother; is there some grand plan here?"

Finally La Veanna raised her head towards her.

"Grandmother?" Tara asked.

"If you continue to see Alexander then you will go, understand?"

But Tara would not allow her grandmother to control her life anymore.

"Why?" She asked.

All she received from La Veanna was a hard grunt of dissatisfaction.

"Grandmother, I will see whomever I desire and love whomever I want. That includes Alexander. So whether I pickup my things and leave with Jeanne or return them back to my room, it surely depends upon you, what will it be grandmother? You or Jeanne?"

La Veanna was losing control over Tara and had to concede. She was wise and would play the odds of regaining Tara's favor.

"Return your things to your room, my dear," she replied.

"What about Alexander?" Tara asked.

With humidity she voiced, "I will not stand in your way. If you still wish to see this young man." Her tone was very strange and in an uncaring tone.

"Now, whatever I decide in the future, it will be of my own decision, not yours, grandmother," Tara said storming upstairs with some of her things to her room. But she pondered over her grandmother's easy postulation.

Shortly later Tara's room was completely cleared out. The poster of a group of singers which Jeanne gave her from California was a miss, leaving a vacant space. The bed had no bedding upon it, stripped bear. The cute black teddy bear Alexander give her was now not in its familiar place between the pillows. Out of the chair which she kept next to her bed was missing last years' birthday card from Jeanne. Suddenly Tara felt one of the costs of being independent. La Veanna had done a job to her room and her psyche. The confused Tara slowly sat upon her bed desponded, viewing the sudden changes in her life since she met Alexander. Tara still vowed she would never let him go. Her hands slowly release her things which were her clothing.

Tara began to cry a storm over the conflict of their relationship. She discovered that by removing Alexander, her life would be a forest. She pounded the walls with passion and anger, fighting the storm in her mind. She had fought for him now there was no turning back. Slowly she dropped down to the floor crying her eyes out. Again she started to pound to floor until Jeanne's shouting outside her window brought her back to some sense of belonging. Slowly she wiped her face of the tears which cover it displaying the torture she was feeling. Taking a deep breath, Tara gathers herself to face the world again.

After a few minutes, she had replaced most of her clothing and shouted out of the window for Jeanne to come up.

Jeanne arrived in the room shocked at the changes. She saw Tara's face which as in a sadden expression. Slowly she replaced Alexander's teddy bear back in its honored place, never far from her friend's heart. Tara replaced Jeanne's card in the chair, explaining just what had happen with her grandmother. Both displayed uncertainty about the future, here once it was brilliant now a sinister cloud hung over them.

"What will you do now?" Jeanne asked. "You know you could have stayed with me anytime."

"Thanks, I know that," Tara said.

"What now?"

"I don't know? But I'm in control of my own life, not her," Tara replied unsure. "Whatever I decided to do, Alexander will be apart of it totally."

"I hope you what you're doing?"

"I guess? You know, I just hope Alexander understands just what he is getting into? Jeanne, you know I would never hurt him."

"You love him?" Jeanne asked as they continue to unpack. "He just touches me and I fall apart."

"Yes, I do."

"My, we've come a long way haven't we?" Jeanne asked.

"Well, I better get dress for work, help me?"

Jeanne nodded and smiled at her to comfort Tara in her decision.

"Look, Tara, don't worry about Alexander. He has a way of figuring out things for himself. The feel affection between both of you is robust. Give it time, ok?"

Tara nodded smiling back.

Later that evening a young lady about sixteen and dress in an alluring sexy white short skirt arrived at the Brickyard to see a man, she gazed at Alexander's bedroom window with interest as she held a very special letter from her superior. The old woman caretaker of the place waved her in through the front door. The young girl displayed the letter and was allowed freely up the stairwell to Alexander's room. She paused a moment then knocked presenting her presents.

Now dressed, he answered the door clear headed and refreshed. Before him was the young lady smiling, stared at Alexander with interest and hunger. Even though she was young, there was something ancient about her, something mystical. It was her eyes which told of the ancient times. They were lifeless eyes. There was no joyfulness of adolescence in her face, just detached manifestation.

"Can I help you?" He asked.

"You're Alexander?" She asked. "You are the one I seek?"

"Yes?"

"I have a letter for you," she voiced handing him a letter.

"Who is it from?"

"Mai Dede, now I must go," she replied backing slowly away. "She desires your presents tonight for dinner."

"Why should I come?" He asked.

"Because you want the truth, correct?"

"The truth?" He asked. "The last time I went for the truth, I almost died. Can she promise my safety?"

"Will you come?" She asked sounding distant.

Alexander read the letter discovering Mai Dade wanted to speak with him as soon as possible. There was something she knew he wanted to know. But this time he would see her on his terms, no alleys. Mai Dede was to meet him there later that evening. He nodded to the girl then reviewed the letter again. He looked up to thank her but she was oddly gone. There was no sign of her; it was as if she just vanished into thin air, as if a dream.

Later Mai Dede arrived at his room wearing a beautiful evening gown in black with a lace collar with a beautiful pendent upon it. She was surely dress to kill. His concern was about Mai Dede. Much to his delight she played off the last time she saw him, expressing regret over their last encounter, convincing him that she was as much danger as he. She explained after hearing what happen to him; there was nothing she could do. Mai Dede paced the room playfully to get his attention. She was a full-figured foe with the dubious distinction of being the hottest hell raiser in town. She was known for her erotic high jinks.

"This is where you and Tara made love?" She asked.

Alexander looked at her pondering how to respond.

"You can tell me, I'm your friend, Alex," she said.

Slowly and seductively Mai Dede climbed into his bed. The dress she worn was tight and pressed upon her firm breast. He could tell she was excited as her nipples forced their imprint for him to view.

"Your not looking at my breast, are you?" She asked jokingly.

He quickly turned his head in another direction. Mai Dede climbed out of the bed near him. Alexander was happily in love with Tara, but Mai Dede made it really difficult for him to be faithful.

"You're a ball of tempting desire, you know that?" He whispered. "Your perfume is arousing too."

"The best way to get rid of temptation is to give into it," she said smiling sinfully, licking her full lips.

Mai Dede would often bump into him, wiggling her hips or rubbing against him sexually. The sent of her sexy perfume and the thoughts of being alone with her forced him to pull back.

"I know that scent?" He asked reflecting upon his kidnapping.

"Well many ladies wear it here," Mai Dede said playing it off.

"We better go," he stated yet thinking of the event.

By this time Mai Dede's groaned as her firm tits, their hard nipples fully erect rested upon his chest. Her sparking eyes were penetrating his in swift fashion. Suddenly she rubbed his shaft completely, cradled his love tool.

"Stop!" He shouted pulling her hands off him.

"What's the matter?" Mai Dede asked smiling.

"You stated that you had something to tell me, now your dress for a night on the town."

"Want to come?" Mai Dede asked.

"To see the town, yes," he answered. "That's all."

"That's all."

"Promise to behave?" He asked.

"Sorry can't do that, but I'll give it a try," Mai Dede said.

Slowly she retrieved her purse and took his hand, leading him out of the room. She had planned to take Alexander over to Basin Street without Tara's knowledge. After escorting him around the underside of New Orleans, Mai Dede struggled to seduce him. But Alexander felt it was all right and could withstand her advancements. Besides, Mai Dede had promised to explain what she discovered about his kidnapping, a puzzle which he wanted answers. Something Tara was giving him a hard time at getting at, the truth.

Many hours later they had a few drinks at the local bars. Strangely all the bartenders knew Mai Dede and were pleased to treat her freely. Alexander did benefit from the wanted attention of her lady friends about town. All his drinks were free yet he wasn't about to get drunk, that he had never done opting only a few glasses. Late they arrived at a reserved large room by Mai Dede. It was on Common Street side of the building, on the first floor, which she equipped in magnificent fashion. The fireplace and mantel were of white marble, and the furniture upholstered in rep and damask, was of highly polished sold black walnut, as were all of the woodwork and floors, which were covered by velvet carpet. The sleeping-chamber of hers was amazing to behold. The place was pleasant and he wondered why she brought him there? She gave him a cold glass of tea and he they both tossed the cooperation. It wasn't long before Alexander became dizzy. The drink she gave him was spiked. And he was sinking under her control ever minute. She got up and looked at him.

"Alex, you're all right? You look like you need to relax," she whispered.

He was suddenly lost in his reasoning, moving closer together; their lips met in heated passions. She reached down to his hard cock through his pants and traced her fingers all around its outline. Caught up in the moment, Mai Dede slowly unzipped his pants and attempted to remove his penis. But Alexander wasn't going to be trapped in this false attraction. He refused to a sex toy for her. He glanced around the room trying to figure the exit? In the left-hand corner was a magnificent étagère, upon which were statuettes, the work of a renowned artist, and small articles of vert betraying good taste, both in selection and arrangement. The hangings of the bed, even the mosquito bar, were of lace, and an exquisite basket of flowers hung suspended from the tester of tube bed. Around the walls were suspended chaste and costly oil paintings. Alexander's consciousness was clearing a bit now, but Mai Dede had started to control it again. The fragrance, the sweet scent was influencing, controlling in nature. Alexander desperately battled to regain control of his own consciousness.

Mai Dede was too strong.

Alexander began to suddenly lean towards the bed, yet managed to not to land upon it. To avert it, he quickly grasped his arms around the bed post in trepidation. Knowing if held landed on bed, he would surely be at the mercy of Mai Dede affections. He knew that Mai was one of the most desirable women he had ever seen. It became clear that he was in a drug state.

She whispered pressing against him from behind, "I've wanted this for a long time, lover boy."

Suddenly Mai Dede pulled down her black evening gown and panties, thoroughly exposing her most intimate areas. Her pace increased like wildfire. There's no telling what Mai Dede, the vixen will do to quench her endless thrust for infinite sexual bliss.

"What's happening to me?" He shouted.

Mai Dede bent over then reached back to guide his stiff prick into her pussy. Her wetness made it easy for his cock to slide all the way inside her. They slowly position against one another, working into a gentle rhythm.

"Oh, yes, Alex. I knew it would be like this!"

He was not in control of his actions.

"Oh, do me faster, now!" She screamed.

It was as if some force was driving him on, making him have sexual intercourse with her. Though his mind could see what was happening, his body and every muscle was all hers to command.

Mai Dede cried out, "I'm coming! Give it to me now!"

Their pace increased much to Mai Dede's pleasure. But suddenly in the heat of her climax, Alexander regained his psychical ability again. Suddenly his eyes could focus on Mai Dede now standing in front of him wanting more. He thought out every reason this should not be happening to him. Yet it was happening and he was having a difficult time dealing with it. Mai Dede began to touch him everywhere, but he continued to struggle. The task was becoming harder to keep his senses again of his surroundings. Still she kept pressing and pressing him. Not allowing Alexander to clear his confused mind.

"Stay off me!" He shouted. "Please stop removing my clothes."

"I want more of you, Alexander," Mai Dede voiced. "Tara will not be around to save you this time, my dear, dear friend. You damn fool."

Slowly she removed a peril handle dagger from her purse near her. She was going to murder him, herself. Making a deadly swing at him, she missed, plunging it into the wooden bed post. But before she could get another chance to stab him, Alexander managed to push her nude body aside in a rough manner, anything to buy time. Still much in a daze from part Mai's spells and drugs, he managed to escape out of the once hidden door.

Moments later running as if he were drunk and with Mai Dede dressed and staying on his trail; following him and waiting until he dropped, he was not about to blackout. The woman was indeed dangerous. Alexander's mind was spinning wildly by now. Just couldn't get it to stop spinning, but his eyes were only now clearing. For each time he'd glance back, Mai Dede seemed to be gaining ground on him on foot. Breathing had become heavy from the encounter and the continued hurried pace caused him to suddenly collapse into a group of prostitutes along a street called Dauphine Street.

He pleaded, "Please...help me."

They just stared.

His face appeared as if there would be no tomorrow. Alexander ended surrounded a bevy of beautiful women eager to shed their innocence to expose the soles of their sexual obsessions.

The ladies just laughed at him horribly. Strange and frightening their laughter seemed. Like a hammer pounding right into his brain. Still he climbed up on one of them, he pressed on, pushing them aside, attempting to make it back to the main streets; hoping to catch a taxi back to the Brickyard. His mind was nearly jelly and unsure which way to go? It has to be this direction he was now fighting with himself. Fortunately, his sense of direction was correct. Clashing onto the streets with his clothes soaked with fear and sweat, staggering into the middle of the streets; Alexander flagged down a fast moving taxi which almost hit him. Quickly and without looking at the driver, he jumped in tired and out of breath. With most speed he glanced viewing Mai Dede just standing there watching him. She'd played with the dagger like it was apart of her. The razor like edges glared, picking up the reflection of the night light from the street lamp just outside the alley.

TARA THE FORBIDDEN FRUIT - 196

Alexander, a young man and well shape muscles was no match for Mai Dede's black magic and sorcery. With his height of six feet tall, he felt there was no event which he couldn't control. He was wrong and it was not yet over, as he felt that all the workouts should by all means protected him. Only to discover even his logic was no match. A tall dark and handsome man with a mind that was ahead of its time, it may have just became his instrument of his downfall? A man that dealt with logical method and facts, a mind which viewed the world as black and white; now founded himself locked in a world of supernatural and forced to face the powers of Black Magic. For the magic of Voodoo would soon engulf him completely into its world. There was no turning back now for him. It was a world of the unbeloved and bizarre world of loving someone from this world.

PART VII
Dangerous Affairs

Mai Dede's dangerous attacks were still fresh on his mind. The thoughts of the past hours made him ponder over leaving, that he had discovered that life in New Orleans was not all it appeared to be. Alexander rested a bit before speaking with the driver. The glass plate before him allowed the driver to be safe from rudely passengers. Alexander knew it was time for some clear answers from Tara and wasn't going to accept nothing else, if he were to stay. Again he misplayed his safety. His likely surprise, safe as he assumed was not to be.

"Where to, Alexander?" The driver asked.

"What?" He asked looked up bewildered of the driver calling him by his name, casting oddness of it to Tara. Too much information was coming in his direction. Just too many possible directions leading to a great goal; what it was he feared the worse. Hell, he doesn't know anymore? Where does one go when he's being pursued by a mad woman? The whole place seem insane at this point to the logic thinking man.

"I not sure?" He told the driver in a horse and weak voice. "How did you know my name?"

No reply.

But before he could give the directions a sudden and scarcely laugh came from the drive's direction up front. Then as quickly as he halted the car, the door surrounding Alexander locked by themselves. The window seemed unbreakable as he pounded at them in an agitated state of mind. Suddenly a green gas filled the passenger accommodation, his entire body became limp, made the attempt to move was a feeble one as he tried to pound at the thick plated glass to subdue the driver. Yet they were like steel weights attached to his limps arms. Sadly discovering Alexander could only move his head around, viewing the street signs outside the back window.

"Now you were warned," the driver voiced, "but you fail to obey us."

"Not again, please," Alexander voiced.

The driver never looked back. With a sudden turn and the car pulled down a back alley, heading to where Alexander surely didn't desire to go. Now he was bound to relive the nightmare again this time with a serious ending. As the street lights of amber color flashed upon the driver's face. Alexander sometimes could glance at the driver's face. There seemed to be a large tattoo upon the side he could see. The driver was taking him to his death, his final resting place.

"Doctor Walker?" He asked.

"At your service, Alexander," he said laughing.

"Why are you doing this?" Alexander asked.

"By now you know Tara belongs to us," he said.

"Belong to us? Who are us?" Alexander asked fading off.

Doctor Walker pounded on the glass between them awaking Alexander abruptly.

"Don't fell asleep just yet sir, we have so much to cover," he said.

"Fuck you!" Alexander shouted.

No to far ladies luck was looking out for him. It came in the form of another cabby. The drivers of the other taxi gazed on with great interest.

"Did you see that?" Jeanne had noticed him from the corner of her eye. "I know it was Alexander, Tara?"

The two business men sitting in the back seat didn't understand their interest. They only wished to get to their personal tour, signaling her to do with speed. "You know what we think?" Her passengers asked displaying irritation for delay.

"No!" Jeanne shouted pulling over to the curb.

"Wait, we've paid to good money to drive us around town," one of the men cried, "Now young ladies, we will not take no for an answer."

"What?" The Tara asked, she eyes turned a fiery red then changed back. The men sat back afraid.

The cabby Jeanne viewed turned the corner too quickly to be sure.

"You really think it was him?" Tara asked looking at her friend.

"Can't be sure?" Jeanne answered.

"We need to be sure," Tara said.

"Why don't you use that power like before?"

"It doesn't work that way."

"I don't understand?" Jeanne asked confused.

"Every time I use it, it takes more control of me," Tara replied frightened and mystified at the same time.

"Something wrong and yet nothing," Jeanne voiced, "I'm just not sure?"

Jeanne paused for moment gazing at Tara.

"You know what I think?"

"What?" Tara asked.

Jeanne replied strongly, "Now if you don't mind getting out."

Tara and Jeanne had had enough of their bellowing and ordered them out of their taxi. The shocked tourists stormed out as Jeanne threw out their money to him abruptly. They recklessly drove off headed quickly in the direction of the taxi in question. Their hoped were it wasn't carrying Alexander as feared.

"You know if we're wrong, we just lost a fare?" Jeanne asked as Tara drove, watching out of the rearview mirror at the upset gentlemen which stood there clinching his fist in great rage. But Tara's mind was consumed upon the taxi now ahead of them. Jeanne quickly fastened her seat belt wondering if she should have said anything about Tara's reckless driving, but she cause the mayhem?

Later Tara had driven them to far out of the way abandon antiquated plantation mansion. From its appearance, it seemed to have been boarded up for a great number of years. The shingles were hanging about to break off. At a safe distant, Tara and Jeanne took cover and watched with concern and curiosity, soon recognizing Mai Dede standing proudly at the now open doorways directing her cohort. She commanded a group of men to deliver Alexander into the mansion. There was several men follow her orders hurriedly without reservation; forcing Alexander out of the car against his will.

Tara and Jeanne could hear Alexander shouting, "Not again!" over repeatedly. At least his senses were still intact. Yet his imagination made him see what his fear demanded him to see.

Alexander noticed a low glow coming from inside the once thought abandon mansion. There was no need for him to put up fruitless struggle; even though he could now move again. Seeing the men holding him, huge in size and too strong to break loose from, he just had to wait for another opportunity to escape; unconfident whether there would actually be one coming his way?

Tara and Jeanne just had to do something? Watching from a safe distance and still very uncertain of how to deal with the dangerous situation; they had to save him.

"What now, Tara?" Jeanne asked as they stood behind a huge tree shooting into the heavens.

Tara waved her closes friend near and whispered a plan into Jeanne willing ears. Hoping whether it would be enough to halt her lover from getting murdered? That was a chance they all were willing to take. They both headed secretly in opposite directions around the huge mansion. Jeanne was to create a small fire on the back porch to get their attention. Hoping this would allow Tara to snatch

Alexander right from under their noises. As Jeanne was busy doing that causing a diversion, Tara had made it to the front porch windows. Inside, Mai Dede had her love sitting down and bonded in front of some candles. But this time he was not blindfold and there was no secret to his captors. Mai Dede wanted him to know just who his life would be ended by upon this night.

"La la, Ma ma da!" Mai Dede shouted.

She slowly lifted the same peril handle dagger above his head. Alexander hated seeing that dagger again in the same night, he had avoided its aim once, but current events didn't promise a second meeting of voidance. Tara outside was wonder what had became of Jeanne? The long wait has caused her to ponder if something had happen to her too.

With a flick of a thought, she caused the dagger to slip out of   Mai Dede's hands. Then she caused the candle to flip over to the floor nearly setting the room on fire, anything to delay the execution.

"Tara, I know you're here!" Mai Dede cried looking around.

Tara didn't reply and remain hiding.

Out back Jeanne had made it to the porch without being noticed. She observed man a woman carrying white towels into the back door. The only light was a kerosene lantern hanging above the porch, waving to the gusty wind. Jeanne sneaked to a nearby pile of wood boxes. She had to wait until all was clear and that chance came a few minutes after the two went in unaware of her presents. She had her chance and took clear advantage of it. Quickly Jeanne approached the lantern, releasing it from its hooks; she adjusted the flames release by a slight twisting of the nod. The glow from the lantern created a ghostly appearance upon her frightens face. She knew both Tara and Alexander's life was resting on her shoulders, failure was not an option. It was then she noticed a can of kerosene loaded to the brim near the boxes. It was used to maintain the lantern about the place. Jeanne got the right ideal, taking a chance to adapt to the situation by barrowing the kerosene. Quietly she spread the flammable liquid around the back porch and windows in a loosely fashion until the can was empty. With the lantern she threw it upon the soaked porch setting it to flames. At first it spread crossed floor then quickly to the walls and windows. She hurried out of site to a wait Tara and Alexander.

"Flames!" Shouted a man from the rear of the mansion.

"I see smoke and flames near the rear!" Another man cried pointing in the same direction of Jeanne's handy work on the back porch. Tara smiled in great relief, not only that Jeanne was successful, but she was also safe. Now it was her turn.

The unforeseen events was about to play itself out. The small flames had gotten out of control and started to swipe through the antiquated mansion made entirely of dry and rotten wood at a commanding rate. It was like the Pit of Hell one of the men screamed. Now everyone was trying best to get out themselves before they were consumed by the flaming beast. A huge beam of flames fell upon a woman just as she had dodged one before her in the corridor. The sizzle of her skin and the burning of flesh filled the air. Thick black and gray smoke rolled its way through the whole haven, clouding everyone's view. Even though others attempted to extinguish the ever growing flames, it was a lost cause. From the sounds of things; the only thing Alexander was pleased about was the flames had not reached him as of yet. Also the faith of his life was put on a much welcomed hold.

Alexander could now see the flames approaching his way in a streaming flair. The corridor before him displayed a tunnel of flames, individuals was jumping around throughout the tunnel for their lives. The spectacle was ghastly to see. Struggling to adjust his view from the heat and smoke, he thought there was a face of flames peering at him smiling. He quickly could see his life at its end. No one was coming to help him as Alexander struggled wildly to get loose. But the ropes were tide too stringent. There was nothing he could do.

Mai Dede and the others left busy fighting the flames in the other room when Tara climbed through the front window. She quickly hurried to the very frighten lover, cutting him loose. The members had now appeared in front of the mansion blocking their escape route. The lovers had to go through the flames.

"Say nothing," she whispered to him then kissed him.

"Tara?" He whispered.

"Quickly, please?" She begged.

He oblige with total confusion.

Holding his hand, Tara pulled him out of the room now filled with black smoke. Before them the corridor too was filled with black smoke; a cloud of flames bellowed along the walls and ceiling before them. Luckily they duck the explosion of heat to follow. With Alexander leading the way they had to find another way out, but Tara argued to hit that beast ahead on that the only was to escape was to go for the throat. Flames were everywhere now and sometimes seem to be like dancers twirling about. There was nowhere to release the heat, to ease its dangerous hold. Suddenly the flames strangely pulled back and went into the walls, back draft. Tara and Alexander gazed with fear seeking its new position. Suddenly it appeared behind them busting its heated anger. There were flames surrounding them now and each knew they had to dig-in, now was not the time to run.

Outside the mansion was bellowing flames from its four floors. The windows had shattered, spurting it glass upon the grounds as men and women ran for cover.

Inside the upper floors were engulfed with flames fueling the lower sections.

Meanwhile Tara and Alexander were covered with a huge wooded desk. They covered their faces with wet towels to help with the smoke. The flames returned with a vengeance blasting at them with force from all directions. The floor rocked violently from the blast consuming nearly all, as they lay against the floor avoiding its deadly flames which rolled like bellowing clouds. Alexander's clothes caught fire as Tara worked feverishly to put them out. His clothes were saved along with little burns.

"Now!" Tara shouted. "We have to go, now, Alex!"

"All right, lets' move!" He shouted.

He got up and they headed through a small opening of the flames. But faith played a dangerous joke on the lovers. The floor beneath Alexander collapsed sending him plunging to the cellar. Surrounding and below him were flames like a beast's mouth attempting to finish him? Hanging on with his left hand for dear life, he reached out with the other to Tara waiting on the edge. She smiled at him reaching her arms lower, nearly falling in herself. With all her strength and without magic she pulled him to safety.

Before them was the corridor to freedom. The area was filled with smoke, strangely no sign of flames. Under one of the doors a thick cloud of smoke dragged out then quickly returns back without them noticing. Suddenly two men ran passed them, seeking escape. They approached the door with reckless abandonment. What they got for their troubles, a suddenly blast of flames consumed them, throwing them against the wall. The flames acted like a creature attacking them as it raced towards them howling, finally killing them, and then strangely pulled back again. Tara and Alexander avoided that door. Instead they went to a side door leading to a room a few feet before them. As they approached Tara pulled Alexander back with concern. He looked on struggling to see through the dense smoke. There, they viewed a dancing twirling flame rising from a crack in the floor. The view causes both to gaze at it in wonder? Both square they could hear howling from the flame as it suddenly spread like rolling waves of water upon the floor. Then strangely it pulled back clearing the way again. They rushed at new opening only to discover the door was lock. Alexander attempted turn the knob but burned his hand. The door with flames about it bellowed outward as if to burst.

    They had to go and now!

    With a strong kick of the door, it flew open and flames shot out like a cannon. They both took cover behind the walls until it backed away. Tara leaped in first without telling Alexander, who was stun by her action to protect him. He attempted to follow but a sudden wall of flames blocked his entrance, throwing him backward in the corridor. The flames would not allow him in as he shouted for Tara. From what he could see, the last room was engulfed with intense heat and flames. But the oddest thing was Tara standing not being touched by the flames, as if the flames were being controlled? Appearing out of the flames, Tara ran out unharmed grabbing his hand and pulled him into the room, leaping through the final door and out into the yard.

Meanwhile, Mai Dede tried to return to the room to finish him off quickly. But discovering she couldn't get near the front room. A large wooden beam in flames had completely blocked the doorway. The entire mansion had come an inferno. Mai Dede felt Tara and Jeanne was the cause of this, a deduction she picked up before all hell broke loose. Glancing around the corridor Mai Dede noticed the whole mansion was inflames. Engulfed in a fiery-inferno, she knew Alexander could not survive. Quickly, she rushed at the last minute out to escape the flames about her. Her feelings were uncertain, yet Mai Dede remained confident of killing Tara's lover in such a horrible matter, cremation. Smiling to herself, she left with the others to notify La Veanna the task.

Meanwhile outside what she hadn't noticed on the opposite side of the burning mansion was three figures standing and watching a few yards away. For there stood covered and through the upheaval Jeanne, Tara, and Alexander in high spirited to be well and alive. The flames bellowed out heat that reached upwards into the heavens. It filled the night skies with majestic brilliance of lights as embers shoot upwards, making the skies appeared like it was the sunrise itself. The flames consumed the antiquated plantation mansion in minutes of it being set on fire by Jeanne. Fortunately, Tara got Alexander out quickly, but not too soon for him before it proliferated. But he remained puzzled? Walking away from Tara, he glanced at both ladies wondering?

Behind them flames were so intense that it gave out unbearable heat, forcing them to move back a bit from it warmth. Strangely, Tara stood there watching it oddly. Then she moved towards him in concern, but he pulled away from her frighten.

"Alexander, what wrong?" Tara voiced bewildered by his actions, standing there watching him with affection and dismay. His was enraged with what had transpired.

"Tell me what's happening here, Tara!" He shouted.

"Tara, what's his talking about?" Jeanne asked.

"You walked through fire like it was air and not be harmed," he said.

"Is that true, Tara?" Jeanne asked.

Tara didn't reply.

"Don't tell me another time!" He glanced at Jeanne direction, which expression was one of perplexed. She was too awaited for the same answers demanded by Alexander.

Tara moved away frightened.

"Well the both of you see," she voiced attempting desperately to get it out, but discovering it was very difficult to do so.

Only just now she partly started to place things right in her own confused reasoning. Tara gazed at him worried. Suddenly like lighting, flashes of her past came forth in rapid pace, flooding her bewilder mind, visions as far back as the birth when she was conceived. This was what La Veanna had feared, the visions. Yet Tara couldn't picture her childhood, there was a gap in the flashes. Soon she came to realized there had never been a childhood for her, all the childhood photographs around the house were replicas of another child's bygone days. It was all an elaborate propaganda created by her grandmother. Now was a time of transparent thought within her own mind and greet the love in her life. Until Jeanne and Alexander came into her shielded life, she would have naively continued to live the lie.

Quickly Tara glanced at him pleading with her beautiful eyes.

"Alexander, I now know that I've loved you for a long time. We both knew of the attraction we felt before we ever met," she voiced approaching him.

"Before we ever meet?" He asked.

"Yes."

"It was you who was in my dreams?" He asked.

"I can't say," Tara said.

"Then tell me what's going on here," he asked.

"First there was emptiness and an endless abyss in my soul. Fortunately, we founded each other and you pulled me out of it, for that, I will always be grateful. Without you, my love, there would be no reason for living," she said attempting to diminish the disbelief of what was to come, realizing that all the grooming and time spent in her was targeted for some horrible plot.

Alexander understood what she meant by feelings for him? Yet couldn't workout what she was getting at? Jeanne watched too with interest. She had trouble in figuring it out too. Both their expressions were perplexed as they watched Tara walk around in a nervous fashion. Suddenly Tara halted, noticing her same reaction, one of a menace nature. Her hands were sweaty with apprehension.

Tara cried out, "You don't get what I'm saying...do you?"

"What do you want us to say, Tara?" Jeanne asked.

"Jeanne, you can't sense or experience what I'm understanding inside, do you? You both think I'm mixed in this somehow? That I may desire to have you killed Alexander. You can't really believe that? I love you, Alex."

Jeanne saw this was getting out of hand, stepping in.

"But, Tara what are we supposed to make of all this? These people consider you as a 'Madonna' if I can use that?" Jeanne asked. 'You can't deny that?"

Alexander stun over the outlandish events could only watch the ladies with nothing to add, what could he say? This whole situation was becoming stressful to him. He didn't come there for this. Let alone fall in love, but it happen. Alexander truly loved Tara.

She walked in an unsure manner towards him, kissing him deeply with affection. This time Alexander didn't withdraw. The warmth was still there in full force. They both stared at each other wondering what to do next? Tara suddenly realized she must enlighten him to what she'd vision and knew what is to be true.

"Jeanne, my best friend for life who never questioned my bizarre actions, maybe its time you should have?" Tara asked. "Alexander, a person who unlocks my life and my heart, bring a true reason for me to be here upon this earth."

"What are you trying to tell us, Tara?" He asked.

"What I'm trying to tell you both is...now hold on to your sanity. What I need to tell you is...I'm to be the next High Priestess. Do you understand me now? That is why Mai Dede has suddenly been in my life creating misfortune, as if she could simply denounce it but couldn't." She continued shouting; whaling out of fear to be liberated from this unwanted and painful destiny.

This came so quickly to both of them, causing shock waves they couldn't believe within themselves; even though they've heard it from Tara, herself. It made no it harder to acknowledge. Standing back from her, Alexander didn't know what to think? He viewed Tara beginning to go into a rage over her life and where she was going. But for some reason she couldn't stop? She persisted, shouting until Jeanne slapped her hard against her face. Then something ungodly unexpected happen to alter their perception forever. With little warning, Tara unknowingly did something the two would never forget.

Her once beautiful eyes turned a deep yellow as her grandmother did before. Her arms reached out towards

Jeanne to strike her down. Yet Tara or what she was, cried out in a horrible scream.

"El! el, ma sa!"

Jeanne began to rise parting her body from the earth under her feet. Gradually she continued rising until even Alexander could barely see of her in the darken skies if not for the flames. Viewing what had occurred he had to attempt something for both their sakes?

"Tara, please stop it," he pleaded.

No reply.

"You're going to kill her," he followed up.

But she took no consideration to his appeal and remained gazing upward. It seemed as if she wanted to force her best friend off the face of the earth. Yet for some reason to him it was not of Tara doing? But some unseen influence other than hers, supremacy from another source, possibly...her grandmother? If this was so then she had regained complete mind control over Tara's consciousness. La Veanna's annoyance and heated rage along with Tara's floating on his passion made her an easy target. Through Tara's thoughts, La Veanna decided to rid herself of Jeanne continued interference and match-making this night. Alexander feared he was next if a halt to resentment wasn't stop. Suddenly Alexander leaps toward to her in hopes of forcing Tara to break the connection. But he became an unwilling victim of La Veanna's psychic powers. For through Tara own mind, she had paralyzed him in his steps.

"Tara, you must stop this!" He shouted. "You must get control back of yourself. Jeanne is your true friend and close partner. If you love...her too, you must..."

Anxiety had stuck in him for Jeanne and there was one more thing he could attempt. He paused for a moment then uttered, "I do need you, Tara."

Tara sharply glanced at him astonished. Suddenly, he could move again. Taking advantage, Alexander cried, "You're not in control anymore, please for me, try to get back. Just try to control your own consciousness. It's all...you...have...to... do."

His request was working and Tara was beginning to relax as   La Veanna lost her control of her mind.

"Alexander, what did you say?" Tara asked looking puzzled at what he had said.

Finally Tara broke completely.

"You really mean it?" She asked.

"Yes."

Now please Tara listened this time and followed his request. Slowly Jeanne's body lower gently back to earth unharmed.

"Forgive me?" Tara asked.

"We do," Alexander said.

"It wasn't me. You have to believe me," Tara replied afraid.

Then her eyes returned to normal, a radiant haze. Gazing to them, Tara still wondered whether or not Jeanne remained her best friend? Plus most of all whether Alexander meant what he said and still desired her? Tara had cause to be concern, for him it was difficult to ever conceive Tara in such a manner. The view was too frightening to behold. He became even more frighten as she approached him.

"Just stay back for a moment, ok," Alexander voiced.

"Please?" Tara pleaded.

"I don't know just what is happening here? Tell me what the hell is happening? People trying, and almost accomplishing their task of killing me, your best friend, Jeanne, shooting to the damn moon like a rocket, and to top it all off, the Tara, who believes she is becoming a damn High Priestess."

"Please Alexander," she cried.

"Alex, please," Jeanne pleaded to resuscitate the damaged relationship. "Tara is telling the truth and you must believe her."

"No, excuse me, to be in witchcraft and I believe her. I've seen it with my own eyes. Hey, I don't what to think anymore? This is way beyond any logic I know, this black magic and all," he complained.

Tara moved towards him trying to comfort his confused and frighten mind. But he backed away from her quickly uttering, "Look, I just have to get out of here, I'm sorry."

"Don't go," Tara pleaded refusing to use her powers.

Alexander rushed away from the two ladies, terrified by what he'd seen. As he ran along the dirt trail, trying to avoid being seen by his captors, his mind was totally perplexed by wanting to leave and not wanting to leave Tara's tenderness. His whole world of which he had much control was now destroyed in one night of bizarre happenings and the days preceding it. All he desired were to just relax; stay out of compromising positions which would upset him. He just wished to live. Now with a new love, Tara which lies to him about being involved in the art of black magic, maybe it was against her will, maybe not?

He would struggle for the next days if he should depart alone or not? He thought. Unsure of what he'd witness, Alexander knew he wasn't ready for this. Also unsure if it was safe to be around Tara, he opted to get away and reflect over the rapid ever changing events which transpired that night.

"What the hell have I gotten onto here?" He asked loud.

His mind searched for answers as inside him apprehension took over. Sweat was pouring down his brow as he continued to run along the path, running until he arrived back at the Brickyard boarding house and into his room in an exhausted state of mind. Quickly he locked the door, bolting it from the inside as if it somehow it gave him some comfort of safety. Yet his mind was still focused on Tara. He pondered whether it was himself doing the remembrance or Tara playing with his mind? His heart was beating so rapidly, he could square the thumping was heard by the people outside in the below street. He peered nervously out the corner of the window, wondering if his captors had followed him. Fortunately, there were not a sign of them, but he could not unwind.

Meanwhile back at the clearing, Tara was still afraid of possibly losing the two. Jeanne had remained and not cast any judgment of her friend. She still cared for them both even though Tara lifted her off the ground.

"Help me, Jeanne?" Tara asked.

"I don't know what to say, Tara?"

Gazing at her, Tara attempted to convey their friendship by her expression of concern. The pressing and friendship soon won over Jeanne's compassion. Jeanne understood her deeply and what was at stake with regaining Alexander's love and trust.

"What do you want me to do?" Jeanne asked. "What about, Alexander?"

"I don't know?"

"You can control him with your psychic powers and bring him back?" Jeanne joked watching closely at her reaction to the question. Tara look at the burning mansion then gazed at Jeanne.

"If I'm to ever love him again and he loved me, I must control this curse. If there were ever to be a future, I have to control it, Jeanne."

"Tonight just leave him alone to think," Jeanne said.

"But…" Tara said.

"Look, if you love him, let him go," Jeanne replied.

"I do love him," Tara cried. "He has to come back to me."

"If Alexander loves you, then he will return," she added.

Tara reached out her arms towards Jeanne and the ladies touched hands. Quickly, Jeanne hugged her best friend, something Tara need badly. The trio was almost complete except for Alexander's presents and Tara missed him badly. The following days would be an important proving point for the two lovers. Like anyone whom lived in New Orleans, knew of Voodoo and its way of life to those who lived in a certain area of town, Jeanne was no stranger to it either and could adjust better then Alexander. But seeing Tara display such powers overwhelmed even her.

"What about Alexander?" Jeanne asked. "I would be going crazy over all of this?"

"I need time to work this out," Tara replied.

"What are you going to tell him?"

Tara began to walk around to the passenger side of the car. Then opened the door slowly, pondering about the question.

"Jeanne, I care for him so much, it burns within me so. You must help me get him back, I need Alexander."

Jeanne nodded.

Aware of their conversation was being observed through Tara's eyes by La Veanna. Tara thought it's best that Jeanne talk to him first. Her hoped that since Jeanne got them together; he may be willing to speak with her more freely without fear? Also Alexander trusted Jeanne a great deal, that could be a plus in her favor, riding on the numerous conversations they had had among each other; it were Jeanne who convinced him to stay longer. But the ladies weren't fooling themselves about the out come. They knew it would be an uphill battle to restore the relationship. Tara was even more determined to investigate just what her grandmother involvement in? She struggled over how La Veanna could cause anymore harm to Alexander, knowing she loved him?

Meanwhile the situation was much different at Tara's home. A knock came at La Veanna's front door late that night. She was rocking in a chair alone, her face pointed to the open window displaying the heavens. Clouds had formed blocking out part of the moon, creating an overcast of strangeness. She knocked three times upon the table nearby loudly, signaling them to enter. The front door opened slowly by itself. In stepped Mai Dede with Doctor

Walker behind her, smiling over their accomplishment of killing her granddaughter's lover.

"Why have the both of you returned?" She asked.

"What do you mean?" Mai Dede asked.

"Fools, you haven't accomplished any task, I've sent you on. Tara has made a fool of you both," La Veanna cried out enraged. "Instead you have caused only pandemonium and deaths."

Confounded and mystified with great concern both displayed trepidation at their welcoming by her. The two stared at each other frighten of possibly coming under the wrath of La Veanna?

"You old woman, you have no ideal of what had transpired tonight," Mai Dede voice moving around the living room like she owned it, arrogant and assertive.

"You have caused many deaths at the plantation. Many of our people died in that fire," La Veanna replied. "You show no remorse, why?"

"You sit here everyday and night upon a decaying throne about to breathe your last breath, now you're claiming we dishonored you, what a forest of statement," Mai Dede spoke.

"Young lady, you're playing with fire," La Veanna cried.

"Could it be you bring shame on, us?" Mai Dede asked acting assure of her deed. "So some had to die?"

La Veanna wasn't going to allow the sassy Mai Dede to address her in such a disrespectful manner. Nor anytime allow any lower queen to attack the dignity she earned. Mai Dede had set in motion the rage which she clearly wished to avoid coming there. She had crossed the line too many times before. La Veanna, the High Priestess sat up in her throne like chair. Bending over slightly towards them with no expression now, she in a weak manner waved them closer. Both Doctor Walker and Mai Dede followed baffle with interest. Speaking ever so softly as her voice was almost gone from years of residing over rituals.

"He, the one in love with Tara, my only granddaughter is not dead," Le Veanna voiced. "He, the one you both foolishly claim victory over his death should give your own lives. For you have dishonored one above you which deserves no such dishonors. I have allowed you to speak and have heard from which you claimed, now you will give one life. But, I will spare one of you and the other shall surely die this night. Let it will be an example for the disgrace you have brought into my home."

In her dark blue ancient dress with large white lace prints in front, rested back slowly, taking a deep and frightening breath, as she collected her thoughts. Suddenly Doctor Walker blinked first, rushing for the front door. Having no desire to leave this earth, he struggled to escape. Yet knowing there was nowhere to hide from La Veanna's psychic consciousness, in his mind the murder would to place. But he couldn't think of anything else to do after failing twice. Mai Dede watched him struggle to his feet. She was herself filled now with apprehension of what was next, wishing she'd never hassles La Veanna. Yet she never made a step to leave like Doctor Walker, knowing better.

La Veanna chanted, "Voudou! Voudou Magnian!"

Suddenly and without warning, Doctor Walker fell on the outside porch. His hands rested upon his tattooed face. His eyes were left wide open as if he seen the devil himself. Killed by a massive heart attack from a multitudinous wave of thoughts thrown his way by her, La Veanna turned towards Mai Dede.

"Forgive?" Mai Dede pleaded falling to her knees. No reply.

Quickly Mai Dede gazed on with horrible fright. She glanced up at the High Priestess hoping for her own life to be spared. Never have she seen   La Veanna so enraged and vindictive. There quickly came a huge wave of humbleness, engulfing Mai Dede now keening before La Veanna. But now it was Mai Dede's turn to feel her wrath. She had witness Doctor Walker's death, now it was time she witness her own. La Veanna bowed her head towards the now humbled Mai Dede at her feet. Raising her hands, she placed them upon Mai Dede's beautiful long silky jet black hair.

"You have a good grade of hair, my child," La Veanna strangely uttered, "You shall have one more chance. Kill the one called Jeanne, friend of my granddaughter. She has been the one which brought them together, let her death be the one death which breaks them apart. She will visit him in the next few days for Tara's sake."

"But Alexander still lives, why must I kill Jeanne?" Mai Dede questioned her in a reluctant and confused manner. The target now was completely confusing her? She thought it should be Tara's lover?

La Veanna turned towards her and replied, "She is on her way to the Brickyard, alone. She means to bring them together again. Now go! Do not disappoint me, Mai."

She then sent her away to halt Jeanne's attempt. Mai Dede stepped over the now limp body of Doctor Walker, not wishing to become a copse herself.

"What about, him?" She asked.

La Veanna just waved her on voicing in a low tone, "There are others who will remove him."

The next few days all was tranquil and there was no sign of Alexander. By the time Mai Dede drove up at the Brickyard, Jeanne had made it to his room already. There she would attempt to convince him to forgo what he had witnessed, to trust his inter feelings for Tara. Though Mai Dede's task was to prevent such a thing happening, Jeanne had a way with words. There came a light knock at his door, which the sounds of it frighten him inside. Realizing the nights before was filled with tension and uncertainty about his future there, Alexander left all the light in his room dark. Yet there remained the pressing issue of Tara? It had been too much for him to adjust to, for any outsider to adjust to.

"There's no one home," he answered through the door.

"Alex, its Jeanne, let me in please," she cried, "Tara and I been looking for you for days."

No reply.

Jeanne continued banging on the door wildly.

"Will you go away? Go away before they know I'm here, Jeanne," he responded.

"Dammit, if you don't open this door…"

Suddenly, it opened slowly at the door as he peer the best he could with the little view presented to him, wondering if Tara was along too? She was not with Jeanne in person, but in heart. His bags were packed and he had called a taxi to take him to the airport in an hour. Whatever Jeanne had to say to him wouldn't be enough. She walked around his room wondering just where to start? The overt bags didn't please her at all and she expressed it with conviction, throwing them onto the floor upset.

"I see your leaving us, why? Are you all right?" She asked.

He nodded. "What about you?"

"Yes?"

"I see you're intact after all what had happen," He responded slightly smiling.

"Why are you leaving?" She asked.

"I have to do what it, Jeanne. My leaving would be for the best of all concern," Alexander said.

"You don't have to do anything."

"Look, Jeanne, I have to leave this place. Understand? They were right all along. Tara and I don't belong together. You nearly died yourself," he explained. "Can't you see, no one wins and no one lose."

"Right?" Jeanne said.

"I don't belong here," he answered.

She refused to allow him the easy way out, refusing to allow his feelings of phobia for Tara to sore what come be. "Then you're really going?" She asked sadden.

He nodded knowing Jeanne deserved an answer after bring them together. Look, I appreciate what you've done for me, for us. But I'm not going to reflect about anything accept home."

Jeanne leaped at him striking him, shaking his body in anger bellowing, "You can leave like this! It's not right, Alexander because I love you!"

Alexander pulled her off him stun by her statement. "What?"

Jeanne paced the floor overcome but emotions.

"Why didn't you tell me?" He asked confused, "Does Tara know?"

"No," she replied, "Tara had eyes for you and you the same for her. I couldn't allow my feelings to interfere with her happiness." Jeanne had dismissed her attraction towards him, for the good of all.

"I don't know what to say?" He asked.

"Say nothing, this is only about Tara," Jeanne answered. "Now we must think about what is next for her, Alexander."

"Still…"

"Still I love you but that is not important now," Jeanne said pacing the floor then turned to him. "We have to save Tara."

"How?"

"I don't know," she added, "but the two of you should be together."

He couldn't hide his feelings for Tara, they were as strong as before, demanding in nature, tender in delivery. Tara couldn't help being drawn into the world of the supernatural, that she and now he was painfully well aware. Both had lived with hurt and could over come their dilemmas if given time. He knew there's more to this. Tara wasn't allowed a choice in the way she wished to live. Now was he will to run out on her? Destroy the relationship they had built? He was hurting inside from the continued attacks aimed towards him.

Jeanne and he knew time was running out on Tara's freedom, that she was battling the odds against her alone. Tara had been protecting Alexander during this battle, now it was his chance to protect her; time for him to alter his thinking? But if it wasn't for him being there, Tara's life would not be in jeopardy. He was not like other people who came there and left. He had gained a close friendship with Jeanne who at this time couldn't restrain the tears. He picked up his bags ready to leave, speechless.

"Alexander?" Jeanne pleaded.

"What do you want from me, Jeanne?" He asked. "I'm only human like everyone else, that's just what I am."

"We need you," Jeanne voiced.

"We can't change we are. You're asking too much for me to accept what I've seen, Jeanne."

"Tara loves you. That alone should count for everything," she added, "I know you've seen their psychic powers and how strong they appear to be, but we can win here if we work together."

His heart suddenly dropped out of wretchedness. Glancing around the darkness of the room, Alexander had to make a decision of his life. Jeanne was right all along but he still resisted. Maybe they can't win, maybe the only thing they could do is go home. The situation would scare anyone into doubt.

"Alexander, I know it does cause deep concern. Damn, I've known Tara for over two years and never knew," Jeanne cried, But don't throw it all away, please. Tara about to give up her life to these people, you can't allow that, you must not."

"I don't know anymore," he said.

Jeanne held him tightly wanting his support, deeply deserving of him. Finally Alexander released his bags as they clashed upon the floor. He knew he couldn't turn away. Even if he tried a stay way, his heart would curse him for life. Somehow he had enlightened Tara his feelings regardless of the out come. Jeanne smiled wiping the tears from her eyes.

"I wish I knew where she was?" He voiced.

"Tara misses you and wants me to tell you, she understands if you wish to save your own life."

"Together we'll help her, ok?" He asked

Jeanne nodded.

"Better yet, take her away from this place, fast."

Alexander agreed and discovered the deep devoted friend Jeanne was to Tara. But Tara was not out of danger yet.

A few days later at another disclosed location in the swamp, Tara had disappeared trying to sort out her mayhem, soul searching. She finally decided to return home more confused than ever. She was a proud woman and walked in as such, wishing to know the truth about her past. That night all lights were out strangely. Even though La Veanna was blind, she kept the lights on for Tara, calling it, a light to steer by.

Entering the front door, Tara listen carefully for any signs of life, none presented itself. She then switched on the hallway lights as it cast her shadow upon the stairway. After only a few minutes, Tara discovered   La Veanna had left without a trace. Still she throughout the huge house she came so well to know, she was now a stranger. There was only silence ringing through its dark corridors. Could what had happen to her caused   La Veanna's death? After a fruitless search downstairs she proceeded to the upper floors. Suddenly she noticed a peculiar fragrance coming from her grandmother's bedroom? Tara placed her hands upon the always locked door, taking a moment to investigate the weird and wonderful aroma. There was an unfamiliar click indicating the door was unlocked. As she opened it with great concern, a rush of the scent pushed passed her, sweet in nature. Taking a deep breath, Tara inspected the bedroom.

There were countless ceremonial objects, similar to the ones found by her and Alexander at the site. All were neatly arranged in their places along the walls. This she had no more doubt about, realizing that Voodooism was a real factor in La Veanna's life, much to her dismay. From the looks of things, her grandmother was the most powerful figure among her people. Along with other things, she discovered evidence of charms, oddly Alexander had one too.

Tara placed her hands on the charms and her psyche spanned off into a psychic vision. Instantly she could see the past drifting before her thoughts. Suddenly she viewed herself in a trance finding one of them on the table, for she was her grandmother. La Veanna placed the charms in a red velvet box. She struggled to vision more, it soon became easier. There was an address written on a note upon the nightstand, someone called Jimmy name was printed on top. That was all she could see for now as the trance faded. Back to reality she glanced around more evidence was discovered, amulets, and magic powders. But the strangest of the collection, was imported from Africa; a large-almost life-size doll which had been carved from a single tree-truck. Painted in brilliant colors and bedecked in beads and gaudy ribbons, this doll formed such an impressive spectacle, and to her so obviously a source of magic. There something else strange which frighten her. Tara's picture was placed on the forehead of the life-size doll. Under her photograph was some writing which read; for the daughter of the house of Turner, first born will be mines. She will become the next High Priestess on her birthday of the month of summer.

"Then she will become immortal and replace me as others have before me," Tara voiced aloud.

This stun Tara for the note was referring to her. She stared at the huge figure with contempt. Searching through more of the papers below, Tara examined an old marriage record of the Turners and discovering she was really the daughter of a person named Karen Turner, a mulatto woman born in New Orleans. When Karen was in her twenties, she married a man named Jacques Turner also a mulatto. Further, the ceremony was strangely performed by a priest named Anthony Alomen against La Veanna desire. Jacques Turner died a year or so afterwards by some unknown cause? Karen Turner went onto live with a quadroon man, Sammy Glapion, son of her grandmother. To this date her grandmother claims there were no records of their marriage. Yet the dairy did show that she had a daughter, and that was Tara, herself. But nothing was ever stated about the night she was born or her childhood, but that there were records of the last two years only. Placing the papers down slowly, Tara glanced around the huge bedroom. Then realized there were to be a ritual ceremony in the coming nights. That would explain why her grandmother wasn't home this night. Further observations exposed to Tara, there was only a few weeks left before her birthday; as she soon began to sense what was in store for her.

Rushing back to her bedroom, Tara desired to leave such a place only grew more desperate. But she now knew of the dangers of staying near the one's she loved, Alexander and Jeanne. Opting not to contact them for their own safety, feeling strongly she brought it all on them, running away was the best she could do. The only reasonable selection was just one, as she gathered some of her things including the teddy bear from Alexander and Jeanne's photo. Not wishing to place Alexander into anymore perils, Tara headed directly towards a special hided location in the swamps. The area was unknown to many accept Jeanne. She hoped it would serve as a safe-house until her birthday passed. Then maybe another queen would be chosen in her place. But she had others wondering where she was? The good guys in addition as the bad ones depending on how ones viewed life itself.

PART VIII
Delusion of Trust

Alexander knew time was running out for Tara. He and Jeanne were at the Brickyard discussing how to approach the pending event. They both were concern about if she would even accept their help, more less, his? The events were about to play out, forcing him to witness Jeanne's last days. After days of searching they couldn't find Tara. In fact no one could. She just vanished from the face of the earth. Tried and desperate, Alexander knew the searching wasn't working, that different route had to be taken.

"What do we do next?" He asked moving towards his bedroom the windows. "I mean we must have another plan, don't we?"

"I don't know?" Jeanne asked. "We've searched everywhere."

"I remember the first time I met her at this cabin in the swamp," she voiced.

"That's it!" Alexander shouted.

"What?"

"The abandon cabin near the clear water pond," he voiced.

"I never thought of that place," she replied, "Let go!"

"Sure, Jeanne, let me get something out of my bag. Why don't you wait for me in your taxi?"

"See you downstairs," she responded.

Alexander watching her leave seemed awkward. Still something was pulling at him, he thought? Across the street stood Mai Dede waiting for Jeanne to return to her taxi alone. If she could get Alexander too, that would perfect. Jeanne was unaware that she was facing the same faith as Alexander. She walked out of the building caught up in thought.

Shortly she viewed Mai Dede tapping her right foot. Both ladies glared at each other with contempt. Mai Dede knew why she was there, but Jeanne remained completely puzzled. She quickly gazed around as she slowly moved towards the car, frighten of the moment. The people who were once on the street were strangely gone? Only three men stood at the base of the Brickyard entrance, acting as if nothing was going on. Jeanne paused then looked up at Alexander's window, wishing he somehow would come to her aid. But if they had gotten him then Tara was surely be lost. She opted to give herself up for the two. Soon she was totally clear of the building and near her taxi. Shaking nervously, she placed her hands on the door handle. Mai Dede suddenly signaled the three men to snatch Jeanne quickly.

"Hey guys off duty if you don't mind," Jeanne joked in vain. "Hey guys, can you read the sign."

Jeanne didn't refuse them opting not to fight. It would have done no good anyway. She just smiled bowing her head at Mai Dede. One of the men grabbed her arms, causing great agony.

"Take it easy, will you!" She shouted.

Alexander happen to glanced out of his window, noticing the rough treatment of Jeanne by the unknown men with her. They quickly carried her off into another car. How foolish he was to allow them to separate. Mai Dede was getting in another car ahead of them. In his attempts to leave the building, Alexander was stopped by the presents of the old landlady. She glared at him with hatred to halt in his foot steps. He ordered her to remove herself from in front of him, but she stood her ground. He wondered how to get by her without hurting the old lady; surely she was buying time for their escape. He knew the longer he stood bayed, the more Jeanne's life was at earnest cost, driving him to a demented state.

"Move now!" He ordered but her expression never changed.

He moved towards her, hearing the roar of the engines outside the building, signaling the kidnapping of Jeanne. Suddenly he moved with speed near the old woman. But with a quick and unexpected slap from her back hand, he was forced backwards with great force. Force as if she had the vigor of the three men whom abducted him. She grinned at the stun young man sinfully. Alexander wiped his brow in confusion and disarray. What horrible strength she posses. His mind pondered, she had the will of the devil inside her. Climbing up off the top of the steps, he attempted to move pass her again, but this time with force, thrusting himself at her. The old woman suddenly dodged him as he rolled recklessly down the stairs. Ending stun and confused, he wondering why she allowed him to pass? Whatever the reason was, he had no time to deal with its complexity. He struggled painfully to his keens and then to his feet. The horrible fall should have killed him there; yet faith had a way of dealing the unexpected hand of life. He rushed stumbling quickly to the front of the building, only to view the two cars driving off. Holding his left shoulder, bruised from the fall, the last eyes he saw were Jeanne's, as she shucks her head not to persuade her. But he couldn't do that. No he dare not allow himself to withdraw from her aid.

What he had foolishly done to Tara in her need, would not allow the same mistake with Jeanne. Standing there bewildered and despairingly he had to do something? Suddenly he noticed the keys were strangely still resting on the outside taxi's door. Not waiting, he catapulted himself into the vehicle. It matter not if it was a trap set by Mai Dede or just a foolish error by them. He drove off as if he were a race car driver, chasing them with reckless disregard of his own safety.

After several hours he and the others ended somewhere in an obscure part of swamps, unknown to him. The car he was chasing was now abandoned on the roadside. Alexander inspected it disappointedly wishing it was the latter. An expression of despair grew at a rapid paste upon his face, replacing any gleam of hope he once had. But there had to be hope, there must be? He thought, struggling within himself. There was a bright moon above his head, casting a disenchanted gloom over the entire area. There seemed to be an unnatural mist, two inches hovering above the ground, engulfing his feet, coming off the swamp nearby. Unfortunately, this was as far as he could go upon four wheels. The rest of the chase would be on foot beyond this point. He'd hoped, not a point of no return. The swamp seemed totally strange and yet very live. Sounds and smells unknown had surrounded him.

"Boy! This is not going to be easy, not one damn bit!" Alexander voiced aloud to himself, attempting to convince himself to drop his paranoia. But there was not option in this case, he had to move forward.

Grabbing a flashlight from Jeanne's taxi he proceeded reluctantly through the hoarse brash and wet lands before him. Luckily, he had the advantage of surprise over Mai Dede and company. They were unaware of his presents in the area. Mai Dede had an hour start over him, which he quickly made up. Watching them from a distant Alexander could now see the site clearly from his advantage point. They arrived at a lake in which the central figure was Jeanne, forcing her to be the focal point of their attention. Most of the celebrants were women, with a few quadroon men, and each carried a burning brand. He moved even closer undetected by those he followed, needing a better view to figure a course of action. Hidden up in a large tree to observe what was happening. He soon discovered there was no way to get Jeanne out there for now, forcing him to wait gauntly.

"What the hell is going on?" He thought to himself observing them.

The women were all dressed elaborately, some of them in bridal costumes, and with extraordinary regard for fineness and purity of their linen. At one end of the group a corpse was exposed. The rites having been commenced, an elderly turbaned female dress in white and red signaled the others. Alexander noticed it was La Veanna, herself ascended a dais and chanted a wild fetish song, to which the others song too. At the same time they commenced to move in a circle, while gradually increasing the time. Soon their clothing and other ornaments were all torn off. He noticed that all had become intoxicated and drunk with reckless madness and yet there was exceptional excitement! Alexander could see baskets of snake whose heads were projecting from the cover hissing. In the midst of the witches, he called them, the pythoness of this extraordinary dance and revel was a young lady, bare feet, costumed. He soon recognized that it was unfortunately and to his great fear, Jeanne! In one hand she held a torch, and with wild, maniacal gestures headed the band. It seemed as if Jeanne had lost all control of her consciousness. In this awful state of nudity, she continued her ever-increasing frantic movements until reason itself abandoned its earthly tenement. In a convulsive fit, Jeanne finally fell, foaming at the mouth like one possessed, and it was only then the mad carnival found a pause.

"Enough!" He cried out.

Just then La Veanna pulled a peril-handle six inch dagger out and held it high for all to see. Suddenly, with reckless concern, she plunged at Jeanne's heart with the cold steel. But Jeanne had awakened and rolled off the table dodging the blade which lodged into the wood table.

"Run!" Alexander shouted. "Get out of here!"

Jeanne did as ordered dashing into the dark night of the woods being chased by two men.

"Leave her alone," Alexander cried out in anger.

"Let her go!" La Veanna ordered.

Soon Alexander realized he uncovered himself to them. Something he hadn't wished, but his rage couldn't be control by his out burst. There still was Tara to be concern about. Quickly, he leaped out of the tree to escape from the rapidly approaching group, which surely didn't desire his presents there. He managed to hide from them and circle back to the ritual site. He halted for a moment as he viewed Jeanne approaching still dazed. He felt the worse had happen to his friend, Jeanne.

"Jeanne, are you ok?" He asked. "Lady, you must survive."

"My mind is clearing now, thanks," she replied hands shaking in fear. She placed them on Alexander's arms. She moaned indicating she was still alive, but was torn half dead from the scene.

All his attempts to bring Jeanne around, she did show signs of regaining her faculties. But by this time, the others were returning to the site.

"Jeanne, I got to take you with me," he voiced.

"Alexander," Jeanne voiced, "Tara is at a pond north of here about a few yards from here, a cabin."

"I have to get you out of here first. Can you get up?" He asked.

"I'm too weak," she responded turned her head.

"Then I'll carry you out!" He voiced strongly.

"No time. No time for me, but time for you and Tara to escape," she uttered in a horse voice, "Time has been our adversary from the start, you know that? Even now it's our enemy."

"I'm taking you out of here, now," Alexander whispered in her ear. With Jeanne in his arms he carried her a few yards and hided behind a bush. The chasers ran passed them unaware of their presents. Clearly they were searching for Tara now.

"Listen to me, Alexander," Jeanne voiced, "I'll be alright, and you have to get to Tara before they do!"

"I can't leave you alone." He voiced.

"It's not too late for me. Please leave before you get caught. Remember, I love you two more than my own life. I guess I've inadvertently prove it?" Jeanne half laughed. "Now I'll be all right here for now. This girl knows a few tricks they don't know. Now go get Tara, please."

"What about you?" He asked.

"I'll see you two after all are safe, ok," she answered. "Now go, she is waiting there, just north of here. They must not find her tonight. It's your turn to turn hero I'm afraid."

He nodded.

Alexander hated to leave Jeanne wiping her beautiful face off. Removing the paints they so brutally placed there, yet shapely applied to her, carefully rested her head down slowly. He had to do something? The thought kept racing through his mind. Jeanne was right about chasing Tara; there was nothing else he could do. The sound of the men became ever more present and near. He kissed Jeanne upon her lips tenderly, uttering in warmth, "Your something else. You've helped Tara and I become one, forsaking your own life. Tara truly has a friend in you. I love you, Jeanne... goodbye." Alexander took his finally gaze at her then rushed back through the bushes to the taxi, heading for help. He never wished to leave her.

She put up a good front of strength as Alexander took off seeking Tara. Shortly after, Jeanne smiled then lost consciousness.

Later, Alexander rough through the swamp avoiding being detected. Still his thoughts haunted him. During the ritual, he noticed it would be the last Voodoo ceremony over which Tara's grandmother would preside. Discovering she was going to be dethroned in weeks. What he had figured were that La Veanna was well over a hundred, too old to perform the onerous duties of her high post. Therefore Tara would indeed replace her, chosen by birth. What Tara had tried to explain to him was totally true. Instead of going after Tara, he decided to get help from other sources.

Hours later he'd arrived with the local police. There they searched the area he specifies, strangely finding nothing of the ceremony or Jeanne's whereabouts. The High Priestess, La Veanna assured nothing was discovered.

"Where are they? They were right here?" He asked confused, trying to express to the offices his seriousness. But the officers expressed there was so much eccentric things happening in their area, it was best that he forgot what he'd seen. That he should be contented it wasn't him. The officer's attitude was in an annoying and joking reluctant manner, unwilling to assist Alexander any further. Seeing he was getting absolutely nowhere. Alexander decided to get Tara out of there. Aware of the weeks before her birthday, he was afraid she would be put through the same ordeal, vowing this would not happen.

Now that he had their taxi, Alexander hurried towards Tara's home fearing the worse. Maybe Tara went home after and Jeanne wasn't in her right to give direction? He had dismissed the notion of Tara being up north. Only thinking if she would forgive him for impulsively running away from her, there was still time to escape? Especially at a time when he was mostly needed, yet the overwhelming proof of the existent of the Voodoo Cult had surpassed even him. Tara had warned him to understand it when the stake turned against them, how foolish he felt. Losing his reasoning, Alexander struggle on what was next? Driving to Tara's home, a strange feeling befell him, no longer protected by Tara's psychic powers, and now acceptable to La Veanna's powerful thought control, he at the mercy of her grandmother if caught alone. Unfortunately for him, the feeling would come true.

From the ceremony, he remembered La Veanna dressed in red and white. Pulling in front of the house, he struggled whether to proceed or not? The same mist which he collided was suddenly at his feet again. It sat upon the front porch like a coat over someone's body. The moon was still high above him lighting the huge house of very archaic design. There were several lights on, one coming from Tara's room, the other from what seemed to be the living room? Alexander wanted Tara and whatever he had to do would not be enough. He stepped in front of the door, it slowly opened by its self. With cautious moves in alerted fashion to anything that may come, he soon caught Tara's scent throughout; hoping it was a sign she was there waiting for him.

"Tara?" He uttered peeking down the dark hall.

No reply.

There was a light just at the end of the corridor coming from a room he viewed from the outside. From the beginning Tara never allowed him to visit her there, always meeting him strangely at the Brickyard or other locations, protecting him. Again he called out her name and still no reply. Now he'd reached the lighted room. Placing his hands upon the threshold, Alexander gazed around the corner.

"Come in young, Alexander," La Veanna voiced. "Glad you have decided to honor us with presents. Please have a seat if you will."

Alexander wasn't too sure what she meant by, we? He had seen no one behind him nor anyone but La Veanna before him.

"It is unfortunate that my granddaughter never brought you with her to my home. The last time you departed in such a hurry. Sadly, we have to meet under such poor conditions, Jeanne's disappearance, you understand?"

Alexander only looked on concern.

"Never mind, have a seat," she cried out to him pointing to a chair at the dinning table. Though the tone of her voice was pouring out demented kindness; Alexander remained totally on his guard of the Voodoo queen. He would not allow her any chance of probing into his consciousness. He'd been down that road before and wasn't planning on revisiting it anytime soon.

"Do you know where Jeanne is?" La Veanna asked. No reply.

"Well, what about my granddaughter?" She asked. No reply.

La Veanna relaxed back in her seat at the head of the table. She concentrated mentally towards Alexander's thoughts. A flash of lighting in the dark consumed her mind, shocking her in bewilderment. Strange, she thought that penetrating his mind was difficult? Someone had taught him to block her thoughts or was blocking them for him; could it be that Tara was with him if not in body but in mind? This La Veanna had to ponder as she pulled back the continued attempt, settling for a draw on the psychic front. She had to get he answers the normal way with no advantage.

"Where's Tara?" He asked wasting no time. But La Veanna only smiled sinfully.

"What have you've done to your own granddaughter?" He added.

"I will tell you in time my, young friend," she replied, "Now we will have dinner. We create such a hunger during our ceremony tonight. Pity you had to interfere, it would have been so grand."

Alexander stood there about to leave, he'd had enough.

"Now I'd asked you to sit down!" She shouted, "Don't force me to say it again. Even though I'm blind, I can surely sense your disposition." There was a red glow coming from her face.

Alexander pondered over what to do now. He turned viewing a huge man at the window peering in. To his right near the door, he viewed another man in the corridor just out of site. With the odds against him the only thing to do was just play along until he had a chance of leaving or seeing Tara. He sat with utmost speed. Suddenly Alexander smells another fragrance in the room, coming from behind the curtains. It was a sweet scent; one he came upon before, but where? His answer came quickly as Mai Dede appeared before him. He jumps within himself surprised to be in her presents. This time she didn't have a dagger that he could see. But she brought some food out of the kitchen to serve them. Mai Dede moved close to him. The scent brought back memory of the past evening, one he wished he could forget of sexual bondage.

She whispered in his ear, "I knew you would come."

"Mai, enough of that," La Veanna ordered. "Now bring him a bowl of hot gumbo and a patter of fried fish."

"I was just discussing old times with an old friend," she joked.

"Go now child!" La Veanna shouted upset over teasing of sexual overtones.

Mai Dede bowed leaving them.

"What's this?" Alexander asked. "A meal before my own execution? How does it goes; yes eat, drink and be merry, for tomorrow I shall die?" But his joking didn't go well with La Veanna, still she laughed slightly.

The meal was brought in and placed in front of them. Alexander only ponders if it was poisoned, eyeing the food and drink.

"Eat?" La Veanna voiced, mood changing from pleasant expression to one of hatred. "WE took time to prepare such a meal and you refuse?"

Alexander could square she could see? Still he refused to take one spoon, placing it aside the plate.

"You don't trust us, do you?" Mai Dede spoke from behind him. She was now rubbing her thighs against his back. Maybe getting off on him, as the scent of eroticism engulfed them.

La Veanna took a spoon of the hot gumbo into her mouth. He then followed with caution slowly. Mai Dede was waved away by La Veanna, but until she gave Alexander a lustful smile of appreciation for his unwilling sexual services. After a couple of minutes, he realized La Veanna was unaware of Tara's whereabouts. Mai Dede entered greeting him with a huge smile, more like a very dangerous smirk, slowly staking the room. With the light from the kitchen, it outlined the very well shaped body of hers, as the dress was very translucent in the background light. The way she moved said there was something different, something lustfully blinding about her. The lady was surely dangerous to his very being. He could sense her demanding aura about her. His eyes could not brake away from Mai Dede. It became more apparent she was playing with his mind again; La Veanna had sense his thoughts of lustful interest too in Mai Dede, smiling slightly. But Alexander refused to be lured into such an erotic man trap.

Suddenly he jumped up from his seat. Some unseen force caused him to accidentally spill the hot gumbo onto La Veanna lap. This caused both ladies to break their telekinetic power off him for a brief moment. And luckily it allowed him to run out the front door, unknowingly averting the same faith of Doctor Walker. Alexander stopped at the door looking back at them then heard a voice ordering him to run. He did unsure of its source, knowing it came from a friendly clairvoyant person.

"Dammit, Mai Dede, find Tara!" La Veanna shouted enraged. "Her telepathic thoughts were here protecting him! What fool I was!"

"What about Alexander and Jeanne?" Mai Dede asked.

"Never mind those fool!" She answered. "They could never harm us!"

Racing off in the taxi, he knew that Tara could be anywhere. The logical conclusion was Tara would be waiting at Jeanne's apartment.

Hour later, Alexander arrived there; all which remained was neither furniture nor signs of Jeanne ever living there? It could not be. He had been there various times, as Tara and Jeanne sat there for hours discussing anything and everything. Glancing around, he noticed a trace of powder along the walls. Treading him to believe La Veanna's people must have cleaned out Jeanne's apartment. This night was a nightmare by all standards, pandemonium of the highest stages of life, pulling him ever way and in every form. Alexander sat down on the now bear floor gazing around the empty apartment. Tara's disappearance consumed his entire mind. Where could she be? He thought. The questions kept hunting him, pounding, spinning and drilling his consciousness. He soon realized he couldn't think clearly and logically anymore. The evening troubles had taken its toll upon him, knowing he needed rest badly. But he couldn't stay there, not there. They were still after him, hunting him like a wild pig struggling to maintain its life.

The next morning Alexander awoke. He discovered the place he founded haven at was inside the girls taxi the rest of the night just outside of town. He climbed out of the taxi gazing about the wooded area. Having no desires of returning to his hotel room for great fear of his life, he now remember what Jeanne had told him and what Tara attempted to explain to him about Voodoo, he had to know more. Several hours later, about 9:00am that morning, he decided to read up on Voodoo Rituals at the town's local library. Yet after arriving only to discover that every book upon the subject had strangely vanished? Not a note or book remained on its self for him to examine. The computer internet service was down leaving him confused. He now wished that he brought his own wireless laptop with him for the trip. It seemed as if someone or somebody wasn't willing to allow him to research the subject.

Suddenly an unnatural feeling engulfed him, as if someone was watching. Chills ran down his back for no reason? It was like an unseen energy of anxiety was attacking him? The staff was all staring at him as if he was a murder, it was time to go. With haste he exited the rear door of the building to void being captured again. It was then he remembered something from Jeanne of Tara's whereabouts, something which could assist him in locating her. He made his way back to the taxi and was about to drive away. Next to the taxi an old homeless man with a grey beard greeted him. He stood there unwilling to leave, watching Alexander with great interest. It was the way he glared which made Alexander very nervous, yet he felt sorry for him passing on a ten dollar bill. Quickly the old man grabbed onto his hand passing on a note.

"Read it," he ordered.

"What?" Alexander asked confused.

"She said you would be logical, pity," he said laughing.

But before Alexander could get a closer look, the old man hurried away leaving the curious note and the unwanted endowment of currency. After a close examination the note was in Tara's handwriting, who expressed not desired to be the instrument of his death.

That the past and coming events were becoming impossible to manipulate. That numerous quadroons were desperately hunting her and soon there would be nowhere to camouflage her being. Tara only requested one important thing from him? That she would turn herself in if no harm would come to them. That she couldn't live with herself if it was she who caused their death. Tara went on pleading that Alexander find to strength to leave her and take Jeanne with him, to return to St. Louis for their wellbeing. She never wished the events to occur, yet it was much to do to their own unwillingness to accept true facts. Sadly Tara pointed out that she knew her lover was afraid of her, deciding it was best for all to say farewell.

The note ended with 'Tara of you soul'.

Alexander paused and was stun over the warmth of Tara's letter and the sorrow she was suffering. He'd had recognized her handwriting and was sure it in-fact came from his vanished love. But what she expressed troubled him greatly. Now he ready to concede to the mysterious hiding place which Jeanne had told him, the place where she first discovered Tara. His heart was still heavy with the disappears of Jeanne. She had told him of a place where Tara would disappear for days at a time before they became good friends. Suddenly it dawned upon him. Hurriedly he drove like a madman through the town. As he drove, thoughts of the past events haunted him in agony. One particular person remained upon his mind, La Veanna.

She was extremely old, which really displayed upon her small frame. Her dwelling was in the reserved quadroon quarter of New Orleans. A woman of superior cleanliness sat quaking with feeblemindedness in an ill-looking antiquated rocking chair, her body bowed and her wild, witch's tresses hanging about her shriveled yellow neck, the Queen of the Voodoo. Alexander heard she was over an hundred, and after seeing her, there was nothing to cast doubt upon the statement. She had shrunken away from her skin; it was like a turtle's. He could scarcely help but see the face, now withered, had once been handsome and remained commanding. There was still a faint shadow of departing beauty on the forehead, the spark of old first in the sunken, glistening eyes and a vestige of imperiousness in the fine, slightly aquiline nose, and even about her silent, woebegone mouth.

Later Alexander had found Tara in a small cabin just off the main path, just as Jeanne said. The place was scarcely higher than its close board fence. In the center of the small room whose ancient cypress floor was worn with scrubbing and sprinkled with crumbs of soft brick a Creole affectation of superior cleanliness. There Tara stood a vision to behold.

"Hi," he uttered quickly yet frighten.

"Alexander?" Tara replied somewhat surprised to see him there.

"Yeah, how are you feeling?" He asked.

"I'm not sure?" Tara answered confused.

"Well as you see, I've received your note."

She moved away from him voicing, "I'm fine, what about you?"

"I feel like a fool...kind of bad...," he responded.

"Who told you of this place? It was Jeanne, wasn't it?" She asked then answered her own question. She gazed at him concerned.

"Don't blame her, ok?" He asked. "It's was my entire fault that she gone."

"What?" Tara asked staring at him confused.

"Don't know, do you?"

"Yes I should have never brought her or you into all of this. I felt her through my entire body and couldn't get there in time to help her. She was like a sister to me, and I knew that she loved you too, Alexander. I knew all the time." Tara explained. "But he lives."

Alexander was glad to behold Tara's beauty again and glad Jeanne's feelings were exposed to the both of them. The attraction had never wavered from them. It consumed their passion almost instantly. Quickly Tara leaped from the table and ran into his arms, wondering if she could help not her but him, when it was surely her which needed a miracle to survive the attacks.

"Alexander, you are not ill, are you?" She cried out watching his eyes as they displayed redness from little sleep and total fear.

"No...No, I'm fine," he answered. "Just need more sleep that's all. Never mind me so much, I feel really bad for leaving you, not understanding."

"No my love, I understand the trepidation," she followed.

"Tara, I love you," he voiced with strong conviction.

"I to you, my love," Tara replied kissing him.

Yet he and Tara knew he was from another place...another time. That his world was one of the reasons and clarity compared to Tara's world of sorcery and mayhem, a world of Voodooism and magical powers. Supremacy of both the queen and of the doctors, practitioners of black magic, where the unreal become real, where the Voodoo worshippers, the priesthood was comprised almost entirely, and principally mulattoes and quadroons. But he couldn't leave her there, even though it was killing him. His heart released its self of her love and passions as Tara had become his ever being. He refused to allow Tara to give up.

"Tara, you asked me once; would I die for you, remember?" He asked.

She nodded.

"Let me show you by taking you home with me. I can keep you safe and warm. What happen to Jeanne doesn't have to happen to you. I wouldn't let it." Alexander pleaded to her. "Jeanne said if ever something happened to her to take you away from here."

But Tara still feared for his life, wanting him to stay away. She expressed she would be unable to accept his death, yet he kept trying, pushing his plans to take her away with him.

"I can't leave! Don't you understand, no?" She shouted at him afraid leaving the small cabin confused.

"Why?" Alexander asked.

Quickly he rushed after her concerned and frighten for her life.

"Please, Alexander," she pleaded.

He grabbed her firmly from the back. His face was on her head as his body pressed against her back. She felt their love exploding as he wrapped his arms around her body which desired him so. Her eyes were filled with torture and devotion.

"Look, can I talk to you? I want to ask you something important and I want the truth!" Alexander asked.

"Sure…what?" She asked.

"Tell me, why did you come here?" He asked leading to something.

She moved away from him.

"I'm tired of fighting them." She said with eyes rested in a strangle manner.

But he wanted more.

"If you want it to be over then I'm glad," he followed.

She turn to him in dismay voicing in agony, "You know I do. Alexander, I never wanted this." But he wouldn't accept that reasoning anymore then accepting him leaving her there.

"Great, so you give up," he voiced upset.

Tara began to walk away from him in confusion.

"Wait, I'm sorry, just upset that's all," Alexander cried. "You know, since I've known you, you've never quit, don't start now, Tara."

She stared at him now displaying tears.

"I don't know what you wish for me to say?" She asked. "When we first approach each other, it was good, now all has turned horribly disastrous. Why?"

"Tell me what is so bad? I know we had struggles, but Jeanne would have wanted us to continue with our lives," he pleaded pushing the issue.

"Alexander, don't you understand, all this time I never had a childhood to call my own. Never knew what it would be like just growing up as a normal child, every damn element of my life manufactured by others. My grandmother didn't have to place this curse upon me, claiming I was something that I wasn't. Damn her and her soul, I wished I've never been born." Tara voiced enraged.

Alexander had to defuse her anger. "La Veanna never lied."

"She didn't, she just never told me what I was becoming. Protecting me from who knows what's out there. Just another damn-fuckin witch being breaded to take over an aging throne of black magic, that's my grandmother, La

Veanna was just someone who held the throne for me to age. I don't desire that, do you understand?!" She cried.

"I understand, but you have to understand you are her heir, and she had to protect you. Look, even though she was wrong...for the correct reason. I believe she still loves you, Tara.

She remained disturb over it all. He could not blame her, still Tara gazed at him frighten bellowing, "That protection doesn't mean nothing. Look, you wake up thinking your normal and your not. You're really a damn witch with extraordinary extrasensory abilities! At times mind-reading comes upon me without warning, hearing peoples thoughts. So what if I had twenty-three years of being a moral woman, no lets make it two years of normal life, the other I'm not sure if I knew what was happening to me at least it would have been real. Maybe I could have halted all of this, maybe Jeanne would still be with us and you wouldn't be endanger?"

"It was real," he replied. "Our love is real."

Tara yelled back, "Nothing is real if you don't believe in yourself or who you are! I don't believe in myself anymore, don't you understand? Once a person discovers they are not, what they appear to be, that's it, it's finished!"

He moved towards her as the morning breezes blew against his face. There was something else she wasn't telling him.

"That's not it?" Alexander asked.

"That is it," she answered hiding her thoughts, concealing her expression. "You're mistaking."

"No it isn't, tell me the truth, Tara?" He asked.

"Why are you putting me through this?"

"Because you have to let it out, Tara," he answered.

"You want to know the truth? The truth is I don't want to see your death. I don't wish to lose the love I have found in you. If they had come to me with this before I met you, I wouldn't care. I've would have left you alone at the airport." Even more tears started to pour from her beautiful face.

"So what? So what if we both die today or tomorrow. So What? We have here everything but the truth. Now will you please tell me what's the truth is, Tara. Dammit, tell me?"

"I'm afraid, you want to hear it. I'm frighten," Tara cried "For the first time, I'm frighten. I do not have control of my own life anymore."

"Is that all? What's wrong with being afraid?"

"It is for me," she voiced.

"Your human aren't you?" Alexander asked.

Tara moved away from him crying and confused. It was like her soul had been jerked away from her.

"I don't know what I am? All I'm aware of is that I'm a tool of the devil, lied to throughout my short lived life here. Now because of it, Jeanne is not here with us anymore."

Alexander pointed out Jeanne didn't force her into anything. That she was grown woman who cared for her and did what she felt had to do. Tara is a woman of great resolve and her guilt was falsely placed. That she didn't have to do what everybody thought she should, for her world was real, that she didn't use her psychic powers to obtain it. Alexander assured her, he didn't believe that. That it didn't matter what he'd believe, but what she had to carry around inside her. Tara had to be strong and believe these people were not going to take things away, afraid that she can't be a woman? Well none of it was true, but it didn't matter what they told her, it didn't matter because she was the one who has to come to grips with it. For after this is all over, it will only be she and Alexander and he just couldn't live like that. Surely they couldn't live in the past. He pleaded with Tara not to allow them to destroy their future.

He had gotten to her soundly, even though he didn't mean to go off on her, but he had to end this conflict she had within herself. Tara stood there pondering, facing him, and staring into his caring eyes. Alexander began to wonder what she was about to say, whether it was for or against leaving? Hoping his message got through to her reasoning.

"Look, Jeanne knew you could do it, so do I. But you got to want to do if for the right reasons." He voiced.

"...and if we die?" She asked.

"Then we die, but at least we die loving each other. With no fear and I believe we can live with that. That's all I can say to you, it's up to you, my love." With his head bowed down, he could say or do no more for her. The choice was all her own now. Slowly Tara reached out her hands to him in agreement.

Smiling away the tears she voiced, "Thanks, my love."

"Anytime," he joked, "anything beyond reason this time."

They stared at one another with great affection as the breeze blew in from the trees which surrounded them. Tara whispered, "I really love you."

"I know," Alexander respond smiling.

Slowly they pressed against each other and pressed their warm yet frighten lips together, displaying their forever devotion and love to each other.

"All right, I'll come with you if you want me to. But we must leave tonight." She added much concerned.

"Why?" He asked.

"Trust me," she just whispered.

Tara knew she had to cross-up her grandmother and Mai Dede. Explaining to him that she would exploit her supremacy over Mai Dede's consciousness, claiming that would be the key.

Later that night both lovers drove passed the burnt down plantation house. They stop and observed the black ashes now spread among the grounds. There were still police tapes where the bodies once fought to live. The cost was too high for all and they knew if they'd stayed, it would surely escalate. Tara and Alexander stood there under the same tree which exposed her remarkable psychic abilities and almost destroyed their love; they had come to turns with the paranormal. Tara had succeeded in using her clairvoyant powers controlling Mai Dede's mind and passed on misleading information to La Veanna, allowing them to leave by the back roads. It seem too simple to do so, even Tara felt all wasn't safe. Alexander knew from the ceremony, her grandmother would be coming after them. The only problem would be when? He only hoped they would be ready for her.

PART IX

The Soul's of Lovers

Days later in St. Louis, Missouri ...

Alexander thought their troubles were over by bring Tara back home. This would prove a costly mistake on his part. To assume life for her would change by moving to a new location was foolish; for Jeanne was the true victim here. There as not sign of her escaping as they searched for them. Yet what amazed him more was Tara's reaction when they arrived at his apartment. The thoughts kept growing with more clarity.

Tara stood in the middle of his living room lost. She had left her birth place in New Orleans for the technical world of St. Louis, Missouri, a world she as not accustom to. Already she missed her grandmother knowing what she was, still she loved her. Tara had to adjust t the strange ways of this city. She only hoped that Jeanne would find a way to join them. A gazed at modern apartment it was clear she missed her ancient room and its politic charisma; she struggled mentally with the adjustment. But she was here now and unsure just how to handle the unwelcome change?

"You know, it's a relief to arrive here uncontested," he voiced placing his bags into his bedroom.

"If you say so," Tara said.

"Now you truth me, ok?" He asked.

Tara gave a half smile of concern.

It was pleasing to finally enter his humble-a-bowl and with Tara on his arms, life was going to be fine. Tara too was much pleased to see her love's world. She had never left New Orleans before now and was a little hesitates to venture beyond its borders. She glanced at Alexander smiling as he gave her the grand tour. This Tara had no reservations about acquainting herself about the apartment. First she moves over to the big screen monitor, flicking from cable channels to cable channels, settling upon a music channel. Then she noticed the black home entertainment center system in the corner, and he proudly explained its function much to her liking. Finally she enjoyed most the music collections he'd gather over the years. But what mostly impressed Tara were the honors placed upon his walls, from all over the nation, degrees, letters of appreciations, and etc. But all his honors appeared to be on the logic side though. This was not a man whom would settle down with just anyone. She thought. And felt proud he had chosen her for passion over his reasoning.

Though Tara had never attended any school, she was taught the basic 3R's; reading, writing, and arithmetic from her grandmother and her assistants. She displayed herself like a child in a cookie jar and all the goodies were all hers. Alexander admitted to himself, she should have been apart of his life well before this. There was no denying her considerable questions which continued to pour out of her beautiful mouth that she was an exciting woman. The modern world of which surrounded him was no match for Tara's laughter.

"What now?" She asked.

"Now, you have to meet Marilyn, she been waiting for you in the other room."

"What?" She asked.

Tara stood there stun by his statement of another woman. A hated expression filled the once cheerful face of hers.

"What do you mean, Marilyn?" She asked with contempt."

Alexander knew he'd better put an end to her reaction quickly. "Will you come with me? I.... think it's time you two met."

"I'm not sure if I want to?" She uttered confused. "Alexander?"

Tara followed slowly into the room behind him, peeking over his shoulder; she noticed no one was in the room? Maybe she was in the bathroom? She thought. Alexander halted in front of a laptop computer.

"What's this?" Tara asked.

"Alexander moved closer the computer citing it was, Marilyn.

Tara laughed then joked, "You mean I'm replacing a machine?"

"Now I would not put it that way," he laughed with her.

"But Marilyn is nice, I mean logical, like you," Tara added.

"Wait a minute there?" Alexander said laughing.

"I bet she can't do the things I can do for you?" She asked kissing him on the neck. "Can she, Alex?"

Alexander smiled agreeing.

"Well be as it may, make yourself comfortable, this is your home now," he voiced. "I have to check my other machine and mail."

"Alexander?" Tara called.

"Anything you need?"

"Well, I'm hungry for the first time in my life, maybe a hot bath, if you have one?" Tara replied.

Alexander kissed her with affection whispering, "Food, we have, but a bath we have not. But I can offer you a shower."

"Fine, just point me the kitchen first," she replied. Grabbing him around his wrist, Tara followed him into the kitchen playfully. After showing her the modern convinces of the apartment, he checked his answering machine, discovering Jimmy has left several massages to call him when he'd arrived. Also there were several other voices from past relationships which never expanded from the biological. A point he quickly explained to Tara. But any other thought of females fell short the scene of Tara's reaction filling his empty home.

"So that's Jimmy, nice voice, though a little on the nerve side, don't you think?" Tara asked looking on with a ham and cheese sandwich and a glass of milk in both hands.

Alexander nodded.

"You know, you have everything here for a person whom decided to live a life alone." Tara joked.

He didn't reply to her statement, knowing she was very perceptive. He had encouraged up a collection of wonders to help forgo the art of human acquaintance, placing them directly to the point, Marilyn.

"I meant you enjoy being alone. That's why some many objects, right?" She asked not understanding she was cutting him deeply.

"I wouldn't say that, but almost?" He finally replied.

"Well, I'm here and we will be happy ever after," Tara voiced.

"What now?" He asked this time.

Tara laid the drink and the food down and ran to him, placing a huge hug upon him. His warmth was taking away the horrors which befell her. "I love you so much, Alexander. I hope we never part," she whispered.

He assured her it will never happen on his watch, expressing they would be friends and lovers forever. He explained that she had to meet Jimmy, a good close friend of his. So Tara hurried to refresh herself before Jimmy arrival at the apartment. But Tara paused smiling then whispering, "Only if you join me." He couldn't refuse such an offer from this gorgeous lady, but stated after he'd made a call to Jimmy.

"Your lost," she whispered moving away.

"Hi, Jimmy, are you there?" Alexander asked watching Tara undress.

"Sure, what are you doing back so soon?" Jimmy replied voice heard on the phone.

"Never mind that, I got something to tell you important."

"What could bring you back, accept work?" Jimmy joked.

"Nothing so painful, and what would you say, a love?"

The news shocked Jimmy greatly, yet his voice was very pleased. "Where is she? Who is she? Tell me more about her?" He asked wanting to see Alexander's mate.

"Her name is Tara and she's, can you believe it, her at the apartment," he answered.

"Well are you going to tell me her complete name or do I have to guess?" Jimmy pushed for more.

"Oh, sorry about that, its just she is so fantastic to behold. Her name is, Tara Turner. Look Jimmy, the future Ms Thomas is calling me into the shower, so..."

"Get you friend. I guess my gift worked after all?" Jimmy joked referring to the charm."

"Whatever you said leave out the supernatural," Alexander said.

"I'll see you later, ok? I really want to see the bride to be, who could have you bagged, my logical friend. See you later." Jimmy voiced then hung up the phone.

Alexander heard Tara running the shower now waiting for him. She was the hottest lady in town to him. Her black hair; her moist, full, lips; and the come-hither look in her hazel eyes were just the beginning. A wiggle of her magnificent hips could set his pecker throbbing. He surely remembered many sultry summer evening with Tara in the back seat of her taxi, in his room and at Jeanne's apartment. It was all coming back to him. Tara strolled in the living room to him. She looked stunning in her black gown they brought on their way up from New Orleans. It was cut low to reveal her pair of bronze mounds. Glancing around, Tara pressed against him and whispered in his ear, "Let's slip out of here, no more phone calls, please."

He could not say no.

The lovers slipped into a small, darken side room. Tara melted into Alexander's arms, her breasts billowing against his chest. As her tongue darted into his mouth, he slipped his hands into her black silk gown, feeling her satiny firm breasts. The nipples stiffened under his rolling fingertips, and Tara inhaled sharply. She lifted her gown, exposing her lovely, saucy knees and bronze thighs. She took his hand. "Feel," she said. There was a naughty tinge to her voice, as she pressed Alexander's hand to her pubic thatch. "No panties," she whispered with a smirk. Then Tara laughed softly, pressing her crotch against his palm. They were kissing hot and hard now. He rubbed her feverish twat. She was damp, and his hand was wet with her honey. Tara moaned softly as he massaged her, letting his finger slip into her slit. While he was doing this, Tara fished in Alexander's pants until she found the treasure for which she so badly seeks. She brought out his dick. "Put it in," Tara whispered. "I want to feel that big cock in me... please," she cried burning inside.

The lovers both were still standing, so he held her left leg up. His shaft slid between her slippery thighs, and he quickly buried himself in her. Lifting his right hips, he thrust into his soon to be lover. Tara clutched his neck, hanging on as she trembled. She leaned her head back and closed her eyes, savoring the feel of his cock plunging into her. They spent several minutes in the room.

Meanwhile, outside the window, Alexander heard Jimmy's car pulling in, causing them to pull back. But both didn't have any desires to stop. Their love was to passionate, they had to run for cover, run for shade.

"Go take your shower, please," Alexander asked kissing her deeply. She obliged wondering why he didn't join her. He explained if so then they would never finish.

Meanwhile outside Jimmy had a flat tire and was delay in coming up the stairs. This was good because the time when it took him to change it allowed the two lovers to cool down a bit, but not completely. In the back room, Alexander was taking his shower after Tara when a knock came at the door. Tara had just gotten out and was wiping her beautiful body off. She answered the door in just an emerald color towel.

"Hi, you must be Alexander's best friend, Jimmy, right?" She asked smiling and dripping wet. "It is a pleasure to meet one of his true friends that not a machine. Will you come in?"

"Sure." Jimmy replied.

"Sorry about the water," she voice breathing heavy.

Jimmy's tongue was hanging out like a dog in heat. This majestic beauty Tara was a sight to behold. Beautifully tone and smooth skin, with a figure that would not quit. Tara carried an aura about her as if she were a queen. Her mannerism stunned the always outspoken Jimmy, leaving him totally speechless for once in his hurried life.

"Oh, I'm sorry for not being dress to receive you. Alexander has told me about your way of dressing here. But you see we just finished showering and I hadn't had time to unpack yet," Tara uttered as she had to pull the small towel tightly around her exquisite body. But Jimmy never responded, gazing at her every second. "Say, are you all right? Jimmy?" Tara asked. "You are Alexander's friend?" Tara asked puzzled by his actions.

Finally he stop staring at Tara long enough to nod yes.

"That good," she replied.

"Jimmy at your service. Please forgive me but your the most beautiful woman I've ever laid eyes upon in my entire life, please believe that."

"Thank you, I guess?" She replied surprised at his stares and reaction. She was different from all others around the city and to Jimmy, Tara was the most enchanting and magical woman he'd seem. He for some reason couldn't peel his eyes off her.

"Is there anymore like you in New Orleans?"
She nodded.
"Tell me more…"

"There's one that would burn your heart out if you allow her to," Tara answered referring to Mai Dede and the way she trashed men's lives.

"Jimmy! Hey, you're making Tara nerves with the stares," Alexander voiced coming into the living room to join her. "Hey what been happening since I've been gone? You see I've met my future wife, Tara. She was born in New Orleans and a quadroon woman. That is a true native, my friend," Alexander expressed proudly.

"It's no big deal," Tara said. "Excuse me please."

Jimmy continued to stare at Tara as she left them to get dress. He whispered, "Hey, partner, is there anymore like her down there? She great! Now if you decide not to make her your wife, allow me the pleasure of asking, Tara."

"Jimmy, Tara more than that, she is my heart and life."

"Ok, ok," Jimmy joked.

"I more then desire her, I love her with every fiber of my body," he explained. "Besides there are things you don't understand about her."

"Well I'm happy for you and wish you many years of joy, my friend, you surely deserve it," Jimmy replied.

Tara returned shortly after changing into some shorts and Alexander's extra larger T-shirt with California emblems upon it. He always purchased his T-shirt far too big for his body, though his frame needed a large with his muscular arms and chest, something which she enjoyed resting upon, it made her feel safe. Tara rested down next to him upon the couch. She wrapped her arms around him in pure pleasure. She had became quickly adjusted to his surrounding, feeling it reflects Alexander's way of life and the way he though.

"Say, why don't we all ahead out tonight, allowing me to treat?" Jimmy asked wishing to foot the bill.

"Not tonight, Jimmy," Alexander replied.

"Yes, we're very tired," Tara followed.

"Well, I understand and I'll see you guys later," Jimmy voiced heading for the door. "Don't thank me, Alex, see you later."

"You have to leave so soon?" Tara asked.

"I have to get to work in the morning," he replied.

"See you later," Alexander said walking him to the door.

Jimmy took one last look at Tara grinning with excitement.

"Goodnight, Jimmy," Alexander said pushing him playfully out the door. "We will see you tomorrow."

Tara and Alexander waved to him leaving knowing he meant well, but the drive had tired them. Instead they went to the bedroom and fell to sleep together.

Late that night Alexander was awoken by the sound of foot steps outside his bedroom window. He didn't disturbed Tara who in a deep slumber next to him. Her face was so peaceful for the first time since they left New Orleans, he wasn't about to awake her now. Yet the steps were coming closer and louder. Alexander sat up in the bed watching the windows surrounding them. Suddenly a shadow passed by the window nearest to the bed. He carefully got out of bed without waking Tara to investigate. The rooms in the apartment were pitched dark, but he knew his way around, opting to retrieve a baseball bat from the closest. He viewed the shadow moving towards the living room and followed quietly and ready. The outside windows were locked except for the one in the den. That was where he would make his stand to protect her.

"You didn't waste anytime, La Veanna," he whispered to himself.

Alexander crawled along the walls hidden by the furniture and the darkness was his aid. The unknown shadow did as expected approached the only open window and began to climb in. He knew the law stated that the burglar had to in before he could act, so he waited. The burglar strangely threw in a set of bags. Alexander was puzzled by actions taking before his eyes forcing him to pull back and only observe. The shadow now a human form recklessly fell to the floor.

"Dammit?" The shadow whispered oddly.

Alexander knew that unmistakable voice.

"Jeanne?" Alexander whispered.

"Alexander?" She whispered back.

Alexander got up and flicked on the room light. There stun was Jeanne smiling flat on her back glad to see him. He smiled shaking his head with joy.

"Jeanne!" He cried smiling.

"Well, aren't you going to help me up?" She joked.

"Oh, sure," he voiced aiding Jeanne to her feet.

Alexander hugged her tightly with affection.

"Ok, I'm fine," she joked. "You caused a great disturbance back in New Orleans. They are still searching for Tara. Even the great La Veanna is out looking for her heiress. You've taken a great treasure my friend. Where is Tara?"

"Wait here, ok?" He asked.

She nodded.

Shortly he returned with Tara half sleep, rubbing her eyes. She followed him in the den unaware of the surprise. It didn't take long before she viewed her best friend.

"Jeanne!" She screamed.

"The one and only," she replied.

They hugged for a long moment with joy until Alexander broke them apart. All three was together again and the atmosphere was filled electricity, the time was 3:00am, but neither cared. After an hour all three were aware of how each escaped. That now was the time to live. Tonight they would not be apart as Jeanne took a shower then joined them in bed. It didn't take long before all three was fast a sleep.

The next morning, Alexander awoke along in the bed. He rolled over looking around the room for either woman. Then he heard the talking of the ladies in the next room. Their conversation was pleasing to behold as he relaxed in bed.

"So you made it out, Jeanne?" Tara asked.

"Had to after you did," she replied. "But I'm surprised that you left New Orleans? Don't you miss home?"

Tara nodded as he prepared the breakfast.

The kitchen was filled with dishes and drinks for all. Toast was popping and coffee brewing. The smells were heaven to the hungry.

"What about Alexander?" Jeanne asked

"What about him?"

"Can you really adjust to his world?"

"I don't know, Jeanne, but I have to try for us," Tara answered. "I met his best friend Jimmy yesterday."

"What's his like?"

"You would like him, I think?"

"Handsome?" Jeanne asked.

"I leave that up to you," Tara joked pouring the orange juice at the table. She waved Jeanne to get Alexander up for her while she finished preparing table.

Meanwhile in the bedroom Alexander had gotten up and dressed. He viewed Jeanne entering the room. She rested against the door frame watching and smiling. Her eyes viewed him nuke briefly.

"Well good morning sleepy head," she joked.

"So it wasn't a dream, I'm glad," he voiced.

"Tara is lucky to have you at her side and thanks for getting her out of there," she uttered with affection. "Now we have to figure out what next?"

"We take a day at a time," he answered.

"Good reply, my dear," Jeanne followed. "Now breakfast is getting cold."

"On my way," he replied readying himself.

Later that day a call came from Jimmy seeking them to go out late that night. All three agreed and decided to meet about 8:00pm.

That night as he left the trio, Jimmy's eyes remained upon Tara's beauty squaring he'd very even anyone like her. Now Alexander thought his actions were funny. Knowing he too had found a prize in Tara and at the same time found a good friend in Jeanne. After introducing Jeanne to Jimmy the two quickly discovered that the attraction was only in the form of friendship. But that was fine since now Tara and Alexander had their two closest friends nearby.

Later at the club on the east-side named, OZ. the foursome arrived looking for a good time. Finding a table, they sat to watch the dancers enjoy themselves. Alexander watched in fun, but memory of La Veanna continued to hunt him. Then there was Mai Dede's sexual attack on him leaving an emotional mark of helplessness. Observing people dancing wildly only hindered his enjoyment reminding him of the voodoo ceremony. Tara gazed over to him, seeing her lover troubled. Placing her hands upon his, she comforted him in this hour of need. He returned a smile back in gratitude. Both watch the carefree form of Jeanne and Jimmy's dancing out on the floor, free spirit they were. The place was very large and crowded; as heat seemed to be the main factor they noticed most. But after a cool drink of a Manhattan long island tea, Tara and him were relaxed. Alexander looked at Tara confused about what to do now? True they had successfully made it back to his home for the time being, but it would only a matter of time before La Veanna send her horrible militias there.

Now Tara would have to learn his way of life, far different from the peaceful surroundings of her home.

"What's wrong?" Tara asked worried about him.

"Nothing, everything fine," he replied smiling.

Tara knew she was a big change in his life. She could tell through the way he kept apartment. Everything was too well organized for her taste. And there was something she had to know about him, wondering if now the time she should ask was?

"Alexander, we need to talk?" She asked reaching out to his face.

"I know," he replied with a serious face.

"No, I don't mean talk about my home but about you," she added kissing him.

"What?"

Tara nodded confirming he was right, reaching for his true feelings. "Can we go to a quieter place? I like the music, but…"

Alexander agreed noticing the pool room had just open. Quickly he grabbed Tara's hand and led her into the sealed room. She glanced around the place then moved over and removed a pool stick. She seemed very trouble about being there? There were issues to settle now, something off her chest. Alexander began to rack the balls.

"No," she uttered.

He looked at her puzzled on the matter. "What's wrong? You're unhappy about coming here?" He asked hoping it was not the answer. Tara picked up the cue ball, gripping tightly. She gazed at it with conviction then at him the same way, bewildered.

"You were lonely, weren't you?" She asked surprising him.

"What, lonely?" He asked in a bedazzle manner.

Tara could tell by seeing it obstructing his life. The way his present yourself, the way he kisses her, there was something missing? Alexander appeared confused demanding to know where Tara was going with this inquiry. He sat upon the edge of the pool table concerned over why now? Tara pulled back a little then moved next to him, sitting. She spoke as a person who was undergoing the misfortune. The lovers acknowledged they trusted each other, but Tara was more intone with her feelings. She couldn't see what in his heart, didn't need her psychic abilities to notice a void in his life. He nodded in agreement knowing that he needed to tell me what was hurting him. Tara knew he was holding back, she could feel his thoughts as much as he could sense hers. The two continued to discuss their feelings about their utmost fears of life. It was something which had to be address if they were to combat La Veanna as a result.

Meanwhile at the airport a storm blew in the form of…

"Welcome to St. Louis, Ms Dede, I hope you and company will enjoy your visit here," the airline clerk spoke, staring at her exceptional figure and gorgeous face. She bowed to him smiling then asked about a place to stay near strangely Jimmy's apartment in the Central West End area. She was companied with two ladies to aid her.

Later, a taxi drove her near an Inn resting a block away in the Central West End. The Bellman placed her bags down and awaited a tip. Mai Dede turned handing him a ten dollar bill, informing him to keep it all. But what he wanted was her heated. She was dress in a beautiful white sun dress which enhanced her figure. The front was very low-cut, inviting a man's hunger of lust. Resting upon her silky long black hair was a black comb holding it off her face. The sunglasses were a deep blue covering her penetrating spellbound hazel eyes. Mai Dede's neck allowed the sweat to drip off a very expensive white and black peril necklaces.

"Well? That is all you can do for me, you may leave," she bellowed in a seductive tone. She stood there torrid, tan and terrific.

The Bellman left closing the door behind him, feeling the aches of having blue-balls. Mai Dede laughed at the poor man's calamity as the two other ladies prepared her clothes. For her came not for a vacation but a special reunion with Tara, knowing not of Alexander's apartment, only aware of where he worked, Jimmy were to be the key to finding her target. The other thing was that she over heard Alexander speaking of Jimmy to Tara once before. She had decided to go through Jimmy in order to find Tara before her birthday. First, Mai Dede had to get to know Jimmy, which in fact would be an easy task since most men prided themselves as a ladies man. But tonight she would rest herself for the game tomorrow, vowing Tara would be founded. There was only three weeks left before Tara's birthday and Mai Dede was counting them very closely.

La Veanna had instructed her on what to do upon locating her granddaughter. A sought of psychic spellbound between each other would be their connection.

Back at the pool room the two lovers discussed their perplexing situation. Both knew they would never be alone without the other being escorted by a friend. Tara lean over and kissed him passionately and deeply over their plan. The two returned into the dance area seeking Jimmy and Jeanne. There Alexander noticed Jimmy speaking with Jeanne playfully. He explain to Tara, that Jimmy expressed to him that he could never find a woman whom could satisfy him completely, one of the reasons that he dates so much, opting to devote his time in finding the right woman.

"Welcome back, you two, "Jimmy shouted above the crowd."

The four sat down near the dance floor.

"Hope you two worked out a strategy," Jeanne said.

Tara nodded with caution.

Again Jimmy rested his eyes upon Tara voicing, "You have the most beautiful hazel eyes I've every seen." Alexander pushed him to get his attention. Tara just smiled at Jimmy's commit as flattery, expressing that women where she came from live are very secretive. They believe in love and never let their man go. So before he decides to take one for a one night stand, she strongly advised him to think twice before doing so, then stared at Alexander as if he told her of his relationships?   Alexander just shucks his head in a confused manner. Then there was silence.

Suddenly a huge sound of laughter filled their table from all four.

"Alexander, would you mind if I asked your lady to for a dance?" Jimmy asked. "I mean you can't keep her to yourself all night."

"No, not at all, that is if she doesn't mind?"

"I would like to very much. Maybe you can teach me your style of dancing? I've asked Alex, but he just keeps promising," she replied.

"Slow tune, "Alexander joked.

"Jimmy, don't leave her alone," he said concerned.

"I'll be fine you two," Tara said leaving with Jimmy.

The two got up and moved to the dance floor. Alexander and Jeanne watch wondering if anything bizarre would happen as before at the ritual area in New Orleans' swamp, one of the reasons why he'd refused to dance with her. He would have desired nothing more, but that horrible day of retaliation for his action at the forbidden area made him ponder the consequences. Alexander remembered Tara's frighten face and her reaction after it with clarity. Now seeing her dance happily with Jimmy pleased him so. Maybe, just maybe it was really all over? Maybe bringing Tara with him released her of the curse, he called it. Alexander and Jeanne stared at the two; laughing, joking, dancing their socks off, a small yet ever increasing grin grew upon their once apprehensive face. It seemed as if Tara was having trouble picking up the new steps, but she for once since being taken away from her home was enjoying herself, total free spirited. The music was loud. The air of the place was exciting. Lights flashed all about the place creating a magical world to get lost in, and become whoever you desired without being punished for your sins. But all Alexander could think about was his jewel, consuming his mind, Tara.

What was in store for her now?

"You wish to dance?" Jeanne asked.

Alexander pondered glancing slowly around.

"Not yet," he answered all the time observing Tara and Jimmy dancing. "I mean, I will later, thanks."

"Well there is a beautiful dark hair woman with long sexy leg to her hips observing you to your right," Jeanne joked pointing to another table.

He quickly and nicely replied, "No."

Jeanne smiled then whispered, "Next time, maybe?"

The woman moved away with class from the near table.

After four tunes, Jimmy was out of breath wishing to rest and have a drink. But Tara wanted more pulling him and requesting strangely to dance more with her. "Alexander said you are a good dancer, was he wrong?" Tara asked Jimmy was too fatigue to replied, trying to keep up with Tara. "I love to dance. It's so stimulating, don't you think? Don't you feel the music stroking through your body?" She cried.

"I tell you what I feel, I feel worn out. Please let's sit down, ok?" Jimmy asked gasping for air.

Tara continued to dance wildly.

"Tara, what's with you?"

"No, I demand more! I want thrills!" She replied dancing wildly all around him. But Jimmy had had enough explaining he was heading for his seat through the loud music, leaving her dancing without a partner, fighting his way through the crowded floor of garish dancers. He stopped at the bar for a drink.

Alexander and Jeanne lost sight of them after the third tune. Now listening to the fifth one Alexander started to become worried. Moving out of their chairs, they moved to a better location. There they stood now upon a high balcony which gave them the advantage of the whole dance floor. After many peering over the crowd, it was Jeanne who discovered a large group of people surrounding someone. There were too many people to see through, too dark to view who was the center of attraction. Suddenly there came a slap upon Alexander's back causing him to plunge over the balcony by the same woman admirer earlier. The balcony was about one story high in the far corner, much out of the way of spectators whom was busy watching the young lady dance. Quickly, Jeanne and Jimmy moved to the edge of the platform. They feared that Alexander had fallen below onto the crowd. The unknown woman quickly lost herself in the crowd.

Peering over the edge, both smiled in relief that Alexander was hanging on to the railing.

"Get me up!" He shouted.

The place was so deafening with music and dancing that no one was had noticed him hanging for his life. With one hand on the rail and the other dangling, the only remaining part of the railing loosening, a single screw which remain was strangely unscrewing itself out of the holding. It was the only thing keeping him from breaking his neck below. With his eyes glued upon that last screw, Alexander wonder why now did it happen to break free? When before, he laid upon it without even signs of worn bolts? It all seemed too bizarre to him? Too many times had he faced life and death only to tell about it? For Tara had brought more than love in his well ordered life, mayhem. Jimmy reached down as far as possible. Still Alexander was out of reach and the last screw had twisted itself upon its last threads. Again Jimmy reached down as he held onto Jeanne's arms reaching too. The only chance Alexander had was to swing towards his hands. If Jimmy attempted to move out on the metal railing it would surely claim all three of their lives. But recklessly they tried, hoping to save him.

Lying flat on his belly, Jimmy slowly worked his way along to railing with Jeanne holding his legs, slowly until he reached Alexander. There Jimmy left hand touched Alexander's right in midair. Alexander struggled his way back onto the railing. A relief consumed his very body, but he was not out of danger yet. For now Jimmy shared his misfortune trapped upon the railing. Every move, every twitch they preformed to remove themselves from their certain faith only sealed their deaths. Again, the black metal railing shuck with their frighten bodies upon it. Slowly Jimmy took the chance of backing up. Alexander followed him at a deliberate turtles' pace. Soon both were off much to their own relief.

"What the...," Alexander voiced angered.

"It was that woman we saw at the table," Jeanne answered.

"Hey, partner, settle down. You act as if you've seen the devil himself?" Jimmy spoke quickly to ease his mind. "Just bad railing."

"Bad railing my ass," Jeanne voiced upset too.

"Where's Tara, Jimmy?" Jeanne asked. "You didn't leave her alone did you?"

"Yeah, you were supposed to be with her? Forget about the railing," Alexander followed upset.

"Hey guys, I was," Jimmy answered. "But she loves to dance and I was too tired to continue.

"You left Tara on the floor?" Jeanne asked stunned.

"Sure, what of it?"

"Dammit, Jimmy!" Alexander shouted. "You're supposed to stay with her at all times."

"What can I say?" Jimmy asked looking on confused. "What did I do wrong here guys? Tara just dancing!"

"We have to find her quick!" Alexander followed.

"I don't get it? What's the rush, I know where she is," he replied pointing.

"Where?" Alexander asked pulling on the vest enraged.

Jimmy gazed at as if he were looking at a wild man. But what he didn't understand was Tara's dangerous past. Something Alexander been through with much agony along with her and Jeanne, her best friend. Jimmy pointed in the direction of the crowd yelling wildly. Quickly Alexander and Jeanne rush passed him fearing the worse, pushing the crowd, trying to get through the too excited group of dancers before them. Finally the three broke through only to view Tara doing a very sexual dance, alone. Alexander stood there staring with a bizarre look upon his face. Tara was spinning as if she was possessed. Suddenly she stopped then gazed at them helplessly. The beautiful blue grown she came with was now displaying sweat from her heated body. Tara danced like as pro, like an erotic dancer. All eyes were upon her as if they were voyeurs seeking more of Tara's exposure. That night Tara had become their supreme vision of sexual fantasies. Her sexual form placed in black pumps brought much praise. Alexander and Jeanne observed knowing she was innocent to the abnormal behavior, but something unknown was driving her on?

The men which were viewing her started to grab at their pleasures. Alexander had to be stopping the feverish exploitation, jumping in the center; he wrapped his arms around her, placing his jacket to cover her now torn dress. But the men kept reaching for her, viewing her smiling at their taunting. Tara refused to stop dancing, she couldn't stop herself. Suddenly the music halted.

Jimmy and Jeanne aided their friend at the Deejay's booth.

"Help me, please?" Tara asked then fainted in his protecting arms.

"We're here my love," he said.

He carried her out quickly with great concern. Jimmy and Jeanne were now waiting at the front door worried. Yet confused to what was happening? Jimmy expression demanded more from his best friend, but Jeanne sharply told him to forget what he'd seen. That they would explain it to him soon as time permitted.

Outside the club the streets were quite as they exited the club. There were no signs of La Veanna's people spying on them, just a few lovers playing and love making at their cars. Alexander and friends hurried across the street to the car.

"Just get the car, Jimmy," Jeanne ordered him.

Jimmy looked on stun uttering, "On the way…"

Shortly the car pulled up and Alexander carefully placed Tara's body in the back. He played with her hair a bit then rested her head upon his jacket which he gladly gave up. "Your be home soon," he whispered leaving her in the back seat with Jeanne as they drove off to his apartment. The argument continued between the three wishing, no demanding to know what the hell was going on. But Alexander refused to comply, opting to side track the many questions directed towards him by Jimmy. Indeed, his friend had a right to know, but neither was too sure how they got into this bizarre situation themselves? There was a vague cry coming from the back seat; a cry of anguish from Tara, very silent, very tiny, yet very commanding. Tara had awaked only to hear the attack of Jimmy and the dodging the questions by Alexander. A strong ringing ran through her head, pounding and pounding to no end.

"Alexander?" Tara asked at the top of her weak voice.

Jimmy responded to the sudden scream by stepping upon the brakes recklessly jamming them. The car twirled out of control towards a huge pillar under the bridge. Jimmy fruitless attempts in stopping the car only created more anxiety to all. Alexander glanced back at Tara and Jeanne, reaching his arms back to aid them.

"Stop!" Tara screamed using her extrasensory powers.

Suddenly the car which was spinning halted just inches way from the pillar. Quickly, Alexander jumped out of the car then pulled Tara from the backseat. They hugged with enormous relief. But Jimmy stood there watching, puzzled by what had happen there? Jeanne leap from the backseat stun at Tara psychic strong will. What kind of hold did this woman had on his friend? Jimmy pondered. One thing he knew. Tara was not a normal woman, most of all, he seen the extreme care of which his best friend expressed deeply towards her, knowing there was nothing he could say to keep him from sinking into whatever she was into. Tara was addicting to him and he to her. Jimmy only hoped it wouldn't cause his friends death. And mostly of all, that Tara really loved him too? Yet watching them stare at each other with great affection caused him only more unanswered question?

"Hey guys, it was a bad trip that's all," Jimmy voiced opting to withhold the inquiry. "Now let get you two home, some of us have to work, while others enjoy a long vacation."

Jeanne kissed Jimmy on the cheek thanking him.

Tara still had tears coming from her beautiful eyes. Alexander whispered gently in her ear, "Don't cry. We will soon be home, safe. I would never allow you to get hurt, I love you too much." Tara, hearing this gave a half smile, knowing the key now was to control her, telekinetic powers. For each time it was used, La Veanna with being very clairvoyant could feel her mentally. Touch her thoughts, and what Tara feared most, she supernatural powers could become a beckon to where she was hiding; a sure psyche trail leading them right to his home.

Meanwhile in the Central West End, Mai Dede was busy doing her favorite pastime, fucking. The Bellman was in her bed attempting to please the sex craved diva. Mai Dede was sweating and hungry for his big cock. She ordered him to put it in her forcing her to morn. The two ladies sat in the room watching causing his to feel nervous. After an hour she wanted more of his sex tool, refusing to kiss, just fuck. He was truly exhausted; weaken by the continued sexual attention demanded by her tedious appetite. Mai Dede painfully called him a pussy and didn't desire t be called a man. This was puzzling to him and the mood change of bitch by Mai Dede astonished him. But Mai Dede kept pushing his button, making him feel insignificant in her presents. With rant and rave he threw her over in bed and pounded her from behind with great force. He thrust in and out of her until he came again. Instead of enjoying the extra action Mai Dede climb out of the bed disappointed, storming out to the balcony. The Bellman just sat there confounded and abandoned.

    Mai Dede suddenly felt Tara's supremacy if only for a short moment. She was standing on the balcony watching over the city, waiting for just what happen that night, waiting for Tara to release her powers. Her long flowing hair blew radiantly in the night breeze like a guardian angel. Just a wisp of silky fabric against her exquisitely sensual body, control all. Dreaming perhaps of the starlit city of New Orleans on the moonless night, she knew now Tara was nearby.

"Now I will have Alexander again," Mai Dede uttered to herself and pleased with the results. "But first, I must meet his trusted friend; Jimmy and he will lead me to the both of you. Jimmy will be the very tool of destruction."

With a sip from a glass of campaign, Mai Dede moved to her bed as a chilly laughter came from her passionate full lips, lying next to her was the poor Bellmen gasping for air with excitement. His heart was torn apart by Mai Dede's thirst of sexual intercourse. He had given all he had and it was not enough. She had drained him dry and was wishing for more. The thought of Alexander kept rising in her lustful consciousness, wanted him badly. It was becoming an obsession of passion to her. Mai Dede was never a woman whom didn't get what she desired. She glanced at the once hard dick of the Bellmen huge in size uttering, "Pity, they don't make cock like they uses to."

Mai Dede waved at the two ladies in the room to rid her of this fool of a man. The ladies quickly dragged him out of the bed. Their strength was powerful to behold surprising the Bellman.

"Get out of my bedroom before I get you fired," she ordered. "Keep that thing you call a dick in your pants next time. For advice, don't lose your day job. If I was you, and I'm Hell glad I'm not, I'll find someone whom I could handle next time."

Suddenly she laughed at the poor soul as he ran out of the room, ashamed and carrying his uniform. Mai Dede had proved she could be a cold hearted bitch if not pleased. Only one man has Mai Dede's attention and Tara had him lock within her passionate heart.

PART X
Yearning

Days later and all were at peace, the relationship between Tara, Jeanne, and Alexander went well. Jimmy was the outcast now, not allowed to know of the entire trip to New Orleans. Though at times Alexander would leak few facts siding on the good side of the vacation there, the paranormal world remained hidden. His sexual romp with Mai Dede, a woman who took control of him, forcing a well educated man, would be difficult to explain for any man. Alexander was a living testimony the forbidden world. Mai Dede was a dangerous woman to confront at anytime, even if one has all their facilities. The event on the balcony shouldn't have happen at the club nor should it? Jimmy and Jeanne as a life saver at that particular moment were at the right place and time. Alexander only wished Jimmy wouldn't place his soul into every leggy woman he met. That being a ladies' man was not what life was about. One day, his womanizing maybe the cause of his death.

Things became normal around Alexander's apartment. Tara and Jeanne would explore the neighborhood, enjoying the sights of the city. It was nice to have the ladies along most of the time, to be with someone he cared about for a change. Not the continue blind dates Jimmy was overly willing to set him up with. Later that same day the two lovers ended on the River Front near the bank under the Arch. There was a pleasing glance from Tara at him, as he held her hands. Soon Jeanne approached them with some bad news from home. Through her contacts she discovered that Mai Dede had been there for some days undetected. Yet her whereabouts was unknown but her mission was clear. All the three could agree on was to lay low and out of site. But Jimmy would be the weak link if discovered at all and Alexander had to speak with him soon. Suddenly, Tara gazed at the river feeling a chill. Something dark was coming their way? Something even she couldn't control.

"What's the matter?" Alexander asked.

Tara just continued to stare at the river with concern. He touched her in the arms as it brought her back to him. He smiled. She returned the same but deep inside, Tara and Jeanne knew a tempest was heading their way. Tara only hoped she would have the knowledge to combat the menace when it arrived.

Meanwhile the tempest was Mai Dede sitting innocently on a park bench across the Camo Logistical Center. It was lunch time and most of the employees were still playing catch up or tossing their hands up in disgust. A closer look inside the offices, there was a name plate of Alexander. Resting at the desk filled with seemly endless stacks of reports to be input, was Jimmy. He'd moved to Alexander's office and mostly his desk, mainly because his was flowing with even more work. What he'd missed mostly was Alexander's ability to move work in and out quickly. Glancing at an antique clock from the 18th century, Jimmy had had enough and was ready for the 'Score Game.' A game he would play while eating lunch in the park, scoring the ladies which happen to pass his way. But this time he would tally figures on someone whom was keeping her own score.

As always, Jimmy rested in his favorite location, a bench on the corner of the park. There, no woman could get pass his observation..The view was wide spread with a huge array of chooses. With each leggy female passing by him, Jimmy wrote his count. Spanning from 1 to 20 and mostly placing them around fifth teen, never had he discovered anyone above.

"I see they don't measure up to your expectations," Mai Dede voiced from over his shoulder playfully.

Jimmy quickly covered up the notes he'd placed in embarrassment.

"Oh no, my dear, don't hide it now. Curiosity is getting the best of me, lately," she spoke again, this time more seductively.

Still Jimmy covered the proof of, his sin, opting to glance upon the pavement before him. But in doing so, he was presented a shadow of great define figure of the woman.

"You're getting the entire benefit of me watching my shadow," she continued to tease him playfully.

"I'm sorry, it's just a silly game I play," Jimmy replied.

"Take a better look of what you seek," she pressed on, now placing her soft warm hands upon his shoulder. The fragrance she gave off only drew him in her seductive trap. Jimmy slowly gazed up at the beautiful voice.

"That's it. I knew you could do it," Mai Dede uttered pleadingly.

He was caught playing the game for the first time. Feeling embarrassed and nothing more to say, he humbled himself.

"What's your name?" He asked.

Mai Dede refused to comply with his aroused intrigue voicing playfully, "In time you will know my name. That's if you're willing to play the game?"

"Game?" He asked.

"My game this time," Mai Dede answered. "What I've seen so far, you've already started, Jimmy,"

"You know me?" He asked puzzled.

"No!"

"But you spoke of my name? Who are you?" Jimmy asked.

Mai Dede didn't reply stun at her mistake. "Oh your ID tag, there." She answered.

"You're something, you are beautiful. Your eyes remind me of someone?" He asked.

Mai Dede looked on smiling the thought horrible suggestion. A slight laughter followed the smile along with a tender rubbing of his neck. "Well, what number would you rate me?" Mai Dede whispered in his ear. Jimmy was stun by her beauty and remained speechless. Mai Dede whispered one more think in his willing ears, "I have to go, Jimmy. But you will see me again if you wish, if you concentrate hard enough," She breath heavily into his ears. Jimmy just stared on with his mouth open surprised by it all. Indeed, Mai Dede was as exquisite like Tara and with the mystery of Tara too? He sat there as Mai Dede moved off him. Still she never told him her name, one thing certain, he wanted her.

It was two days since he met Mai Dede in the park. Jimmy attempted through many means to locate her, always failure. But the one thing he failed to do was to inform Alexander of her. The following day at the office he saw Mai Dede again, waking walking down the hall in a most seductive manner. Hurriedly, Jimmy caught up with her. She glanced at him as they rested near a water cooler.

"Hi, Jimmy," she voiced playfully.

"Now you must tell me your name?" He asked.

"Alexandria," she answered moving away slightly.

"Alex for short, I like that," he replied.

"No, it's Alexandria," Mai Dede replied strongly.

Jimmy smiled excitedly from her response but could not receive no more. Mai Dede had passed him a fictitious name to cover up her being there. It was not time, not now for her to expose herself too soon. Mai Dede's foot was in the door, less on Jimmy heart of lust. Suddenly a secretary broke up the conversation needing him to finish up a program.

"Look, uh, are you working here or just visiting?" He asked.

"Just visiting a friend I met in the park."

"Wait before you go. Can we meet for dinner or something?" He asked, "Maybe meet some good friends of mines, Alexandria?"

"We will see, Jimmy?" Mai Dede replied with levity. "Do me a favor and don't tell anyone about me yet, ok?"

"Why?" Jimmy asked.

"Tell you later, but no one, ok?"

Jimmy nodded lusting after her.

She had done it to him again, playing hard to get, yet playing her entertainment perfectly with his covetousness for her. The game of obsession, something no man had ever escaped, but there was one exception, an exception which torn at her ever since she met him in New Orleans, Alexander, the one that got away. Though Mai Dede used her consciousness to forced him to have sex with her, Alexander's will power had commanded her attention; a watchfulness which she couldn't dismiss with a smile or a magic charm.

"Alexandria?" Jimmy asked intruding her thoughts.

"Yes?"

"Why not tonight?" Jimmy asked viewing her in a trance. Finally she smiled then backed off, passing him a kiss. Then she was gone. Jimmy stood there watching her turn around the corner vanishing again.

He placed a call to Alexander to inform him of meeting Alexandria against her request.

"Hello?"

"Alexander, guess who I met?" He asked. "No! Let me tell you, a lady named Alexandria and she's above every number I've every written down."

"Fine, Jimmy so when does Tara, Jeanne and I met this, Alexandria?" Alexander asked.

"Sorry, I need some more time with her alone."

"Tara says, hi," Alexander voiced.

"Tell the ladies hello too," he replied. "Look, their on my back to get these programs done. Why don't you cut your vacation short and join me?"

"No way," Alexander joked. "The ladies wouldn't allow it.

Tara and Jeanne smiled at him pleased with his chose of words.

"I'll see you soon, take care," Jimmy final words were hanging up.

"Later," Alexander spoke to the phone.

Later Tara and Alexander were resting and listening to some ballets off the CD player. Her mind was at rest since that night at the club, feeling more at home with him. Also with Jeanne nearby, all was well. She was glad that Jimmy has found someone, considering maybe they all could have dinner sometime? Alexander with his arms around Tara warmly smiled agreeing.

"Well better leave you two alone," Jeanne voiced.

"Jeanne?" Tara replied.

"No, you two need some quality time together," she joked.

"What about you?" Alexander asked.

"I'll be fine," she answered getting up and heading for the extra bedroom. "Besides, it's been a long day, goodnight lovers."

""Night, Jeanne," he replied.

"Sleep well," Tara followed.

Tara rose to him citing she was hunger, wondering if Alexander felt the same. He gazed at her confused pondering to go out and get it, pointing to himself jokingly. Tara parted her heated lips uttering softly, "please?" He didn't want to leave her alone this close to their birthday. Too close to the horrors they were forced to leave behind; for anytime those same horrors could rear its ugly head. He pleaded with Tara come with him, but she pointed out Jeanne as just in the other room, no need to be concerned? Still Alexander expressed he would feel better if she went with him. Again Tara pointed out Jeanne would protect her, joking she had a taste for crab legs. Finally she pushed him to get ready to leave. Tara sat there listening peaceful to the music which eased her to another world. The soft ever growing tunes gripped her soul in countless and tender ways. Alexander returned ready to leave bowing down he kissed her passionately.

    Tara smiled waving him on mischievously.

    Later Tara's body now resting on the numerous pillows placed upon the floor. After several sweetheart tunes she was totally inundate. It carried her soul throughout its raises and falls, through its every changing melody of affections. Suddenly Tara rose up and begun to dance in her feet, spinning, waving her arms like a graceful opera play dancer. It so consumed her mental state that she never noticed what was happening to her.

    An hour later, Alexander had just returned with the cuisine and drinks, only to view an out of the ordinary sight, as he entered the apartment…

Tara was dancing a most beautiful and graceful style. It was as if she were floating a few inches off the wooden paneled floor. He stood there in silence, not announcing his presents. With the food resting in his arms, Alexander placed them next to the base of the door, as a great smile came upon his once passive face. Passive from the continued conflict they had endured. From his view, he could see all of Tara which moved the furniture from the center of the room prior, allowing her moving space to flow in her seductive movements. The moonlight was beaming upon her exceptional form through the window. What a find. He thought to himself, proud of Tara's adjustment in his logical world. She had proven her willingness to accept him completely, though her world to him was another matter. One he would have to accept inevitably. The two had hidden the taxi in his underground parking space since his car was being overhauled, trying anything and everything to protect Tara from the unknown. But what he viewed shocked him even more…

As Tara danced to the soft engulfing music strangely her body began to rise above the floor, nearly two inches at first. Then with faster more graceful moves, she rose higher until she was a full twelve inches high. Tara had defined the laws of gravity. He was stun at the awesome sight. Jeanne had heard the strange sounds too and joined Alexander's side. Still Tara had not noticed them in the room, prancing about with reckless abandon. Then there was more music coming from somewhere else? Yet it wasn't? There seemed; musicians, organist, violinist, fiddler; flutist, harpist, fifer, trumpeter, piper, and drummers; as carols piled upon carols recited their lullaby, harmony upon harmony combining to an enchantment of orchestrated bliss. Alexander and Jeanne had an ear for music but this was beyond any performance of music they had every heard. It was pleasure giving. They thought. Then there came a brilliance which could only come not of the earth.

    Suddenly one of the bags fell over on the floor, breaking its tuneless sound into the room. Tara glanced in the direction of the sound viewing Alexander and Jeanne standing there staring with amazement mixed with confusion and humiliate. Yet she continued floating and now moving towards their direction. Slowly she reached out her hand to Alexander pulling him gently to the center of the floor which she'd cleared. Jeanne slowly backed away allowing them time alone and closed the bedroom door behind her smiling. The music began again engulfing them both. He soon realized it was Tara which was controlling the tunes, transposing the CD player into instrument of affection for him. She floated around him as he twirled about following her in perfect movement. They glazed at each other with great affection as she started her regression to earth. Slowly Tara landed in his awaiting arms. She slide gracefully as Alexander wrapped his arms around her.

"That how you make me feel, graceful," Tara whispered in his ear then pressed her lips upon his.

What he'd had seen, he had accepted from but something had to be done. Tara smiled with amazement sighing, powers.

"Alexander, each hour, each day, I'm discovering more and more of my powers. It is wonderful yet scary?" Tara said stun. "You know, late at night while all the world is safe within their dreams...my spirit walks the shadows late at night, an empty feeling creeps into my soul and I feel so lonely. Sometimes I can see their dreams, their nightmares."

"Tara?" Alexander asked concerned.

"No you don't understand, you and Jeanne have changed me. I would give it all up, if it could bring you safety." Suddenly she started crying from the anguish of possibly losing her best friend and her forever love.

"Look now, everything will be fine. Now stop with the tears."

"I can't, sometimes when I'm alone; it all comes back to me even stronger. I could have lost both of you." Tara voiced sadly.

"But you didn't," he replied, "We're here with you."

"I know my love, but I've had visions, it's just a matter of time!" She yelled. "Something about a blue stain goblet? I don't know?"

He pulled Tara closer, hugging her from the anguish of the visions.

"To Hell with the visions," he shouted.

"What?"

"We will rewrite them, ok?" Alexander asked

"We will?"

"Damn right, we will," he replied in the strongest tone he could muster. "I love you and powers or not I will fight to keep you. You can take that to the bank and store it away for life."

Tara pushed aside her visions this time for love, hoping what her lover said could really override what she'd seen in her dreams, as they hugged each other, but Tara's face displayed a great sadness of reality knowing her visions had never failed her yet. The truth could never be held back. She though. Just as the year must end in December and a new one begin in January; deep inside she knew their relationship was headed for damnation.

"I'm hungry, lets eat," he voiced reaching for the bags of food.

"Ok, I'm too," Tara replied lighthearted, hugging him lovingly.

"I believe I got everything here…"

Tara watched him prepare the food upon the dinning table with sadness. What was in store for him? What could she do to prevent him from dying? The thoughts of these questions haunted her every waking moment and sometimes into her dreams. But she placed upon her face a convicting cheerful half grin, covering up the true expression of destiny before them. Hoping the more she came into her powers, it would benefit them all. Feeling dispirited that it nearly came too late for Jeanne; for that, Tara cursed herself and her world.

The next day the sun was shining into one of the windows of the Camo Logistical Center. At the desk Jimmy had devoted himself to clearing up the back log of work. Since meeting Alexandria the Game he called it wasn't in his blood anymore. Her appearance caused him great reservation in pursuing any other women. Replacing the game were continued nightmares forcing him to only consider Alexandria, Mai Dede saw to that playing with his mind, controlling it at will.

"Hey guy, what are you doing?" Mai Dede asked Jimmy as she entered his office or more less Alexander's office.

Jimmy smiled wondering where she'd been the last few days.

"Alexandria, I'm caught in a mess here," he replied fooled by the fictitious name Mai Dede gave him days before.

"I thought you first name was Jimmy?" She asked playing with Alexander's name plate. "Who is Alexander?"

"Oh, it is Jimmy. This is not my office. It belongs to my best friend who is on vacation," Jimmy replied staring at Alexandria, not able to perform his work around her. Her scent filled the room with affection.

She was wearing a short black skirt with a red silk blouse and black pumps. With dark shades upon her face, Alexandria was truly a bewildering woman. It was the first time she had laid foot in Alexander's office. Touching things of his with the utmost care, and with clairvoyant powers, she could vision him plunging his dick into her heated and waiting pussy. Mai Dede gazed about the office, picturing Alexander working his ass off. His computer resting alone on the corner of his glass desk which it sat upon was so clear to her. All his files were neat and well ordered, so logical. Suddenly Mai Dede locked Jimmy in his office. She moved around his desk and behind him, massaging his neck. Jimmy was being seduced and liked every bit of it. With a hard twist of his chair Jimmy sat there facing her in front of the windows. She waved him not to speak and he gladly obeyed. With a first gentle kiss, Mai Dede had her target then pressed her full lips again, this time with great passion on his. She reached down unbuttoning her pants. Then slowly she raised her skirt and mounded her prey.

Jimmy didn't struggle but allowed the vixen to seduce him in his office. This was a great dream becoming a reality to him. A many of nights he dreamt of this woman's body touching his, and now it came true in the best way. Her body was perfect in shape and warm to the touch. Her breasts sweated with sexual drips resting upon his face. She placed his hard dick inside of her enthusiastic retreat waiting to be pleased. With a short thrust, Jimmy's rock hard tool was inside her. They were like animals wildly fucking each other in a reckless manner. Each time Jimmy was ready to come, she pulled away teasing him and prolonging his erejection, a sexual skill she acquired over time with many suitor.

The sexual encounter went on what seemed hours yet only minutes. Finally Mai Dede allowed Jimmy to release his sexual juices. She moaned with excitement and feverish pitch until she came upon him. The office files were tossed from the desk and onto the floor in their heated passion, neither cared. Jimmy wanted more but Mai Dede had other plans leaping off of him. She pulled her shirt back down and smiled with a sinister grin. She playfully fastens her blouse always watching him like at hawk seeking its prey.

Jimmy stunned and exhausted looked in lost and betrayal.

"What was that about?" Jimmy asked.

No reply.

"Then did you think about going out?" Jimmy pleaded.

"Going out?" She asked in a confused manner. "Yes, the club and dinner, I'm still thinking, Jimmy."

"Well I don't know anything about you, Alexandria?"

"We have time to get know each other," she answered playfully. "Good things come to those who wait. Well, I'll be seeing you, Jimmy."

"You're not leaving already? You've just arrived."

"Sorry, I have something to do," she said.

"I have to tell you that ever since I've met you, I can't sleep. I dream about you every night having hot passionate sex," Jimmy followed jumping out of his seat. "You can't do this to me again."

"Nothing fair, my dear Jimmy," she said.

"But…"

"I won't be far," she smiled then left him unsatisfied wanting more.

Mai Dede's eyes were like pools of fire, waiting to consume by him. Jimmy tried to press her on where she was staying. But she wisely side step his request. It soon became a skill of which she controlled Jimmy, only allowing negligible information to satisfy his strong will to know. His thoughts were only of Alexandria now as his work begun to suffer and he had not seen his friends in days. He was obsesses with Alexandria being. There were a daily meeting of sexual endeavors between the two at the office and other strange locations like carwashes, parks, and secret places. Jimmy's body was truly giving out due to the daily desires of Mai Dede.

One late night as usual Jimmy ventured to the club depressed over not being able to reach Alexandria. He had no more taste in playing his number games on women. No more bench lunches, nothing. He struggle going into the club that night. Ever since he met Alexandria in the park that day, she has possessed his consciousness. People were dancing and have fun. Jimmy was just watching and not willing to play along with the festivity. His mind was being continually fed drink after drink attempting to wash away the haunting vision of Mai Dede known as Alexandria to him. Finally after several hours he had enough as he requested his coat at the checkout counter. The place just wasn't the same anymore. There were attractive females coming on to him, but they weren't Alexandria. And surely weren't Alexander's love, Tara, the most beautiful woman he'd ever seen.

"Alexander, you lucky fool," he voiced aloud to himself toasting his friend on his find. "I find one and she vanishes, my fuckin luck."

An attractive woman joined him at the bar.

"Jimmy?" She asked. "Is that you?"

He looked up to see Sandy Johnson an old friend of his.

"Sandy, hi," he replied half dazed.

"Long time no see," she voiced. "Can I join you?"

"Not tonight Sandy," Alexandria said moving in. "Be a good little girl and leave us adults alone."

"Excuse us, but how did you know my name? Jimmy, who is this woman?" Sandy asked.

Jimmy's eyes brighten at Alexandria's presents.

"Jimmy what's going on here, you said you would call me days ago, remember?" Sandy asked. "You've just disappeared. No one has seen you for days. Does she have something to do with your disappearing?"

Alexandria stood there rubbing Jimmy's neck like an owner with her dog. And Sandy knew something was wrong? Not too far from the truth.

"Jimmy are you all right?" Sandy asked looking at Mai Dede with contempt. "You don't look that well?"

"He's fine," Mai Dede answered.

"I'm not talking to you, whoever you are?" Sandy voiced strongly. "Maybe I should call Alexander about this; maybe he could straighten the matter?"

Mai Dede slightly waved her fingers and suddenly Sandy lost her voice. She struggled but in attitude to speak while looking at Mai Dede.

"What's wrong?" Mai Dede asked smiling. "Cat caught your voice?"

Jimmy still daze looked on confused.

"Sandy, speak with me," he said concerned staggering from to much to drink. His senses were questionable.

Mai Dede lifted Jimmy to his feet.

"You're leaving so soon?" Alexandria allies Mai Dede voiced behind him. "Let me help you stand."

"You're here?" Jimmy replied somewhat surprised to see her there. "I missed you last night."

"Well, I thought I visit this dance club," Alexandria asked. "It's so lonely at my place. I just need to be around people, you know?" She continued sweetly.

"Sure, sure I know," Jimmy replied smiling, lightheaded.

What made the situation even more exciting was she seemed untouchable, beyond reproach. Jimmy longed to take her in his arms again, but he never really expected it to become a reality. That night he would get his chance again.

Sandy soon got medical help as a staff worker help her out of the room and into the back room. Mai Dede just watched smiling as Sandy's face displayed total fear of her.

"What about Sandy, should we check on her?" Jimmy asked.

Mai Dede stood there then kissed him wrapped in his arms.

"She'll be fine in a couple of days, don't worry," Mai Dede answered. "Sandy's sudden condition will pass when she decides to keep her mouth shut and stay out other peoples' business."

"Well, I was headed back to my apartment," Jimmy voiced.

"That would do fine. I mean, mind if I come along?" She asked.

"No, I like that very much."

"Fine, shall we go, never was into dancing anyway," she joked.

"I know what you mean. After seeing Tara dance, she placed a new meaning on the word," Jimmy added.

Unknown to Jimmy, his statement hit home for Mai Dede. As she pressed him to tell her more, but he was too busy thinking about her, a plus, but also a hinder to her mission there. Opting to dismiss the subject for now, she hoped was to find some information at his home on the whereabouts of Alexander. She could never get back into Alexander's office and there was already too much exposure at this point. Though she had been there only a week, Mai Dede had only ten days to locate Tara and bring her back to New Orleans before her birthday. The drive was a pleasant one for Jimmy having Alexandria next to him was an added blessing. She was wearing a black dress ending at the upper part of her thigh. She was always dressed classy, one of the main things he approved of, the other sexual attractiveness. To keep his attention, she continued to display her leggy legs in a manner to arouse him making it hard for him to maintain his concentration upon the road ahead. Alexandria never spoke a word during the drive, only gazing at her victim and licking her full sexual red lips, which matched heated yearning.

Later they attended a well known dinning location in the West End. Jimmy hadn't stopped running around all day, and by the time he met Alexandria at the club it was almost 9:00pm. Now he would have to put out again to satisfy Mai Dede, something his body didn't need. The two sat at a private table in the far corner.

"You must be really hungry," she said with a tone of warmth he hadn't detected before. Alexandria's sexy smile which played at the edges of her full inviting full lips mouth made her more attractive than ever. Though Jimmy wondered how she knew Sandy and now his hunger.

"Are you reading my mind?" he joked.

"Are you asking if I'm clairvoyant?"

"I don't know?" He replied. "Are you?"

"Don't be an ass, Jimmy," she said.

"Look I don't like it when you call me names, I've told you before," Jimmy said upset. "You play with my emotion day and night!"

"I'm so sorry Jimmy," Mai Dede voiced playfully. "Forgive me?"

"Just don't call me names, ok," he said.

During their appetizers a huge man appeared at their table with the desire to remove Alexandria from Jimmy's side. From the looks of things, he wasn't willing to take no for an answer. His hands were larger then Alexandria's face. After being refused by both she and Jimmy, the huge man refused to leave, causing a disturbance in the club. He shouted at Alexandria that she was a bitch and should be treated as such. This Mai Dede didn't needed, unwanted attention. She viewed Jimmy's angry beginning to boil over. He stood up to the demanding stranger, facing him to protect Alexandra, but clearly the strange would have mopped the floor with him. And his condition wasn't the best due to   Mai Dede's desires.

"Look, Sir we are here just for a drink," Alexandria said.

"You don't have to explain anything to this intruder," Jimmy said.

"Bitch, you think you're too good to eat with me?" The stranger said in anger. "Well, what you have to say about that?"

Alexandria's temper rose to a fever pitch. She stared the stranger down with pure contempt forcing him to nervously back down from her.

"Since you can't respect our time, then you'll have to pay the price," she said in a fiercely tone. "No one calls me a bitch!"

The stranger began to raise his fists. Jimmy gave a swing and hit the stranger in the face with no damage. Alexandria concentrate on the stranger's face casting a spell knocking him down to the floor with an unseen apparition. He attempted to get up but oddly he began choking, grabbing his throat as if someone or something unseen was fighting with him on the floor. Jimmy stood there confused that his abnormal reaction. Finally the man's body went limp, eye open wide. A bartender witnessed the event checked for signs of life, there was none? This strong huge man had expired before their eyes by an unknown force.

"Pity," Alexandria voiced stepping over the body.

"What about him?" Jimmy asked stun.

"What about him?" Alexandria asked. "I'm hungry."

Much to his surprise, she suggested they get some lobster and crab at Red Lobster and hurry to his apartment.

Later…

Jimmy's apartment could be described as a comfortable bachelor place, decorated very sensible, with shag rugs; less sophisticated as reflected by Alexander's apartment. Though much larger than his. He lived in a sprawling space filled with style and an overview of the glittering city lights. The entrance near the living room, combing marble pillars on both sides created a sense of drama. In the living room, there was a huge French black stone fireplace to keep warm. The paneling in the living room concealed his television and stereo system. Alexandria made herself at home throwing her rap upon the couch.

"Where are the drinks?" She asked.

"What?" Jimmy asked.

"Where's...you're...drinks?" She asked again.

"Over there to your left," he replied confused.

Alexandria threw open the doors as if she own the place herself. The highlight of the apartment was the bedroom. It was truly a work of art, a twentieth-century viewpoint. Checkered bird-eye oak enhanced the walls of the bedroom. There were two table lamps by a well known designer. Next to the chair are 1933 nesting tables. Upon the windows, silk damask drapery fabric in a bronze color, mo-hair velvet on desk chair and bronze leather chair. The selection of furniture and decorative objects by no means favor Art Deco exclusively.

Upon one of the tables were writings of her name, Alexandria. She picked it up and waved it at Jimmy in a playful manner voicing, "You've been thinking about me. I like that in a man."

Jimmy had nothing to say about it all, it was moving too fast for him. But he couldn't restrain his lust for her. Mai Dede knew she had him lock, stock and barrow. If she wanted him to bark like a dog, Jimmy would at the slightest hint. She moved back to the living room, teasing him every step of the way. Feeling quite appeased after two glass of fine aged wine, he sat next to Alexandria on the couch, feeling great waves of heat passing between them as their legs touched. At that point, if she was dangerous he didn't care. To him, they were but two people about to become lovers. Jimmy felt so good just to relax from the work of the office. They always sent him here and there; it was hard on his legs. Alexandria sighed as she stretched out, putting her beautiful head in Jimmy's lap. His cock began to pulse in his jeans, throbbing against the back of her neck. Without a word, she reached up and placed his hands onto her firm breasts. Alexandria's nipples were taut, firm, and very erect against his touch.

    Her legs moved seductively against the soft mohair velvet of the couch. His hands slipped between hers legs, and she melted against his bold fingers as he unzipped the side of her dress and massaged her mound against her silk panties. He could feel her heat through the panties' thin crotch. Her hands slid up his arms to stroke his shoulders, leaving imprints of her nails. She loved him nearly to death that night. As it was always her plan to do so. Many hours later, Mai Dede lifted herself out of the bed. She had no worry about Jimmy awakening, wearing him out earlier. She searched his apartment for clues of Alexander's whereabouts. Suddenly she noticed Jimmy's phone book above the fireplace. She eyes grew with the thought of finally having what she search for. Opening the pages and flicking through it wildly, she finally came upon the treasure she seeks. Much to her surprise, Tara and Jeanne's was right next to Alexander? Mai Dede knew they were close, but soon realized their plans relocate.

A sudden sound came from out of the bedroom as she torn the page out and rushed back.

Jimmy half sleep glanced up at her.

"What time is it?" He asked resting in bed.

"About 2:00am, love," she replied staring wildly at him in the dark.

"What are you doing up, Alexandria?"

"Stay there, I have to be going anyway, lover," she voiced rushing the commit from her mouth. Then dress in a hurry.

"I'm so tired? Will I see you tomorrow?" He asked smiling; still he could only see her beautiful form in the dark.

"Maybe?" She answered knowing her wouldn't.

She got what she came for, his soul. And if he pushed her any further then he would be a victim. She moved over him in a strange manner, whispering, "Now go back to sleep, yes a deep sleep." Jimmy did as she asked strangely. She had place a curse upon him, rubbing his forehead gently inducing him to sleep. With a few spoken words, his soul was gone. He was luckily Mai Dede had allowed him to live that night. Her target was Alexander not this fool. She thought storming out of the apartment with the torn paper of information of the apartment address and unlisted phone number. The night indeed brought great results for Mai Dede, now it was time for her to face Tara.

It took only a half hour for her to arrive at the apartment that night. The convertible sports car pulled in front of Alexander's dwelling. Mai Dede stared up; there were only the lights from the television glowing out of the front of the window. She smiled strangely in their attempt to hide from them. Thinking to herself; tomorrow will be her day from now on, days of terror which would engulf the trio.

"Ranggg....," the phone sounded.

"I'll answer it," Tara voiced rushing to the phone.

Alexander was busy playing with his electric chess game with Jeanne and joking playfully.

"Hello?"

"Hi Tara, we missed you," a voice came over the phone.

Tara stood there stun by it and puzzled? She was sure it sounded like Mai Dede? Slowly she placed the phone back upon her ear. Then listen further to the voice.

"What do you want?" Tara asked.

"Tara, you failed us and we don't like that," the voice stated.

"You have the wrong number," Tara voiced aloud.

"You've could have went along with us with no problem, shame on you," the voice added.

Tara suddenly slammed the phone down with great fright. Her mind must be playing tricks upon She thought. Could it be that La Veanna's had to power to reach beyond? Was it really her grandmother calling? What once was a relaxing evening with her love Alexander and friend Jeanne; now had turned into a living nightmare. Again the phone rang but this time she refused to pick it up. Refuse to even come near it's continue sounding which caught the attention of Alexander, more to the point of irritation from his point of view.

"Pick it up please, Tara," he requested.

"Tara is something wrong?" Jeanne asked.

"No," Tara nodded.

Tara stood there shocked. Finally she moved again back to the phone, her hands now shaking in trepidation. This influence, if indeed it was coming from her was not welcome.

"Tara?" Jeanne asked.

"It could be Jimmy, haven't heard from him in days," Alexander voiced making this move in the chess game. "Pond to Queen three…check!"

Tara glanced towards his direction confused on what to do?

"Yes?" She spoke in an unsure manner.

"Hi, Tara, where's Alexander?" Jimmy voice came over the line to her relief.

"Jimmy!" She yelled.

"Tara? Are you there? Say something?"

"Oh, sorry…I must have been daydreaming," she responded happily.

"Daydreaming? You're starting to sound like Alexander"

"You want him, right? I'll get him for you," Tara answered.

Tara carried the phone and handed it to Alexander. She stood there staring at him wondering whether or not to tell him about the phone call from the voice? Alexander had seen enough to last a life time to her, one more bizarre event could push him away from her, she feared. His reaction at the earlier plantation's fire should never be again, too many deaths, too many victims.

Alexander took the phone and went into the bedroom to talk.

Tara climbing into his rocking chair reflecting upon phone call, could La Veanna be there from New Orleans, and if so, it could cause her friends' life? Jeanne joined her concerned over her latest reactions to the earlier calls. She sat across from Tara in support.

Meanwhile in the bedroom...

"What you say?" Alexander cried on the phone. "Where have you been? We're concerned about you."

"Alex, she beautiful. She passionate and hot blooded," Jimmy answered gleaming over the phone. "She even has haze eyes like Tara."

"Slow down, now can you at least tell me her name now?"

"Oh, yeah, Alexandria, fresh isn't?" He asked.

"Where is she now?" He asked.

"She left about an hour ago. But let me ask you something?"

"What?" Alexander asked.

Jimmy pause then uttered, "You know when its right but you know its wrong too? I mean, I think I love Alexandria? The way her eyes stare at me...you know, their similar to Tara's, only a little more peculiar. I don't know how to explain it? The woman won't give me her address or phone number, can you figure that? All I have is her first name, Alexandria. Am I tried? The woman had worn me out."

Alexander told him to get some sleep and that he was not making much sense. Hanging up the phone, he looked for Tara, only to discover her ball up in his rocking chair shaking of trepidation. It was as if she had a fever. He hurried to Tara's side in comfort her.

"She been like this since the earlier phone call," Jeanne voiced. Tara gazed at him as if she heard a ghost, a phantom from the past.

"Your ok?" He asked with concern.

Tara waved him off indicating she just needed time.

"Let me handle this," Jeanne asked him.

Alexander nodded backing away.

The next several days were more of the terrible calls. Alexander noticed Tara emotions were on the edge most of the time. At times she would lash out without reason then ask forgiveness; citing it was just nerves. He wondered if it came from the closeness of their birthday. Never knowing of the phone calls coming in on his private line, maybe he could have foreseen the up coming conflict, one which would pitch Tara against Mai Dede with only one victor. Knowing that the prize being Alexander the next unsuspecting sacrifice.

Late one night he and Tara were listening a series of love tunes off the Compact Disk player then an outburst came outside of his door. The clamor startled the trio as if they were being invaded by an army, nearly shaking the door off its hinges. Then there came the shouting coming from Jimmy, excited about something. The way he was acting brought much worry to the group and certain trepidation. His continued reckless attempt to get them to answer the door paid off as Jeanne rushed to the door with Alexander's blessing.

"Jimmy what the Hell?" Jeanne voiced shocked at his look.

"You looked as if sleep was a stranger to you," Alexander followed.

All conclusions were right as Tara gliding her drained and worried comrade to the sofa. Tara hurried to the kitchen for a glass of water. She had seen this subservient condition before in New Orleans and only inflicted by Mai Dede. She was the only woman known who could bring a man to his knees in such a ghastly matter, leaving him just a shelf of a man, a lifeless piece of clay for her to flatten or reshape at her will. The alter ego of   Mai Dede, Alexandria had destroy Jimmy mentally and left him for dead. He was confused and sexually battered. Jimmy grabbed Alexander's shirt pulling him close and crying. He knew Alexandria would never even call again. Despondently he loved her and missed her bewitching affection. Clearly to all, she had stolen his will to live. Tara had returned into the living room with the glass of water, never far from ear length.

Alexander thanked her taking the glass.

Tara watched on with great interest as Jimmy tried to explain his troubled short past with Alexandria. The more Tara listened the more she understood that Mai Dede was up to her old tricks. They were tricked too not considering the name Alexandria and Alexander so similar. Something she had feared from the first time she heard the voice. Tara stood there gazing into the ceiling strangely. What Mai Dede left of Jimmy, it could have happen to her love. This, Tara would not allow. It was time to confront Mai Dede or she would witness another love tragedy, her own. The following morning, Jimmy had slept over their apartment. Tara had to place a spell upon him to rest at last, blocking Mai Dede's nightmares. Taking away a little of the distress, but not the broken heart he suffered at the hands of Mai Dede. During the night several times Jimmy had to be attended to for his fear, loud screaming kept them awake most of the night. Ramping on in his sleep, shouting out Alexandria's names time and time again with loneliness, his screams could be heard out in the quite streets.

What was left behind in New Orleans, now pledge Tara in St. Louis? She never confused the issues of reality, never stood blind to the rush of agony coming their way. Something had to be done. She thought. What she'd feared was coming true. First it was the bizarre phone calls which she somehow kept from all. Now it was his friend being attacked through the heart. She had already lost her home and feared that here was next. Again like clock work the ghostly call came through, but this time Tara picked it up prepared to deal with Mai Dede. She was free to speak as Alexander, Jeanne and Jimmy had gone earlier shopping. This would leave her room to move.

Tara voice was indeed stronger than before. This Mai Dede noticed at once, but attempted to continue her game. Tara only gave her silence from the other end forcing Mai Dede to confront the issues. Now surprised about her finding out, Mai Dede struggled to regain the upper hand. Tara continued the mental attack pointing out what she had done to Jimmy should have never had happen. Tara expressed she was looking forward to their enviable confrontation. Mai Dede went one step farther telling Tara where to find her and she would be waiting. Mai Dede's games went too far and Tara decided to put an end to them. Mai Dede hung up the phone. Tara held the phone against her breast wondering how to confront Mai Dede? Hoping just words alone would force her back home, allowing them to be at peace and out of harms ways. If Mai Dede was pulling her into a trap then the other had to know. She had made up her mind not to tell the others of the pending meeting, fearing their interference; nor willing to explain to Jimmy that Alexandria was really Mai Dede. Opting to reserve her feelings through his trying times, Tara couldn't allow the recovery end.

    Mai Dede had flattened his ego and done a great job of it. Though Jimmy was like a boy playing with the hearts of others, he never leaded them on about how he felt about them, always placing his views on the table before they went further in the relationship. Jimmy was never the same since meeting Alexandria, playing the number game, and never venturing into the park for lunch. He would now need time to pull himself together. If   Mai Dede could do this to Jimmy, surely Tara hoped to protect her love, Alexander from the same faith; but time has away of ether healing or destroying? That surely remained to be seen. There remained the crusade against Mai Dede's continuing meddling into their affairs. It had to stop that night. The time was nearly eight o'clock in the evening. Tara was confused on how she could get away from her protectors of the apartment to meet her adversary, without using any spells.

Later, Alexander and Jeanne were in the living room reading books. Tara notice how peaceful their minds and life appeared. Still the underline feared they felt could not be so concealed. She could sense their emotions battling within them, the inter beast which consumed her. Alexander glanced up at her smiling. She returned it willingly but with reservations. She did have the power to place him into a deep sleep but opted not to control him in such fashion; it would only mystify the issues. They both demanded that their love would be pure with no outside assistants. As the evening became longer Tara had to leave them somehow? Suddenly an ideal came to her, dressed in jeans and a white blouse Tara slowly approached him hoping if her plan would work. She knew it had to.

Tara crossed her arms breathing slightly heavy from wonder.

"Alexander, can I have a word with you?" She asked in a very low tone.

He nodded placing the book down upon his lap. The rocking chair which he was resting in halted at the sound of Tara's voice.

"How's Jimmy? I didn't get a chance to see him this afternoon?"

"Fine," he answered.

"I'm sorry," Tara spoke.

"Sorry about?"

"About Jimmy's condition, he really cares for her?"

"A little too much if you ask me," Alexander replied. "The doctor claims it would take several days before he could return to work, something about a nervous breakdown or depression?"

"Look, I have to go out, you don't mind? All of this pressure of our up coming birthday is playing harsh on my nerves, and Jimmy's condition is one to ponder over? I want to get something special for him and deliver it to the hospital," Tara uttered hoping he would accept her reasons to departing from the apartment.

"Say I'll come along," Jeanne voiced staying up.

"No, no that's alright, Jeanne," Tara replied sharply.

"What?" Jeanne asked.

"I mean that I need to do this myself, ok?"

"If you wish, I guess?" Jeanne asked.

"Thanks," Tara voiced smiling with trepidation. "This I must do myself guys."

Time was at a must now and working against her every moment she talked with them. She feared if ever Mai Dede came into contact with the ones she loved, it surely could be the death of them.

Alexander nodded his head in approval to her suggestion, kissing her with loving care. Yet his mind pondered over her true intentions? He came to know Tara well when it came to hiding her feelings, but he had to allow her space to exercise her demons. Tara, herself wondered if she could really past off the anxiety which consumed her as Jeanne watched her closely, knowing Tara was hiding something dangerous from them?

"You're sure you won't need a friend?" Jeanne asked.

"What she has to do, has to be done alone," Alexander answered for her waving on.

Tara quickly deciding to exit before anymore questions was directed her way, and to the hospital and the recovering Jimmy. To get her there Alexander was honored in caring for Jimmy's vantage 1965 black mustang, a sports car which Jimmy and he restore with pride, with a four on the floor stick shift, Tara had mastered it well. Back in the apartment Alexander looked at Jeanne and her him then both nodded and exited the place. As Tara drove off, they took the taxi which was hidden. The skies were raining that night, causing the streets to shine from the city's street lamps. The hissing of the tires running along the soggy road seem as if it were the only sound allowed. They kept a good distant behind Tara in the mustang, only wishing to see just where she was heading. One thing they knew, Tara did head for the hospital.

Later after at the hospital visiting hours were over but Tara had to see Jimmy. She had to know if Mai Dede still had some connection with his illness. There was a male attendant near his room as she approached, asking if she could know the whereabouts of Jimmy's room. He examined the records announcing Jimmy was in the mental ward, informing Tara, she could not visit him until the next morning, but she had to see him before confronting Mai Dede. A must in forcing this crusade, slowly she gazed into the man's eyes and uttered in a very tone, "Go right on in. Here's the keys the ward." A flash of bright light came from her eyes then quickly faded. The man repeated the same, word for word. Tara had taken over his mind with little if none resistance. Then she told him to relax and sleep and strangely he followed her mental suggestion, slowly resting behind the desk and into a deep slumber.

She headed to the mental ward hurriedly.

There Tara discovered Jimmy standing at the small port window on the door. It seemed as if every essence of his being which made him a man was withdrawn? Tara placed the keys into the locked door then moved into the room, picking up the chart. She read the report and discovered the doctors had no ideal what was wrong with him, but Tara knew gazing into Jimmy's eyes for a minute and in that short time found the heart of the problem. Mai Dede had taken it and lifted him in agony. His soul was gone. Tara guided him, to the bed and sat him down carefully. Slowly she brushed his hair to claim him down.

"Jimmy, do you hear me?" She asked.

He just mumbled in a frighten state of mind.

"Jimmy, I know there is something left in you, bring it out." She whispered into his ear. "I need what's left of your consciousness to help you."

No reply.

"Please just hold on for one more night," she said.

Suddenly Jimmy began to shake wildly, but Tara held on to him tightly with concern. Clearly the unsettling sight of Jimmy's condition was appalling to anyone. No more laughter, no more lustful foreplay, all which remained was tears from his heart. Shortly after Alexander and Jeanne had followed her to Jimmy's room. There they observed with interests and great concern from the monitor at the floor's desk, never revealing themselves during Tara's visit. They knew Tara was the only person whom could help Jimmy now, as they gazed on with interest. To interfere now would only do more harm. Jimmy had placed his trust in Tara's hands.

Tara placed her small smooth hands upon his heart. Suddenly flashes of his encounter ran through her mind like fatal blows of detestation. First there was happiness than horrible darkness. There were continue sexual abuse was numerous. Jimmy glanced at Tara with not apprehension but attachment, somehow in his state; he knew what she was attempting to do.

Tara whispered, "Jimmy, tell me what I'm here for?"

Jimmy stared at her trying to force the words out of his mouth.

"That's it. I know you want to tell me what I'm here for," she repeated.

Her desires were to get him to allow her into his damaged soul, to allow her to heal him partially and bring him on the road of recovery. Jimmy started to sob even more as he sat up against the bed board for support. Still Tara pressed on. She had to get inside his reasoning, for there were no limits to her psychic powers she couldn't use more or it would damage him.

"I gave her everything, Tara," Jimmy weeps.

Tara smiled at his commit; she had broken through Mai Dede's spell.

He continued, "Alexandria promise me forever, but her left me."

"Please tell me," Tara whispered to him.

Jimmy stared on trying to speak more of his affliction. His heart was pounding wildly now. He explained that he lie to him self that Alexandria would stay. He should have known better. She took his life from him, that Jimmy had lost his very soul. Tara promised that she would get back his essence. Jimmy continued bellowing why was the reason she left me? Did she find someone else? She took his complete life, but still she left him alone. A many of nights he'd weep alone for her, until he couldn't take it anymore, everyday, more and more of his soul vanished a he slept. Jimmy screamed out in anguish needing her.

Tara quickly held him tightly explaining he had to be stronger than her, that they needed him, expressing after tonight, he would be back as he was. Tara knew she couldn't pull Jimmy together alone. She had to have faith in his strength. Jimmy bellowed uncontrollably in mental torture. He was dying of loneliness inside. It appeared he wouldn't last the night? Tara pressed upon him that he must hold on. That Jimmy was not being punished, but spoiled by someone who played with men's hearts. Understand that Jimmy was becoming exhausted. Tara laid him on the bed until his soul has returned to him. Jimmy rested upon his pillow as asked by Tara.

Out in the corridor Alexander and Jeanne moved away from the monitor and hurried out of the building to their vehicle to await Tara. What they seen only enforced their appreciation for her will.

Tara gazed at Jimmy one more time, knowing he would die that night if Mai Dede wasn't stopped. She had seen Mai Dede in his psyche, controlling and planning his assassination. Leaving the room, she locked the door and headed down the corridor to her car. In his room there was silence, no more weeping. Suddenly he got up from his bed. Walked over the window and stared out of it in a bizarre way. His soul was out there in Mai Dede's clay shaping hands. With a closer look of his reflection in the mirror, his eyes were red from the continued weeping. All that remained was several tears running down his aimless appearance.

Later Tara drove away from the hospital in a hurried fashion; closely followed by Alexander and Jeanne. Though the wipers were in bad shape, poorly keeping the mist off the windshield, Alexander managed to keep Tara's sports car rear lights in view. After an hour they soon noticed they were in Jimmy's neighborhood. May be Tara gotten lost returning home? He thought. But after passing Jimmy's apartment, that thought rolled off their mind like the rain drops off the windshield. Soon Tara arrived at the Carton Hotel several blocks down the street. This puzzled Jeanne's mind very much? What was she doing there? Who did she know? Something was very peculiar about this scene? The questions just kept pouring into their already confused minds. Yet both Alexander and Jeanne made no move to interfere with Tara's bizarre actions. Sitting very patently with exceptional interest, they gazed on in a brief moment, the weak working windshield wipers would clear the rain and allow him to see. What they was viewed remained to be seen. There were too many unanswered questions? But tonight, maybe tonight they felt at least some would be?

Tara had parked the car in front of the Carton Hotel in a rush, unconcerned if anyone noticed her. Whatever was driving her, Alexander and Jeanne had to find out. Tara was like a woman on a mission.

Inside, the front desk clerk noticed Tara approaching her. Voiced, "You must be Tara?"

She nodded that he was correct.

"Your from New Orleans?" Tara asked.

She nodded.

"Where your boss?" Tara asked.

"She is waiting for you in Suite 186. You may go right up," she added in a ghostly manner. Nearby a Bellman sat blank in a chair. Mai Dede had gotten to his mind. Tara stared at him sadly knowing Mai Dede treated men like toys, mentally adjusted to server her every whim; something Alexander had joked about people whom life was controlled by others.

Tara proceeded cautiously up the stairs, knowing Mai Dede for theatrics; she wished not to rush into any of her horrible games.

Meanwhile Alexander left Jeanne in the automobile and entered the hotel a few minutes behind his lover, over hearing the suite's number. There was no need for him to rush after Tara at this point. However, he'd wished not to be too far behind, just in case. Tara finally came to a door. Upon the gold plate Suite 186. She strengthens her constitution to deal with Mai Dede. Hoping she wouldn't lose her temperament and take vengeance for all who was debilitated by Mai Dede's enchantment. That would surely play into Mai Dede's hands, knowing as long as she remained nonviolent; she had a chance of not losing domination and possibly losing Alexander? She was the only line of defense blocking Mai Dede now. In the past Mai Dede was held in check by La Veanna, but she was now unleashed and very dangerous. Tara started to place her hands upon the double huge beige doors. The gold plate representing the suite's number gleamed upon her clear apprehension. She glanced around the now empty corridor leading the suite as if wanting to be somewhere else. Further away, she noticed the massive bay windows at the end of the corridor. The mist of the precipitation just as Alexander's car had fogged the vista. There was a hazy afterglow of the lights outside from the street lights.

"Come in, Tara," Mai Dede's voice echo through the corridor.

"Funny," Tara yelled, half smiling out of skepticism.

Suddenly the two door open allowing Tara to pass. Tara took a deep wondering breath then entered. Mai Dede knew Tara would come on account of her friends. Tara stared on directly into her eyes with contempt. The room was shadowy as a small glow of candles lights was emulating, but enough to allow the ladies to view each other clearly. Tara walked around the room in a strange manner, touching and looking for any sighs of Doctor Walker presents unaware of his death. She decided to remain on guard for any tricks directed towards her. Mai Dede poured her a glass of sherry but she refuse to accept any of it, fearing that it maybe drugged? Something she knew Mai Dede was a master chemist. The two ladies didn't speak a word at first, opting to tried to feel each other out.

Tara spoke, "You play a sick game with lives that don't belong to you particularly souls which other posses."

Mai Dede gave a slight laugh at first then came a dangerous smirk.

"Games as you call it are for fools who have time for nothing else. What I do with my time, well never mind," Mai Dede answered. "I proved a service."

"You invest in the souls you've collected and I'm here to stop you," Tara voiced with pride.

"Pity, Alexander put you up to this?"

"You leave Alexander of this, witch!"

"Look who's calling a kettle black or shall I say, really a soulless witch?" Mai Dede joked glaring at Tara.

"A witch, I'm not nor do I plan to be one," Tara shoot back.

"Poor little princess," Mai Dede joked. "What a waste!"

"No matter what my dear grandmother's plans are, I'm going along with them. La Veanna may have created all of this, but I'll end it right here and now with you." Tara infuriated.

Mai Dede countered by responding, "You have no chose. What's done is done. Similar to Doctor Walker's death, he didn't play by the rules so he is history." Mai Dede attempted to bring Tara's emotions to a broil but failed. She wanted so badly to battle with her, to see if she could overcome Tara's powers, something which had to be tested by herself and what better opportunity than now.

With Tara conflicting feeling of affection for Alexander, she was weakening even more with distraction.

There was only silence in Tara's direction. Mai Dede couldn't understand it? What was Tara waiting for? The cards had been played? The stage was set in motion? But Tara never lost control.

Meanwhile outside the door, Alexander arrived at the suite unnoticed by the two. The door was left halfway open revealing the two women in a heated argument. He watched on as the Mai Dede continued verbal attacks against his love. But much to his surprise, Tara was holding her own until…

Mai Dede had one more card to play. She willingly brought Alexander into their conflict. Tara didn't answer displaying any expression trying to confuse her. Mai Dede played with the past encounter of their sexual rump. Tara jump at her direction landing in front of Mai Dede pointing out he would have nothing ever to do with her. Suddenly Mai Dede let out an enormous laugh shocking all. Even Alexander felt the powers of her outside; with a voice which echo throughout the room.

"Alexander and I were lovers. I bet you didn't know, Tara?"

"You're a damn, liar," Tara replied. "He would never betray me."

Mai Dede poured it on citing, "I never needed to lie about a man. You, Tara should know better. Of all the people whom claim to know me. You know me best. I've had him before your stupid rescue."

"I don't believe you," Tara screamed.

"Alexander would never hurt me so."

"Are you sure?"

"I'm very sure!" Tara responded upset.

There came a smirk upon Mai Dede's face. Now she knew Tara's lack of conflict was about to play in her hands. Tara's emotions were getting the best of her, the weak link in her impressive coat of knowledge, adoration; truly a powerful force but also a cribbing one to handle. Alexander was watching and listening the whole while. Wishing he could tell Tara the real truth about his and Mai Dede's encounter. But still if Tara were to stand strong, it had to be brought out from within. Several times he would glance about wondering if anyone was coming down the corridor, no one? None had shown and the conversation continued among the ladies.

"You think his yours? Well I got news for you," Mai Dede yelled, "That man is going back with me, also you. But you know that?"

"You got to be kidding," Tara replied. "We're not going anywhere!"

"Oh yes you are. La Veanna sent me here just to find you two now that I've done that, it's only a matter of time."

"Well, go back and inform her, I love him and we're staying." Tara responded. "You take too many chances around me, Mai!"

"Enough of this, Tara! First, I'll take Alexander then you will be next," Mai Dede laughed. "You know the fumy thing about all of this. You can't guard him or Jeanne twenty-four hours a day, my dear. Eventually I...will ... have him for life. Alexander will be like a puppet on my string!"

Suddenly Tara screamed so loud, she voice erupted the very walls surrounding her, even more thunderous than Mai Dede's laughter before. No, she repeated in enraged. Sudden winds out of nowhere befell upon Mai Dede, throwing her against the walls. Mai Dede only smiled and returned a wall of flames. The room which was solid now became four dimensional in all respects. Where there were floors, vanished leaving them hovering in midair, sustained by thoughts only. What walls remained was now vanishing too and replacing them was an endless space of stars. Alexander's only clasp of reality was the door frame which he now held on with great conviction, fearing he would be lost like the objects in the room. If one was to view the room. There remained only the frame of the door connecting the supernatural to the factual world He glanced behind him to the corridor and viewed it as non-changeable. But when he returned his eyes back into the room things were different Tara was now high above him. Mai Dede was a several yards away facing her. The two ladies were squaring off at each other. He knew there was nothing on his part that could benefit Tara. This whole situation was too peculiar for his taste, something which Tara had feared.

"You've pushed it to this point, why?" Shouted Tara in a commanding tone, her eyes was full of contempt and rage.

Mai Dede replied in a strong tone, "You can't hide what you are! You are not like them, we are not like them. La Veanna has ordered you home and your coming!"

"You're wrong? I will fight you with the powers which I despised," Tara yelled.

Mai Dede knew what she was doing. The battle waged on with lighting bolts coming from the heavens. There seemed to be a pair of eyes peering below them. The same red eyes during Tara's birth with glowing heat they seemed to give out, as Alexander stared them too with great concern wonder whether they had something to do with the conflict before him. Tara didn't desire to harm Mai Dede, but knowing she had to be destroyed. Mai Dede yelled lifting up her hands; bring forth a huge ball of fire, than threw it with commanding force at Tara. But Tara vanished from the area, reappearing behind her. There she raised her arms and drove a huge lighting bolt into Mai Dede's unprotected back. The sudden action sent Mai Dede to her knees in anguish. She let out a scream that chilled anyone soul. Numerous bright balls of lights shoot out of her, changing into ghostly white bodies in mist forms. They were the souls of those who she possessed. They were now released and heading back to their true owners. Tara viewed Jimmy's very essence happily on its way to enrich him again.

She had done it! Her promise to Jimmy was now complete, but still it would take time for him to recover.

Tara floated back in front of Mai Dede concerned that she may have killed her? Suddenly a loud laughter came from above them. The eyes sent a strange yellowish beam of light directly into Mai Dede's limp body. She jerked wildly and uncontrollably as her body gave a glowing shell surrounding her once limp body. Tara looked on with great interest and surprise, perplexed would be a better word. She heard the laughter before knowing what it was. Too many times, she had spoken with it at the lake and in her dreams, but always during the trance. Now she started to remember her dreams oddly. But this time Tara was totally conscious of its horrifying presents. The laughter suddenly halted when she refused to concentrate. Tara gazed at Mai Dede's face viewing discovering the laughter was now coming from her; whatever wickedness was in the room decided to make its present known through Mai Dede, voicing its demands.

"You have done well my child. Any guardian would be proud to have you as their child," Mai Dede voiced possessed.

Tara's anxiety factor rose rapidly.

"I am not a child!" Tara yelled. "I will not believe that?"

"Not yet, but you will be," Mai Dede replied.

"I reject you!" Tara shouted.

"There may have been a time when you could have gone…"

"What time?" She asked.

No reply.

"Who are you?" She asked.

"It is time for you to come home, back to New Orleans, Tara."

"I will not come!" Tara shouted.

"Enough of this delaying, child! I have waited long enough!" Mai Dede shouted in anger and irritation.

"Waiting?" Tara asked confused.

"Yes, waiting," Mai Dede answered. "Waiting for you to come of age. Waiting for you to rid yourself of Alexander."

"What does he have to do with this?" Tara asked.

No reply.

"I demand to know what Alexander has to do with this." Tara asked strongly trying to figure out a way of ending this nightmare.

"It's time to come home, Tara. Too much time has already passed away."

A strange smile of conviction came upon Tara's face. "Then I'm not a witch? I'm still as human as anyone else? I still have a chance?" Tara asked.

"For now…" Mai Dede voiced in possessed fashion.

"I have out grown you haven't I?" Tara added. "You don't have anymore control over me than during my actual birth?"

The voice suddenly became oddly silent and reserved from anymore of Tara's questions. Whatever it knew, it wasn't willing to allow Tara to drill it for more. It was true, Tara had come into her own; for the unknown voice which spoke with her for so long had confronted her finally on equal terms. But it underestimated Tara's heart. That heart which grew into an affection of a young man, Alexander. It alone shielded her from the voice mind control. It alone made Tara stronger then expected. Her head went up proudly and with confidence, she had faced the entity which created her for its own dangerous proposes and faced it down. There was a chance it could be all over? There was love standing, now obstructing the unnatural. There was hope? Tara thought knowing she was the master of her own faith and nothing was going to stop their lasting relationship.

"Enough, let there be light!" Tara shouted.

Suddenly the fiery eyes began to fade into the darkness. The floors appeared solid and strong below them. The walls which were only stars before returned to their pale green color again. The ceiling above turned into a mist then became solid again. The furniture which had strangely floated aimlessly was now placing its self where it once sat. As for Mai Dede, she regained her mind and strength, only to withdraw in a corner from fear of Tara's exceptional supremacy. Tara, herself had descended earth bond again. What she had learned that night wouldn't escape her consciousness again. Alexander witnessed the entire events unfolding before him. A huge smile came upon his face of relief fro his love, Tara. It too seemed that they had beaten the odds. Now there was nothing standing in their way, but he's decided not to interfere opting not to alarm Tara of his presents. Slowly backed out the corridor to join Jeanne and explain the magical thrills he witnessed.

Meanwhile in the room, Tara had Mai Dede punishment to hand out. What that punishment would be was in questioned? She didn't know what to do with Mai Dede?

"What now?" Mai Dede asked shaking.

"What to do you ask?"

"Do? If you're not careful…" Mai Dede whispered strangely.

"What do you mean, careful?" Tara asked.

"You will see…," Mai Dede voiced sounding dazed.

Tara pointed out that the rape of her lover will not go unpunished. That Alexander didn't fall for her like the others, only showing that love had a place in both worlds; for that Tara spared her life. But expressed in rage that Mai Dede never cross her path again or the next time she would not control her anger. Mai Dede gave her some advice that there will be others. But Tara was determined to overcome any enemies that confront them.

"Mai Dede, go home," Tara final words were.

Mai Dede backed into the corner of the dark room laughing with two other ladies. Suddenly they vanished fading in the darkness of shadows, leaving only their phantom residue resting upon the wall. Tara had gotten good at her craft, maybe too good; for La Veanna was mentally observing the entire conflict. Unfortunately Tara was unaware of this unwanted intruder. Her mind was too clouded by love and strong desire to return home to Alexander. Now La Veanna had placed a falsehood into Tara's consciousness. Now she was easy prey for the pickings when it was truly time to come to her birthplace.

Several hours later Jeanne went to take Jimmy home that night. Jeanne thought Alexander and Tara needed time alone deciding to remain at his apartment for the night.

Alexander returned home alone and exhausted, but seeks to impress Tara. He created a heated snack for her as she walked in with a smile of accomplishment on her face, ridding them of Mai Dede's interference and bring Jimmy back into the sane world. Alexander kissed her deeply with passion glad the ordeal was finally over. Tara too was pleased to see a warm loving face again after the abrasive conflict.

PART XI
Vanishing Affair

Weeks passed and the threats once were before them vanished.   They thought it was all over. They were surely and dangerously wrong. Alexander and Jeanne decided to give a birthday party the following weekend; for Tara began to display signs of missing her way of life in New Orleans and hungered to be around them. She soon relaxed as Alexander comforted her and reassured her that he would always be around. He should have known better then to bring attention by way of a surprise birthday party would lead them into trouble. They were both blinded by love. Mornings passed, Alexander had to leave to establish things for the birthday party. This would involve leaving Tara alone. He gazed at her resting in their bed and kissed her. Tara mourned in pleasure of the attention given to her, wrapping her arms around him. Suddenly she notice him dress and readily to leave. He sat next to her as Tara moved even closer to him for warmth.

"Where are you going?" She asked in a low sleepy tone. Her voice not yet willing to conceded to welcoming the world.

"I'm going to pick Jimmy and Jeanne at the hospital, he's being released today from his final treatment," he answered.

"Wait, I'll go with you, just give me moment," Tara voiced.

"No, rest for now. I won't be long."

Tara gazed at him smiling. "Remember your promise to me," she whispered. "Don't forget it."

"What promise?" Alexander asked.

"Well, that you will never leave me," Tara replied with eyes half opened from a wild sexual exchange between them the night before.

"I remember," he answered kissing his love.

Yes Alexander remembered every place they had gone to. Never parting from each other, but this time they made a huge mistake. Tara had went back to sleep feeling safe a peace in mind not allowing her psyche to blemish their sexual encounters.

Later the two went to lunch. At a small luncheon place, Alexander and Jimmy discuss his adventure into the supernatural world of New Orleans. As the conversation went into major detail, Jimmy couldn't believe what he had heard from his best friend's encounter, but understood the reason for concern to protect Tara. The entire situation though it all seemed out of the ordinary to him, couldn't sweep it aside since he himself was quarry to the show aggression. Alexander and Tara failed to do was to inform him about Mai Dede's actions towards him, both fearing he may have a relapse and lose him again. Worse yet, seek to find her again. Also they never talked about Tara's conflict, a mistake.

"What's wrong?" Jimmy asked drinking tea.

"I love Tara so much, you know. I guess I will watch over her. What else can I do? Tara took a dangerous chance with her own life coming here," Alexander expressed worried.

"My friend, you better be careful," Jimmy voiced with concerns. "Where is she now?"

"With Jeanne," he answered, "We take turns being with her."

"You have to ask yourself, would that be enough?"

Alexander took the sound of his voice and the way he expressed it in a fearsome manner. The two dismiss the danger for the moment and started to work out the plans for Tara's and his birthday.

Meanwhile at the apartment, Tara had awoken alone. Jeanne was still sleep on the other room across from hers. Tara slowly placed her hands over to Alexander's side of the bed, only to discover he was still gone. She glanced over again and viewed him with a dagger in his heart. Blood was everywhere in bed as Tara, herself laid in the pool of blood. The room was full of her people from the many rituals her had witnessed. There were old women, old men, young women, young men, children with hollowed out eyes blind to their training, and presiding over all, La Veanna reaching out her hands to Tara. Suddenly with frightfulness, she screamed at the top of her lunges. Alexander luckily had just arrived back to the apartment when he heard the screaming.

"Tara, where are you? What's wrong, Tara?" He asked.

"Tell us what's wrong?" Jeanne asked entering the bedroom.

Alexander and Jeanne leaps into the bed with her. Tara's eyes stared at the bloodily body resting next to her, shaking all over and out of control with anxiety.

"Calm down, we're here with you, just relax for us," Alexander asked.

"Tara you were just dreaming," Jeanne added.

Tara finally took her eyes from the spot and gazed at them unsure. She body was covered with sweat from panic. She then gazed back at the spot but the dead body was gone? The light white cotton gown was now clinging to her shapely form. She thought they've killed her lover. Thought she was too late to help him. When she awoken Alexander was dead, maybe a dream, maybe a sign of things to come? She begged him not to leave her again to wake alone in a half deranged state of mind. Clearly the coming of the birthdays was taking its toll upon her mentally. They knew it and agreed never to leave her alone again.

"Alexander, Jeanne promise me," Tara said.

"I promise you from the bottom to my heart," he vowed. "Jeanne?"

"Yes I too promised," Jeanne said.

Yet Tara didn't smile at first then gave a half smile in relief.

"Now kiss me, Tara," he playfully demanded. "We have along day ahead of us, ok." He added happily.

Tara leaned over and kissed him with rapture. Yet he could still feel her shaking body.

Jeanne smiled leaving them alone.

Days passed and it was now one day before Tara and Alexander's birthday. Tara had discovered about the surprise birthday partly the trio of friends had planned. After finally convincing Alexander the party would be ill advised and that nightmares continued to plague her, all concerned decided to pull out of the party honoring Tara's wishes. Jeanne again decided to stay over Jimmy's apartment leaving the lovers alone.

Alexander later that night noticed Tara's nerves were on edge and it was apparent her psyche was warning her of threats. As Alexander slept, Tara awoke from the uncertain sounds of the dark night. She stared at her lover sleeping as she struggled, herself.

"Alex," Tara voiced shaking him slightly. "Alexander, are you awake?"

"Yes now, problems?" He asked now adjusting to view her.

Tara stared at him confused.

"Do you really love me like you've said? I really need to know this?" Tara asked. "Before..."

Tara was very concern about her up coming birthday. He held her closely uttering, "Look, no one is going to take you away from me. Understand?"

Tara sat up in bed next to him troubled.

"And if ever they did, I would chase them to Hell and back, no matter what they place in front me," he said smiling.

Tara nodded.

"We've rewrote the meaning of love, and I'll love you to the ends of earth, through the fire. Through any wall, for a chance to be with you, I'll gladly risk it all," he vowed.

"Than if they take me away, will you come after me?" Tara asked holding him tightly. "I feel no matter what we do. They will come."

"Sure damn will," he replied strongly with passion.

Tara hugged and laid a passionate kiss upon him.

"I will never leave you, Alexander, no matter what."

"I hope it never comes to that, my love," Alexander replied.

Tara placed her hands behind her pulling up something in the dark. "Do me a favor and wear this," she whispered relaxing in his arms, feeling very much secured from her nightmares of demons visions. He agreed reluctantly, wishing to ease her mind. It was looked like as tiny sliver heart, about a half of an inch in size. She told him not to pay any attention to it and rest. Tara removed the one sent to him and replaced it with the charm around his neck.

It wasn't long before they fell into a deep slumber. Yet inside Tara's consciousness, she cried, knowing it was just a matter of time when her protection would not be enough

Late that night two threatening figures revealed themselves. One was a mulatto's man and the other, Mai Dede. Unfortunately, Tara's passion for Alexander had weakened her psychic powers to resist enabling La Veanna to control her mind during her sleep. She too had controlled Alexander's, mind that night. Mai Dede had a smirk upon her face staring on pleased at what was about to happen that night.

Morning came as usual as Alexander awoke only to discover Tara was strangely not at his side. Thinking she may have gotten up earlier, he pulled himself out of bed and headed towards the kitchen searching for his beloveth, but she wasn't there? Suddenly he started to worry fearfully screaming out her name only to discover a "gris-gris" outside his apartment door. Now he knew why she gave him the amulet to wear the night before. It was to protect him from such an attack. Yet she didn't protect herself from being controlled. He shouted enraged. Rushing through the apartment in desperation of hoping he was wrong.

Tables and chairs were knocked over in a wild tantrum. Finally it was apparent the conclusion was they had Tara. Suddenly his legs lost their ability to support him. Sliding down against the kitchen wall, he had the "gris-gris" in his hand, clinching it tightly; Alexander threw it out the window.

"This cannot be happening to us?" He said aloud.

He didn't know how long he'd remain upon the floor that morning passed out. Time passed and now it was late afternoon by the time he fully recovered. There he sat staring into space, not moving from the spot. A sudden knock came upon his front door, yet he was unable to move, unable to create the strength needed to answer the calling. He'd lost all desires of living.

"Hey! Is anyone there?" Jeanne and Jimmy yelled outside the door.

No reply.

"Say, you two, comes answer the door! I know you're in there!" Jeanne said. "We're coming in ready or not."

Still there was no reply.

Jimmy soon became concerned and began to look outside, noticing the taxi still parked in the rear from last night. After glancing into the apartment from the outside, both he and Jeanne noticed the living room was in disarray? Suddenly he started banging at the door. When that did no good, he forced his way in by colliding with the front door with his shoulder. They soon viewed Alexander just sitting there on the floor daze.

"Hey, partner? What happen here?" Jimmy asked, glancing around the place for Tara.

"I'm taking a look around, Jimmy," Jeanne said. "You make sure he's ok."

After looking around, there seemed to be not sign of foul-play of any kind, yet his friend sat there stun from something?

"Alexander, where's Tara?" Jeanne asked keening near him.

Alexander finally responded in a very weak state, "They took her?"

"Took her?" Jeanne asked confused.

"Yes." He responded dazed.

"Are you sure?" Jimmy asked.

Alexander gazed up at him with a wild expression. "New Orleans," he said, "They've got Tara."

Jeanne looked at Jimmy concerned.

"You have to help," Alexander cried.

Jimmy looked on stun voicing, "We will, but first, we have to get you up from here."

Both Jimmy and Jeanne pulled him off the floor, got him a glass of water, and covered him out. Alexander explained the circumstances to them of the concerns which Tara feared. But Jimmy refused to go along with his wild theories, believing in it the first time he was told. Jeanne as totally convinces and they needed Jimmy on their side, opting to allow some skeptic view.

"What now?" Jimmy asked.

"The only thing," Jeanne answered.

"Are you crazy?" Jimmy asked. "He could get killed!"

"We must go after her," Jeanne said watching their expression. "We maybe Tara's only hope at this point?"

Alexander began to dress for the trip. Jimmy thought this was a disastrous ideal, but he unfortunately was aware of the bond of deep love Tara and his true friend. Still he tried to talk them out of going, but to no avail. Both Alexander and Jeanne were set on going with or without his blessing.

"When are you going?" Jimmy asked seeing them packing.

"We're driving down in an hour," both cried at the same time.

"So I guess there's no talking any of you out of this?" Jimmy asked, his hands shaking over what was to come.

"We've been through this before, Jimmy," Jeanne explained, "But we need you here if anything happens to us, ok?"

"Look, Jimmy if anything happens to us...well, you know..," Alexander paused then voiced, "...don't come after us, ok."

Jimmy stared at them as if his best friends were writing off their lives?

"You're for real about what happen down there?" Jimmy asked with a bizarre look upon his face.

Both nodded and continued to pack their bags.

"This got to be so outlandish?" Jimmy said watching.

Alexander paused for moment whispering aloud, "I have to get her out of there."

"Wait here guys, I'll be right back," Jimmy asked.

"Where are you going?" Jeanne asked.

Suddenly Jimmy left the room explaining he had something for them in the car, something to stem the tide; arriving back in a very short time and presented a weapon. It was a fully loaded 45-automatic weapon with case.

"Take this with you. You may need it more than I?" Jimmy said handing it to Alexander to place with his things. "Please, for me."

"Get that thing away from me!" Alexander shouted not willing to posses it. "Besides, we will be dealing with the unknown. This weapon is in the physical nature not the magical nature and that's what we're up against. It's all in the mind, my friend."

"What about the body?" Jimmy asked.

"And if I'm correct, Tara would not allow anything to harm us anyway, Jimmy," Jeanne added gazing on with embarrassment.

Alexander saw the turmoil in his face bellowing.

"Well, you had to be there to understand, Jimmy," Jeanne said.

But Jimmy wished they would carry the weapon, but it would do them any good in fighting unnatural magic.

"Look, at least allow me to come with you?"

But both repudiated his request. It was now between them and La Veanna for her granddaughter, Tara. Both thought. Jimmy shouldn't have to deal with this predicament. Tara was missing and there were no need for another.

Jimmy was concerned about him voicing, "I'm sure you are aware of what you're doing. I wish you God's speed, you will need him."

"Wait, allow me to come?" Jimmy asked.

"No! I mean not this time," Alexander answered.

"We must do this alone, besides," Jeanne said closing her bags. "We have also the charm you gave Alexander? It found Tara once, maybe it can produce again, we pray. Besides we need you to tell the story if something happens to us."

Indeed Jimmy remembered it, smiling and giving his blessing as Alexander and Jeanne left the apartment.

Outside, both place their bags into the taxi hurriedly. Jimmy observed them from the upstairs windows, in his hand the weapon. "Hell who would believe what happen here anyway?" He said aloud.

"Hey, Jeanne, you take care of yourself and him," Jimmy shouted, "Alexander, you still owe me for a baseball game. I want to collect!"

A slightly but huge smile upon Alexander's face, knowing it was Jimmy's way of wishing their quick and a safe return. But as he sat at the wheel with Jeanne at his side, the smile halted. They had a dangerous task before them, but it was ether stay or allowed La Veanna to keep

Tara? There was no real choosing in the matter, Tara would be saved.

By nightfall, he arrived in New Orleans. Unfortunately it was Tara's birthday and fortunately they were not detected. Or was it that anyone actually cared? Everyone involved deeply in the ritual ceremony was at a secret site in the swamps. Luckily, Tara had told Alexander of the location during their long walks before. It was an hour before midnight and time was running out for the two lovers. In common with previous Voodoo queens, La Veanna made many changes in the ritual; abolished the snakes which had always formed the basic elements of Voodoo worship, adjusting to the first time of an in hostility queen. By the time they arrived the ceremony was well on its way in an ancient barn. Jeanne was instructed to meet him later and to ready herself for their departure.

Alexander was too late, maybe? Hiding as he had done before, watching with great interest from the back of the room and hide some boxes, attempt to find Tara's location at the ritual. Seated on a high stand with their legs crossed beneath them were about twenty-five men and women, the men in their shirt sleeves, and the women with heir heads adorned with the traditional head handkerchief or tignon. But Alexander needed to move from the spot before he could be spotted by the guards. Moving around the out-skirts of the camp, and looking for Tara He could see the center of the floor, there was spread a small table-cloth, at the corners of which two tallow candles were placed, being held in position by a bed of their own grease. Some curiously wrought bunches of feathers were the next ornamentation near the edge of the cloth, and outside of all several saucers with small cakes in them. Alexander noticed that the only person enjoying the aristocratic privilege of a chair was La Veanna who sat at in one corner of room looking on the scene before her with an air of dignity. She said but little, but beside her two old and wrinkled ladies whispered to her continually. Alexander assumed they were her aids.

There an opening in the ceiling oddly.

What interests him the most was the instrument which had a long neck, and its body was not more than three inches in diameter, being covered with brightly mottled snake shin. This was the signal to two young mulatresses beside him, who commenced to beat with their thumbs on little drums made of gourds and covered with sheepskin. These tam-tams gave forth a short, hollow note of peculiar sound, and were fit accompaniments of primitive fiddle. He noticed it was as if to inspire those present with the earnestness of the occasion, the old mulatress rolled his eyes around the room and then, stamping his foot three times, exclaimed, "A present commencez!"

Rising and stepping out toward the middle of the floor was, Tara. She looked so handsome and was everything attractiveness comes is, but he soon noticed something wrong about her. Nervous with restrained gradually became louder and louder, a song, one stanza of which ran as follows:

"Mallel couri dan delser."

"Mallel marcher dan savane."

"Mallel Marche' su piquan dorel."

"Mallel oir ca ya di moin!"

Since being with Tara, Alexander learned some of their languish. From what he knew, which was little, it could be translated as the following:

"I will wander into the desert."

"I will march through the prairie."

"I will walk upon the golden throne."

"Who is there who can stop me?"

Soon Alexander feared it was getting out of hand as his concerns about Tara's welfare grew vastly.

"No!" He shouted but not running away this time.

Just then Tara heard his voice and turned towards him, staring at him, Tara attempted to break free from such horror. There was a clear night's sky above them. The night ceremony was cloudless. Suddenly Tara stop singling in view of her lover's passionate pleading. She gazed upward, and then screamed and fell into his arms. Yet following her collapse, the crowd saw a huge black cloud scudding swiftly across the hitherto empty night sky. In a moment it had obscured the full moon, and a murky twilight descended, while a faint breeze rustled the tops of the trees and stirred up little eddies of dust in the unpaved opening. Several members screamed in sudden terror. But before he could carry Tara away La Veanna refused to let thing end.

"Mullat a Tootoo!" La Veanna shouted.

Suddenly Alexander couldn't move anymore. Each step he attempted to make was now paralyzed. Unable to help him, Tara remain locked into the ceremony. Her consciousness now was going away from her again. She stood there and fought to break loose from the ritual, but sadly failed. She returned in a deep trance being controlled by La Veanna. Tara moved back to her place at the ceremony. All Alexander could do was watch as he did before during Jeanne's near death. A memory he wish never had happen. His voice was suddenly gone and he was unable to speak with Tara, but had an ideal.

"Tara, if you can read my thoughts and I know you can, please fight back," Alexander's thoughts went out to her.

No reply.

"Dammit, Tara hear me!" He shouted in his mind.

Tara head turned his way only letting out a slight tear of despair.

Now all he could do was gaze on with great anguish. La Veanna gave a smirk at his pity attempts. Rising and stepping up again out towards the middle of the floor, Tara began to sing again. As she sang, Tara seemed to grow in stature and her eyes began to roll in sort of a wild frenzy. There was ferocity in every word, boldness and defiance in every gesture. Keeping time to her song the tam-tams and fiddle gave weird and savagely monotonous accompaniment that it was easy to believe was not unlike the savage of Africa. The sight was amazing to see, as Alexander found it hard to believe. When it became time for all to join in the refrain, Tara waved her arms, and then from every throat went up, "Mallel oir ca ya di moin!" She had scarcely ended the fourth stanza before two women, uttering a loud cry, joined their new leader on the floor, and, these began a march around the room. Watching Tara marching, he tried continually to break the mind control. Still no good resulted from it. As he listened on the song progressed, an emaciated Tara stepped out, and amid the shouts of all, fell in behind the others. This last addition to wild dancers was the most effected of all, and in sort of wild delirium she picked up two of the candles and marched on with them in her hands.

Tara arrived opposite the old queen, La Veanna as she gave her something to drink out of a blue stain flask, the same flask in her visions. After swallowing some Tara retained a mouthful which, with a peculiar blowing sound, she spurted in a mist from her lips, holding the candle so as to catch the vapor. Alexander noticed it was alcohol as it blazed up, and to him this attempt at necromancy was hailed with a shout. Then commenced the regular Voudou dance with all its twisting and contortions, Tara fell exhausted to the floor in frenzy and frothing at the mouth, and the emaciated young ladies he loved was carried onto a table lifeless. Then she was death by all counts. Alexander's mind was now full of hatred for La Veanna and her Voodoo cult. Tara was murdered and taken from him forever. He yelled in anger and blackout.

The next morning Alexander awoke near a small pond tired and beaten. He had now recovered from the blackout during the ceremony. His mind was still fuzzy, but one thing was sure, Tara was dead. His thoughts were that he had failed. He started to wander around the area in confusion. Pondering how could he had allow them to take Tara right from under him? Why didn't he stay up that night before their birthday? Why surely didn't they murder him? There were plenty of chances which had failed. But last night it would have been an easy task. Suddenly a chilly voice spoke from behind him, but Alexander couldn't see whoever was there. A haunting feeling came over him of strong presents.

Someone was there?

Glancing around, he heard foot steps behind him. Soon La Veanna, Tara's grandmother appeared before him in all her ceremonial splendors. She looked on with great compassion for him. Something Alexander would have never thought possible.

"Go home, Alexander," La Veanna ordered. "There is no more that you could do here."

But he demanded answers.

"You had a chance of killing me, why didn't you?" He asked getting up from the ground.

"No more questions," she only replied.

"Yes! More questions, I need more!" He yelled.

La Veanna turned to him with contempt now. Alexander's rigid view of not letting go enraged her.

She cried out, "I spared your life because of Tara."

"Why?" He asked.

"Because she loves you and I couldn't take that away from her, understand?" La Veanna asked. "There some things we can't control."

"Wait you said she loves me?" Alexander asked confused. "Don't you mean loved me?"

No reply from La Veanna.

"Tell me what's going on, La Veanna?" He asked

"Tara would only return willingly if allowed you were allowed to live. That is why you are still here to breathe this air. Don't mistake this for kindness, young man."

He gazed at La Veanna upset more over playing Tara for a simpleton.

"The deal you gave her was unfair," Alexander said.

"Unfair to whom?" She roared back with a hard tone.

"Dammit, to the both of us," he replied with tears in his still tired eyes, and totally mystify. "Don't you see we were one? We were happy. You had no right to stop that. No damn right."

La Veanna listened to him as he marched around upset.

"We had the right long before you were ever born," La Veanna said turning and following his voice. "I should have never allowed Tara to mate with you. But no more questions. You have already caused too much misfortune with your mending. Because of your love for her and Tara's love for you, changes had to be made."

"I just want to know why she had to die." He asked.

La Veanna just walked away from him.

"Alexander, Tara is my granddaughter and you were her first and last love. She never will care for anyone as she has cared for you," La Veanna said pausing there. "Tara loved you very much and it is best that you go home with that memory."

"I can't do that," Alexander voiced.

La Veanna sadly shuck her head then move along the pond to the huge fawn, she finally whispered, "I could have easily killed you last night if I so desired."

"You were right, but understand we made a promise to Tara," Alexander responded.

"We?" La Veanna asked halting. "Jeanne has returned to New Orleans, interesting. We must deal with this quickly."

"Jeanne and I are not afraid of you," he said.

"Go home, and take Jeanne with you," La Veanna voiced walking with aids around the huge fawn and vanished.

Alexander rushed over but couldn't find a trace of them. He stood there more lost than before. Something kept tugging at his mind, the way La Veanna spoke about Tara, there had to be more? Maybe what he saw was an illusion. Maybe he was supposed to think Tara had died? Oddly Alexander could feel it in La Veanna's voice, her movement, the way she expressed her sympathy. He had to find Jeanne before they did and hoped she kept out of sight?

PART XII

To Hell and Back

Later that morning Alexander could have accepted La Veanna's order and his heart was forcing him to rethink it all. Logic could possibly cost them their lives, but it too was driving him to know more. It seemed like ascension of spirits within his very soul, as if Tara, herself was calling him from her grave? Yet Tara's body like the others were never founded, leading him to the conclusion, she could still be alive somewhere? Alexander started to remember little clues after talking to La Veanna at the pond or whether she allowed me to talk. It left a deep abyss in his heart, leading him to the conclusion, it wasn't over. It couldn't be. He decided to explore such a theory, hoping his gut feeling would be genuine. By all logic, Tara should be dead, but for the first time, he opted to leave it behind in desperation of wild obsession as his mind took him back.

It was like Tara was lifted off the face of the earth? Surely, Alexander couldn't get any information from La Veanna. But as he stood there pondering, there was one other person which knew as much. He decided to seek out Mai Dede for questioning, and had heard around town she was resting in the nearby swamp area cabin.

Shortly later reluctantly, Alexander didn't wish to see the evil spirited and sassy, yet sexual, Mai Dede; pressing on against La Veanna's desires. Mai Dede knew of his presents and wishes to see her, a smirk came over her beautiful face when he had arrived. She was sitting upon a huge flat black smooth stone, just buying time for his arrival. The sun was baking everyone that day. Yet there appeared a small over cast, placing a shadow abnormally over her. Approaching her, Alexander knew he had to be very careful. Tackling with Mai Dede's psychic powers proved fruitless. But he knew not to allow her thoughts into his consciousness; for if that were to happen then he would relinquish his soul to her. After seeing what happen to Jimmy, it wasn't happening to him.

The two gazed at each other, one with desires for his affections again, though taken, the other with contempt and wariness.

Mai Dede was as beauty in its essence. She winked at him smiling and pleased to see Alexander.

"So, you've finally came back to me of your own freewill," Mai Dede said relaxing. "What a very reasonable surprise. If you asked me, you should have stayed with me that night when you ran foolishly away and just when things we're getting interesting, my love."

Alexander only watched for weakness.

"Why so silent?" She asked, her voice was in its usual seductive tone, and still it somehow seem to penetrate his very soul. Mai Dede started to moan from passionate thoughts and to use ability of her psychic powers. Alexander's mind began to wonder into flight of the imagination. He was being drain of his soul and sexual being.

"Enough!" Alexander shouted shaking off her probing of his mind, "Mai Dede, that's not going to happen."

"I see, Tara has taught you well about our telepathic abilities," Mai Dede said sadly. "Pity, we could have had so much pleasure."

"Whatever your sick sexual desire maybe, it won't come from me," Alexander said upset. "Need some information from you."

"I know why your here," Mai Dede voiced.

"I didn't see you at the ceremony last night why?" He asked wondering.

"There were other things that needed to be attended to," she answered, resting seductively upon the black stone, waving him closer.

But he refused strongly.

TARA THE FORBIDDEN FRUIT - 400

"Maybe you could tell me whether you've seem, Tara around?" Alexander asked.

"You are probing where you shouldn't, Alexander."

"It is odd though, her body were ever founded. Even your local police acted as if they've tried too; that surely being a story within itself, don't you agree?"

Mai Dede rose up and pressed her body against him lustfully. He stood his ground to the cat like Mai Dede. She leaned again against him playfully this time.

"Tell me, Alexander why should I help you?" She asked.

"Because I need it?" He answered. "Because, a queen your not."

"I see?"

"Why is that?" He added. "If Tara is really dead, then who is queen?".

Alexander gazed on trying to read Mai Dede's expressions. One gift which he mastered himself. The expression was one of celebration then self righteousness with a blend of contempt towards his suggestion.

"You must not take me as a moron," Mai Dede said. "It surely would be a big mistake on your part. Now, if you don't mind, I was busy and you've interceded in my work."

"Work?" Alexander asked.

Mai Dede seemed upset and moodily.

"Did I say anything wrong?" He asked.

"Please leave now!" Mai Dede yelled turning herself away from the contemplating man. "I have no more to say."

Alexander moved closer to her gripping Mai Dede's arms from behind. With his mouth pressed against her neck.

"You know more than your willing to said," he whispered.

"No, nothing," she replied in a weak manner to his touch.

"Tell me what is scaring you so?" Alexander pressed.

"Just leave me alone. I don't want to be here anymore," Mai Dede said becoming frightened, suddenly withdrawing inside. "I don't want to play anymore."

The once aggressive lady was now hiding in fear of something? There was no reason in trying to drive his point further. So with a gentle thrust, he let her go telling her to remove herself from his present. Oddly, she started to laugh at him wildly, regaining her sinful ways. Even though he got nowhere, it was still worth a try. Still, Mai was exquisite to see again.

Later his continued search investigation only brought more frustration. The questions Alexander asked received around town only forced him into a maddening rage of desperation. Most of all Jeanne was no where to be seen? She had vanished just like Tara. The taxi was left abandon outside of town. Days went into nights with the same result, both ladies were lost. Alexander didn't shave or bathe. At nights he would just sit on the balcony of his hotel room watching the streets below in a daze at the Old Brickyard. His health was depleted and most of the time he was unable to get up in the morning, and when he couldn't sleep, he would just sit in his chair in his dark room staring at the wall.

Late one night he had return again from an unsuccessfully search of Tara or Jeanne, exhausted and perplexed, he strangely went to the bathroom. There Alexander filled the tub with water until it was nearly over flowing. He stood there staring at the water bouncing off the walls of the tub. His intelligence was fried and befuddled to why he filled it so high? He went into the living room in a daze. Behind him in the mirror Mai Dede's face appeared smiling then faded. Suddenly his thoughts became clouded and excruciating. He began to throw objects around the room in heated rage. His face expressed a tempter that would rival any fiery prized fighter. The chair near the window was smashed into the corner of the room. The glass water vase met its faith being thrown against a mirror. Suddenly Alexander dropped to his knees in anguish holding now Tara's snapshot. The water from the tub had over flown onto the floor and into the next until it touched his legs. Slowly Alexander look at it then touched it gently, as if being drawn to it. He stood up and moved to the bathroom desolately.

With a twist of the knob, the flowing water had stopped. He again stares at the tub now filled and undressed dropping the photo. It flowed to the wet floor below him, flowing out the door to the other room. Alexander slowly climb into the tub nude and rested his back into the heated water. Then without mercy, he sank his head under the water...

A shadow entered the bathroom turning into Tara. Alexander had been under water for five minutes and his air bubbles were nonexistent. Tara's spirit was silent and pulled him, now comatose from the bathtub. She gave him mouth to mouth until he recovered choking up water. Then as she appeared her vanished into the shadows of the room, leaving Alexander alive to ponder why? He struggled off the floor and noticed Tara's photo now hanging on the cracked mirror. Under the photo a message in mist form on the mirror citing, 'STILL ALIVE,' and it slowly faded away. He took another closer look at mirror again another mysterious message appeared from the beyond citing, 'YOU ARE MY POWER, MY PASSION, MY PAIN.'

The message disappears gradually...

Alexander smiled in fright turning to the tub then to the photo. He had managed to survive death, now he had to manage his own nightmare.

Later that morning he had warned Jimmy not to come. Still Jimmy fought the order with words over the cell phone, but Alexander got his wish. Jimmy remained in St Louis for now.

Alexander knew if he didn't find them soon, their deaths could be by his own hands. He decided to finally press the locals even if it cost him his life. The search to find Tara was not to be ended in failure. For every time he reached out for help. There was a monster of aloneness eating him away slowly, his heart wounded by both Tara and Jeanne's disappearances. The room which he and Tara played in mirrored his own living mausoleum of her. Alexander used a cyber café to contact Jimmy face to face.

Jimmy stood waiting for the displaying view. He too was saddened by the lost of the ladies.

Alexander appeared on the screen in Jimmy's office in St. Louis, his best friend looked like a madman. His heart was in New Orleans and now lost it there.

"How are you doing?" Jimmy asked.

"Unsure my friend," Alexander answered.

"I take that Jeanne and Tara are still missing?"

"Yes," Alexander responded in a weary tone.

Alexander clearly needed rest.

"Want me to come and get you?" Jimmy asked.

"No, I need a little more time here."

"You look like a ghost," Jimmy said.

"I guess your right. I'm tired, very tired." Alexander voiced walking away from the screen.

"Hey pal, I can't see you?" Jimmy shouted.

"Sorry, lost my thoughts," Alexander replied.

"Take a good look into the mirror and get yourself together," Jimmy responded. "If you don't, I'm coming down there."

"Ok, ok I'll do it, just stay there from now," he replied.

"Pool your logic to help you, not to hinder you," Jimmy added preparing to log off. "As long you survived they survive."

Alexander returned in a listless fashion, only to feel a great emptiness never felt before. There has none playing music or cooking. No one to say, they missed him. He had to go rest and say goodbye to Jimmy abruptly. The cyber connection was closed. Alexander eyes displayed a serious case of redness. He left the cyber café and walked back to the hotel over five miles away. There he looked at himself in the mirror. The view he saw was of a man who was becoming a ghost of himself, weak, listless, and very confused on why it all happen? He was to a point of barely being able to walk to the shower. He didn't remember much since that day.

Another two days passed before he could recover fully from the stressful ordeal, though Tara and Jeanne still played upon his mind with zeal, it took Jimmy to clear his thoughts.

Late nights were no comfort to Alexander as he struggled from nightmares of Tara. Of them being together when thing, were at their best, then shocking realities of her being killed at the ceremony brought thing to reality, causing sometimes violent reactions thrusting him into the wakening world; only to force him into tears of loneliness. Many times he would break out in an uncontrollable cold fever, resulting in a screaming frenzy. His night shirts would be socked with sweat of anxiety.

One morning he was having lunch in his room. Something inside himself forced him to peer out of his windows? There Alexander noticed a beautiful woman walking down the block below. Strangely he found himself smiling. The woman seemed to carry herself and look like Tara from the back. He couldn't remove his eyes off her, and continued to stare for some reason until she reached the corner. A bizarre thing happen as she reached the corner she slowly glanced at him.

"Tara?" Alexander cried out stunned.

Running down the stairs, he attempted to catch up with her, but as soon as he'd reached the corner, the mysterious woman which looked like Tara had vanished. For a moment he thought he was going crazy? But in days which followed, the appearance continued causing Alexander to remain there. The nights were now filled by having pleasant dreams of him being with Tara. It soon became an obsession within his mind as if they were never apart from each other's embrace. Yet it was draining him, driving him insane again, forced Alexander's consciousness to be pushed beyond reality and into the fourth dimension.

Until one night he couldn't bear it anymore. The ticking of the clock sounded louder and louder his eyes became glued its slow moving hands. His mind was being frantically torn apart by emotions. Flashes and more flashes kept rushing into his mind, as if Tara, herself was placing them there with reckless abandon.

"It's too much!" He yelled jumping up from bed. "You're consuming me alive!"

The sounds and visions kept growing. He hands pressed the clock against his face displaying pandemonium until his mind couldn't absorb the visions of Tara anymore, falling into a deep but painful slumber. His body laid there lifeless to any observer. His mind floated in a sea of dreams. Later that night a dark and mysterious figure approached his bed in silent fashion. In the left hand was the dagger which nearly exterminated him. The peril handle dagger reflected the little light which beamed in from the windows. Slowly the dark figure moved around Alexander's bedroom observing him with peculiar intrigue. Then suddenly it leaned over him and raises the dagger above him. Alexander's eyes open suddenly and surprised.

Though he couldn't see well in the dark of the room, he quickly focused upon the female figure which stood above him. A closer look and he could see her eyes, then he knew but couldn't believe his own eyes, Tara returned to him, now was his tired mind was playing a terrible trick in a most horrible manner?

The figure halted its movement.

"Tara? Is it really you?" Alexander asked, hoping.

Out of the darkness, the female figure moved into a beam of light from the outside window revealing it was indeed Tara. She was just as beautiful as before they parted. Placing the dagger next to him, Tara moved back towards the window confused to why she came. He looked on stun to see her.

"Alexander, I have returned to ease your mind," Tara voiced soft yet strong tone. "I have heard your calls to me, night after night. Know of this, I will always love you forever and they will never take away the spirits of me to you."

Remaining speechless through it all and unsure rather she was really there. Alexander could only observe her ghostly being. Slowly he reached out his hand towards the ghostly image of Tara. But she was intangible, as his hand which desired her so willingly passed through her like air, leaving him in a disappointed state of mind. Like before other dreams; she would vanish, but this time Tara stayed.

"My love, I am sorry that you cannot touch me," Tara voiced. "For I too desire it so."

Tara then moved towards him with grace and tears in her passionate eyes.

"Your world is not of mines anymore. Therefore you will discover it is hard to understand why I must remain here. All alone, my place should be among my people, and I have been chosen from birth to watch over them. Your world would be unable to apprehend to us, Alexander."

He stood there listening and observing with great interest.

"I really do love you, but you must forget; for I'm so attached to you that every time you dream about me or think about me, I am there with you. Maybe if we had met in another place, another time in life, it would have been good for us," she explained sadly.

Alexander had begun to see Tara's world and most of all, understand her. Understanding, that Tara had never left him and would be in his heart forever. They gave each other a smile of felicity then she turned back to the window, thinking.

"For you, my true love. I will become moral for this one night and this night only," Tara whispered to herself knowing the sad results of her action.

Alexander tried to hear what she was speaking of but couldn't. Tara was speaking with another in the room.

Alexander could not see through her anymore? Within seconds her body became solid before his unbelieving and tired eyes. As she placed her hands upon the window frame; it gave way to her pressure. He looked on with confusion. The wind which blew the curtains through her now moved unhurriedly off her smooth face. Tara leaned towards him and kissed him with great passion and desire, knowing it would be their last night together. He too returned the affection with desire even greater than hers. Tara whispers seductively into his ears, "Oh, I longed to be at your side for so long, to engulf myself within you. To hold you so tightly and make love to you once again."

"I too wished for this night a many of times," he said.

Tara paused pulling back then uttering, "But you must understand."

"What?" He asked.

"Alexander, there's a price to pay," Tara said sadly.

"No, no more for now just you and I," he voiced.

Halting Tara from speaking by pressing his lips upon her full rousing lips, he smiled at her, caressing her heated body; making love for the last time unknown to him. Their love began in a slow drive then elevated into a blasting glory. The night was an enjoyable one for them as they bath in the afterglow. The heat in the room became like a steam room. Yet through it all he wondered why Tara had the dagger? Curious over whether or not she intended to murdered him? The only reason he had figured were he had learned the secrets of her world, and strongly considered an out cast by her people. But for some anomalous reason he wasn't fearful of his life. Now he was with the woman of his life, as Tara offered herself in mind, body, and most of all soul. Tara's attention towards him causes her began to cry as she lay upon his chest bathing in the afterglow; alarming him to questioned her why?

"What's wrong? Why do you cry?" He asked removing her hair from her yearning eyes. "Are you afraid to go back?"

Tara gazed at him with concern uttering, "No, that's not it. I'm not afraid of that. I'm only sorry that we must part from each other, that's all."

"It doesn't have to end this way," he pointed out.

"We both know better," Tara quickly added hugging him.

Alexander gazed back at her wishing that things could be different, yet knowing it could never happen, feeling that he could no more adjust to her world as she to his. Black Magic had surely locked Tara into their life of spirits. The world of the supernatural had robbed her from him.

"I know that you must do what is expected of you. They've done this to you, bastard,' he cursed her culture.

His mind in grossing anguish staring into those loving eyes of Tara's, those eyes which hunted him almost to his own death, but if he could change ever meeting her, he surely would decline.

Tara wrapped her arms around him in need.

"Alexander, you may not understand this but since this all happen. I seriously feel I was chosen for a reason to be the High Priestess," Tara explained. "I mean there is a higher reason even my people don't know."

Her head now resting upon his huge chest as she played with her soft hair; twisting it around and around with her index finger, she was attempting to justify why she could not stay with him. Moving closer to him in bed, Tara turned her head upwards and kissed her lover.

"You know, maybe I can change the way things are there?"

"What?" Alexander asked confused.

"No, my grandmother has been doing this for many of years. Maybe it was my destiny to rule over the old ways of life and bring it into the future? Make it, respectable in someway?" Tara explained.

As she continued to talk, Alexander noticed the change in her, a certain attitude of superiority and maturity; most of all, a reason for living in such a way.

"Tara, look, may be I could visit you one day?"

"No!" Tara yelled with concern.

The scream caused him to wonder greatly, wanting an answer from her jaded and peculiar response. He jump out of the bed and headed to his window; feeling a sharp pain of depression within him. His heart became a piece of rejection of her love. Tara gazed at him crying, hating what she had become. But knowing a truth of which she didn't wish to present to him. The side of the bad part of her reign of being a High Priestess in the Voodoo world. More like a curse placed upon them whom reined Tara climbed out of the bed slowly towards him worried; touching him, but Alexander acted foolishly and rejected her affection towards him. All he knew was the desire to see her, maybe

TARA THE FORBIDDEN FRUIT - 415

once in awhile. Maybe just passing through her home in New Orleans, expressing this strongly to her, still she refused his request strangely.

"You do not wish to view me," Tara voiced.

He was stun at her reaction and confused? Yet he could feel in her voice that something wasn't right. Something Tara was not telling him and he was set on discovering what it was?

"Look at me," he ordered.

"I can't," Tara said trying to turn away.

But he wouldn't allow her, placing his hands upon her crying face and wiping away her tears.

"Tell me why?" He asked.

"Why what?"

"Dammit Tara, don't play me for a person to pull the wool over somebody's eyes. Tell me dammit why can't I see you again? What is it you're not telling me?" Alexander asked. "I desire a remedy from you!"

"You really want to now why?" Tara asked upset.

"Yes, tell me why?" He pushed. "I thought I meant something to you?"

"Dammit, you do my love, you surely do!" Tara screamed crying.

Tara pulled him to the front of a huge mirror in the bedroom. A mirror which he had seen her so many time brush her lovely black hair; as it displayed her beauty upon this earth. He stared at Tara for a moment. Very pleased to see her in all she youthful splendors. Free to touch her as last, which he hungered for day and nights.

"You're as you were before you vanished, beautiful," he uttered in her ears. "Just as I remembered from the first day I met you."

Tara abruptly pulled away from him.

"Look please," she begged.

"Ok, I'm looking," Alexander said puzzled by her actions.

Her yells tormented by reality.

"No! Look beyond your heart at the real me, as I really am, now," Tara said quietly turning him towards the mirror.

There he viewed an old wrinkled skinned woman dress in the same gown as Tara. The image stunned him so. Quickly Alexander glanced at Tara only to discover a young beautiful woman. Then again took another look into the mirror, the same results, and an elderly woman before him.

"This is what is real. What I have become since being Queen. Even though my mind remains young, my body became old rapidly," Tara explained. "What they called an unexpected condition due to love."

"What happen, why?" Alexander asked.

"My love, I couldn't endure the ceremony to avoid this. But if I had then I surely would have forgotten you, and I promise you, I would never leave you, never in heart and in spirit."

"I see, because of me," he said sadly.

"You know what's funny?" Tara asked.

"What?" He asked.

"Mai Dede thinks it very amusing," Tara added with a grin.

"But the mirror?"

"I am using my powers to maintain this youthful body you are accustomed too," Tara explained.

"There must be something that could restore your youth, your beauty?" Alexander asked. "Don't tell me there's not a way?"

"There's nothing I can do for now, my love," Tara answered. I maybe trapped forever in this decaying body. Would you still care for me in this condition?"

"It doesn't matter and you know it," Alexander answered.

Tara moved away from the mirror to the bed and sat down.

"That is why Mai Dede was laughing so hard, she knew all the time. Tara, no matter what you appear as, my love is from the inside, not out," Alexander said stun at the two images presented to him.

Tara only weeps more with her head down in indignity.

"Please, my don't do this to yourself. I doesn't matter one way or the other. We will find a cure for this aging, I promise, Tara."

There was nothing the lovers could do. That was why Tara didn't come to him when she heard him calling her at first. It was she which passed by hotel in humiliation. She should have known better, feeling like a fool. But her desires were for him to remember her as before the curse. Tara hugged him with great concern, mixed with passion. Sudden there stood another figure appearing in their room. It was a woman holding a tiny light; more like a tiny star which originated in her hands. It seemed like it was pulled from the heavens. Yet he couldn't view just who held it. Slowly the glow from the hands revealed an elderly woman. From the figure, Alexander could square it was La Veanna, Tara grandmother looking under the weather.

"La Veanna?" He asked.

"My children, I am dying," she said. "My time is coming to an end."

"Why are you doing this?" Alexander asked.

"Do you both desires for things to be as they were?" She asked.

It was as if La Veanna was examining their minds. It was now clear it was La Veanna as she rose from the chair out of the shadows, sightless. She waved to Tara to come close. But Alexander refused to allow her to go blocking her path. Tara gazed up at him smiling.

"Tara?" He asked.

"I will be all right. She would never hurt me. Please allow me to go?"

Alexander released her, watching Tara mover closer to La Veanna, hoping it wasn't a mistake.

"Come here my grand child," La Veanna cried.

"What do you wish of me?" Tara asked.

"Only to help you, that were all I wanted ever," La Veanna replied.

"Then I will come," Tara said moving towards her.

Slowly La Veanna placed carefully into Tara's hands the tiny glowing star. It had a chilling sensation at first then warmth followed. It gave Tara a refreshing feeling of youth inside her, as she gave a sigh to its healing powers. La Veanna explained that if Alexander wished for Tara's beauty and youth to return everlastingly, she wouldn't remember him ever again; the cost of the healing powers. Stating it was the price of restoring what she had. Also she too explained that the love which Tara has for him had caused the rapid aging of tissues during the ceremony. Tara's heart was not pure and had become poison by their love for each other. She still maintained strongly that their relationship should have never happen.

"What do you mean?" Alexander asked. "We were meant for each other."

"Understand your affections and love for each other was too great! That is why Tara suffered this faith," La Veanna replied enraged. Now you two must make a decision."

"What decision?" Alexander asked.

"Whether to change or remain as things are? That is all, nothing more," La Veanna said. "For my health is fading fast and I needed to know now; for tomorrow is not

TARA THE FORBIDDEN FRUIT - 421

promised to me anymore. Sadly you win Alexander and at the same time lose."

"Don't Alexander," Tara pleaded with him.

Alexander couldn't allow Tara to remain in such a horrible fashion, now knowing it was because of him, she suffered. Looking at Tara as she gazed at the tiny star she held, Tara's mind was at peace. He reluctantly refused until La Veanna added Jeanne in the deal. She knew where the young woman was and was willing to offer her back to him. Now there were two main reasons for Alexander to accept the covenant, but they both had to leave New Orleans. Alexander sadly nodded his approval. Suddenly Tara glanced at him fearing she would lose him forever and that was a price she was unwilling to pay.

"I won't forget you, Alexander," Tara said. "Grandmother, I will remain as I am no deal and release Jeanne."

Aware of Tara's life must come first, his own desires, Jeanne's life, and love had to be put aside; for Tara's life, there will be others; if not him then one of her own kind. But in order for the hex to work, both had to agree to the conditions. Tara still refused to allow La Veanna to perform the spell. Time was passing by as the clock displayed 3: 00am. Tara started acting peculiar, wishing to leave in a hurry. Soon Alexander discovered the reason in a painful scene. Time had expired of Tara's holding of the youthful form. Her body started to transform in the way she was viewed in the mirror. It shocked him to see what was before him, opting to attempt to force her into accepting her grandmother's request.

"Wait, La Veanna, just allow us more time?" He asked worried she would leave.

La Veanna nodded choking from the illness.

Alexander returned to Tara. Her body was weak and her face ancient.

"Tara, look, we have no chose now," he explained. "Jeanne is involved with her life. You understand?"

Tara won't let go of her convictions.

"The time is now for you to live and not for me, but surely for you and your ideals, remember?" Alexander pleaded.

He held Tara's decaying body; she finally agreed and signaled her grandmother to do so, yet reluctantly. Alexander moved back by request of La Veanna. He gazed at Tara's once gleaming eyes and waved La Veanna to start.

La Veanna began to mutter several words:

"Maii Comi stai..."

"Corni Oha mai mai!"

Suddenly Tara began to scream as if her insides were being ripped apart. Then a blinding brightness engulfed the once darken bedroom. The sound of her screaming was so loud, causing such a vibration, breaking every window in the apartment and beyond. It was like an explosion, bursting outwards toward the streets below. It was three in the morning and the neighbors surrounding the area were unsure of what hit them. As for Alexander, he had lost his hearing for a moment, going deaf. But as fast as the bellowing started, it soon passed. Shortly he regained his hearing and the bright lights which blinded him disappeared. The ending results were amazing! He glanced up only to view Tara transformed back as before. Her youthfulness and beauty now took away the aging wrinkles. Her body started to strengthen up to prefect perfection again.

"Your back?" Alexander asked touching her face happily and caringly. My Tara is truly back."

Tara only gazed at him sadly. His eyes displayed tears of lightheartedness.

"Yes, its true, my love. I'm surely back," she replied smiling.

La Veanna looked on at the two smiling.

Alexander turned to her frowning.

"Tara, time to take your rightful place at home," La Veanna demanded.

Tara quickly stared at Alexander with the saddest of eyes, not wishing to leave him; eyes which he'd never seen before.

"Soon Tara's mind will forget you, Alexander. Be prepared when the time comes, as for Jeanne, she will be released to your care as promised," La Veanna explained. "Take care, Alexander!"

"Alexander?" Tara cried.

"Yet I will grant the both of you the remaining night to share only," La Veanna added.

With nothing else to say, La Veanna walked towards the same chair in the darkness. Her body suddenly faded into the shadows, then vanished. The two could only stare at each totally lost for words as they hugged each other.

The next morning, Alexander's mind was at rest with the world. He thought. But he still felt dispirited for Tara's life. Understanding her life as the only way she could maintain. Her people had their life regardless of the other. At least he knew what and experienced true love. He tried to explain it all to himself, yet could not absorb what had transpired last night. Temperament became over bearing and insulting towards the way Tara's peoples lived. Those people almost killed him with their gullible attitudes and strong belief in superstitions. He couldn't feel happy, joy; maybe send them a welcoming card?

He didn't perceive what actually happen there could end so dreadfully. Just like all the others, what they believe in is not right nor was he willing to accept their way to life? But his knowledge of their way of life, proved a great challenge. He almost lost because of Tara's love. Alexander stared at the peril handle dagger which Tara left behind, vowing to remained in his possession; for he knew that Tara's affection was his Forbidden Fruit of life itself, posses its own ritual. Forbidding by their two ways of life, its structure in which to exist, yet they had the fruit of love, but deep inside they would never forget each other.

PART XIII
The Eye's of Love

Maybe the dagger of Tara was calling him somehow? She always had a way of expressing herself in a commanding manner. The dagger was of love which he came to called it. It was telling him something? What, he didn't know, but he had to get to the bottom of it.

Three days later that morning, Alexander venture out the hotel. The people were carrying on with their daily duties in a regular leisurely fashion. The heat in the region was just as torrid. Time here in New Orleans to him had never changed and probably wouldn't. He didn't know what to expect? He just had to appease his mind and wait for Jeanne to appear. Standing at the same spot, searching for a taxi in front of the hotel, he viewed two ladies with baseball caps on not so far. He shouted trying to their attention as the likeness resembled Tara and Jeanne. His heart was racing at a faster pace then his reasoning. Finally he reached the taxi before they departed. Suddenly in a reckless fashion, he leaped in front of it, forcing it to stop abruptly.

"What's the matter with you?" The lady drive shouted.

Alexander stared at them through the front window.

"There's plenty of other taxi here," The other lady said.

It came apparent he was surely wrong. From the back, they look like Tara and Jeanne, but he was allowing his heart to rule his reactions.

"Oh, I'm sorry for causing you such a delay. I just thought, never mind," he spoke in a depressing low tone.

The chill which Tara felt before now ran through him surprisingly. Where should he go? He thought. Where would he find Jeanne and Tara? It all seemed the same to him, horrifying and yet oddly magical. Glancing around, Alexander decided he would find Tara at her grandmother's home. Then he out of the corner of his eye, he witnessed a peculiar sight, Jeanne? He thought.

"Jeanne, is that you? Alexander asked getting a closer look.

She nodded smiling from a distant.

Alexander was overjoyed finding his friend alive. But could it really be Jeanne, with a serious case of renaissance, rebirth? Rushing through a group of people, he finally caught up with the woman. Her back was in front of him, tapping her eagerly upon her shoulder, not sure of what to say if it was her. Jeanne slowly turned around as her beautiful face flashed at him with a smiled.

"Jeanne it's really you!" Alexander shouted with excitement a joy.

"Alex, you're alive and safe," Jeanne cried in joy somewhat overwhelmed in seeing him there.

"La Veanna told me, never mind that," he voiced.

Jeanne smiled then hugged him with affection. "Alexander, I thought they've killed you. But seeing you now, I'm glad to see it wasn't true."

"What going on?" Alexander asked.

"La Veanna died two days ago."

"What?" He asked.

"They claim it was by natural causes," Jeanne explained.

"Where is Tara?" Alexander asked.

"Don't go there, Alex," Jeanne warned him. "I know where Tara is but you shouldn't go."

"Never mind that, just please take me to her?" he asked.

During their walk, she explained that it was Tara who ordered her release. He learned to see things with a very open mind; for anything could happen, not to dismiss things in a foolish manner. Later they soon arrived at

Tara's home. Jeanne explained that La Veanna's death strangely was no shock to most living there, leaving Tara the whole estate and wealthy. Alexander demanded to go alone, only wishing to feel his way through it. But Jeanne remained bother about something? Her expression was one of serious concern. She jerked Alexander to get his attention.

"What is it?" He asked confused by her manner.

"There is something you should know," she answered.

"Well?"

"Tara is not the same," she spoke in a saddening tone.

Alexander pondered what action to take in a sadness and despair situation.

"Tara will not remember you, understand that," Jeanne added. "She totally changed since you've known her."

What Jeanne was saying was true. Yet Alexander consciousness could only focus upon the house before him, wanting only to see Tara.

"Look, I still must see her alone. Will you stay here for me?" He asked in a worried tone.

Jeanne nodded reluctantly.

TARA THE FORBIDDEN FRUIT - 430

The last time Alexander was at this house was during the meeting with La Veanna, a very unpleasant experience at that.

"If you must, then go ahead," Jeanne voiced.

Knocking upon the front door, Alexander couldn't help staring at the door knob strangely. His mind became confused over just what he would say. If Tara mind was indeed changed, what of their promise to La Veanna? Could she reach out from the grave and curse Tara? Soon the knob started to turn and the door slowly open.

"May I help you, Sir?" Tara spoke as if she didn't recognize her only love.

He remained speechless from the glow of affection he felt for her.

"Do I know you?" She asked, this time in a puzzling manner.

Alexander stood there gazing at her beauty still unable to reply. Flashes of visions ran through his head at a rapid paste, visions of their being together, of their loving and caring, and of their joy of life. The two just stood there gazing at each other strangely. Just then Jeanne jumped in seeing he was having problems.

"Tara, this man was interested in buying your home. I told him it wasn't for sell, but he insisted in meeting the owner," Jeanne explained.

"Well I just inherited from my grandmother and I'm afraid that I'm not sure what I going to do?" Tara voiced smiling.

"He loves it so much," Jeanne voiced. "Isn't funny he just had to see it close up?"

Alexander regained his thoughts and took the signal from Jeanne finally as Tara came on the porch.

"Yes, the house is so exquisite to behold," he followed.

Jeanne knew to which he was expressing his feelings for and strangely, Tara felt it too.

"I'm sorry but she is right. The house is not for sell. My grandmother was buried a few days ago," Tara responded. But her mind continued to ponder about him. "Are you sure I've haven't seen you before?" She repeated staring at him. Her feelings were pulling wildly in all directions.

Alexander glanced at Jeanne than at Tara. He knew better then to push his feelings upon her.

"I'm sure, well thank anyway and have a very fruitful life, goodbye,"

"Yes goodbye," Jeanne added.

"I hope you have a joyous," he added.

"Look, I don't know your name, what is it?" Tara asked.

Jeanne looked on concerned. What if she remembers?

"It doesn't matter, it doesn't really matter," He said waving Jeanne on to leave. "Please. Lets go."

"I'll explain later," Jeanne replied to Tara standing there lost.

Alexander left with Jeanne to the airport from Tara's home. She smiled at him happily he would allow it to end.

"It was best. I'm glad you said nothing about your past relationship. You do understand, don't you? You know for a moment, I thought she was remembering. Well, you have to leave here, Alexander," Jeanne said.

At the airport Alexander kissed Jeanne farewell, knowing that Tara was in good hands. But being left at the airport, he couldn't disregard what she had added. Tara was remembering. This hunting statement continued to annoy him greatly. Annoying him to the point of not wishing to catch the plane home, staying there pondering over the matter. His heart still ached for her.

"Sir, your ticket please?" A ticket agent uttered.

Alexander only made it to the gate area, reluctantly.

"What? He responded staring at the runway.

"Your plane is about to take off without you, Sir."

Alexander's foolish heart had got him into love again. He had to see Tara one more time. Maybe it wasn't too late? He thought.

"No, I've changed my mind. Sorry for the delay," He said. "I'll catch a later flight to St. Louis.

Hurrying through the gates then arriving at a rental car booth, Alexander was hunted by the affection of his heart for Tara. Driving towards her home, his mind wondered about whether Tara really remembered him? Yet after thinking it over, his mind halted on the attempt to question her.

Hours later he arrived at the home, deciding to stay out of sight for moment, watching from behind the outer well kept gates; there Tara appeared resting comfortably in a rocking chair upon the porch. Alexander smiled at the sight joyfully. His heart started to pump at a rapid paste. She seemed to be in a daze relaxing with not a care in the world. She was gorgeous to behold again, much to his satisfaction. La Veanna had kept her promise in restoring her youth and her position. Suddenly Tara senses him standing outside the gates and stop rocking.

"Excuse me, I thought you've left. Is there anything else you desire?"" She asked presenting an uncertain desire to speak with him and intrigued by his second appearance before her. He caused her to feeling a very strong and seeks a special attraction towards him, a feeling which confused her so? But Alexander knew they couldn't ratify such feelings. Yet he demanded to know.

"May I speak with you?" Alexander asked. "That if you don't mind?"

"If you tell me your name?" Tara asked.

"Alexander," he spoke in a very soft tone, wondering just how to approach Tara with the up coming questions.

But what he forgot was her ability to read his thoughts.

"Fine, but still my home is not for sell. But it's not the reason of which you've returned, is it?" Tara asked gazing into his wanting eyes.

Alexander felt as if she were trying to extract his true thoughts, a task which should have been easy with her psychic powers, but for past reasons of consuming emotions for him, her supernatural powers couldn't explore his thoughts. By her expression, this caused her an enormous sense of confusion within her being. She gazed upon him pondering then asked, about him.

"Maybe you can tell me why I feel apprehension yet excitement from you?" Tara asked standing now and resting against the pillar holding up the porch.

"What's wrong?" Alexander asked.

"It's creating misgivings within me so," Tara replied.

Alexander realized she couldn't read his thoughts nor control him like others which surrounded her. This allowed him an advantage to question Tara on evenhanded and very equal terms. Still he remained spellbound by their past and her magnificence. The love they once had share before would soon play a profound part in his questioning.

"I understand that you're single?" He asked.

Tara nodded.

"Are you happy?" He asked in a careful and soft directed tone, hoping he wasn't causing any trepidation from her, watching Tara withdrawing a bit from him, oddly wishing she did have the power to examine his mind; it may have made things much easier to express.

"My grandmother strangely won't allow it," she said.

The conversation continues during the entire day. They got to know each other to a certain point of their life. Tara quickly discovered she had a strange liking to him. They laugh and had unyielding fun. Suddenly Tara glanced at him stun for a moment, as she gazed deeply into his eyes. She was thinking about something now her telepathic powers were able in breaking through his wall of thoughts placed there by La Veanna. By this time, Tara had sat next to him, closer than before. The smell of her aroused him so. She gazed at him as if her wanted to kiss him passionately but pulled back. She too sensed his essence near her, one of which her own body desired before. The wind was blowing softly through her black hair, caressing her face at times, resting only a moment upon her smooth and beautiful face. She still was rich with affection for anyone they laid themselves upon, her full lips of lust, wet and moist to the touch. Tara would sometime wet them as she talk, an act which only brought great expectation to her mate.

Every vague movement only builds more glowing thrush of erotic and adores suggestions towards him. She couldn't help it. Tara knew Alexander was strangely bringing it out of her. It was the only way she could hold her heated body from consuming him. This stranger which

TARA THE FORBIDDEN FRUIT - 437

she opens up to was majestically exciting her so; Tara didn't know why?

Alexander knew they were so close to the end now. Both their dream were now played out. How many things could they said goodbye? There was no way to rewrite their ending. Someone had to say goodbye. They couldn't continue living a painful falsehood, knowing they would always love each other. Tara gazed at him dispirited. The man is a strange in her thoughts. For some apparent reason she cannot remember his name or see his face. Yet strangely Alexander's spirit was within her to this day. Also his love and understanding to a great extent.

"Alexander, you may not apprehend what I'm saying, but I'm at peace with myself, finally," Tara voiced.

She rested back gazing at the clear blue sky.

"I understand, Tara," he said.

Alexander still wasn't sure whether he should come between Tara's peace and La Veanna promise they made to her? It was a chance which had to be considered with commanding attention. All could backfire and leave Tara as the victim, but one thing did come to his attention; Tara should be left alone now to live her life without him. The cost was too sizable the attempt it. He promised to himself never to interfere in exchange for her life.

Tara turned her head towards him as if wanting to kiss him.

"While, I must be leaving if you don't mind," Alexander said pulling away. "But I'm glad you're at peace again, please believe that." He felt the trade off was worth it.

Tara smiled as if she knew something he didn't.

"I see it in your eyes that you mean what you say. Yet wish not to leave, why?" Tara asked. "Alexander, it seems of easy to utter your name and brings a glowing feeling of warmth inside me. Tell me, what is it you know of which I do not?"

Tara's question confounded him for a moment, pausing and gazing into her beautiful eyes. Alexander knew it was really time to leave before all was lost. Getting up from beside her, he wanted to give her a replied that she wanted. His heart demanded it. Standing in front of her, he finally uttered, "I know you are a very intelligent and beautiful woman. Far above any who would dare to address you wrongly, a caring and feeling person which will care for her man beyond any other."

"What is it you're trying to tell me, Alexander?" Tara asked.

"No, let me finished please," he asked.

Tara nodded holding back what was really on her mind. Tara wanted him to say it. She pleaded in her heart, badly. He never knew that only he could break the curse placed upon her, that the curse was ended. He moved around the porch trying to express just how to say what had to be said, looking at his love again. He knew he'd loved her all alone.

"I hoped that we will always be friends," Alexander said.

"You mean friends in love?" Tara added smiling.

He paused then spoke, "Yes."

But Tara's words sank deep.

"I feel we can be that," Tara replied, "But that's not what you want to say...is it?"

"I know the life you are in is not of your choosing. Yet it makes you glow evermore, reflecting upon others surrounding," he said smiling.

Tara stood there concern over losing him.

"Oh, Tara, life has so much to offer you, just open your mind," Alexander voiced as tears began to appear in his painful eyes, causing him to withdraw.

"What's wrong? Tell me?" Tara asked holding him upon the arms.

"I must be going now," Alexander expressed sadly.

Tara gazed at him as she wiped the tears gently off his face.

"I know, Alexander, I understand now," she replied as if she knew of his agony.

Something inside her was telling her not to let go.

"Alexander, never mind," Tara said.

"I have to go now," Alexander voiced sadly.

She reached out and held his hands placing them now upon her heartbreaking face. Watching Alexander ever so gently with her heart focus upon his, the sensitive touches of their hands were creating an everlasting bond for life. Flashes of the past ran through her mind, of playfulness, of peril, of obsession, and of escapade. Her mind could see it all from birth to death of La Veanna. Instead of revealing her thoughts, Tara strangely with held them from him.

"Alexander, I will be happy now, thank you," Tara said pulling him closer to her.

"You are a beautiful lady," he responded slightly smiling with joy and heart.

Tara explained that he must go for the both of them. Neither was willing to state what was obvious. Alexander noticed she had become very rested and peaceful in his arms. Now the tears had halted, not fighting to escape her past. Tara's eyes were seeing him as if she knew whom he was. As if she knew he would return to her one day. But it could have been in her heart which she was engulfed in. Someone had to be strong now.

Finally, Alexander forced himself to back away. But Tara wouldn't return to the porch, moving with him, hugging him passionately in a loving fashion.

"I will miss you greatly, Alexander," she voiced. "Now you must go home for the both of us, before we..."

Breaking apart from each other's embrace, the forbidden lovers gazed one more time into each other's eyes then Alexander turned away from her. She herself couldn't tell him that she now remembered nor could he do the same knowing his promise.

"Be happy, Tara. Please always be happy," he expressed leaving her.

Tara just stood there staring at him like it was a horror which came back to haunt her, the horror of a love that had to be halted by the world of Voodooism, and two different cultures. As tears now replaced the smiles that once was there, they loved each other so.

Driving off to the airport, the dust of the road left behind a very special love of Alexander's life. Tara, herself knew it too. Maybe the deal they made with La Veanna was wrong? Maybe the price was too high for all? Maybe Tara and him could have discovered a way of turning things around? Now neither of them would know if everlasting love would have been as sweet. What he did discovered was that it can be just as bitter to the taste. La Veanna started out against them all along, placing considerable obstacles in their way to true love. To put it in prospective, all was against the intermarriage of culture. They both won Tara, yet they both lost her. The endearment of each other wasn't enough. The battle of good verses evil with its ceaseless struggles had them trapped in the mist of it. Maybe Tara's grandmother knew all along the out come? Alexander and Tara may never know. Still they had a chance and that chance would come from Jeanne that same day.

    Later Jeanne went to Tara's home and had a talk with her over the Alexander issues. Tara was sitting on the porch staring at the sun, Jeanne approach with interest of her abandonment.

    "Hello, remember me?" Jeanne asked waving.

    Tara looks at her smiling.

    "Jeanne, right?" Tara asked.

    Jeanne nodded.

"I remember everything now," Tara added. "You were, I mean are my best friend."

Jeanne approach and sat next to her.

"When did you start to remember?" Jeanne asked.

"When he came back the second time," Tara answered smiling. "When I touched him, I knew he was my lover, and I saw you as my friend."

"I see, did you tell Alexander?"

"No, but we both knew inside, just didn't allow the truth to come out," Tara said getting up from, the porch. "Where is he now?"

"Should be at the pond for a last time look," Jeanne answered. "You going after him? And what about La Veanna's curse?"

"There is another who could accept the responsibilities and set me free," Tara answered smiling. "Give me an hour and I'll meet you and Alexander at the airport if I'm successful."

"If not?" Jeanne asked joining her.

Tara only smiled with assurance and ran off through the gate.

"Don't forget if I'm not there, leave for all sake," Tara shouted. "Tell Alexander nothing of this, promise me?"

TARA THE FORBIDDEN FRUIT - 444

Jeanne ran to the gate nodding and concerned.

Later at the Mai Dede townhouse a knock came at the door. Tara was greeted with a great deal of respect from the staff as she entered. Mai Dede came down the stairs to greet her. She was confused by the visit and troubled by Tara demeanor. She led Tara into the study and the ladies had a deep demanding conference. After a half hour the conversation was over. Mai Dede stood at the doors stun yet pleased with the results of the talk.

"So is it a deal?" Tara asked.

"I have to think about it?" Mai Dede said taking a stiff drink.

"Need to know now?" Tara asked.

"You're willing to give it all up, for him?" Mai Dede asked stun. "Do you know what you're giving up?"

"Supremacy, I don't care anymore," Tara answered.

Tara knew if her plan failed there may never come a day another. That life will continue apart for the lovers. The Forbidden Fruit was now true to its name. But now it had an added meaning; that being the exquisite Tara. She knew Alexander would never meet her again. The powers of sorcery wanted to regain its control over her. What she feared if she stayed would come true. The supernatural powers of Voodoo with it incantation and idolatry would had taken over what was left of their relationship. It was time to break free and join her beloved.

"I need to know now, Mai Dede?" Tara asked one more time. "Will you take over my reign as High Priestess?"

Mai Dede stood there pondering…

Meanwhile at the airport Jeanne and Alexander were waiting to board the plane for St. Louis. The passengers were packed in the corridors with far too many bags. Jeanne continued to watch for Tara but no sign of her brought deep concern. Alexander sat near the huge bay windows watching the outgoing planes. He was sad and lonely when Jeanne joined him.

His remembrance of Tara's inspiration, spirit and impression would cast an everlasting picture upon his consciousness. His apartment was even more an empty abyss to go to. His impression upon her would leave a beatified and enchanted feeling throughout her reign as High Priestess. He thought. That once she was mortal and experienced true mortal feelings and most of all, love, she must give up pleasurable ness for the painfulness of reality. Alexander still kept the peril handle dagger. He just couldn't get rid of it. There's no life's lesson to be learned in all of this, though his life and Tara composed of personal affections. They were at the wrong place, but at the right time. And what did happen to them could never take away from the love which was built within them. Because no matter what other's do, they would always love each other! Alexander leans back into his chair, finally at peace with himself.

"Alexander?" Jeanne asked.

"Yes?"

You know if there was a way, Tara would find it," Jeanne said. "I mean, she loves you very much."

Alexander shucks his head sadly.

"It just wasn't meant to be, Jeanne," he replied.

"Never give up," Jeanne voiced looking around for Tara.

No sign of her.

The passengers were now boarding the plane. Jeanne had a second waiting at the gate for Tara, but it seemed it will never be used. The gate clerk waved them on being the last to board.

"Well, farewell New Orleans, may your days and night be peaceful," Alexander voiced aloud. "Tara wherever you are, I love you."

TARA THE FORBIDDEN FRUIT - 447

"Please wait a little longer, Alex?" Jeanne asked.

"What for, Jeanne?"

"Never mind, we better get on the plane," Jeanne said giving up on Tara appearance.

They boarded the plane and took their seats. There was an empty seat next to Alexander and Jeanne sat to his left. The bell sounded for takeoff and they were given their instruction. Both watched the door close slowly then it jammed. Two of the Air Crewmen were called to help close it. Alexander rests his head back and closed his eyes. Entering the plane was Tara with bags in toll, with a glance at the door and a glow; it became unlocked and closed with eases. She moved down the allies until she face them.

"You know what Jeanne?" Alexander asked eyes shut.

Jeanne smiled at Tara standing over them.

"What Alex?"

"I could square I can smell the scent of Tara," he said smiling. "It as if she is here. I must be totally in love or insane. She is my Forbidden Fruit." His eyes were closed.

"May I get to my seat?" Tara asked.

Alexander looked up totally surprised and overjoyed.

"Please," Alexander replied moving for her.

Tara took her seat next to the window on his right side, Jeanne on his left smiled at them.

"Sorry, I know I promised you not to use my powers, but Screener are such a bitch here," Tara joked. "Thanks Jeanne for the ticket."

Alexander said nothing still shock to see his love.

"Well aren't you two ever going to kiss and make up or what?" Jeanne asked laughing. "We have a long one way flight home."

Alexander and Tara kissed each other with great passion.

"Alexander, you are my power, my passion, and my pain," Tara whispered in his ear and caressing her lover. "Forever, my true love."

"It really was you?" Alexander said referring to the bath tub event where he nearly lost his life. He handed her the two charms from around his neck representing alpha and omega there. Tara took the charms securing the reminders of adoration and jeopardy away forever not to be revisited. She placed them in a velvet box. But Tara knew she could never turn her back completely from her past in New Orleans; that it would always haunt her and she needed to be on her guard. Yet she looked forward to her future and new life with them in St. Louis.

Tara and Alexander would always be as one, for they discovered that each other was the Forbidden Fruit of the other.

"What about your position," Jeanne asked referring to the High Priestess. "If not you, who then?"

"Well since my grandmother death, I now totally control matters; the one thing she sort of forgot to inform me of. Therefore, I made a deal with the Devil herself," Tara answered staring out the window.

"What?" Both Jeanne and Alexander asked shocked.

Tara only smiled.

"You didn't?" Jeanne asked grinning.

"Well, are you going to tell us, what deal?" Alexander asked strongly and perplexed. "Who would want such a position as High Priestess?"

The stewardess asked them did they want a drink. Jeanne waved her away politely only desiring the truth from Tara's grinning lips.

"Please tell me, you didn't, Tara?" Jeanne asked with enthusiasm.

"Mai Dede," Tara said laughing. "Since she was willing to give her soul, so be it. What better person to reward than one whom actual through her actions of retribution brought us three together, made us even stronger?"

"I knew there was a reason why I love you," Alexander said kissing her. "Forever, my love." Tara kissed him with great passion and desire.

"Forever it will be you and I," Tara voiced with enthusiasm.

"Stewardess, may we have three drinks please?" Jeanne asked.

The drinks were brought and they toasted…

"May our new life bring joy and happiness," Jeanne said.

"May our new love bring peace and understanding," Tara said.

"May our love never grow apart and fade," Alexander said.

With the toast over they drank.

In the velvet box the two charms became luminosity, displaying its energy shaking wildly in Tara's hands. The charms through the pure supernatural willpower of Tara contain them causing the precarious threat to faded. Suddenly the plane rattled violently upsetting the trio and creating a slight case of the unnerving. It was as if the powers that be from Hell itself were reaching out; not yet forgiving of their protégé willful disregard of her birthright. A message came over the loud speaker that it was turbulence. Tara relaxed in Alexander's arms feeling safe. The trio would rest all the way to St. Louis. They were silent thinking of their decision to leave then suddenly laughed with joy...

    Tara vowed never to tell them that she was now immortal and that the powers that be would one day rise up again against them. It would a secret she was willing to take to their graves. For now she would enjoy the peace and the love of Alexander…

FIN

ISBN 141203903-7